Along the Shore

Also by best-selling author Rochelle Alers

The Book Club series

The Seaside Café

The Beach House

The Innkeepers series

The Inheritance

Breakfast in Bed

Room Service

The Bridal Suite

"A Christmas Layover" in *The Perfect Present*

www.kensingtonbooks.com

DAFINA BOOKS are published by

Kensington Publishing Corp.
119 West 40th Street
New York, NY 10018

ISBN: 978-1-4967-3544-7
First Trade Paperback Printing: August 2022

ISBN: 978-1-4967-3546-1 (e-book)
First Electronic Edition: August 2022

10 9 8 7 6 5 4 3 2 1

Printed in the United States of America

Along the Shore

Chapter 1

July 29

I've done it! I've finally made the decision to move to Coates Island, North Carolina. It has taken me more than a year to think about leaving Connecticut, and now that I've put everything into motion, I know I've done the right thing. Now it's time I let my book club friends know.

Cherie Renee Thompson reread what she'd written. She'd begun keeping a journal at fifteen, a month before enrolling in the prestigious prep school where she'd been awarded a full academic scholarship. Days after moving into her dorm room, she'd found herself writing down her thoughts and reactions to what had become an entirely different lifestyle. After the first year, her entries decreased from one every night to three or four each week. And, most times, it was to release her frustration about having to live in two worlds: one when interacting with students who benefited from unlimited funds from their wealthy parents, and the other when returning to her old neighborhood, with low-income housing, where crime and poverty had become the norm rather than the exception.

Capping her pen, Cherie dropped it and the journal into the tote on the passenger seat. She started up her car and headed in the direction of the bridge connecting the mainland to the island, and five minutes later she maneuvered into the parking lot of the Seaside Café for the last time before returning home.

Home.

The word conjured up memories that had made her into the woman she had become. Connecticut was the state where she'd been born, raised, educated, worked, and lived; however, it had taken just two visits to Coates Island, North Carolina, for her to conclude she hadn't been living but existing. She got up every morning to drive to the childcare center where she was the parent coordinator, and eight hours later, she returned to the two-bedroom condo in a gated development to read or watch television before readying herself to go to bed.

Alone.

It had been almost five years since her breakup with William Weylin Campbell III, and although she'd exorcised him from her life, she still found it impossible to purge him from her head. Cherie lost track of the number of times she'd wanted to call Weylin, just to hear his voice; however, after their last encounter, the two had promised never to contact each other again.

Their agreement would also serve to remind her what she'd sacrificed to give Weylin what he'd wanted because she'd believed she would always have a part of him. How wrong she'd been, because in the end, she had been the only loser.

She'd lost the only man she'd ever loved, and she'd lost the child they'd made together. And it wasn't until she'd delivered her son—a baby she would never hold—that she realized she'd traded the child she'd carried for nine months, in a period of weakness and madness, for a lifestyle she'd always dreamed about. She'd made a deal with a man who had concocted a plan she'd been unable to refuse.

Shaking off the memories, Cherie walked into the restaurant. It was nearing closing time for the lunch crowd; two couples were still seated at one table, laughing hysterically. The Seaside Café, family owned and operated, the only eating establishment on the island, was a favorite hangout for locals and vacationers alike.

She spied Kayana Johnson-Ogden as she came out of the kitchen, and she had to admit, and not for the first time, that marriage agreed with the former psychiatric social worker who operated the restaurant with her brother, Derrick Johnson. Kayana's chemically straightened hair, covered with a white bandana, ended several inches above her shoulders. Her nut-brown complexion was darker than it had been at the beginning of the summer season, which meant that, after leaving the café, she was spending more time outdoors with her husband.

Kayana stared at her. "I thought you left a couple of days ago."

Cherie approached Kayana and looped her arm through her friend's. "That was my plan . . . until I decided to go house hunting."

Naturally arching eyebrows lifted. "House hunting where?"

Cherie's smile grew wider. "Here on Coates Island."

Kayana's jaw dropped. "You're kidding."

"No, I'm not."

Kayana studied the petite woman with a mass of black curls framing her gold-brown face. Her large, light-brown eyes with flecks of green shimmered with excitement, and the corners of her normally petulant mouth had curved into a smile. To say Kayana found Cherie Thompson complex was an understatement. She wondered what had happened to the young woman to sour her outlook on life.

"Come with me to the patio, where we can talk without folks eavesdropping," Kayana whispered. She led Cherie through the restaurant's dining area and slid back the pocket doors to an area where diners were able to take advantage of the magnificent views of the beach and the Atlantic Ocean. She sat and waited for Cherie to sit down opposite her. "What made you decide you want to live here?"

Kayana had asked because there weren't that many young adults living on Coates Island, which had a recorded population of about four hundred permanent residents. Those born and raised there usually left once they graduated from high school or college, leaving their parents and grandparents to rent bungalows and cottages to summer vacationers to supplement their fixed incomes.

Cherie rested her hands on the tabletop and laced her fingers together. "There's nothing keeping me in Connecticut. You know, I've quit my job and plan to go back to college to get a graduate degree in early childhood education. Rather than enroll in on-campus classes, I've decided to go the online route, and that is something I can do regardless of where I live."

Kayana knew Cherie had resigned her position at a Connecticut-based childcare center and had mentioned she wanted to become an elementary school teacher, yet hadn't indicated she planned to relocate. Perhaps, she mused, the beautiful young woman had finally gotten over her relationship with a man that appeared to have left her in a perpetual funk. There were times when she lashed out at her or the third member of their group, Leah, without provocation.

She wanted to ask Cherie if moving was what she needed to put some distance between her and her ex, but decided not to broach the topic. "Have you found a house?" she asked instead.

"Yes. The realtor wanted to sell me one of the new condos that went up several years ago, but when I told her I was currently living in a condo and wanted a structure where I didn't have to see my neighbors coming and going, she took me to several properties like your brother's. I finally decided on one with four bedrooms, three and a half baths, that's approximately a five-minute walk to the ocean. It's a lot more room than I'll need, but I love the open floor plan concept, and what really sold me was the fenced-in backyard. Once I saw it, all I thought about was adopting a fur baby and letting it have the run of the backyard."

Kayana smiled when she registered the excitement in Cherie's voice. "It sounds as if you have everything planned out."

Cherie cocked her head at an angle. "I hope so."

There was a vagueness in the three words, and Kayana wondered if Cherie still had to convince herself that she was doing the right thing. She remembered when a developer had wanted to put up a string of condos and waterfront homes, but the members of the town council had voted down his original proposal. After a series of lengthy meetings and negotiations, the developer received approval to build condos with no more than eight units and a half dozen single-family homes. Generations of Coates Island's residents were opposed to an influx of new people, other than the returning vacationers from late May through the Labor Day weekend, whose permanence would dramatically change their idyllic island.

"When do you think you'll be able to move in?"

Cherie ran her fingers through the black curls falling over her forehead. "It's not going to be until the end of the year. The owner and his wife are in the process of negotiating building a house in Hawaii to be close to their daughter and grandchildren."

"You must be talking about Jeremy and Katherine Murphy." Kayana was familiar with the older couple, and rumors were floating around the island that the retirees were planning to relocate to the island of Oahu. They'd vacationed on Coates Island for several years before permanently retiring on the island, and now they were leaving to be close to family members. They'd frequented the restaurant on weekends during the off-season and rarely interacted with other residents.

"So you're really serious about living here year-round?" she asked.

Cherie nodded. "Living here will allow me not to have any distractions once I go back to college. Besides, there's nothing in Connecticut that's keeping me there."

"What about your family, Cherie?"

"What about them?"

Kayana paused when Cherie answered her query with a question. And to say it had undertones of defensiveness was an understatement. "Won't you miss them?"

Cherie stared at her clasped hands atop the table. It was a question she'd asked herself over and over since she'd decided to relocate, and each time the answer was a resounding *no*!

"Not really," she admitted honestly. She glanced up and met Kayana's eyes. "I've never really had a good relationship with my mother, and it worsened when my oldest brother was killed during a drive-by shooting." She ignored Kayana's gasp of surprise.

After Cherie was enrolled in the private prep school and witnessed a lifestyle that was the complete opposite from the one in which she'd been raised, she'd blamed her mother for not defending her when the folks in Edwina's social circle called her a stuck-up ho, bougie bitch, or even worse. Not once did Edwina Thompson open her mouth to refute them, which only served to widen the rift between Cherie and her mother.

Cherie had what she thought of as a love-hate relationship with Edwina. She loved her mother because she had given birth to her and attempted to raise her the best way she could, but she also resented her because Edwina refused to better herself. She also refused to name the men who had fathered her children, which made Cherie reluctant to become involved with any of the boys in her neighborhood for fear she would be dating her half-brother or a cousin.

"I'm so sorry you lost your brother."

Cherie closed her eyes as she attempted bring her fragile emotions under control. It was never easy for her to talk about losing her older brother. "I'd been pleading with my mother to move out of the neighborhood where we lived because it had become a cesspool for drugs and crime, but she claimed she didn't want to leave her friends. Even after she buried her firstborn, she still refused. Once I graduated college and got a job, I moved into a studio apartment, and I found myself constantly preaching to my younger brothers that they had to stay in school and keep away from gangs. Thankfully, they listened; both were able to get into military academies, and this past May, they graduated from West Point and the Air Force Academy. I paid for my mother to fly out to Colorado with me, and it was the first time I ever saw her cry, and that was enough for her to talk about taking college courses so she can get a higher-paying job and move into a better neighborhood."

"Didn't you tell me that your mother had earned a GED?" Kayana asked.

Cherie nodded. "My mother is very smart, but what she lacks is motivation. I think seeing her sons become commissioned officers was the impetus she needed to change her lifestyle. Although when I told her I could get her a position at the childcare center, she turned me down, saying she wanted to find something on her own."

A smile parted Kayana's lips. "She sounds like a proud woman."

Cherie made a sucking sound with her tongue and teeth. "It's more like false pride." She didn't want to tell Kayana that she'd bought Edwina a used car because she'd had to take two buses to get to the diner for her late shift. Edwina had rounded on her, saying she didn't need her handout until her boss threatened to fire her if she was late one more time.

"I just wanted to stop by to let you know that next year you will have two permanent book club sisters."

Kayana slowly shook her head. "I could not have imagined when we met for the first time that Leah would leave her husband and move in with my brother or that you would relocate here when young men and women can't wait to leave Coates Island."

"Well, this thirty-something woman has had enough of the bright lights of the big city, and I'm now looking forward to, as they say, living my life by my leave."

Reaching across the table, Kayana covered her hands with one of her own. "Good for you," she said before removing her hand. "Will you have a problem selling your condo?"

"No. There's a waiting list for two-bedroom units."

"I suppose that solves your problem of trying to unload one property before you can buy another one."

She didn't tell Kayana that moving to Coates Island would be a renaissance, the rebirth of Cherie Renee Thompson, who would begin her life anew where she would be in complete control of her destiny.

Cherie knew relocating would solve a lot of her problems. And the first was distancing herself from Weylin so that she wouldn't have to read about him in the local newspapers or see his image during a televised segment covering local and national politics. He'd been sworn into Congress as a representative six months before his thirtieth birthday, and less than a year later, he'd revealed that, after seven years of marriage, he and his wife were now the parents of a mixed-raced infant son through a closed adoption. What he'd neglected to inform members of the press was that he'd fathered that child with a woman with whom he'd had a clandestine affair for more than a decade.

Born into wealth, Weylin had it all: a beautiful wife and son, and a political career with endless possibilities, while Cherie was left with a condo in an exclusive Cos Cob, Connecticut, enclave and enough resources to allow her to live quite comfortably with or without employment.

Cherie still could not believe she had waited until she was thirty-four years old to do what she'd needed to do to make herself happy rather than concentrating on others whenever she reevaluated her life every ten years, beginning when she'd celebrated her fifteenth birthday. The events of that year were branded into her memory like a permanent tattoo. Unconsciously, she shook her head as if to banish the painful decision she'd made that had changed her life.

Pushing back her chair, Cherie stood, Kayana rising with her. "I have to leave now because I plan to stay in Philly overnight before heading out again tomorrow afternoon."

Rounding the table, Kayana hugged her. "Drive carefully, and don't forget to text me when you get home."

Smiling, she pressed her cheek to Kayana's. "Yes, Mama. Now you take care of your wonderful husband and give him my regards." The year before, Kayana had married a man who had moved from Massachusetts to retire on the island.

A rush of color darkened the cook's face even more. "I will. Do you mind if I let Leah know you're going to move here?"

"Of course not. Although we probably won't officially reactivate our book club until sometime early next year, I'm really looking forward to it."

Kayana smiled and nodded. "So am I. Derrick and I have decided to close the restaurant for two weeks around Christmas and New Year's, so hopefully you'll move before that so we can help you settle in."

"It all depends on Mr. and Mrs. Murphy. If I unload my condo before closing, then I'll put my furnishings in storage down here and check into a motel on the mainland."

"You don't have to do that, Cherie. You can always stay in the upstairs apartment now that Leah is living with Derrick."

"Thanks, but no thanks. Staying on the mainland and

checking out the neighboring towns will help to familiarize me with my new surroundings."

"Why spend money when you can live here rent-free?"

A beat passed before Cherie said, "It's not about money, Kayana. If it was, then I never would've been able to quit my job before securing another. Money isn't the problem. Changing my life is."

Kayana's smile was more of a grimace. "Okay." She hugged her again. "Don't forget to text me to let me know you arrived safe and sound."

"I will."

Cherie left the patio, walked out of the restaurant, and got into her car. As she drove along the bridge linking the island to the mainland, Cherie shuddered noticeably, as if she'd been dowsed with a bucket of ice-cold water. In that instant she wondered if relocating—or, if she were being honest with herself—running away from all she'd known was the best course of action. Her eyelids fluttered as she blinked back tears. It was something she would never know unless she did it.

As planned, Cherie checked into a Philadelphia hotel, showered, ordered room service, and then watched a cable news station until she turned off the television around two in the morning. She slept in late, checked out, and was back on the road by five. It felt liberating not to have to set the alarm on her cell phone as a reminder that she had to get up and go to work.

Years ago, Cherie had arranged with her mother to allow her twin brothers to stay over with her on weekends once she moved out of the studio apartment and into one with a bedroom. The boys took over the bedroom, while she slept in the living room on a convertible sofa bed. Straight-A students, both boys had talked about enlisting in the army to take advantage of the military's educational benefits, but Cherie had another plan for them once she realized her affair with

Weylin Campbell had benefits beyond his securing apartments for her in his family-owned properties. She'd solicited his assistance as a congressman to get them into military academies. And when they'd received their acceptance letters, she told her lover that there wasn't anything she wouldn't do for him, unaware that he would take her up on that promise.

She pushed Weylin and what had been their fifteen-year relationship out of her mind as she maneuvered into the lot of the twenty-four-hour diner and parked in one of only a few empty spaces. She called her mother, something she rarely did, to inform her she would meet her at the diner, knowing it would be the last time they would get together in person for a long while.

Chapter 2

Cherie walked into the diner and spied her mother sitting at a table in a far corner, talking to another waitress. At fifty-two, she was still an extremely attractive woman, and despite giving birth to four children, her petite body was still slender, a body type Cherie had inherited from her mother. That was their only physical similarity other than their eye color. People in her old neighborhood had called Edwina Kitty, the latter because of her shimmering, gold-green eyes and flawless mahogany complexion.

"Would you like a table or booth?"

Cherie smiled at the man monitoring the front. "No, thank you. I'm here to see Edwina Thompson. She's my mother," Cherie added when he continued to stare at her.

"She's on her break. You'll find her at one of the back tables."

Cherie nodded. "Thank you." She headed for the rear of the diner.

Edwina saw her and stood. She said something to her coworker, who glanced over her shoulder at Cherie, then slipped off her chair and walked away. "Come and sit."

Cherie took the chair the other woman had vacated. "I'm not going to take up a lot of your break time, but I felt you should hear from me in person that I'm planning to relocate to North Carolina."

Edwina looked at her as if she'd spoken a language she didn't understand before her expression changed—became crestfallen.

She lowered her eyes. "Why?"

"Because there's nothing keeping me here."

"What about me?"

"What about you, Mom?" She answered Edwina's question with one of her own.

"I can't believe you're deserting me, too."

Cherie stared at her mother as if she'd taken leave of her senses. But the acerbic words on her tongue vanished the instant she saw tears welling up in Edwina's eyes. It was only the second time she had seen her cry. Her mother hadn't even cried when they'd buried her firstborn. It was as if she had been in denial, believing Jamal wasn't dead but sleeping and would wake up whenever he chose.

However, it wasn't like that for Cherie, and she knew her brother wasn't coming back; the bullets from a high-powered automatic weapon had hit vital organs, killing him instantly. Her tall, handsome, kind older sibling, who'd had dreams of enlisting in the military, was murdered a month before his enlistment, and those responsible were never arrested. It was as if the neighborhood upheld the code that snitches get stitches. Even the girl he'd presumably been sleeping with denied she had been involved with him.

Reaching across the table, she grasped Edwina's hand. "I'm not deserting you, Mama." She closed her eyes once she realized it had been a long time, much too long, since she'd called her that. "I'm buying a house in North Carolina with enough bedrooms that if you want to come and visit you can." She said visit rather than live because Cherie knew her mother would never consider leaving Connecticut. She'd been born and raised there, and it was also because of the connections she had with distant relatives and lifelong friends in the neighborhood.

Sniffling, Edwina blinked back tears before they fell. "Why North Carolina? Why can't you buy a house here in Connecticut? I know you were talking about selling your condo, but I didn't think you would move a thousand miles away."

Cherie smiled. "It's not a thousand, only seven hundred miles. It's about a twelve-hour drive nonstop."

"Why North Carolina?" Edwina repeated.

The seconds ticked before Cherie said, "It's where I feel alive, Mama."

"Alive? Are you saying you feel dead here?"

A hint of a smile tilted the corners of Cherie's mouth. "I'm only speaking figuratively. I went to Coates Island on vacation these past two summers, and for the first time in a very long time, I didn't have to live my life by a clock. I slept and woke whenever it pleased me, and if I decided to spend the entire day in bed reading, that's what I did. I also met two older women who helped me to see myself in a different light."

"And what's that, Cherie?"

"That I should take control of my life and do what is good for Cherie Renee Thompson."

Edwina blinked slowly. "And you don't think that's what you're doing now? You have a job you enjoy, and you live in a wonderful development that you don't have to leave for your daily needs. What more could you want?"

"I want to become a teacher."

"You can't do that in Connecticut?" Edwina questioned. "After all, you did graduate with honors from Yale."

"I know that, Mom."

She didn't need her mother to remind her that she'd earned a full academic scholarship to the prestigious Ivy League college. But what Edwina failed to realize was that she'd studied around the clock to maintain the necessary grades to not lose the scholarship—and to prove to herself that she was worthy of becoming the wife of the man whom she'd loved more than herself.

"So why don't you go back there for your graduate degree?"

"I don't need another degree from Yale to prove that I wasn't a fluke. I've spent the past twelve years working at the same place, and now it's time that I transition from being a parent coordinator to a classroom teacher."

"When are you going to hand in your notice?"

Cherie smiled. "I resigned in May."

Edwina's jaw dropped. "You've been out of work for two months?" Cherie nodded. "Do you plan to get another job while you go back to college?"

"If I work, then it will be part-time. I'd like to become a full-time student and hopefully finish in two years. If not, then I'll sign up for two courses each semester until I graduate. Of course, I'll have to do some student teaching and take a test for certification if I plan to teach in a public school. And if I'm really ambitious, then I'll have to decide whether I want a doctorate degree and perhaps teach at the college level."

She didn't tell her mother that teaching in a private school was not an option for her. Spending four years at a private prep school had taught her that if parents had enough money or increased their endowments, teachers were pressured to pass their kids with grades they hadn't earned.

Cherie realized she'd shocked her mother with the plans for her future. It had taken months after leaving Coates Island the year before for her to reassess her life, and she had concluded she'd been wishing, hoping, and praying for what would never become a reality. She'd fallen in love with Weylin at fifteen and had spent half her life fantasizing spending it with him.

He'd become her first and only lover, and she knew she

would never be able to exorcise him completely until she put some distance between them. The place where she could reinvent herself was Coates Island, North Carolina. Cherie would move into her new house, and while she decorated it to her taste, she would reunite with her friends for their monthly book club meetings. She'd also planned to improve her cooking skills. There were so many recipes she wanted to try and perfect before hosting a book discussion.

"I know you don't hear it enough from me, Cherie, but I truly am proud of you. If I'd had your focus and strength when you left home at fifteen to attend that private school, I doubt whether I would've let a boy talk me into sleeping with him without using protection."

Cherie went completely still before she slumped back in her chair. It was the first time she'd heard Edwina talk about the boys and or men she'd slept with. Whenever she'd asked her about the fathers of her children, Edwina had become mute. It was as if she didn't want to open the door she'd closed once she'd given birth to her sons and daughter.

"Mama—"

"I know you've asked me over and over," Edwina interrupted, holding up a hand, "about your father and my sons' fathers, and one of these days I'll tell you. Once you decide to start a family. But not until then."

Cherie wanted to tell her it was much too late for that because she'd already given birth to a son. She forced a smile instead. "I see your boss glaring this way."

Pushing back her chair, Edwina stood, Cherie rising with her. "That's because my break is over."

"I'll call you, and we can arrange to spend some time together before I leave."

Edwina smiled, nodding. "When are you leaving?"

Cherie's smile matched hers. "Not until the end of the year. The current owners are building a house in Hawaii; they project that we can close on the sale of their current property around mid-December."

Cherie hugged Edwina, then left the diner. She knew she'd surprised the older woman when suggesting they get together. Although they lived in the same state, it wasn't often that they would see each other in person. Recently, phone calls and text messages had become the norm. She would send Edwina gifts for Mother's Day, her birthday, and Christmas, but made up every excuse she could not to visit her.

There had been a time when she'd refused to take her mother's calls because Edwina only contacted her whenever she'd needed money. It wasn't until she'd secured the job waiting tables at the diner that Cherie realized Edwina was serious about becoming gainfully employed; she had even hinted about enrolling in college. Cherie wasn't certain as to what Edwina wanted to study, but just talking about it was a positive step in the right direction for her fifty-two-year-old mother.

As she returned to the parking lot to drive home, Cherie realized she'd turned another corner. She'd finally made peace with Edwina, and she'd been the one to extend the olive branch when she'd invited her mother to come and visit her in North Carolina.

If circumstances were different for Cherie, she would've asked Edwina if she was willing to relocate to Coates Island with her. And if need be, she would withdraw funds she'd put aside for her retirement and purchase a condo for Edwina.

However, what Cherie did not want to do was put undue pressure on Edwina.

And if Cherie were truly honest with herself, she would've admitted that Edwina was the better woman, despite her circumstances, because she'd elected to raise her children the best she could, while Cherie had agreed to give up her child for money to embrace the lifestyle that had always evaded her.

What Cherie did not intend to do was sink into a morass of self-pity again because she had no one to blame but herself. What she had to do was look ahead and plan a future that would give her what she needed to achieve fulfillment.

December 20

It's been a while since I've recorded anything, but today is special. I am leaving Connecticut—this time for good. I never would've thought or imagined I would leave everything familiar to embark on a journey of renewal. I know my mother thinks that I'm running away, and in a way I am. What she doesn't realize is that I must leave or spend the rest of my life pining for something I could never have, and nothing, and that includes a man, is worth that. I don't want to grow old and angry, which I have become over the years, when it would have been easier to accept the reality that I am who I am, and that Weylin is who he is. I'll be closing on my new home in a couple of days, and that day will be like every festive holiday rolled into one.

Cherie closed the journal, capped the pen, and slipped both into her tote. The weeks and months had passed quickly for her once she'd gone through her closets and packed up what she wanted and needed, while donating items she hadn't worn in years to her favorite charity. It had been the first week in December when she'd received a call from the realtor that a closing date had been set for the twenty-first. Three weeks had given her enough time to close on the condo with a buyer who was willing to wait until she'd vacated the unit. She had contracted with a moving company to ship the contents of the condo to a storage facility in Shelby, North Carolina, and then spent a week sleeping on an air mattress and eating out or ordering in.

She had also kept her promise to hang out with Edwina. They'd taken the Metro-North railroad into Grand Central Station to shop and sightsee in New York City.

Cherie had shared things with her mother that were a long time coming. Her attitude had become "better late than never"; she realized that if she weren't relocating, she would never have the memories of enjoying their time together.

She looked around the empty apartment for the last time. She'd stored the mattress and several changes of clothes in the cargo area of the SUV for the nonstop drive to Wilmington, North Carolina, where she planned to spend the night before leaving for Coates Island the following morning. Retrieving her cell phone, she tapped Kayana's name for a text message:

Cherie: I will close on the house on the 21st. Hopefully, I will get to see you before you shut down for the Christmas holiday.

She did not have to wait for Kayana's response.

Kayana: We are not closing until the 23rd. Can't wait to see you. Once we return, Leah and I will plan a special dinner to welcome our book club sister back—this time for good.

Cherie eyelids fluttered as she blinked back tears. She never counted as friends the girls at the private prep school or the ones she'd interacted with at Yale. It was the same with some of her former coworkers. Once they'd discovered where she lived, some were bold enough to question how she was able to live in the gated development on her salary. Rather than tell them off, Cherie decided not responding was more profound. It was enough to leave them guessing . . . and to leave her alone.

It had taken two forty-something women to make her aware of who she was and could be. She thought of them as friends and older sisters who did not bite their tongues when dishing out advice and opinions, and that was more than enough for Cherie to seriously give them some thought.

Cherie: Hugs and kisses.

Kayana: Same to you.

She slipped the phone into her crossbody bag, picked up the tote, and with one last glance at the empty space, she walked out, closing the door behind her. And when she started up her car and drove out of the development for the last time, it was without sadness or regret. It had taken days, weeks, and then months after leaving Coates Island this past summer for her to conclude there was nothing keeping her in Connecticut.

She did not have a mortgage on the condo, and she was only responsible for maintenance fees that were a fraction of what she would've paid for a one-bedroom rental apartment in a middle-income neighborhood. Then she had the money she'd received for selling her son. The Campbells were to Connecticut real estate as Bill Gates was to Microsoft, and knowing this, Cherie had established the terms for her giving Weylin an heir, though it had taken a while for her to come to the realization that she'd been nothing more than the surrogate for a childless couple.

Cherie did not know if Weylin had told his wife that he'd been carrying on an affair with another woman for more than a decade, but apparently that hadn't mattered, as Weylin and Michelle Campbell allowed the press into their home for the first time as parents. It had been the first and last time the Campbells had allowed photographs of their son, and for that, Cherie was grateful.

She tuned the Honda's satellite radio to a station featuring classic dance selections from Studio 54. The upbeat tunes were the perfect thing to take her mind off what she'd left behind, while she attempted to concentrate on what was to come.

Chapter 3

Cherie checked into the boutique hotel in Wilmington, ordered room service, then took a quick shower before it arrived. She'd stopped only once during the drive to refuel, order strong black coffee to remain alert, and take a bathroom break before getting behind the wheel again to make it to North Carolina before eight. One of her pet peeves was driving at night when she was unfamiliar with the road.

The shower was what she needed to offset her fatigue; she patted the moisture from her body with a thick terrycloth towel before applying a lightly scented body lotion and slipping into a pair of cotton pajamas. She picked up the television remote and turned it on at the same time that there came a knock on the door and a male voice announced room service.

After signing the check and closing the door behind the grinning man, she removed the plastic top on the plate, which held a smothered chicken breast, garlic mashed potatoes, and steamed broccoli. The aroma of the mushroom gravy wafted to her nose and reminded Cherie that she hadn't eaten anything since the night before.

She finished eating and set the tray outside the door. There was no need to place the DO NOT DISTURB placard on the doorknob because she planned to check out before ten. The chicken was good, but it could not compare to what she'd eaten at the Seaside Café.

One thing Cherie intended to do was to improve her cooking repertoire. It wasn't as if she was completely clueless when it came to knowing her way around the kitchen, but if she wanted to keep up with Leah and Kayana, she knew for certain that she had to up her game. She also was realistic enough to know she would never be able create the dishes Kayana and her brother, Derrick, prepared for their patrons because they'd had years of practice in replicating the recipes passed down from their mother and grandmother. Discussing books while eating incredibly delicious appetizers, along with exotic libations, had been the highlight of her summers on Coates Island.

Her first year vacationing on the island was a reality check for Cherie. Leah and Kayana must have thought her a sullen, spoiled young woman who said whatever came to mind without regard to their feelings. What she hadn't been able to tell them was that she was still grieving her baby.

This past summer, she'd strived to be better. She had forced herself to think before opening her mouth, and most times, she was successful. Both women often reminded her that she had what it took to get any man she wanted.

Wanted.

Who and what she wanted were and had always been beyond her grasp, but she had been too blind to see or acknowledge it. Why had it taken so long for her to face reality?

Cherie brushed her teeth, and then returned to the bedroom and got into bed to watch the rerun of an old sitcom. Ten minutes into the program, her cell phone rang. Leaning over, she plucked it off the bedside table and went completely still when she saw the name on the screen. Had he forgotten about their last conversation? Something told her to let the call go to voice mail. That she didn't want or need to talk to the caller. But curiosity won out as she answered it.

"Hello." The single word was flat, emotionless.

"Why didn't you tell me you'd sold the condo? My father called me earlier today to inform me that the unit has a new owner."

"I didn't know I had to inform you about something that belonged to me. Remember, it was a condition of our deal." Cherie smiled when she heard heavy breathing coming through the earpiece. "You're a little late, Weylin, because I sold the unit several weeks ago, and the buyer was generous enough to let me live there until I was ready to leave."

"Where are you?"

The proprietary hint in his query struck a nerve with Cherie. Her former lover had no right to question her whereabouts. After all, they had ended their fifteen-year relationship more than four years ago with a promise they would never speak again.

"That's none of your fuckin' business."

"Where is this nastiness coming from, Cherie?"

"Oh! You think I'm nasty because you question me as if I'm obligated to keep you abreast of my whereabouts. Let me remind you that I'm not your wife, so don't confuse me with Michelle, because I don't look or sound like her. Good night and goodbye." Cherie ended the call and slipped the phone under a mound of pillows.

Her face was on fire as she struggled to control her temper. She could not believe Weylin's audacity, questioning her about something that had belonged to her. He wanted a baby, and she had given him a baby, and in return, she got the condo free and clear—or so she'd thought. The phone rang again, and this time she let the call go directly to voice mail.

Cherie was angry with herself that Weylin still had the power to make her feel things she did not want to feel. His call had shattered her contentment. The euphoria she'd experienced when getting the call from the realtor had dissipated like a drop of water on a heated griddle since answering Weylin's call.

Biting her lip, Cherie stared at the flickering images on the television screen. Hanging up on Weylin was something she never would've done in the past. Then, she'd been too grateful to hear his voice when he'd send her coded messages as to where they would meet for their liaisons, all the while marveling that no one ever suspected them of carrying on a clandestine affair. She was known as a friend from their prep school days and then as a classmate at Yale.

Cherie had even joined his campaign as a volunteer; she'd agreed to telephone registered voters once Weylin challenged the popular incumbent representative for his congressional seat. She remembered the day because, hours before, her gynecologist had confirmed what she'd suspected all along: she was carrying Weylin's baby.

They'd talked about having a child together, and she'd agreed, but that was before he'd blindsided her with the news that he wanted to adopt the child as his own because his wife was unable to have children. This disclosure had rocked her to the core. When they'd discussed her becoming pregnant, she'd thought it was to produce their love child and not his and Michelle's. It had taken Cherie several weeks to formulate a plan, one in which she would get what she wanted and her lover would get what he wanted. Weylin had agreed to the condo but had balked at the amount she'd requested. What he hadn't realized was that she wasn't the same old Cherie that had dropped everything at his beck and call, or agreed to whatever he'd demanded.

She knew she'd shocked him when she'd said it was all or nothing, that she would keep her baby and raise it on her own, and there was no guarantee she wouldn't reveal the identity of the father of her child at some time in the future. It had taken Weylin less than a week to agree to what she wanted, and by the time she'd completed her second trimester, she had moved into a unit in one of the most exclusive enclaves in Cos Cob, Connecticut, and had received stock options in Campbell Realty Corp., which she promptly sold back to Weylin's family's company for more than six figures.

Fortunately for Cherie, her pregnancy wasn't evident to those with whom she worked because she'd gained only fifteen pounds.

Cherie waited until the beginning of her final month before putting in a request and was granted a leave from her job for personal reasons. Most of her colleagues were aware that she'd lost a brother due to street violence and knew she had always taken vacation for several weeks beginning with the anniversary of his birthday.

She'd remained cloistered in her condo, only leaving for appointments with her obstetrician, and when it came time for her to deliver, it was at a private hospital in a remote town near the Massachusetts border. She'd been admitted to the hospital as Janine Richardson rather than Cherie Thompson, and within minutes of delivering a healthy five-pound, six-ounce baby boy, the carefully orchestrated sham was over.

Cherie shook her head again. She refused to let Weylin's call affect her. She was moving to Coates Island and into a new house, and was going to reconnect with two women she'd come to admire and claim as friends.

Friends.

Her lips twisted in a cynical smile. She had befriended a girl in the neighboring apartment before she'd left for prep school; however, whenever she returned home during school holidays or a recess, it was as if the girl wanted nothing to do with her. Then came the whispers that she thought herself better than them because she spoke differently and preferred to stay home studying rather than hang out with other kids her age.

What they didn't understand was that she was on scholarship and had to maintain her grades or lose the coveted grant. At first, she was upset by the alienation, but once she met Weylin, she didn't care if they spoke or even acknowledged her. He had become her world and everything she wanted and needed. In hindsight, Cherie knew she had not only been vulnerable but starved for acceptance and blond, gorgeous Brad Pitt look-alike William Weylin Campbell III had fulfilled her fanatical fantasy.

Although she'd continued to sleep with him once he'd married, unknowingly she'd begun to change. First, it was the demand for expensive birthday and Christmas gifts, which she'd sold, depositing the money into her safe deposit box. Then it escalated into large sums of money—which he was willing to give her, and which she had used to purchase savings bonds in various denominations. Her fear of being poor had become an obsession that was the driving motivation to get whatever she could from Weylin.

But it was his plea that they make a baby together that had her figuratively walking on air. Her rationale was that, if she couldn't marry him, then having his child came a close second—all of which detonated once he admitted he wanted the baby for his wife.

It was apparent that Weylin had underestimated her when his family's attorney called her a scheming, manipulative ghetto bitch because he had been so certain that she would continue to bend to his client's will. Ghetto bitch or not, Cherie had had enough. Enough of becoming a floor mat for a man she would never be able to claim as her husband.

Cherie had told herself never again. Never again would she trust a man, and she was now resigned to live her life as a single woman, doing what she wanted and what was good for her emotional well-being. She flicked off the television and the bedside lamp and settled down to get some sleep before her drive to Coates Island to close and take possession of her new home.

* * *

Cherie walked up the steps to the two-story house with off-white vinyl siding, robin's-egg-blue shutters, a gunmetal-gray slate metal roof, and an expansive front porch. The structure had been built to withstand hurricanes and tropical storms, though they rarely, if ever, struck the island. Unlike the beachfront homes, her house wasn't built on stilts.

She unlocked the front door and stood motionless, staring at the yawning space with highly polished wood floors as the scent of lemon wafted to her nostrils. The former owners had arranged to have the floors redone and the house cleaned from top to bottom, because not only had Cherie met their asking price, but she also had been willing to wait for them to complete building their house in Hawaii.

An overwhelming feeling of joy held her captive as she struggled to draw a normal breath; she closed the door and walked through the entryway and into the living room with a wood-burning fireplace. The family room off the living room also had a fireplace. The open floor plan concept was perfect for living and entertaining, and she couldn't wait to host a book club meeting in her new home, but that wasn't going to become a reality until everything she'd ordered was delivered. The condo's living room furnishings would go into the family room, and her bedroom furniture would occupy one guest bedroom. The table and chairs in the condo's dining area were perfect for the alcove in the expansive eat-in kitchen. She still had to order a bed, night tables, and dressers for another of the two guest bedrooms, and the smallest of the four bedrooms would eventually become a home office.

Cherie had ordered a new queen-size mattress to replace the one on which she'd slept when she'd moved into the condo, while she had also ordered a king-size bed, triple dresser, chest-on-chest, and a padded bench seat she planned to position at the foot of the bed in the master suite. She climbed the carpeted staircase to the second story. The enormous second-floor master bedroom had a spacious sitting area and French doors that opened out onto a balcony that offered views of the ocean; it was the perfect place for her to begin and end the day.

The en suite bathrooms in the master and one of the guest bedrooms were a spa retreat, with freestanding rain showers, soaking tubs, double vanities, and built-in shelves for storing towels and beauty products. She returned to the first floor and opened the door to the built-in refrigerator to discover it spotless; its only contents were two open boxes of baking soda.

Cherie had retraced her steps to her vehicle to unload her luggage when she spied a woman waving to her from a house across the street. Smiling, she returned the wave, and the tall, slender woman took it as a signal that Cherie wanted to meet her.

There was something about woman as she came closer that reminded Cherie of Leah because of her red hair and freckles. The woman's smile was still in place when she extended her hand.

"Kate Murphy told me you would be moving in today. I'm Bettina Wilson."

Cherie took her hand. A network of fine lines deepened around Bettina's brown eyes. "Cherie Thompson."

Bettina pulled the bulky sweater around the blouse she'd paired with well-worn jeans and tattered leather moccasins. "I couldn't believe it when Kate told me a young woman was buying her house because we don't get too many young folks willing to settle down here on the island. Once my kids graduated high school, they were out of here. My husband and I decided to stay after we retired. I happen to like my home, as well as the fact that we don't have to leave to go on vacation to some tropical island when we have it right here." She paused to wave to a slowly passing car with SHERIFF emblazoned on the side door. "That's our new deputy sheriff, Reese Matthews. He really isn't new to Coates Island; he grew up on the mainland. He went into the army right out of high school and came back last year to join the sheriff's department, where his cousin is the chief."

Cherie hadn't spent more than two minutes with the woman to conclude she was a gossiper, and for her, that was one of the drawbacks of living in a small town. Most folks knew something about someone, and it was probably just a matter of time before Bettina gleaned things about her Cherie did not want her to know, and that meant she had to be very careful whenever they had a conversation.

"It's nice to know that the island has police protection."

Bettina nodded, her short reddish curls moving with the motion. "There's hardly any crime here on the island. It's on the mainland where the deputies are kept busy."

Cherie glanced at Bettina's house. It wasn't one of the newer structures on the island but appeared to be in good condition. Window boxes and a wraparound porch added to its quaint charm. She'd spent her first vacation on the island in the local boardinghouse, and earlier in the summer, she'd rented a bungalow because she had come to value her privacy.

"It's nice meeting you, but I need to take some things inside. I want to settle in before the movers bring my furniture tomorrow." Other furnishings were scheduled for delivery over the first three weeks in January.

"You're more than welcome to join me and my Andy for dinner tonight if—"

"Thank so much," Cherie interrupted, "but I have plans to eat with some of my friends tonight."

Bettina gave her a wide-eyed stare. "You have friends on the island?"

"Yes. It's the reason I decided to move here."

The other woman's eyebrows lifted. "Oh, I see. If that's the case, then I better let you get on with moving in. The invitation is open for dinner. I do make a delicious kidney pie, if I say so myself."

"Thanks again for the offer," Cherie repeated. She wanted to tell the woman she rarely ate organ meat, but did not want to appear ungrateful. And she was glad that she'd mentioned she had friends on the island because hopefully Bettina would take the hint that she did know people on Coates Island with whom she could socialize.

Bettina nodded. "I'll let you go get settled in. Remember, if you need anything, I'm right across the street."

Cherie just wanted the woman to leave her alone so she could unload her car. And she also wanted to drive to the Seaside Café before it closed. It took three trips for her to unload the cargo area of the Honda CRV before she slipped behind the wheel to drive the short distance to the café.

Girl, what have you gone and done? Cherie felt a shiver of apprehension eddy through her as she stared out the windshield. It was as if she could hear her grandmother's voice chastising her whenever she'd gotten into something she'd being warned to stay out of or away from. Was Grandma chiding her for running away rather than staying and fixing her life?

Chapter 4

Cherie maneuvered into a parking space at the Seaside Café and then walked around the building, which was erected on stilts, to the front door. Aside from the white van with the name of the restaurant emblazoned on the doors, there were four other vehicles in the lot, all bearing North Carolina license plates. It was a reminder that she had to exchange her Connecticut plates for ones from her new home state.

She opened the door and entered the dining area. It was apparent that Kayana and Derrick had changed the doorbell ringtone from the distinctive Big Ben gong to wind chimes. She hadn't taken more than two steps when Cherie spied Leah Kent coming from the direction of the kitchen.

"Well, as I live and breathe. I can't believe you're really here," Leah said, her drawl confirming that she'd grown up in the South.

Cherie smiled. "I know you didn't believe me when I told you I was going to move here."

"Kayana kept dropping hints, but to be completely honest, I really didn't believe her." Leah extended her arms, and

Cherie walked into her embrace to press her cheek against the older woman's.

Cherie inhaled the scent of the tall redhead's perfume mingling with the smell of yeast clinging to the apron she'd put on over a long-sleeved T-shirt and slim-fit jeans. And because she was working in the café's kitchen, Leah had covered her strawberry-blond hair with a white bandana.

Pulling out of the embrace, Cherie said, "Well, I'm here in the flesh, and this time to stay." It felt good to say that; before leaving the island earlier that summer, she had said it in jest, not knowing whether it truly would become a reality. "If you could walk away without a backward glance, giving up the historic mansion, fancy dinner parties, and the bling, to move here and work in a restaurant, then the decision for me to uproot myself was a no-brainer."

Leah made a sucking sound with her tongue and teeth. "You left out the cheating, lying, and verbally and physically abusive husband."

When first meeting Leah Kent, Cherie resented that she had what Cherie always wanted: a wealthy husband and children, unaware that the woman had spent thirty years married to a man she'd despised. Now, in hindsight, she was ashamed that she hadn't always gotten along with the recently widowed former headmistress for an exclusive Richmond, Virginia, private all-girls school and had sometimes attacked her without provocation.

Cherie glanced around the dining area. "Is Kayana here?"

"Not yet. This is Derrick's two weeks to cook, and that means Kayana will come in just before closing to clean up for the next day."

She noticed a rush of color stain Leah's pale cheeks when she mentioned Kayana's brother's name. The redhead had always liked the handsome widower, and once she moved to the island, she and the single father had gone from friends to lovers and were now living together.

"I came in to see you guys, but to also eat lunch and pick up something for dinner."

Leah gestured over her shoulder at the buffet table with its trays of hot and cold dishes. "There still may be some baked chicken and braised beef ribs left. We just packed up several takeout containers for the sheriff's office. Select whatever you want while I get some to-go boxes from the kitchen for you." She paused. "By the way, where are you staying?"

"I closed on my house this morning. I'm expecting the movers to deliver my furniture tomorrow morning."

"You're staying in an empty house?"

Cherie bit back a grin when she saw an expression of horror freeze Leah's features. "It's empty in the literal sense, but I did bring an air mattress, folding chairs, and a card table with me."

"There's no way in hell I am going to let you sleep on the floor, Cherie. You're coming home with me and Derrick. You know we have three extra bedrooms that no one sleeps in."

"Thanks, but I'm good."

"You're not good, Cherie," Leah insisted.

Cherie did not want to argue with Leah. She'd done enough of that in the past. Now that she was going to live on Coates Island, she needed a comfortable and stress-free relationship with her book club friends. She didn't mind if they disagreed when critiquing a novel, but she wanted none of the rancor that had been so apparent the first year she'd come to the island. And she didn't need a therapist to tell her that she was still harboring a lot of anger and guilt for selling her baby to the man who had lied to her when he said he'd wanted her to have his child so they would forever be bound together.

"I was sleeping on the floor before I left Connecticut. I'd arranged to put everything in my condo in storage down here while I waited for a confirmation date for closing on the house, so I'm sure I can survive one more night."

Leah narrowed the topaz-blue eyes in her lightly freckled face. "Well, if you say so."

Cherie flashed a bright smile. "I say so."

"As soon as you're settled in, Kayana and I are going to host a housewarming party for you." She held up a hand when Cherie opened her mouth. "Mama has spoken and means no back talk."

Cherie couldn't help but laugh. Leah's voice had taken on the tone she'd heard countless times when mothers chastised their children, some demanding complete obedience. Leah, fifteen years her senior, was old enough to be her mother—that is, if she'd had her children at fifteen rather than nineteen.

She curtsied as if bowing to royalty. "Yes, Mama."

Throwing back her head, Leah laughed loudly. "Go and get something to eat before someone else comes in and cleans us out." The words were barely off her tongue when the door opened, and a man wearing a gray uniform and holstered handgun walked in. It was obvious he was law enforcement. Leah nodded to the tall, dark-complected man. A matching gray, wide-brim, Western-style hat was pulled low over his forehead. "We just finished your order, Deputy Matthews. I'm going to get it from the kitchen."

Cherie gave the man a quick glance before averting her gaze and making her way over to the buffet table. When she'd met his eyes, there was something in his intense stare that made her feel slightly uncomfortable. She attributed it to his not seeing her before. And when Leah had addressed him as Deputy Matthews, she realized he was the same man Bettina Wilson had identified as Reese Matthews, the island's newest deputy.

There was no doubt he would stare at her. After all, she was a stranger moving to an island with approximately four hundred permanent residents. Cherie was aware that many of the homeowners left the island to check into extended-stay rentals or went to live with relatives during the months of June, July, and August.

There were half-empty trays of chicken, beef ribs, yellow rice, mashed potatoes, string beans with smoked meat and white potatoes, smothered cabbage, succotash, and bowls of macaroni salad and coleslaw. There were more than enough selections for her lunch and dinner.

Reaching for a plate, she busied herself, filling it with chicken, potatoes, and smothered cabbage. She heard the door chime, and when she glanced over her shoulder, she discovered the deputy had left. Picking up a knife, fork, and napkin, Cherie found an empty table away from the other diners and concentrated on eating.

The Seaside Café had earned the reputation of serving some of the best southern cuisine in the county. The Johnsons' macaroni and cheese, creole fried chicken and buttermilk waffles, and potato salad were customer favorites. They were also Cherie's favorites in addition to Derrick's lasagna, meat loaf, and barbecued spareribs. Whenever they'd gotten together for their book club meetings, Kayana and Leah went all out when it came to preparing small plates. Cherie had assumed the role of mixologist whenever she concocted alcoholic and mocktails.

The first summer she'd come to North Carolina for a vacation, their book club had met every Sunday afternoon, but this past year they'd changed it to once a month. It had taken the pressure off Leah, who, because of family emergencies, had divided her time between Richmond, Virginia, and Coates Island. In the end, they'd met only once for a book discussion, with a promise to resume the following year.

Cherie wasn't certain what the new year would bring for the book club now that Kayana was married and Leah was living with Kayana's brother. Leah hinted that she and Derrick had talked about marriage, but the widowed couple were in no rush to tie the knot. Derrick had been widowed for a few years, while Leah had recently lost her philandering husband. The former teacher had also admitted that she had symbolically divorced her husband years ago and that he'd done her a favor, passing away when he did, to spare her the angst of going through a long and no doubt contentious divorce.

As the single one among the trio, Cherie was more than willing to agree to whatever schedule Leah and Kayana proposed. If they wanted to wait until the summer to start up again, that would give her time to decorate her home and research colleges for online degree courses.

She finished eating and then picked up the takeout containers Leah had left on the table, along with a shopping bag bearing the restaurant's logo. Cherie filled one container with macaroni salad and coleslaw and the other with yellow rice and braised beef ribs.

"Is that all you're taking?"

Cherie turned to find Leah standing only a feet away. "Yes. I plan to drive to the mainland to shop for groceries after I leave here to stock my fridge. Once I'm settled in, I'll go back and buy enough to fill the pantry."

"Aren't you going to wait for Kayana?"

"No. I still need to shop before it gets too late." She didn't tell Leah that she wanted to be indoors before sunset. Not only didn't she like driving at night, but she also felt more secure being home after dark. It was something that had come from her childhood. Her grandmother had cautioned her to be home before the streetlights came on because the neighborhood wasn't safe at night. And as she grew older, Cherie knew her grandmother was somewhat paranoid because if something bad was going to happen, it didn't matter what time of day it was, but it had been so engrained in her that she continued to adhere to the warning.

Cherie missed her grandmother as much as she did her brother. Gwendolyn Thompson had been her most vocal supporter and cheerleader. She'd been the one to encourage

Cherie to ignore the snide remarks about her believing she was better than the other girls in their neighborhood—because she was. Her Grammie hadn't lived long enough to see her graduate from high school. Most folks said she'd died from grief. For a week following Jamal's funeral, Gwendolyn refused to come out of her apartment and barely touched the food Edwina left for her. Three months later, she died in her sleep. The coroner said it was natural causes, but Cherie knew her grandmother had willed herself to die because she'd doted on her oldest grandson.

Cherie knew it would take time, but living on Coates Island would allow her to view life differently.

Reaching into her crossbody bag, she took out a bill and handed it to Leah. "Let me know if this is enough to cover my food."

Leah pushed the bill into the pocket of Cherie's jacket. "Your money is no good here," she said in a quiet voice.

"If you say so," Cherie whispered.

"I do say so." Leah smiled. "We're closing the day after tomorrow for a couple of weeks. Will we see you again before then?"

"I doubt it, Leah. I have so much to do in the house before I can begin to settle in."

"Take your time, sweetie. As they say, Rome wasn't built in a day."

Cherie smiled. "You're right about that. Give Derrick my best, and I'll see you guys when you get back." She pressed her cheek to Leah's, turned on her heel, and walked out of the restaurant.

She returned to her car and thought about stopping at the house to put the food in the fridge, then changed her mind. The temperature was in the low forties, cool enough that the containers with the food wouldn't spoil before she reached home.

Driving more than a mile to a supermarket to purchase groceries was something Cherie would have to get used to.

Living in a gated community with onsite shops had spoiled her. She either walked or drove the short distance to pick up whatever she wanted or needed, or went online to have the items delivered directly to her front door.

Humming a nameless tune, she reveled in the emotion of unadulterated freedom she likened to a baby bird leaving the nest for the first time, soaring with reckless abandon. Yes. She was free to interact with whomever she wanted, and free to begin her life anew without regard to others.

She drove along the bridge connecting the island to the mainland without encountering another vehicle either coming or going and decelerated to less than twenty miles per hour. There was a sign indicating she was entering the Village of Coates Island and another displaying the speed limit, which was monitored and enforced by the sheriff's department. The Village, as the locals referred to it, was typical of the downtown business area in many small towns. There was the ubiquitous town square, with granite monuments with the names of the fallen men and women who had served in past and recent wars, and mom-and-pop stores catering to locals and vacationers alike.

Earlier that summer, Cherie had taken the jitney to the mainland to familiarize herself with the area once she'd contemplated—and it wasn't for the first time—if she would relocate to the island. There was something about strolling along the narrow cobblestone alleys behind the small shops; a few bore signs indicating they'd been established when the colony had been under British rule.

During their first book club meeting, Kayana had given her and Leah an overview of her family's history on the island, going back to the eighteenth century, when North Carolina had been an English colony. She had been entranced that the Johnsons' roots ran deep in Coates Island. Kayana, Derrick, and their sister, Jocelyn, were direct descendants of a pirate and a free woman of color. Every time Cherie had thought about tracing her own ancestry, she had been reluctant because she didn't know the identity of her biological father, and she did not want to open a Pandora's box and release a plethora of shocks and the answers to the countless questions she needed to ask Edwina. She'd decided that, if she was going to begin her life anew, she would have to forget about her past.

Coates Island's mainland had a documented population of more than thirty-eight hundred residents. It claimed its own school district, town council, police department, jail, and court. During her first trip to the island, she'd learned that she had to apply for a vacationer's sticker, park in a designated area on either the island or mainland, and wasn't permitted to drive on the local roads beginning with Memorial Day weekend through Labor Day. Nonresidents got around by walking or riding jitneys or bikes. Cherie's short-term plan was to change the address on her driver's license, apply for a resident sticker at the town hall, and purchase a bicycle for exercise.

She parked her car in the lot behind the supermarket. It wasn't as large as a twenty-four-hour superstore, but it had everything she needed to stock her fridge and pantry. Cherie leisurely pushed the shopping cart up and down aisles, filling it with cleaning supplies, canned goods, dairy, baking items, and fresh produce. She stopped at the meat section and selected packaged chicken, breakfast meats, and a variety of beef and pork products, and then lingered long enough in the housewares aisle to pick up a saucepan, a frying pan, and several serving pieces. Although she was expecting the boxes from the condo to be delivered the following day, Cherie knew it would take time for her to unpack and put everything away. Her priorities were the kitchen and bathroom, and setting up one of the guest bedrooms, where she would sleep until the furniture she'd ordered for the master bedroom arrived.

She paid for her purchases, loaded the cargo area of the SUV, and headed back to the island. At her new house,

Cherie tapped the remote device attached to the vehicle's visor, and the automatic garage door opened smoothly. The former owners had given her two remotes and the programmed code to the garage door. Not having to get out of her car to open and close the garage door was a much-needed convenience.

There were a few other details Cherie had to put into action before settling comfortably into her new home. The house was wired for Wi-Fi, and she needed to sign up with a company for online, telephone, and internet access. She backed into the garage, shut off the engine, and tapped the keypad on the wall to close the door. It took several trips for her to unload the bags and carry them up the four stairs and into the kitchen.

By the time Cherie finally put away the groceries, the afternoon shadows had lengthened as dusk descended on the island. She reheated the food from the Seaside Café and sat on the folding chair at the card table to eat. She knew it would take time to turn the house into a home, but then again, all she had was time. Time to decorate, time to become acquainted with the mainland and island, and time to determine which college she would select to continue her education.

She finished her dinner, then went upstairs to shower and change into a pair of sweats. Cherie covered her feet with a pair of thick cotton socks, picked up her cell phone, and went to sit out on the porch. The former owners hadn't taken with them the all-weather Adirondack chairs with blue-and-white cushions in various prints and designs that were a match for the shutters. Along with the balcony outside the master bedroom, the porch was a perfect spot to begin or end the day.

The scent of saltwater wafted to her nostrils with the rising wind off the ocean. The temperatures had dropped appreciably with the onset of dusk, but she loathed getting up and going inside to get a jacket or heavy sweater. How different, she thought, from when she'd sat on her condo's balcony to watch cars enter and leave the development. Not only didn't she have to encounter any of her neighbors or engage in chitchat with those who had tried unsuccessfully to get to know her intimately, but to those who had been bold enough to ask her how she could afford to purchase a two-bedroom unit, she'd responded that she'd had a wealthy benefactor who had rewarded her for looking after his son. None knew that she'd been involved with the property owner's son.

Her cell phone rang, and she answered before the second ring. "Are you calling to check up on me?" she asked Kayana, teasingly.

"You know I am. After all, I have to make certain our book club sister is okay."

Cherie smiled. "I'm fine, Kayana."

"The offer still holds if you want to stay in the upstairs apartment until you're settled in."

"Thank again for your concern, but I am really okay here. I'm glad you called before going away because I'm thinking about having some of the rooms painted. Could you give me the name of someone reputable I could use?"

"There is someone we've used a few times. He has a business on the mainland. After we hang up, I'll text you his name and phone number. When you call him, let him know that I recommended him to you. His name is Sylvester Connolly, but everyone calls him Sly. He's a perfectionist, so you may have to put up with his idiosyncrasies and get familiar with his mercurial moods."

Cherie laughed. "If that's the case, I'll make certain to stay out of his way."

"You learn fast. I'm not going to keep you, but let me know if you need anything before we leave."

"I don't think so. I really appreciate you thinking about me, but I want you and your boo to enjoy yourselves. And if you can't be good, then please be careful."

Kayana's sultry laugh came through the earpiece. "Unlike

you, there is no risk of my getting pregnant, so we don't have to be careful."

The mention of pregnancy rendered Cherie temporarily mute. She'd gotten pregnant once, and there was always the possibility that she could do so again, yet it was something she refused to think about. And if she did decide to have another child, the circumstances were certain to be vastly different from the first time. Not only did she want to bring her baby to term and keep it, but she also wanted to be married and have her child grow up with two parents.

"Right now, having a baby is not on my to-do list."

"Perhaps not now, Cherie. But what about in the future?" Kayana asked. "Maybe you'll meet someone, fall in love, and start a family. Leah and I can take turns babysitting whenever you need to take some time to yourself."

Cherie smiled, although Kayana couldn't see her. "You have it all planned out for me, don't you?"

"Why not? Leah and I are booed up, and there's no reason why you shouldn't be, too."

"Right now, I don't have time to be, as you say, booed up. I have much too much on my plate to get involved with a man. Give me a few years, then I'm certain I'll get there."

"I'm glad you're keeping your options open. I know you probably don't want to hear it, but you're a lot more enjoyable now than you were when you came down here last summer."

"I know I wasn't very nice to Leah. At the time, I was dealing with my own shit, but that's behind me now." Cherie didn't want to admit to Kayana that relocating was the best thing she'd done to put her past behind her.

"Good for you. Leah and I were talking about when you want to begin holding our book club meetings again."

A beat passed. "I'd like to begin again in the spring. That will give us a lot more time to read several books before the summer season when you guys will really be busy."

"How often do you want to meet?" Kayana asked.

"Once a month works for me," Cherie said. "It takes the pressure off trying to finish a book in a week."

"I'll let Leah know. I've held your ear long enough, so I'm going to hang up now. Have a very merry Christmas and a fabulous New Year."

"Same to you."

That said, Cherie ended the call. It wouldn't be the first time she would spend Christmas and New Year's alone since her brothers left to attend the military academies, but this time it would be different. She planned to gift herself with a piece of jewelry to commemorate a new beginning and prepare a special dinner with champagne to celebrate the new year.

She would be alone, but not lonely. Not when she'd spent more than half her life alienated from her prep school and college classmates and those in the neighborhood where she'd grown up. She was glad that she'd rekindled some connection with her mother and truly looked forward to the time when Edwina would come down to visit with her.

Her grandmother was gone, Jamal was gone, and her twins brothers had embarked on a life in the military, so that left Edwina, and Cherie hoped they could have a normal mother–daughter relationship sooner rather than later.

The solar porchlights came on automatically as she got up and went into the house. She planned to go to bed early and get enough sleep to be ready for the movers, who were scheduled to arrive at eight the following morning.

Cherie carried the air mattress to the smallest of the four bedrooms, inflated it, then covered it with a sheet, lightweight blanket, and comforter. Sleeping a few feet off the floor reminded her of the time when she'd slept on a rollaway cot in the bedroom she'd shared with her mother. Their apartment had two bedrooms; her brothers had occupied the larger of the two, while she had shared the other bedroom with her mother until she'd left to attend prep school. And whenever she returned, she'd opted to sleep on the cot rather than with Edwina, who tended to snore if she drank alcohol.

Cherie brushed her teeth, washed her face, then slathered on a moisturizer before stripping off her clothes and walking down the hallway to her temporary bedroom. Tapping the wall switch, she dimmed the overhead light until there was just enough illumination to make out the mattress bed. She set the alarm on her cell phone to wake her at six, because she wanted to be showered and dressed before the movers arrived the following morning. She didn't mind sleeping on the floor because in another twenty-four hours she would sleep in a bed in her new home for the first time.

Chapter 5

An hour after the movers unloaded everything from their van, Cherie stood in the middle of the family room. A year before, after returning from Coates Island, she had contacted an interior decorator to confer about making changes in her condo. At the time, she'd believed giving her living quarters a new look would lift her sagging spirits. The decorator had recommended replacing the black leather sofa with an oyster-white leather sectional unit and suggested she order framed black-and-white photographs of plants and flowers, and a variety of green and flowering plants. It'd worked for a while; then she realized new furnishings and/or redecorating weren't the answer.

She smiled. The condo's living room furniture was perfect for the family room, and the round oaken dining room table and four chairs fit well in the kitchen's alcove. The movers had positioned the pieces in the bedroom where she'd directed them, and they were effusive in their gratitude when she generously tipped them for their efforts. Now all she had to do was unpack boxes. She'd unpacked several boxes labeled BATHROOM SUPPLIES when her cell phone rang. It was the painter, calling her back after she left a voice-mail message for him.

Cherie answered the call before it rang again. "Hello."

"This is Sly. Did you call me?"

Her eyebrows lifted slightly with his rough tone. "Yes, Mr. Connolly."

"It's Sly."

She hesitated. "Okay, Sly. I did call you because Kayana Johnson gave me your name and number. I just moved in, and I'd like to have my walls painted."

"What color are they now?"

"White."

"That's boring."

Cherie smiled. "I agree. I'd like various shades of blues and greens."

"How many rooms are you talking about?"

"The house has four bedrooms, a family room—"

"Enough!" he said, cutting her off. "I'll have to come and see what I'm working with. Give me your address, and let me know when it is a good come to come out."

"You can come now." Cherie felt it would be better for him to paint the before the furniture she had on order was delivered.

"Give me your address. And I'll bring the book with the blues and greens you're looking for."

Ninety minutes later, Cherie had selected the colors she wanted for the walls, along with the trim. Sly had complimented her choices, saying she had a good eye and that the pale colors were serene and spa-like. He wrote up a contract, with a promise that his crew would begin painting two days after Christmas, while estimating it would take no more than three days to complete the project. Cherie found this agreeable because it would give her time to unpack and make the house feel lived-in before the end of the year.

She had stepped out onto the porch, watching the painter's van drive away, when she spied Bettina crossing the street, coming in her direction. Cherie smothered a groan. She wanted to go back into the house but knew that would be rude. She wondered if the woman was a busybody or lonely now that her children had left home, hoping it was the latter.

"Good morning," Bettina called out, smiling.

Cherie returned her smile. "Good morning."

Bettina stood on the first step. "I noticed that the movers delivered your furniture earlier this morning. Do you need help putting things together?"

"No, thank you. They put up everything for me."

"Good for you. I saw the painter driving away. Do you plan to paint?"

Cherie counted slowly to five before answering. The woman reminded her of some women in the neighborhood where she'd grown up who were permanent fixtures in their apartment windows. They got up early and hung out of the windows for hours, observing everyone coming and going.

"Yes, I do."

"Good for you," Bettina repeated. "I couldn't understand why Kate wanted white walls with light-colored floors. And when I asked her about it, she said it was easier for her to see the dirt. The lady was one strange bird. She and that husband of hers kept to themselves, which made me think they were in the Witness Protection Program."

Good for them, because it kept people out of their personal business, she thought. "There are some advantages to being in Witness Protection."

Cherie hadn't realized she'd spoken her thought aloud. Bettina didn't know that Cherie had never been open with strangers. Other than the people in her neighborhood, everyone else knew very little about her, and that included classmates, coworkers, and her book club friends.

Bettina blinked slowly, and then leaned closer. "Are you saying that is your situation?" she whispered.

Cherie wanted to laugh in the woman's face, but knew that would be rude. "No comment," she said instead, wishing Bettina would take the hint and keep her distance. She didn't mind Bettina being friendly or even neighborly, but resented her unwelcomed nosiness.

An expression of concern flitted over the older woman's features. "I'll understand if you're trying to get away from an abusive husband or boyfriend. My younger sister had the same experience. She finally was able to escape her abusive husband when she upped and moved to some little town in Idaho that barely made the map. So I'll give you your space, but if you ever need help or someone to talk to, just remember I'm right across the street."

Cherie forced a smile. "Thank you. I still have to do some unpacking—"

"Go on in, honey," Bettina interrupted. "I need to get back to the house and finish wrapping gifts for my grandkids. Andy and I decided to drive down to Orlando to spend Christmas with my daughter and her husband. We plan to stay there until after the New Year. So if I don't see you before we leave, you have a Merry Christmas and a Happy New Year."

"You, too." Turning on her heel, Cherie went into the house and closed the door.

She sighed. Knowing she wouldn't have to deal with Bettina for more than a week felt as if she had been given a reprieve, and she knew there was no way she could stay home during the day and have unannounced visits from the obviously bored woman who reminded her of the women in her old neighborhood. Those who were either retired or unemployed had developed a culture of minding everyone else's business, and were as adept as tabloid reporters in searching out gossip to repeat over and over.

Cherie's grandmother had said there were a day crew and a night crew of idle women monitoring the comings and goings of everyone in the neighborhood. They knew who was cheating, stealing, hooked on drugs, and/or abusing their elderly parents, wives, or girlfriends. As hard as they'd tried, none of them was able to identify the men that had fathered Edwina Thompson's children.

She thought about Edwina's promise to tell her about her father. *One of these days, I'll tell you, once you decide to start a family. But not until then.* And several times since Edwina's vow, Cherie wanted to tell her mother she was the grandmother of a boy that she would never hold or claim as her own. That her only daughter had sold her son for a better way of life, and that now, in hindsight, she realized it was wrong to trade a human life for material goods. And she couldn't accuse her mother of keeping secrets, because she was also guilty of the same. No one knew she'd had a child, and if they did, they never would have been able to identify the father. Other than at public events, she and Weylin were never seen together.

Stop thinking about the past and concentrate on your future, the silent voice taunted. Cherie knew she couldn't change her past, so now it was incumbent on her to map out what she wanted for the rest of her life. She would turn thirty-five in March, and by that time, she would have set up her house for total living and relaxation. And by that time, she hoped to have selected the college to enroll in online courses to obtain a graduate degree and become a classroom teacher. She decided to unpack a few more boxes before driving to the mainland to open a bank account at the local branch and do some last-minute Christmas shopping.

Reese Matthews parked his cruiser in an alley, got out, and walked along the mainland Village's downtown business district. He hadn't taken more than a few steps when he saw her heading for the bank. It was the woman he'd seen talking with Bettina Wilson and then again later that afternoon in the Seaside Café. He knew it had been rude to stare, but something wouldn't permit him to look away the instant he met her jewellike eyes.

Coates Island was small enough for most folks to become familiar with one another. Since returning to Coates Island, he'd discovered a couple who had retired on the island and was now selling their home and moving to Hawaii. Reese had to admit that he was mildly shocked to discover a young woman had purchased their house when, over the years, there had been steady flow of twenty- and thirty-somethings leaving the island for better employment opportunities.

He had returned to life as a civilian nearly a year ago, and it had taken him four months to feel completely comfortable with his new lifestyle. He still wore a uniform and carried a firearm, which had made it easy for him to transition from Army Ranger to a local deputy sheriff, but that's where the similarities ended.

It had taken more than twenty years for Reese to come to appreciate his hometown. Growing up, he couldn't wait to leave, to discover a world outside of Coates Island, North Carolina, located several miles south of Wrightsville Beach, and when the army recruiter visited the mainland's high school during career week, he couldn't resist the recruiter's pitch to be all that he could be as a soldier in the United States Army.

His grandparents did not try to dissuade him from enlisting, but had offered him an alternative: enroll in the ROTC. Their dream was for him to graduate from college, because it was something Reese's mother hadn't been able to do.

He'd graduated with honors and entered the army as a second lieutenant and, twenty years later, was honorably discharged with the rank of captain. He had served and protected his country honorably for two decades, and now it was time for him to protect his hometown. He marveled that very little on Coates Island had changed since he'd left at eighteen, returning only when he had extended leaves.

The current census recorded the mainland's residents at thirty-eight hundred inhabitants and the beach community another four hundred permanent inhabitants with a combined total population of forty-two hundred. It was a small town with small-town sensibilities. Shopkeepers still decorated their windows to reflect the various holidays; there were no fast food restaurants to compete with the Seaside Café; vacationers were not permitted to drive on local roads during the summer season; and most businesses were owned and operated by generations of family members.

He'd returned home whenever he was granted leave; the last two times were to bury his grandfather and, seven months later, his grandmother. Only a few relatives were his last link to his mother, and once Reese informed his cousin that he was submitting his discharge papers, the older man urged him to return home and join the sheriff's department, where he was now chief. The offer was a no-brainer. He would move into the house where he'd been raised by his grandparents and embark on a second career in law enforcement.

"Good afternoon, Deputy Matthews."

Reese smiled and touched the brim of his Stetson in acknowledgment. "Good afternoon, Mrs. Kenny."

He'd attended high school with the older woman's daughter, and in the past, she would've called him Reese, but now it appeared that those who'd known or grown up with him preferred to address him as Deputy Matthews. Mrs. Kenny was married to the pharmacist at the local drugstore, and his pharmacist nephew had recently left a national drugstore chain to assist him.

"Are you going to be around for the lighting of the Christmas tree?" she asked.

"Most definitely."

The highlight of Reese's childhood had been accompanying his grandparents on Christmas Eve to the town square to wait for the mayor to throw the switch that would illuminate thousands of lights on a twelve-foot live Norwegian spruce. It was a time when the entire island turned out for caroling, live music, dancing, and gifts, donated by the merchants, for all children under the age of twelve. Coates Island during the Christmas season resembled a Hallmark movie without the snow.

The first time he'd been granted leave for Christmas and he'd returned with his new bride, she'd complained constantly that she'd prefer to spend the holiday in the Caribbean rather than in a dead-ass town with a bunch of boring-ass folks. Monica had announced this in the presence of his grandparents, which had shocked Reese; he'd believed she would've been more respectful of them. His grandfather hadn't said anything; it was his grandmother who later said she didn't like the woman and predicted that if he didn't divorce her, she would make his life a living hell. However, he hadn't heeded the warning, and years later, Monica did make his life hell when she'd attempted to put his rank as an officer in jeopardy.

Reese thought of his homecoming as bittersweet. His grandparents, who'd raised him from an infant after the death of his mother, were gone, while the house that had been willed to him was filled with wonderful memories that were imprinted on his brain like a permanent tattoo.

His grandmother had insisted he call her Gram instead of Mama, because she revered the title, was kind, even-tempered, and protective of him, while his grandfather, whom he'd called Papa, was a hard taskmaster who demanded nothing short of perfection when teaching Reese everything he knew about carpentry and how to frame a house. He knew his grandfather truly loved him despite his reluctance to exhibit affection.

"Don't forget, Deputy Matthews, that I'll be looking for you on Christmas Eve."

Mrs. Kenny's voice broke into his thoughts. Reese smiled again. "I'll definitely be there."

He was assigned to the 4:00 p.m. to 12:00 a.m. shift to cover the tree-lighting ceremony; as the last hired, he was scheduled to work most holidays. The sheriff's department staff included the chief and four deputies who rotated eight-hour shifts five days a week with two days off. Reese spent his days off in the workshop on the property behind his house. The instant he picked up a circular saw or touched a wood chisel, he recalled the many hours he'd spent in the workshop, watching Papa cut and sand a piece of wood for various pieces of furniture. His grandfather had taught him to identify different types of wood and their uses. And Reese knew that, if he hadn't joined the military, he would have become a master carpenter like Raymond Matthews.

Reese walked the four square blocks that made up the downtown business district. The shopkeepers had swept the sidewalks in front of their businesses and picked up any debris that had collected along the curbs. Years ago, the local chamber of commerce had embarked on a beautification program to install awnings over every shop and replace the existing lampposts with those resembling gaslights from the Victorian era. The cobblestones along the alleys were restored, and decorative brickwork covered the sidewalks throughout the entire business district.

Reese had lived and attended school on the mainland, but what he remembered most about growing up on Coates Island was crossing the bridge linking it to what locals called the island. There wasn't need to drive to a larger city to hang out at a mall because the beach had become his playground. He and his friends jogged along the sand, swam in the ocean, gathered driftwood to start a fire to roast s'mores; when they were exhausted, they fell asleep until the sun dipped beyond the horizon and the air cooled, signaling it was time they return home. Teens still tended to congregate on the sand, listening to music until sunset or sometimes later. However, no one was permitted on the beach after midnight, and the regulation was strictly enforced by local law enforcement.

He walked into the supermarket and made his way to the deli counter to pick up something for dinner. Normally, he would've called in an order to the Seaside Café, but with them closing for two weeks, he would alternate using the supermarket's deli or cooking for himself. Although he had breaks and lunch and dinner hours, Reese preferred eating in the breakroom at the station house. His current shift began at eight in the morning and ended at four, and once he was home, it usually took a while for him to unwind, and he didn't want to spend time cooking.

"What can I get for you, Deputy?" the man wearing a colorful tie-dyed bandana asked.

"What's good, Mike?"

The elderly man glared at him under lowered bushy eyebrows from behind the counter. "Why in blazes do you ask me the same damn thing each and every time you come in here?"

Reese dipped his head, hoping to conceal the smile tilting the corners of his mouth. The deli man was all bark and no bite. "Inquiring minds need to know." He wanted to remind Mike that the only time he came in to order was when the Seaside Café wasn't open for business.

"Know, my ass."

Reese's eyebrows lifted slightly. "My, my. Aren't we touchy today?"

Mike sighed and closed his eyes. "I don't mean to take my bad mood out on you, Deputy. I just had one of my full-time workers quit on me. How do you call in and say you're not coming back anymore without a warning or even an explanation."

Remorse replaced Reese's teasing. Michael Fennell had become a permanent fixture in the deli section once the supermarket expanded beyond the meat and produce departments. He was aware that Mike came in early to prepare dishes for those wishing to purchase more than cold cuts and cheese.

"I'm sorry to hear that."

"Enough about my problems." He waved a hand in dismissal. "The smothered pork chops are really good. I made 'em myself. It was my grandmama's recipe."

"I'll take that, along with the steak fries and garlic green beans."

"Good choice, if I have to say so myself," Mike said, chuckling under his breath before he sobered. "If you hear of someone, anyone, needing a job, please tell them I'm looking and willing to pay more than minimum wage."

"Have you considered hiring two part-timers?" Reese questioned.

Mike paused. "No. What are you getting at?"

"Hire a retiree for the morning hours and a high school student for the afternoon."

"Hey, I think you're on to something," Mike drawled, grinning from ear to ear. "I'm going to put an ad in the *Clarion*. Thanks."

Reese nodded. He took the bag, made his way to the checkout, and paid for his purchase. Minutes later, he retraced his steps to where he'd parked the cruiser. His shift would end, barring an emergency call, in three hours, and he was looking forward to returning home to unwind.

Crime on Coates Island was negligible when compared to other towns, but that was not to say there weren't break-ins, car thefts, underage drinking, and an occasional assault. Almost all of the criminal activity was on the mainland, while calls from the island were usually attributed to domestic disputes that were quickly resolved once a uniformed officer arrived.

Once Reese made the decision to return to Coates Island to live, he had to ask himself if he would be content not moving every few years. He'd lost count of the number of bases he'd been assigned to during several deployments, the number of countries he'd visited during his twenty-plus years of active duty. The first month, he slept twelve or more hours a day, watched endless hours of television, and when he did leave the house, it was to sit on the beach. That had become his time to reflect on where he'd come from and where he wanted to go.

He'd asked himself the same question over and over: Can I spend the rest of my life on Coates Island? It was a place that, when he was a teenager, he couldn't wait to leave. His hometown had become too small, a place where one day blended into the next without change. He got up every morning to attend school, returned home to do homework, and on weekends, he worked alongside his grandfather, even when there were times when he'd wanted to hang out with his friends.

Fast-forward, and the answer was apparent. Yes, he could. He'd survived several deployments and had returned physically whole and grateful that he'd been given the opportunity to embark on a second career to protect and serve his hometown.

Reese enjoyed reconnecting with people he'd known all his life and becoming acquainted with some of the new residents who had moved to Coates Island. He enjoyed his work as a deputy and had settled comfortably in the home where he'd grown up.

He'd just turned down the street when he saw her again. This time, the woman he'd seen talking to Bettina Wilson and then later, that afternoon, in the Seaside Café was pointing to something in the window of the jewelry store. Reese didn't know why, other than her natural beauty, he found himself intrigued with her. He knew it was easy enough to discover her name by walking into the office of the town clerk and searching through the deeds for the name of the owner of the property that once belonged to Jeremy and Katherine Murphy. Or run her license plate number through a national database. He quickly dismissed those tactics, which he thought of as snooping and wholly deceptive. And there was the possibility that she was either married, engaged, or cohabitating. Without warning, the woman turned and met his eyes before she opened the door to the store and disappeared inside; at the same time, he did not break stride. He made it to the alley and got inside the cruiser.

It had been a while—in fact, a very long time—since a woman had attracted his rapt attention like this stranger had. The first and last one he'd married. *Act in haste, repent in leisure.* Reese still could not understand why his Gram's wise sayings flooded his mind when he least expected them. However, if he had heeded her warnings, they would have saved him a great deal of heartbreak and disappointment.

He started up the car and headed back to the station house to put his food in the refrigerator. The town hall had been erected on a block a quarter of a mile from the business district. It housed the mayor and town clerk's office, the local court, and the sheriff's department, including a single holding cell.

"Sweetie, I thought you went out for lunch." Petite, with sparkling blue eyes, never married, Elizabeth Henry called everyone sweetie, because she claimed she was never able to remember names. She'd cut her shimmering white hair into a becoming, chin-length bob.

Reese smiled at the woman manning the front desk. Elizabeth had been an employee of the sheriff's department for more than forty years and had worked under three sheriffs during her tenure. She'd been hired right out of secretarial school and, over the years, had become a computer whiz. She was quick to say that Chief Parker Shelton was the best. Elizabeth had threatened to quit and/or resign several times, but once Parker was elected, she'd decided to stay on until, she claimed, the Lord called her home, which she hoped wasn't for a long time.

"I did, but I'm back. I have to catch up on some reports before I leave later this afternoon." He didn't tell the receptionist that he'd prepared breakfast for himself—grits, eggs, bacon, and toast—and the meal was enough for him to keep up his energy all morning and afternoon.

Elizabeth waved a blue-veined hand. "You're the only deputy who gives me his paperwork on time. The others play catch-up just before the chief has to submit the reports to the mayor's office for their town meetings."

"I suppose I'm a little inflexible after serving in the military for so many years."

"Inflexible or not, I told the chief that if he doesn't get on the others to give me their reports on time, I'm not going to kill myself working overtime inputting them into the computer."

Reese knew that if Elizabeth complained to Parker about the deputies, there would be hell to pay. His cousin was laid back and easygoing, but there were occasions when he'd become a drill master, barking orders and expecting them to be followed without question. This was a side of the retired drill sergeant he'd witnessed once and did not want to see again. He stored his dinner in the refrigerator and then retreated to his cubicle to type up a report from the prior day before returning to his shift. He'd issued three parking tickets and written up a report of graffiti scrawled on the rear doors of the hardware store and the bookstore. Most merchants were opposed to installing cameras in and outside their businesses, a topic that had come up for discussion during prior town hall meetings. However, with the proliferation of graffiti appearing on school property and now in the business district, the mayor and town council members were seriously considering passing an ordinance to secure properties from vandalism.

Reese finished typing his report, read it over, and then uploaded it to Elizabeth's computer. He planned to drive over the bridge to the island and then return to the mainland before clocking out for the day.

Chapter 6

Cherie, reclining on the chaise in the family room, stared at the images on the flat-screen TV mounted above the fireplace. Christmas had come and gone, and the rooms were painted in calming shades of blues, greens, and grays. The cable company had connected the Wi-Fi for access to the internet so she could begin researching colleges for her online degree.

She'd thought about enrolling in next year's fall semester, but then changed her mind to put it off until spring of the following year. That would give her time to settle into her new home and lifestyle. She'd been out of college for more than ten years, and she wanted to make certain she was emotionally ready for required reading, completing papers, and eventually student teaching.

It was New Year's Eve, and it wasn't the first time she would celebrate the holiday alone. But this year would be different. She was where she wanted to be, and she was certain what she wanted for her future. Cherie never could have imagined, when she'd opened a magazine and read the article about vacationing in North Carolina, that calling the rental agent handling vacation properties would change her life. The woman told her that all the bungalows were rented, but there were vacancies at the boardinghouse.

Then she'd been in a dark place. It was the anniversary of when she'd given up her son, and she had to get away—anywhere. Two days later, she'd emailed the signed contract to the agent and wired funds to cover the summer rental.

She'd made many decisions in her life, and summering on Coates Island had been one of the best. So much so that she'd returned this past summer, and it was enough for her to conclude it was where she wanted to live.

Her cell phone chimed a familiar ringtone. Smiling, she picked it up and tapped a key. "Happy New Year!" Cherie could hardly contain the joy she felt at that moment. She'd been waiting for her mother to call her.

"Happy New Year to you, too, baby. I've been so busy working that I didn't have time to open my mail. When I opened my bank statement, I saw that you'd deposited money into my account. Why so much, Cherie?"

"I want you to save it for when you move." There was silence on the other end of the connection. "I'm serious, Mom. I really want you to think about moving away from the neighborhood. If you find a place where the rent is more than you can afford on your salary and tips, I'm willing to subsidize you."

"Where are you getting all this money, Cherie?"

There was no way she was going to admit to her mother she'd been paid to give a man her child. "Don't forget that I worked, Mom, and also invested well." And she had. She'd traded her body in exchange for getting what she could from a wealthy man. What she refused to do was think of herself as a prostitute. Her relationship with Weylin went beyond having him pay her for sex. They'd had an affair for years, but things changed once he'd blindsided her with the demand that she give up the baby they'd made through the intimate act of making love. He'd sought to soften his petition when he'd admitted over and over that she had given him what Michelle couldn't—and that didn't only include a child. He told her that, if circumstances had been different, he would've married her.

"I don't know why I keep forgetting that. Do you have plans for tonight?"

"Yes. I'm staying home. Tomorrow I plan to roast a pork loin and make smothered cabbage, black-eyed peas, and cornbread."

Cherie had grown up believing black-eyed peas, or Hoppin' John, on New Year's Day would bring a prosperous year filled with luck. Green leafy vegetables were thought to signify wealth, and cornbread also represented wealth because it looked like gold.

Edwina's laugh came through the earpiece. "I'll never understand my children's preference for southern food and traditions, even though whenever they open their mouths to speak, everyone knows they're from New England."

"Speak for yourself, Mom. It was Grammie who kept the traditions her mother had brought from the South during the Great Migration." Cherie's great-grandmother had passed on before she was born, yet she never tired of her grandmother talking about the traditions practiced by generations of African American women in the southern region of the country. "Are you going to tell me that you're not going to make a pot of black-eyed peas."

"I'm not cooking this year. Pamela called to let me know she's having a little get-together, and I told her I would come and bring dessert."

Cherie nodded, even though her mother couldn't see her. Pamela was a distant cousin they only got to see at weddings and funerals. And Cherie didn't know what had changed to prompt her to invite Edwina to her home for the holiday. Pamela didn't attempt to conceal her disdain for her lowly relatives and always looked for every opportunity to remind everyone that she'd married well. And marrying well did not involve inheriting money; her husband had hit the jackpot at a slot machine for seven figures at a local casino and subsequently purchased a five-thousand-square-foot house overlooking the Connecticut River.

"What brought that on?"

"Stop it, Cherie! I know what you're thinking. Pamela runs hot and cold, so I'm going take her at her word and show up with a pound cake and a couple of sweet potato pies."

"And I won't say what I'm thinking. My only resolution for the coming year is to think before I speak. Have fun, and give Pamela my best."

"I will, baby. I am so proud of you, and as soon as I earn a few more vacation days, I'm going to drive down to visit you."

Tears filled Cherie's eyes as she struggled to bring her fragile emotions under control. She wished she could have had this relationship years ago when she needed to confess to her mother about her ongoing affair with a married man and that she'd given up her only grandchild because she'd wanted a better life for herself.

"Thank you, Mama. I love you."

"I love you, too."

The line went dead, and she knew Edwina had hung up. She sat motionless, willing the tears not to fall. Cherie knew that, if she did cry, it would open wounds that had healed, albeit slowly and leaving scars. She'd spent years resenting Edwina not telling her who her father was, and she still couldn't understand why her brother's murder had remained a cold case, while loving and losing Weylin and the child they had made together. She had missed a close mother-daughter relationship, which had evaded her for years, but now that they were given a second chance, Cherie would do everything within her power to make it work.

Cherie pulled into the parking at the rear of the Seaside Café, picked up the two small shopping bags off the passenger-side seat, and walked around to the front of the building. Kayana had sent her a text saying that they were back and open for business and she couldn't wait to reunite with her book club friends.

The cold and rainy weather could not dispel her joy at getting out of the house. The company had delivered the living room and master bedroom furniture a week earlier than originally confirmed. However, she was still waiting on the dining-area table and chairs, which were on back order. She'd noticed Bettina standing on her porch watching the activity, and once the workers left, she surprised Cherie when she revealed she'd been hired as a part-time counterperson at the local supermarket's deli section. Bettina admitted she didn't need money but had to get out of the house, even if it was for a few hours, because her retired husband expected her to wait on him hand and foot, as if she were his personal maid. Bettina complaining about her husband reminded Cherie of some of the women when she'd worked at the childcare center. Despite their complaints, they appeared content not to change their situations. And now she understood why Bettina sought out her company so often. She'd wanted to put some distance between herself and her demanding husband. It also wasn't the first time Cherie was thankful she wasn't involved with someone. If she'd had a relationship with a man after she'd broken up with Weylin, she doubted she would've uprooted her life and moved away.

Cherie skipped up the steps and opened the door to the sound of wind chimes. Kayana and Leah were carrying trays from the kitchen. Both were tanned from vacationing in the Florida Keys.

"Happy New Year!"

They set down the trays and formed a group hug. Cherie gave each a small shopping bag. "It's just a little something I wanted to give you for Christmas."

"You didn't have to give me anything," Leah said.

"I'm with Leah," Kayana agreed, "even though we did bring you something back as a housewarming gift. But we've decided not to give it to you until you invite us over. That's when we'll open your gift."

"That's going to be sooner rather than later because most of my furniture has been delivered. I'm just waiting on the dining-area table and chairs. Other than that, I'm now looking for accessories. I went online and found a shop in Shelby that stocks area rugs, throw pillows, and bar stools for the breakfast bar." Cherie still hadn't decided how she wanted to set up her home office, and she'd stacked boxes of unpacked books, DVDs, and CDs along every inch of wall space in the smallest of the four bedrooms.

"You sound as if you've been busy while we were away," Leah remarked.

Cherie smiled. "I must admit, I've been having a ball decorating the house. By the way, I just came over to give you your presents and to ask if I can work here until I begin taking classes. I don't expect to be paid," she said quickly. "I need to do something other than sit home all day and spend hours in front of the computer shopping online or watching television. Right about now, I'm a tad stir-crazy."

Kayana shared a glance with Leah. "Are you sure you want to work here?"

Cherie nodded. She waited until Leah returned to the kitchen to say, "Very sure. I can bus tables and clean up after you guys close."

Kayana crossed her arms under her breasts. "I'm certain

Derrick won't mind the extra help, but there's no way you're going to work here without us paying you."

"I don't need the money."

Kayana shook her head. "It's not whether you need it, but we can't have anyone work here without putting them on the payroll. What we don't need is problems with the tax folks."

"What if you pay me minimum wage?"

"That'll work. When do you want to begin?" Kayana asked after a pregnant pause.

"Tomorrow." Cherie knew Kayana and her brother, Derrick, were co-owners of the Seaside Café, and that meant she had the authority to hire and/or fire an employee.

"Okay, Cherie. You're hired. I'll have to get the paperwork for you to fill out a W-9 for your tax information. Once you complete that, Derrick will add you to the payroll. Paydays are every other Wednesday. You can opt to be paid by either check or direct deposit."

"Direct deposit is more convenient. I'll bring you a copy of a check tomorrow."

Cherie had opened an account at the bank on the mainland and written a check to transfer all the funds from her old bank to her new one. Changing her address with the post office and closing out the bank account represented a final break with her past.

Kayana nodded. "This is my week to cook and Derrick's to clean up. But now that you're coming on board, he can stay home."

"What time should I come in?"

"We close at two, so try and get here around one-thirty."

Cherie sucked in her breath, then let out a sigh of relief. When she'd asked Kayana whether she could work at the café, there was no guarantee she would agree. "Thanks, Kayana."

"There's no need to thank me. I would like to thank you because the weeks I don't cook, I can stay home and read instead of coming in and cleaning up to prepare for the next day."

"Have you thought about what books or genre we're going to read for our discussions?"

"No, but we can talk about that tomorrow after we close. And thanks again for the gift."

"You're welcome. I'll see you tomorrow." Cherie left the restaurant to drive to Shelby to look for area rugs and throw pillows.

She didn't want to admit to Kayana that her obsession with decorating the house was her way of compensating for wanting and never owning a dollhouse, like some other young girls she'd known. There had been a time when some of the girls in her neighborhood were getting dollhouses for Christmas or their birthdays. When she'd asked Edwina for one for her eighth birthday, her mother claimed she did not have the money for the one she'd selected; it was like a mansion, with multiple rooms and floors. Then Edwina suggested buying a kit to build one out of balsa wood, or Cherie could wait until she'd saved enough money to buy the one she wanted. Years went by, and her mother hadn't saved or had enough to buy the only thing Cherie had ever asked her for. It had become one more thing she'd added to the list of things she'd resented when it came to her mother, because Edwina always found money for her Friday-night card games. Sometimes she would win, but most times she came home without a penny. This is when she would disappear for hours, and when she returned, it was with enough money to last her until she received her monthly check from social services.

Cherie's new home had become her adult dollhouse, with multiple rooms and floors for her to decorate as she saw fit. However, the house on Coates Island wasn't a fantasy; it was real, and Cherie was more than content to live in it alone. Marrying or becoming a mother again was no longer a priority.

Leah revealing the most intimate details of her thirty-year marriage was a wakeup call for Cherie, and she learned that not all that glitters is gold. When she'd first met the headmistress of the private school for girls, and seen the size of the diamonds in Leah's ears and on her wedding band, her resentment for Leah ran deep because she had what Cherie had always wanted: to become the wife of a wealthy man.

Tapping a button on the steering wheel, she tuned the radio to a station featuring show tunes, and she sang along as she drove slowly over the bridge to the mainland. In a couple of days, she would celebrate her first month on Coates Island; she had familiarized herself with most of the small shops, but it was in Shelby, the county seat, where Cherie discovered there were fast-food restaurants, as well as chain and big-box stores.

She drove off the bridge and decelerated. There were no streetlights or stop signs but a few posted speed limits, and she forced herself not to drive more than twenty miles per hour or risk being pulled over, ticketed, and mandated to appear in traffic court. Cherie slowed even more when she spied the deputy who had come into the Seaside Café to pick up an order the day she'd closed on the house. He was talking to a young woman who appeared totally enthralled with what he was saying. Then, without warning, he turned to look her way, and Cherie quickly averted her head as she continued driving. She peered up at the rearview mirror and saw that he was staring in her direction.

"I am not speeding," she said under her breath. And she had no intention of driving more than the speed limit until she turned onto the county road leading to Shelby.

Living on the island during the off-season was very different; there were no or very few vacationers. Now there was the possibility that she would run into the same people over and over, and she was certain that, once she began working at the Seaside Café, she would become more than familiar with the restaurant's regulars.

She made it to Shelby, pulled into a space in the shoppers' parking lot, and inserted enough money in the meter for the two-hour limit. Cherie was able to select the stools for the breakfast bar and flat-screens for the two guest bedrooms and the home office, and arranged for their delivery; she loaded throw pillows, bed dressings, and area rugs into the cargo area of the SUV.

It wasn't until she'd returned home with her purchases that she heard her inner voice telling her she was becoming a shopaholic. That the house had become an obsession that had begun years before and was now a fixation. And Cherie didn't need a therapist to tell her that she'd equated owning property with being better than those with whom she'd grown up. For her, not having to pay rent in a low-income neighborhood meant that she'd made it. That she was entitled to all she'd acquired since graduating from an elite prep school and a prestigious Ivy League college with honors. However, she knew that owning a home on Coates Island would never have been possible if she'd hadn't slept with a wealthy man and subsequently sold her son to him.

She sat on the floor in the family room, her purchases strewn around her, and knew a time of reckoning had come for Cherie Renee Thompson. All the material goods, the stack of bonds in a safe deposit box, and the priceless baubles she'd been given—and couldn't wear in public and had been forced to sell—did not bring her the emotional contentment she'd been chasing all her life.

She lost track of time as she sat, eyes closed, the back of her head resting against the seat cushion, and replayed her life in her mind. She silently applauded herself for her accomplishments, and chastised herself for scheming, manipulating, and blackmailing a man who was just as obsessed with her as she had been with him. But, in the end, the user became used. Weylin had turned the tables on her when he used his clout to recommend her brothers for military academies and then to get the baby his wife was unable to give him.

When she finally got up off the floor, she knew she wasn't the same Cherie who had woken up earlier that morning. Like Leah Kent, she had been given a second chance at life. Leah had left a historic mansion in Richmond, Virginia, to start over as a baker in a small café off the coast of North Carolina, while she had left an exclusive gated Connecticut community to come to Coates Island to work part-time in the café while studying to become a classroom teacher.

Falling in love, marrying, and starting a family were no longer priorities. Now her sole focus was to teach young children.

Cherie woke to the sound of tapping. She sat up, looked around the room, and then slumped back to the mound of pillows cradling her shoulders. There was a sliver of light coming through the accordion shutters at the French doors, and she realized that the tapping against the glass was sleet.

She raised her arms above her head, moaning softly as she rolled her head from side to side. Lying in the California-king bed, the firm mattress cradling her body, she chided herself for agreeing to start work at the Seaside Café later that afternoon when she wanted to spend the day in bed reading. But that couldn't happen until Sunday, when the restaurant didn't open for business.

The Carpenters song "Rainy Days and Mondays" came to mind. But unlike in the iconic song, it wasn't Monday, and Cherie wasn't feeling down. In fact, her life was perfect. She was living in her forever home. Reaching for her cell phone, she noted the time and decided that if she didn't get out of bed, she would go back to sleep and then have to rush to make it to the restaurant for her first day of work.

* * *

The wind was blowing the driving rain sideways, and the umbrella did little to protect her when she got out of the Honda and walked to the front of the Seaside Café. Holding the umbrella lower, she didn't see the figure coming toward her until it was too late; she struggled to keep her balance and would've fallen if a hand hadn't caught her upper arm.

"Sorry," she mumbled.

"There's no need to apologize."

Cherie shifted the umbrella to see who belonged to the deep soothing voice. With wide eyes, she stared up at a smiling Reese Matthews. He wasn't in uniform; he had on a poncho with a US Army insignia and matching baseball cap. Seeing him this close made her aware that the deputy was an extremely attractive man. It was no wonder the woman she saw him with the day before was grinning like a Cheshire cat.

"I wasn't looking where I was going, Deputy Matthews."

Black silky eyebrows in a mahogany-brown face lifted slightly. "You know my name?"

"Yes. I heard Leah call you that the other day when you came in to pick up an order."

He smiled, exhibiting perfectly straight white teeth. "That means you have one up on me, because I don't know your name."

Cherie knew it wasn't possible to withhold her name because all he had to do was ask Leah or Kayana who she was. "It's Cherie Thompson."

He extended his hand. "It's nice meeting you, Cherie. And I'm Reese Matthews."

Switching the umbrella to her left hand, she offered him her right. "It's nice meeting you, Reese. I have to go, or I'm going to be late for my first day of work."

He released her hand. "I don't want to be responsible for you losing your job. I suppose I'll be seeing you around."

Cherie smiled. "I'm certain you will."

She left the parking lot and climbed the stairs to the front door as pinpoints of heat dotted her cheeks. She didn't know if Reese Matthews was married or single, yet she'd found herself ogling at him like the woman she'd seen him with the day before. It was something she'd accused Leah of when she couldn't stop staring at Kayana's brother, unaware that the two would become a couple.

Cherie liked Reese's large dark eyes, which were as mesmerizing as the timbre of his mellifluous voice. It contained a drawl that made her listen intently to its cadence and enunciation, and she concluded he had a voice for radio. She forgot about Reese when she was greeted by Kayana, who escorted her into a room where she was given a bibbed apron and a bandana. The owners of the Seaside Café had a hard-and-fast rule that all cooks and servers were required to cover their hair.

"Business has been slow today because of the weather," Kayana said as she opened the walk-in refrigerator and set a tray of marinating chicken on a shelf. "We had a total of five customers, and they all ordered takeout."

"I met Reese Matthews in the parking lot."

"Not only is he a steady customer, but he's known as one of Coates Island's most eligible bachelors."

Cherie didn't react to this information, because despite finding the man attractive, she had no intention of fawning over him like the woman she'd noticed yesterday. "Is your brother counted among the eligible bachelors?" she teased.

Kayana chuckled. "Not if Leah has anything to say about it. While we were on vacation, I overheard them talking about setting a wedding date."

Cherie secured the ties of the apron around her waist. "They both are widowed, so what's stopping them?"

"It's Leah who wants to wait. Derrick has been widowed for more than five years, while it won't be a year for Leah until this summer."

"Are you saying she's changed her mind?"

"I think so. I managed to convince her that there's nothing keeping them from becoming husband and wife. Even my niece, Deandra, says she's looking forward to the day when Leah will be her stepmother."

"Are you saying she wouldn't mind having a—"

"Don't say it," Kayana interrupted, frowning. "One of these days you'll come to see that Leah isn't that much different from you or me. I think of her as a sister-girl of a lighter hue. If you hadn't cut your vacation short last summer to return to Connecticut, you would've met one of her sons, who just happens to be engaged to a mixed-race woman of color."

This disclosure did shock Cherie. "Like Mama, like son," she drawled.

Kayana's frown deepened. "There's no need for you to be so cynical, Cherie. As a black woman, I always found myself attracted to black men, and that's why I married one. I will be the first to admit that I was devastated when James cheated on me and had a baby with another woman. Although I didn't want anything to do with another man, it had nothing to do with race. Then Graeme Ogden walks in, and for a year, I never gave the man a passing glance. Then when he came back the next season, it was to buy a vacation home. I had no idea he'd moved here to get close to me."

Throwing back her head, Cherie laughed. "It worked, didn't it?"

"No shit," Kayana drawled. "And if it hadn't been for my brother threatening to kick Graeme's ass because he believed he'd done something for me break up with him, that brought me to my senses."

"Was Derrick serious?"

Kayana nodded. "Very serious. Derrick has appointed himself the protector of his sisters, and when my sister broke up with her husband, he drove down to Florida to confront the man."

Now Cherie was intrigued. "Did he do the same when your left your husband?"

"No, because he claimed I could take care of myself when it came to James. It was different with Graeme, because Derrick got to see our relationship play out over the summer."

"Were you in love with Graeme at that time?"

"Yes, I was. I asked him about going back to Massachusetts at the end of the season, and that's when he told me he wasn't returning. He admitted he'd resigned his teaching position and had retired on Coates Island. That's when I lost it, Cherie. Before that, we'd talked about trust, because neither of us had trusted our exes, and then he admitted to being in love with me and that he was hiding another secret but couldn't tell me unless we were married."

"But you did marry him, Kayana."

She smiled. "Yes, I did. Initially, I felt as if he was using the ploy as leverage to get me to marry him, but when I realized I didn't want to spend the rest of my life without him, I accepted his proposal. And now there are no secrets between us. I'm no longer a practicing psychiatric social worker, but I'm going to give you the same advice I gave Leah. Do not get so deep into a relationship that love supersedes trust. You can fall in and out of love. But once you lose trust, the relationship usually can't be made whole again because you're always suspicious."

Cherie felt as if Kayana was talking directly to her. She had fallen in love with Weylin, and then he'd deceived her. She'd trusted him when he claimed he wanted her to have his love child, never imagining he'd planned to raise it not with his lover but his wife.

"One of these days, I'll ask you to put on your social worker's hat, but only when I feel comfortable enough to tell you my secret." She paused. "Now, tell me where I should begin cleaning up."

"I'll show you where we keep the cleaning supplies. You can begin by wiping down the tables and sweeping the floors.

After that, you can clean the restrooms. Meanwhile, I'll take care of the kitchen. I should be out of your way before you begin mopping."

Smiling, Cherie gave her a mock salute. "Aye, aye, boss."

"One more reference to my being your boss, and I'll fire you."

"Got it!"

Chapter 7

It took Cherie two weeks to feel like an employee of the Seaside Café. She had a key to the rear door, and Derrick had given her the code to the security system. She usually arrived around one to watch Kayana and her brother prepare dishes for the next day and waited for diners to leave before she began cleaning off tables and chairs.

The fixed price for the all-you-can-eat buffet was lower during the off-season, and seniors were half-price year-round. She had also become familiar with the regulars who came in most days at the same time. One elderly couple admitted they no longer cooked other than to brew coffee and make toast, and the food at the café sustained them for the entire day. Cherie noticed that occasionally Kayana would fill a to-go container with food for them to take home, and she suspected they were on a fixed income, like many of the retirees on the island. Now she understood why so many of them rented their homes to vacationers during the summer season.

Cherie had also become familiar with a middle-aged man with cold blue eyes and a receding hairline; he came in several days a week around noon and lingered until closing. He sat at the same table and selected the same items every time. That didn't bother her as much as his staring. At first, she suspected he'd seen her from somewhere, but quickly dismissed that notion. Despite the fact that he was what she thought of as nondescript, Cherie was certain that, if she knew him from somewhere, she would've recognized him because of the glacial iciness of his eyes. And whenever her eyes met his, he would switch his focus to one of several muted television sets placed around the dining area. She waited until the last diner left, then locked the door and turned over the CLOSED sign.

Reaching for a remote device, she turned off all the televisions but one, tuning it to an all-news cable channel, and turned off the closed captioning. It was her time to catch up on what was happening around the world while she cleaned up.

Derrick came out of the kitchen and pushed his tattered painter's cap off his forehead. "I'm frying up a tray of Creole chicken for the sheriff's department. They're throwing a surprise get-together for the chief's birthday. By the way, I made up some mac and cheese, and if you want, I can put some in a to-go container for you, along with the chicken, as soon as it comes out of the oven."

Cherie affected a dreamy expression. The Johnsons were renowned for their Creole chicken and mac and cheese. "Please and thank you."

Derrick smiled. "Consider it done." He sobered and adjusted his cap. "I don't know if Kay told you, but we really appreciate you cleaning up because even when Kay and I alternate cooking every two weeks, we still come in after the café closes to clean up so we can get a jump on the next day's menu."

"I really don't mind, Derrick, because it gives me something to do before I go back to school. I worked for twelve straight years, and I still wake up the same time every morning as if I had to punch a clock."

Cherie liked Derrick Johnson. Kayana's brother was brainy, tall, dark, and handsome, with a matching set of deep dimples. And it wasn't the first time she realized why Leah had been attracted to and fallen in love with the drop-dead-gorgeous and very talented cook. Whenever she saw them together, Cherie realized they complemented each other. Derrick hadn't denied Leah the freedom she needed to become a mature, independent woman capable of doing what she loved. The former schoolteacher and headmistress was now enjoying life as the Seaside Café's baker.

"I know the feeling. Once I left Wall Street and moved back here, I found myself still on New York City mode until my mother told me it was all right to slow down and stop living my life by a clock."

"How long did that take?"

"Probably about six months." He smiled. "I better get back to the kitchen—that chicken can't fry itself."

Cherie nodded. If Derrick and Kayana appreciated her cleaning the restaurant after closing hours, then she also appreciated them for paying and feeding her. Every night, she went home with enough food for dinner and lunch the following day. She didn't know how they did it, but Kayana and Derrick prepared enough food each day but with little or no leftovers. Their methods were in keeping with the plaques on the walls around the restaurant: WASTE NOT, WANT NOT. And if there were leftovers, they called the local church's outreach to pick up the food for their soup kitchen.

Fifteen minutes later, she shut off the television and heard music coming from the kitchen. Derrick had turned up the volume on a channel featuring music from the sixties and seventies. Her mother loved the music of Stevie Wonder and had named her Cherie for his "My Cherie Amour." Cherie's music compilation paled in comparison to her book and movie collection, and once she set up her home office, she planned to have enough shelves on which to display them.

She hummed along with some of the more familiar tunes.

There were times when Edwina would play the same CDs over and over, while sitting in a darkened room with a bottle of beer. This was when Cherie knew her mother was in a funk and refused to talk or go near her. It would go on for days, and then, unexpectedly, she would emerge smiling, as if nothing had happened. The first and last time Cherie had suggested Edwina see a therapist, the discussion had ended in a shouting match between the two women. She knew her mother needed help, but also knew that wasn't going to happen until Edwina admitted that she did.

It was close to four when she finished her chores and put everything away. The aromas of spicy chicken and mac and cheese wafted to her nostrils as she walked back into the kitchen.

Derrick handed her a large shopping bag. "I put a few extras in the bag for you."

"Thank you, Derrick."

Cherie removed her apron and bandana, placing both in the receptacle for soiled laundry, and slipped her arms into a puffy coat. She looped the straps of her crossbody over her chest and, clutching the shopping bag, took the back staircase leading directly to the parking lot. She'd just closed the door when a large figure loomed in front of her, and she wasn't given time to react when a hand snaked around her throat, fingers tightening and making it impossible for her to scream or draw a normal breath. Objects floated in front of her eyes, and just when she felt herself going limp, the hand fell away, and she slumped against the side of the building.

"Move and I will blow your brains out!"

The buzzing in her head vanished, and she recognized the voice. It was Reese Matthews. He'd come along in time to save her from someone attempting to assault or possibly kill her. Her vision cleared, and she recognized the man who came into the restaurant and couldn't take his eyes off her. It was obvious that he had been stalking her.

Reese came over to her as she stood as straight as she could. "Are you all right?" he asked in her ear.

Cherie nodded. "I think so," she said, recovering her voice.

"I want you to get behind me and don't move."

"Okay." That's when she noticed he was pointing a gun at her attacker.

Reese shifted the automatic to his other hand without taking his gaze off the man blinking and humming to himself. "Get face down on the ground. Now!"

The man obeyed, his body jerking as if he'd been hit by a jolt of electricity, and Reese thought the man who had attacked Cherie was either physically ill or mentally disturbed. Reaching into breast pocket of his sheepskin-lined jacket, Reese removed his cell phone and tapped the speed dial for the station house. It took less than thirty seconds to relay a message that he needed someone ASAP to come to the parking lot of the Seaside Café.

He felt a lump in his throat when Cherie buried her face in his jacket and released a strangled cry. Reese wanted to comfort her, but knew he couldn't take his eyes off the man; he didn't know whether he was feigning being crazy to get the upper hand and jump up and attack them both. And he hadn't issued an idle threat. He would've shot him—not in the head, but in both legs to prevent him from getting away.

"It's okay, babe. You're safe now."

Minutes later, he heard the wail of a siren coming closer and closer. It was rare that lights and sirens were seen and or heard along the beachfront community. He quickly relayed what he'd encountered to the uniformed deputy, who put the man in handcuffs while reading him his rights and then escorted him to the rear of the cruiser at the same time Derrick emerged from the restaurant.

"What the hell is going on here?" Derrick shouted.

"It appears as if one of your customers was waiting here to attack Cherie."

"Is she all right?"

"She claims she is."

"Please don't talk about me as if I'm not here," Cherie said. Her voice was low, void of emotion.

Reese tucked the automatic handgun into a holster behind his back and turned his full attention on Cherie, who was massaging her throat. He called on all his self-control not to take her into his arms to offer some comfort. "Do you want to go to the hospital to be checked out?"

"No. Thanks for asking, but I am okay." Again, she spoke in a monotone.

Derrick walked over to Cherie. "Did he hurt you?"

She rested her hand against her throat. "I'm certain I'll have a few bruises where he tried to choke me, but other than that, I'll survive."

"I want you to take the rest of the week off—"

"I don't need—"

"Don't argue with me, Cherie, or so help me, I will fire you. Reese, can you see that she gets home? I'll bring the food over to the station house."

Reese took Cherie's arm. "Do you think you'll be able to drive?"

She glared at him. "Yes, I do."

He bit back a smile when she exhibited a modicum of spunkiness. Bending slightly, Reese picked up the bag she'd dropped. "You head out, and I'll follow you."

Derrick patted Reese's shoulder. "I'm glad you came along when you did because that crazy sonofabitch could've really hurt her. I'd noticed him hanging around longer than most folks, but didn't think too much of it, because it's off-season and business is slow. It's only during the summer that we don't allow people to use the place as a hangout. They sit, relax, eat, and then leave."

"I don't recognize him, so either he's new to Coates Island or he's just passing through. But once we book him, we'll find out who he is and hopefully where he's from."

"What going to happen after that, Reese?"

"We'll contact the sheriff in Shelby and have him transferred to their jail," Reese explained as he watched Cherie start up her Honda and drive out of the lot. "I have to leave now. I'll call you later to catch you up on what's happening with everything."

Cherie drove slowly while taking furtive glances in the rearview mirror to see the daytime running lights from Reese's pickup. She'd lied to him and Derrick. Her throat felt as if it was on fire; she'd been nearly strangled to death, and it hurt each time she attempted to swallow. And she did not want to think of what would've happened if Reese hadn't come along to rescue her from someone who was obviously a madman.

There had been a time when her internal radar was on full alert whenever she encountered someone she didn't know or ventured into some sections of her former neighborhood. It was as if blocks were parceled out like land grants for different gangs, and the unspoken word on the street was that you entered at your own risk. But she wasn't living there, hadn't been for years, yet her life was threatened on an idyllic island almost a thousand miles away.

Kayana had called her cynical. And she was. She'd spent half her life wanting to better herself and live in a place where she didn't have to install three or four locks on her front door to thwart intruders or carry pepper spray to repel a would-be-attacker. There was one good thing she could say about her old neighborhood. No one had ever attacked her or offered her drugs.

Cherie reached home, tapped the remote device under the visor to raise the garage door, and drove in. She waited for Reese to park his vehicle in the driveway and follow her into the garage before pressing the keypad to close the garage door.

"Don't move," he ordered in a quiet voice. "I want to check the house before you go in."

Cherie wanted to tell him she doubted if anyone had broken into her home. However, she was too emotionally drained to argue with him. She needed a cup of tea and a warm bath before she got into bed. Hopefully, she would sleep long enough to forget how close she'd come to being strangled.

Reese returned, and she stared at him as if he were a stranger. He'd removed the hat that had covered his black, cropped straight hair. She forced a smile. "All clear?"

He nodded. "Yes."

Cherie took off her coat, hanging it and her crossbody on a peg in the area outside the kitchen, Reese following suit. Then she tapped a switch that turned on the trio of pendants over the breakfast bar. "I'm going to wash my hands before putting on some water for tea. Would you like some?"

Reese set the bag with the Seaside Café logo on the floor near the refrigerator. "Before you do that, I'd like to take a look at your neck." He cupped her chin, gently raising it. He smothered a curse and slowly shook his head. "The bastard deserves a real ass-kicking, and I'd like to be the one to give it to him."

"No, please," she said quickly. "There's been enough violence. After my tea, I'm going to take a bath and then go to bed."

"I'll wash my hands and make the tea while you get some ice for your neck."

Cherie nodded. She wanted to tell Reese that she was safe now and that he could leave because she needed some space to process what she'd just gone through. That she feared if he stayed she would weaken and beg him not to leave her. She'd always prided herself on being strong and able to face any situation, whether good or bad. She'd acquired an overabundance of confidence in her thirty-four years that had given her what she needed to navigate the road called life.

* * *

Reese found the half-bath and stared at his reflection in the mirror over the vanity. When he'd checked every room in the house before allowing Cherie to enter, he was awed by the meticulous furnishings in the house. The shades of blues and greens on the walls, with pale contrasting trim, gave the spaces a zen-like feeling. Everything, from the bed dressings to the area rugs and accessories like table and floor lamps, had him wondering if Cherie had employed the services of a professional interior decorator. Even the framed black-and-white photographs of plants and flowers lining the wall going up the staircase to the second story added an inviting and homey touch.

From the first time he'd spied Cherie talking to Bettina outside the house that had belonged to Jeremy and Katherine Murphy, she'd intrigued him. And then when he was able to see her up close, he'd found himself completely enthralled with the dark-haired, hazel-eyed beauty.

He'd also discovered that he was no different than some of the other residents of Coates Island who were gossiping about the young woman who had purchased the Murphy house rather than one of the condo units. She'd become an anomaly because most home sales were attributed to retirees, like the Murphys and Graeme Ogden. He, Derrick, and Kayana Johnson were a few of the exceptions.

Derrick had moved back with his pregnant wife to help his mother run the Seaside Café. Kayana returned years later to assist her brother after their mother retired. And Reese had returned, after ending his military career and following his grandmother's passing, to move into the house she'd willed him and join the sheriff's department, where his older cousin was the current chief.

At forty-two, he'd had a valid reason for returning. What, he mused, was Cherie Thompson's reason or excuse for moving to Coates Island? Was she running from something or someone? Did she know the man who had attacked her? Or had she done something to someone, and they'd ordered an attack on her as retribution?

The questions were a jumble of confusion in his head as Reese washed and dried his hands on a cobalt-blue towel; he hoped to find some of the answers once the perp was questioned. He walked out of the bathroom, retrieved his cell phone from his jacket, and sent a text to his cousin, saying that he was going to be delayed and that Cherie Thompson's name should be left out of the arrest until he questioned her about her knowledge of the attacker. He didn't have to wait long before Parker replied:

Copy that.

Reese found Cherie leaning against the countertop with a bag of ice wrapped in a dish towel pressed against her throat. He knew she was in pain, yet she'd attempted to put on a brave face. "How is it feeling?"

Her smile was more a grimace. "Better."

He approached her and took her hand that held the ice. The marks on her throat were bright red. "Do you have anything in the house for pain?"

"No. I usually don't keep drugs in the house."

"I'm not talking about medical marijuana, Cherie." Her face flushed with his mention of marijuana. Had he hit a sore spot? Had she been involved with a drug deal that had gone bad and she'd had to leave home and hide somewhere remote? "Don't you have any over-the-counter pain medication?"

"Yes. It's in the upstairs bathroom."

"Do you want me to get it?"

She shook her head. "No. I'll get it."

Reese registered the resignation in her voice. He realized she'd been traumatized and knew this wasn't the time to question her about her attacker. "I'll stay with you until you drink your tea and take your bath. I'm going to leave because I have to work the twelve-to-eight shift. But I promise to be back tomorrow afternoon and will check in on you. I'm off in a couple of days, so if you need me to run errands or help you cook, then I'm your man."

Cherie blinked slowly. "You cook?"

"Of course, I cook. Who do you think feeds me?"

"The Seaside Café," she retorted. "You come in enough that I figured you couldn't put together a meal."

Reese laughed. "That's because my shift changes every other week. I'm the last hired, so I don't have any seniority, and that means sometimes I'm eating dinner at four in the afternoon or eight in the morning."

"But doesn't it help that your cousin is the chief."

His eyebrows lifted. "So, you know about that?"

"Yes. Bettina Wilson told me."

"What else did she tell you about me?"

"Nothing. I don't like gossip or people who gossip. It can only cause trouble."

"The only thing I'm going to say to you is get used to it. Here on the island, everyone seems to know everyone else's business, while it's not as prevalent on the mainland."

"Where do you live?"

"Fortunately, on the mainland."

Cherie set the bag of ice in the stainless-steel sink and filled an electric kettle with water. "You think I'm less fortunate because I live along the shore?"

Reese crossed his arms over his chest. "Of course not. It's just that I prefer living where folks don't monitor my comings and goings. There's one road to get on and off the island, and once someone becomes familiar with your vehicle, they can tell you how often and what time you come and go. It's different on the mainland. The homes are built with enough space between them so you can't smell what your neighbor is cooking. We have a school campus for grades beginning with kindergarten and up to and including twelve. There's also a downtown business district and an area for local authority. In total, about forty-two hundred citizens make up Coates Island, and I like to think it's a wonderful place to raise a family and perfect for retirees."

Cherie plugged in the kettle. "If it's so wonderful, then why is there an exodus of young people once they graduate high school?"

"They want what most young people want—life experience. They want to have careers and to visit places they've only read about or seen in travel ads. They want to attend professional ballgames, and go to concerts and clubs. The only time we have movies on the island is during the summer, when they show films in the town square, and that's for the benefit of the vacationers."

"Are you saying that if you had a multiplex theater with at least three screens, then the kids would stay?"

"That's not what I'm saying, Cherie. The bottom line is job opportunities and careers. We have shops where the business is passed down through generations, but even that is no longer a guarantee, and shop owners are forced to either work longer hours or hire someone they don't know because they tend to be suspicious of anyone who isn't local."

Reese watched Cherie take down a teapot and two cups and saucers from an overhead cabinet. Her movements were slow and measured, as if she were a puppet being pulled by a puppeteer when she opened another cabinet to remove a small glass jar filled with tea bags. He knew if she didn't take something to alleviate her discomfort, she wouldn't be able to fully function.

Moving quickly, he rested his hands on her shoulders. "I'll take care of the tea while you go upstairs and get your pain medication."

Turning her head slowly, Cherie glanced up at him. "Honey, sugar, lemon, or milk?"

Reese cursed under his breath. She was asking him what he wanted in his tea while still attempting to play the flipping martyr. "Lemon and honey."

It was first thing that came to mind. He wanted to tell

Cherie that he usually laced his hot tea with bourbon, but this wasn't one of those times. Not only was he scheduled to work later that night, but he didn't want to show up at the station house with the smell of alcohol on his breath.

He'd been responsible for planning his cousin's surprise fifty-fifth birthday. The date coincided with his fifth anniversary of being sworn in as chief. Although Parker despised surprises, this was one occasion Reese couldn't let go by without some fanfare, even if it was a small gathering.

"Reese?"

"Yes?"

"I'd like you to promise me one thing."

Smiling, he angled his head. "Only one?" he teased.

"Yes, one for now."

"What is it?"

"After I take the acetaminophen and drink my tea, will you please leave so I can take a bath."

"I leave and what, Cherie? You go into hysterics because after a while you can't keep up the tough girl act." Reese knew he'd struck a nerve when she glared at him.

"For your information, I don't get hysterical." She closed her eyes and blew out a breath. "I need to be alone so I can process what just happened to me."

"What you don't need is to be alone."

"Look, Reese, I don't need a babysitter. I've been on my own even before I graduated college. I've had a lot of ups and downs in my life, and like the others, this too shall pass."

"Are you telling me this isn't the first time you've been attacked?"

"It's the only time I've been attacked. And I must thank you for coming along when you did because things could've turned into something much more tragic."

"Do you believe in destiny, Cherie?"

A beat passed before she said, "I do now."

Her answer meant she hadn't believed in it before tonight. Reese had arranged for one of the other deputies to drive to the Seaside Café to pick up the food because he'd wanted to keep his cousin away from the station house long enough for Elizabeth to finish decorating the chief's office. However, when Parker began complaining that he had to get back to the station house, Reese had no alternative but had to tell him about the surprise celebration.

"I'll leave, but only if you give me your cell number." Reaching into the pocket of his jeans, Reese took out his cell phone and handed it to Cherie. "I'll text you rather than call, and whenever you wake up, you can return the text." He waited as she tapped the keys with her information, then returned his phone. "I'm going to have to take a picture of your neck as evidence." She tilted her head back, and he took three shots in rapid succession. "I'm done."

"Thank you," she said, smiling.

Reese returned her smile. "You're most welcome."

Chapter 8

Reese returned to the station house in time to see Parker Shelton thanking everyone for making his fifty-fifth birthday a memorable one. He winked at Elizabeth when she smiled at him, and then turned his attention to his cousin. At fifty-five, the never-married, retired Marine Corps drill sergeant was an incredible physical specimen. He stood an even six-foot and worked out every day; whenever off duty, weather notwithstanding, he could be seen running along the beach.

Thirteen years Parker's junior, Reese felt more like his younger brother than second cousin and had always looked up to him as his mentor. And it was Parker's counsel he'd sought once he'd made the decision that he wanted a military career.

A slight flush darkened the chief's khaki-brown complexion. "And I'd like to personally thank the deputy who is responsible for this impromptu get-together. What do you know? He just happened to walk in." Everyone turned to look at Reese and applauded.

He gave Parker a snappy salute. "It's not every day someone gets to be double nickels along with celebrating their fifth anniversary as chief on the same day."

Parker's light-brown eyes sparkled like newly minted pennies. "You've got that right."

"You're the best chief Coates Island has ever had," Elizabeth shouted. "And I've been here before some of you were born, so I know what I'm talking about."

"No one is disputing you, Miss Elizabeth," countered Ian Burrows.

Reese had learned that Ian had hoped to be promoted to chief before the mayor appointed Parker to the position. However, months after his being sworn in, Parker selected Ian to be assistant deputy chief.

Parker crossed his arms over a crisp gray shirt. "There's enough food here for everybody to take home, so don't be shy. Miss Elizabeth will pack up whatever you don't take and store it in the fridge. Now it's time we get back to protecting and serving. Reese, I'd like to see you in my office."

"Don't worry, sweetie," Elizabeth whispered to Reese as she approached him. "I'll make a plate for you before these vultures devour everything."

"Thank you, Miss Elizabeth."

She patted his arm over his jacket. "You know I'll always look out for you."

"And I you," he whispered. "Got to see the chief before he reads me the riot act."

Reese entered Parker's office and closed the door. He admired his cousin because he didn't give him preferential treatment because of their familial relationship. He was just another deputy expected to follow a direct order, and the only time he wasn't the chief's subordinate was away from the station house. Then they were family.

Parker pointed to a chair facing his desk. "Please sit down."

Reese complied and gave his boss a direct stare. "I know you want to talk about what went down in the Seaside Café's parking lot. And right now, I don't have much information to give you other than a man attempted to strangle one of the restaurant's employees."

"Did you interview the woman?"

"Don't you mean interrogate, chief?"

Lacing his fingers together, Parker rested them on the top of the desk. "No, deputy, I meant what I said. We interview victims and witnesses and interrogate those we arrest and charge with a crime."

"No, I didn't interview her, but I will tomorrow. Right now, she's too traumatized to recall everything that happened to her." Reese was aware that if he had insisted Cherie talk to him about the incident, she would've shut down completely. She didn't say anything while drinking her tea, then unceremoniously had asked him to leave so she could be alone.

"What do you know about her?"

"Not much," Reese admitted truthfully. "I know she bought the Murphy house on the island, she had Connecticut plates on her vehicle before she exchanged them for North Carolina's, and that she works at the café."

"Full-time?"

"No. If I come in around noon, I usually don't see her, so I have to assume she's a part-timer."

Leaning back in the leather executive chair, Parker closed his eyes for several seconds. "The man we have locked up in the back refuses to talk."

"Does he want an attorney?" Reese asked.

"No. And he wasn't carrying any identification, but once we ran his photo and prints through the national criminal database, we discovered he has a long rap sheet that goes back to when he was arrested at twenty for shoplifting. He's committed a lot of petty offenses over the years, but nothing on his record indicates violent assault."

"Where were these crimes committed?"

Parker glanced down at the printout on the desk. "Anywhere and everywhere. He's been arrested a few times in Cleveland, Ohio. Jackson, Mississippi. Memphis, Tennessee.

The last one was three years ago in Birmingham, Alabama. They were all misdemeanors, and the most time he's ever spent in jail is ninety days."

"Well, he's going to spend more than ninety days behind bars for assault."

Parker nodded. "I agree. But first we need the victim's statement before I call Shelby P.D. and have him transferred to their jail to be arraigned."

"I'll try and get that from Cherie tomorrow."

"Don't try, deputy. Just get it. We don't need folks gossiping about a woman being assaulted in broad daylight. Talk like that will negatively affect tourists wanting to come here if they don't feel safe." Parker ran a hand over his face. "Something keeps nagging at me."

"What's that?"

"Why did she move here?"

"Her name is Cherie Thompson, chief. Do you usually ask folks why they move here? For that matter, why do they decide to vacation here?"

"I happen to know her name, deputy. But wasn't it you who didn't want it bandied around until we're able to get a statement from her?"

Reese had noted the hard edge creeping into Parker's voice. "Yes, because I want to protect her before folks on the island get wind of what happened in the café's parking lot. But that's not going to be easy after they saw and heard lights and sirens." He revealed what Derrick had told him about the man hanging around the restaurant.

"Don't you think it's a little coincidental that this piece of shit shows up after Miss No Name moves here?"

"No, I don't."

He didn't want to believe that the woman with whom he'd become enthralled after catching less than a half dozen glimpses of her over the past month had been involved in something that had put her life in jeopardy.

Parker gave him a steady stare. "You have exactly twenty-four hours in which to interview the victim and write up your report. And please impress upon her that she must be willing to testify against her attacker or we'll be forced to let him go. Meanwhile, I'm going to talk to Derrick about his employee."

Reese's impassive expression did not reflect his increasing annoyance. He didn't know why Parker wanted to target Cherie as the reason for the attack and not some pervert who decided he saw something he wanted and went after it. He'd overheard the talk about Cherie moving to the island. Some were whispering about her living in the house alone, while he'd consciously ignored the gossip that she probably was hiding from a stalker boyfriend or an abusive husband. Whatever her reason, it was personal. And when he did get the chance to interview her, his questions would focus solely on the attack.

Pushing back his chair, he stood. "I'm going home to get some sleep before I begin my shift."

Parker glared up at him. "Twenty-four hours, deputy."

Reese nodded. He knew they wouldn't be able to hold the man in jail if they weren't able to charge him with the assault. And, for Reese, releasing him to possibly attack another woman was not an option.

Turning on his heel, he left the office and retreated to his cubicle, where Elizabeth had left a napkin-covered paper plate and a bottle of water. He uncovered the plate to find fried chicken, mac and cheese, potato salad, candied sweet potatoes, and a fluffy biscuit. There were a lot more carbs on the plate than he usually ate in one meal, but there was no way he was going to pass up the café's legendary Creole chicken and mac and cheese. While he was on active military duty, Reese hadn't strictly monitored what he ate, but it was different as a civilian. He'd traded meat and potatoes for chicken, fish, and lots of fruits and vegetables. He took his jacket off the coat tree and slipped into it before picking up his plate. He would eat at home before returning for his shift.

Twenty-four hours. That was the time allotted to him to uncover the details about what had happened in the Seaside Café's parking lot.

The doorbell rang, and Cherie glanced at the clock on the microwave. It was ten minutes before nine. As she went to answer the door, she sent up a silent prayer that it wasn't Bettina, because if her neighbor had an inkling of the incident in the Seaside Café's parking lot, she probably would ask her a myriad of questions she had no intention of answering.

Cherie opened the door, and it wasn't Bettina but Kayana and Leah standing on the porch. "Good morning."

Kayana gave her a narrow look through the glass on the storm door. "Is it?"

"Aren't you going to invite us in?" Leah asked.

She unlocked the door and opened it. "I'm sorry. Please come in."

Cherie wanted to tell them she wasn't ready to receive visitors, not when she looked as if she hadn't slept in days. After taking a bath, she'd gotten into bed, and instead of sleeping, she'd cried until she had dry heaves. She'd relived the frightening scene in the parking lot over and over until exhaustion finally claimed her and she fell asleep.

When she saw her reflection in the mirror earlier that morning, her knees almost gave way. The imprint of the man's fingers were clearly visible on her throat. Moving around like an automaton, she'd completed her morning ablutions and slipped into a pair of sweats and thick cotton socks. Reese told her he was coming back after his shift, and when she'd opened the door, she expected to see him and not her book club friends.

Kayana stepped into the entryway and caught her arm. "Stop and let me take a look at your neck."

Cherie tilted her chin and was totally unprepared when Kayana snapped a picture of her throat with her smartphone. "What are you doing?"

"That's evidence of what that crazy bastard did to you."

She closed her eyes and didn't tell Kayana Reese had already photographed her neck as evidence. "I'm trying to forget what he did to me."

Leah brushed past her. "That's not going to happen for a long time, Cherie. Even after the bruises go away, you'll not forget how close you came to losing your life." She held up two canvas totes. "Enough talk about lunatics. I'm making brunch."

"Brunch at nine in the morning?"

Kayana grasped her hand and leaned closer. "Please don't fight with Leah this morning. When Derrick told her about that man choking you, she had flashbacks of when her ex tried to strangle her before he pushed her down the stairs."

Cherie bit her lip. Leah had made a passing reference to her husband physically abusing her but hadn't gone into detail about his attack. She did mention that she had to be hospitalized after falling down the staircase in her home. Accidently falling was very different from being pushed.

"Okay. I won't fight with her. I wanted to invite you guys over after I got my dining-area table."

"Sorry about upsetting your plans because we're here to take care of you in advance of you hosting a housewarming. And we intend to spend the day. We want to plan for our future book club meetings."

"But aren't you guys working?"

"No."

"Didn't Leah go into the café to bake?"

"No," Kayana repeated. "Derrick decided to close today. Chief Shelton wanted to come to the restaurant to get a statement from him about the incident. My brother thought it would send a bad message to customers to see the chief's car at the café, so he opted to close."

"Couldn't he take his statement over the phone?"

"Chief Shelton is totally by the book. For him, it has to be in person."

"I have a confession to make."

"What's that, Cherie?"

"I'm glad you and Leah are here."

Kayana dropped a kiss on her damp hair. "And I'm glad we decided to come. By the way, you home is absolutely gorgeous."

"I agree," Leah shouted from the kitchen. "It could be a layout for an architectural magazine."

Her friends complimenting her about her home was overshadowed by their concern for her well-being, and she knew for certain her decision to move to Coates Island was one of the best she'd ever made. Leah, once she was discharged from the hospital, left Richmond to come to Coates Island to recuperate. Kayana and Derrick had welcomed her with open arms and insisted she live in the apartment above the restaurant. Cherie was certain if she'd been attacked in Connecticut and had fled to the island, Leah and Kayana would do the same for her: offer her their protection and sanctuary.

"You guys do whatever you do in the kitchen. *Mi casa es tu casa.* I'm going upstairs to get a scarf to cover up my neck. Every time I catch a glimpse of myself in a mirror, I can't help but think about that monster choking me."

Kayana washed her hands in one of the double stainless sinks. "Derrick told me that if Reese hadn't come along when he did, you probably wouldn't be standing here talking to us."

Cherie nodded. "I was close to blacking out when I heard Reese threaten to shoot the bastard."

"And he would have," Kayana confirmed. "Reese spent more than twenty years in the military as an Army Ranger. And I can assure you he wasn't issuing an idle threat."

"You should think of the man as your guardian angel. He was at the right place and at the right time," Leah said, giving her a sidelong glance.

Cherie nodded again as she recalled Reese talking about destiny. He'd believed he was destined to be in that parking lot at the exact time she was being attacked. "Either guardian angel or superhero."

Leah angled her head. "If he's a superhero, who would he be? Superman? Batman? Captain America or Spider-Man?"

"Black Panther," Cherie said, "because not only is he a superhero, but he's also a king."

Kayana dried her hands on a paper towel. "I would have to agree with you. Reese's family is considered black royalty on Coates Island. Like my ancestors, his were also free people of color even before the Emancipation Proclamation. He also comes from a long line of master carpenters. Maybe one of these days, he will tell you about his folks and their contribution to the island."

Cherie wasn't certain she wanted or needed to know more about the deputy. She'd consciously shut herself off from the opposite sex, yet there was something about Reese Matthews that whispered she was lying to herself. Notwithstanding his gorgeous face and body, she'd experienced flutters in her stomach whenever he entered the restaurant. It was as if she had been watching and waiting for him to come, and when he did, she had to call on all her self-control to pretend to be interested in her tasks rather than give him furtive glances. If their eyes happened to meet, he would affect a half smile with a barely perceptible nod of acknowledgment. She didn't know why, but she was mesmerized by his deep, soothing voice and entranced by the scent of his masculine cologne.

Thinking about him quickened her breathing and elicited a wave of heat that began in her face before slowly working its way down to her chest. Then, without warning, her breasts grew heavy, and she swallowed a moan as the region between her thighs pulsed, and she couldn't believe what was happening to her. Yes, it had been years since she'd slept with a man; she'd encountered men that had expressed an interest in dating her, yet none had affected her like Reese Matthews. Why him? she mused. What made him so very different from the others?

"I'll be back in a few minutes." Her statement was breathless, as if she'd run a long, grueling race.

She had to put some distance between herself and her friends before they noticed the flush suffusing her face. She did not want to dwell on Reese because she feared losing focus and the reason she'd relocated. She had left Connecticut to put her past behind her. And that included exorcizing a personal relationship that nearly destroyed her emotionally. It had taken a while for Cherie to admit that the aptitude she'd exhibited academically was vastly superior to her ability to choose wisely when it came to a romantic liaison.

She found a blue silk scarf in a drawer with several others, looping it twice around her neck and then tying it in a neat bow over the sweatshirt with the fading Yale logo. She left the bedroom and walked into the en suite bath. She picked up a wide-tooth comb and pulled it through the tangle of damp curls. Now she felt better prepared to interact with her friends without them staring at the angry red bruises. If she'd known in advance that she would have visitors so early that morning, she would have applied ice and concealer to minimize the puffiness and dark circles over and under her eyes.

Cherie turned off the light and went downstairs. Although she hadn't expected Kayana and Leah to show up, deep down inside she was happy they'd come to check on her. Because that's what real friends do.

Chapter 9

Cherie recovered from a fit of hysterical laughter and dabbed the corners of her eyes with as napkin. "Was your husband really naked?" she asked Kayana, after she'd given her update about an incident that had occurred when they'd sailed down to the Florida Keys.

"As naked as the day he came into the world."

Kayana revealed that Robert Duvall was Graeme's favorite actor, and he'd memorized every line of the actor's dialogue from *Apocalypse Now.* Leah and Derrick were still asleep in their cabin when Graeme got out of bed, butt naked, and went up on deck just as the sun was coming up and yelled, "I love the smell of the ocean in the morning." And when someone yelled back that they liked it too, he lost his footing as he scrambled down the ladder and wound up with bruises on his legs, lower back, and abrasions on his scrotum. And when she'd asked him about them, he claimed he hadn't wanted to talk about it. It was after they'd returned home that he finally confessed to her about the incident.

"Was he aware that your boat wasn't the only one moored at the island?"

Kayana took a sip of the mango-infused champagne, her eyes crinkling in a smile over the rim of the flute. "There were no other boats around when we'd dropped anchor off Bahia Honda key late that night, so he must have assumed we had that side of the island to ourselves."

"When Kayana told me about it, I laughed so hard that I actually peed my panties," Leah said, grinning. "Derrick told me I was wrong to laugh, but you know how guys stick together when it comes to jokes about their family jewels."

"And Graeme's were gloriously on display that morning," Kayana added. "I wanted to ask him if he'd learned his lesson but didn't want to add more embarrassment to injury."

Cherie liked the former widowed high school math and economics teacher who had moved from Massachusetts to North Carolina because he'd found himself drawn to the co-owner of a restaurant on an island that barely made the map. And it was apparent he knew what he'd wanted and gone after it, unaware that Kayana wasn't interested in becoming involved with a man—at least not romantically. Cherie didn't know what the tall, gray-eyed man had said or done, but apparently it worked: within six months of their first date, they'd become husband and wife.

She wondered what it was about vacationing on Coates Island that had changed lives and futures. The first year Graeme Ogden visited, his idea was to rent a bungalow and enjoy his summer recess. The following year, it was to retire from teaching, purchase a home on the island, become romantically involved with the co-owner of the Seaside Café, and marry her.

It had also taken Leah Kent two trips to the island to realize she had to change her life and find a man who not only loved but respected her. Cherie had begun to believe the island was restorative because she too, after two trips, had decided to make it her forever home.

And she was looking forward to their book club discussions, where she experienced a satisfying camaraderie with the two women in their late forties, a closeness that she'd been unable to achieve with women her age. She didn't regard Kayana and Leah as mother figures but as mentors for how she should try to live her life.

Kayana's twenty-year marriage had ended once she'd discovered her husband had fathered a child with another woman, and Leah was finally willing to give up her glittering lifestyle as the wife of a judge, to walk away after thirty years of marriage to a much older man who'd controlled every phase of her life. Cherie knew that if they were willing to give up men they'd loved and married, then it should've been a no-brainer for her to completely exorcise her former lover from her heart and her head. And now she felt comfortable enough to admit to her friends that she was a work in progress.

"Have you guys decided where you're going to celebrate Christmas this year?"

Leah and Kayana shared a glance. "Derrick and I decided to marry next Christmas Eve, but we're not certain whether it's going to be in Florida, where his daughter and other family members won't have to travel for the event."

"I told Lee she and Derrick could marry in Florida, and then honeymoon in Dubai, like Graeme and I did."

"How was it?" Cherie asked.

Kayana closed her eyes, smiling. "Incredible."

"Graeme's wedding gift to her was incredible," Leah drawled. "When she showed me the thirteen-millimeter South Seas drop pearl earrings capped in yellow diamonds, I nearly lost my shit."

Cherie and Kayana laughed. "Now you really sound like a sister when you talk about losing your shit," Cherie said.

Leah sighed as she shifted into a more comfortable position on the sectional's chaise. "Aren't all women sisters under the skin? We get paid less than men for doing the same job, and there so many other things I want to bitch about, but I don't want to ruin my buzz talking about it."

Cherie raised her flute. "Talk about a buzz. These mimosas are delicious *and* lethal. You guys can go upstairs and sleep it off before you even attempt to get behind the wheel, because I will *not* take the blame for providing you with alcohol if you get stopped for driving drunk."

"You don't have to worry about that. We intend to hang out here today until we wear out our welcome," Kayana announced.

"I did say *mi casa es tu casa*," Cherie reminded them. Brunch was nothing short of perfection. Kayana made eggs Benedict, substituting pastrami for Canadian bacon, with Hasselback potatoes, and Leah's French toast. She'd sliced challah bread, stuffed it with cream cheese, and topped it off with a bourbon-maple syrup. They'd emptied one and a half of the three bottles of champagne. And after cleaning up the kitchen, they'd retreated to the family room and literally collapsed on the sectional.

Cherie set her flute on a glass coaster on a side table. "Speaking of weddings and gifts, have you worn your earrings, Kayana?"

"Not in a while. I'm waiting for a formal affair. I've been dropping hints for Leah and Derrick to have their wedding in Newburyport."

"What's in Newburyport?" Cherie questioned.

"Graeme's ancestral home."

Her eyebrows lifted. "Ancestral like in Leah's Kent House?"

Kayana shook her head. "I don't know because I've never been to Kent House, but Graeme's family's home is also listed on the National Register of Historic Places. It is a beautiful Victorian mansion filled with priceless Turkish and Aubusson carpets, porcelain vases, Baccarat chandeliers, Tiffany lamps, and vast collections of fragile bone china, silver, and crystal."

"Did you know about this before you married him?" she asked Kayana.

"Yes. He told me about growing up in Newburyport and attending private schools and college in Boston. His mother was what folks call old money, while his father's family were blue collar, and as an only child, he inherited everything. What I didn't know was that he'd retired from teaching and wasn't returning to Massachusetts at the end of the summer season. That's when, as Leah put it, I lost my shit. Meanwhile I was sleeping with the man, spending more nights at his place than in the apartment above the restaurant, and he hadn't said a mumbling word about living year-round on the island."

Leah stared at Kayana. "The fact that he'd bought a house on the island should've given you a clue, Kayana."

"Some people have purchased houses and condos as vacation properties. Look at you, Cherie. This home could very well be your second home. You could have a job where you're able to work remotely and have the option of working here or in Connecticut."

Cherie laughed. "I really don't have it like that," she lied smoothly. Her friends didn't know she did have enough resources to maintain two residences, but it would result in her withdrawing money from her retirement account. "Leah, have you thought about having your wedding at Kent House?"

Leah gave her a stink eye. "Hell no! Once is enough. Alan and I were married at Kent House, and it was more like a wake than a wedding."

Cherie shifted on the leather cushion and folded her legs into the lotus position. "That was then, and this is now. Your ex is gone, and so is your witch of a mother-in-law. I know you gave the house to your sons, but it's time for you to begin new traditions. Have Caleb and his fiancée talked about where they want to have their wedding?"

"Marisa has talked about having it at Kent House."

"There you go," Kayana drawled. "If your son and his fiancée plan to marry at the family estate, then so should you, Lee. And weren't you the one who said you were never accepted by Richmond's so-called crème de la crème because there had been a time when your family lived in a trailer park?"

Leah nodded. "And they never let me forget it. If I hadn't married Alan, they would've expected me to step off the sidewalk to let them pass. I felt like a hypocrite during Alan and my mother-in-law's funeral, pretending I was grieving when, deep down inside, I wanted to tell everyone that I was free at last. Free from Adele's condescending bullshit and free from Alan flaunting his whores and disrespecting the mother of his sons."

"That's why you should have your wedding at Kent House," Cherie told Leah.

Leah closed her eyes and let out a breath. "Don't you think folks would talk about me remarrying a little more than a year after Alan's passing."

"The hell with those sows!" Kayana shouted. "I don't understand you, Lee. The very people you're concerned with didn't bother to hide their contempt because they felt they were better than you, while their cheating husbands had long rap sheets with endless names of women they'd fucked."

"I'm with Kayana," Cherie said, chiming in. "Fuck those fake heifers. I'd make certain to send out invitations to the folks I did get along with, and within days, the word would be all over Richmond that recently widowed Leah Kent was getting married again. And I'm willing to bet that, when you show up with Derrick, most of the women will be craning their necks to get a look at him, and those who do will have to go home and change their wet panties."

"Cherie!" Leah's face had turned beet-red.

"There's no need for you to get all red in the face, Leah, because you know it happened to you whenever I caught you making googly eyes at Kayana's brother."

"I wasn't the only one looking," Leah said defensively.

"I admit that Derrick is fine as hell, and even if I was interested in him, nothing would've happened."

"Because he's not white?" Leah countered, angrily.

A beat passed as Cherie glared at Leah. Then a hint of a smile tilted the corners of her mouth. "Touché. I suppose I deserve that for some of the nasty things I've said to you. And no, it's not because he's black, but it's his age. Derrick is old enough to be my father." Derrick had mentioned he was looking forward to celebrating his fiftieth birthday in grand style.

"I hope we've settled that," Kayana said under her breath.

"It's settled," Leah and Cherie said in unison.

"Now back to you marrying my brother, Lee. Are you going to have the event at Kent House?"

The redhead sat straight. "Why not? Even though I told my sons I would never live there again, they expect me to come and visit. And once Caleb and Marisa make me a grandmother, I probably will visit them more often."

Cherie unfolded her legs and stood. "I'm going to get a pad and paper to write down some things you'd want for your big day. After that, we need to talk about what books we want to discuss for our upcoming book club meetings."

Leah waved a hand. "We have more than ten months to plan for my wedding. Right now, I think we should concentrate on our book titles."

"Lee's right, Cherie. If we're going pick up where we left off last summer, it's time we decide what we're going to read."

Cherie sat down again. "Last year we only discussed my selection, *The Alienist*, because Leah had to go back to Richmond. But I did manage to read all three titles."

"So did I," Kayana said. "I really enjoyed *Love in the Time of Cholera* and *Memoirs of a Geisha*. But it was *The Alienist* that I loved so much that I had to read it again."

"Do you have any ideas, Leah?" Cherie asked.

A beat passed before Leah asked, "What if we select books with movie tie-ins? We read the books, then view the films to see how well they translate into film."

"I'm in," Kayana said.

"Me too," added Cherie, sharing a fist bump with Kayana.

Leah drained her flute, then set it on a coaster on the glass-topped end table. "Do we all have to choose the same genre?"

"I don't think we should," Cherie replied. "That would make it too parochial."

"Cherie's right, Lee. Someone can choose a legal thriller like *The Firm*. Or one of Tom Clancy's espionage titles."

Cherie said, "I like Clancy's *Clear and Present Danger*, but y'all know I'm into period dramas, so I'm going to select Dennis Lehane's *Live by Night*."

A beat passed as Kayana appeared deep in thought. "As a foodie, I'm going to pick *Like Water for Chocolate* by Laura Esquivel.

Leah pulled her lower lip between her teeth. "I've never read that one."

Kayana smiled. "Then you're truly going to be in for a treat when you read it. We've confirmed *Live by Night* and *Like Water for Chocolate*. What's your book and movie tie-in, Lee?"

"For me, it's a tie between *The Jane Austen Book Club* and *The Thorn Birds*."

"*The Jane Austen Book Club*," Cherie and Kayana chorused, then exchanged another fist bump. They'd read and analyzed Austen's *Pride and Prejudice* the first year they'd met as a club.

Leah smiled. And it was obvious she was quite pleased with her choices. "It looks as if Miss Austen is up for discussion again. And this time it will be all her titles. Are we going to read the books first, and then view the movies, or the other way around?"

Cherie decided to speak up first. "I suggest reading the books, and whoever is hosting the title is responsible for showing the movie. Once the film is over, we can analyze both, keeping in mind that some books don't translate well into film and vice versa."

"That sounds good to me," Leah replied. "What about you, Kayana?"

"I'm on board with it. The next thing we need to resolve is when and how often we should meet. Cherie?"

She felt two pairs of eyes on her, and knew Leah and Kayana expected her to come up with a schedule that would prove workable for everyone. "We can keep last year's schedule of meeting one Sunday afternoon each month."

"Which Sunday?" Leah asked.

"The last Sunday." It was the first thing that popped into her head.

"That's doable," Kayana agreed. "When do you want to hold the first meeting, Cherie?"

Cherie hid a smug grin. It was the first time Leah and Kayana had given her the lead when making determinations about the club book. "March." It was now the end of January, and she predicted she would be able to read all three books in the eight weeks.

"March it is," Leah confirmed.

"If it's all right with everyone, I would like to host the first meeting," Kayana volunteered. "And I'm going to attempt to make some of the Mexican-inspired recipes in the book."

Cherie applauded. "You definitely won't get an argument from me."

The highlight of their get-togethers was the food and drinks that accompanied their discussions. And she knew she had at least eight weeks to up her game when it came to cooking for her to officially host her first meeting. In the past, she'd been responsible for supplying the beverages and, occasionally, dessert. *Live by Night* was set during Prohibition; alcohol was the focus during that era, and she wanted to come up with drinks that mirrored that period in history. Cherie had never been much of a drinker because she'd witnessed firsthand how drinking too much had affected her mother, so there were months and years when she would never have anything alcoholic. She much preferred a mocktail.

"That makes two of us," Leah said in agreement. "If y'all don't mind, I'd like to claim April. After watching *Bridgerton* three times, I'm obsessed with desserts, so be prepared for a sugar high when it comes my turn to host."

Kayana lowered her eyes. "I have to confess that I binged on all the episodes the first time and then waited a couple of weeks before watching one episode every other day. What about you, Cherie?"

Her eyebrows lifted slightly. "What about me?"

"Did you watch *Bridgerton*?"

Averting her gaze, she stared at the decorative fireplace screen. "No comment."

Leah wagged her finger at her. "How many times, Cherie?"

Biting back a smile, she said, "No comment."

"Dam-yum!" Kayana said, drawing out the word in two syllables. "It had to be more than three times if she's not willing to fess up, Lee. And it means she's got you beat."

Her gaze swung back to the two women. "Okay. I admit watching it whenever I was in a funk."

"And how often was that?" Leah asked.

"Too often. After a while, I knew I had to do something or end up old and angry. I'd quit my job because it was no longer fulfilling, and then when I drove down here last year, I felt like I'd been reborn. That's when I knew relocating and starting over was what I needed for my emotional stability."

"How long has it been since you were in a relationship?" Kayana asked her.

"Too long."

"I need a time frame, Cherie."

"Almost five years."

Leah moved off the chaise to sit next to her. "That's much too long for a woman your age."

She met the bright-blue topaz eyes. "Didn't you say that

you and your husband hadn't shared a bed or bedroom in over ten years?"

"Yes, I did, but that was by choice. I could've slipped into bed with him, and he would've welcomed me with open arms, because it would blow up his ego knowing that his wife still desired him. But it didn't happen because I'd had enough of his tomcatting, and I was afraid he'd give me an STD."

"And it's by choice that I'm currently unencumbered. I—" The chime of the doorbell preempted what she wanted to say. "Excuse me, but I must get that."

"Don't get up," Kayana ordered. "I'll see who it is."

At any other time, Cherie would have resented someone usurping her in her own home, but this situation was different because she realized her friends were being overly protective. Her last protector had been her older brother, Jamal. He'd told guys in their neighborhood not to mess with his sister or they would have to answer to him, and she wondered if his edict, not that he'd been sleeping with another boy's girlfriend, had been responsible for his murder.

Chapter 10

Reese stood on the porch, waiting for Cherie to answer the door. When he'd driven up, he noticed the late-model Audi belonging to Leah Kent. But when the door opened, he was slightly taken aback to find Kayana standing there.

"You're not working." Her question was a statement.

"Not right now," Reese admitted. He only wore his uniform when on duty; pullover sweaters, jeans, and boots were his customary off-duty attire. "I'd like to talk to Cherie. Is she all right?" The query was pregnant with concern.

Kayana closed the door and pulled him aside. "She appears okay. But something tells me she's putting on a brave face, so try not to come on too strong when you question her."

"What makes you believe that?"

"As a former psychiatric social worker, I've had clients who tended to mask their trauma and pretend they were okay. Leah and I came here to keep her mind off what went down yesterday. I'm telling you this because Cherie's our friend and we really care about her."

Reese wanted to ask Kayana if she was experiencing some guilt and responsibility because the man had been a customer at her restaurant, and he'd attacked Cherie on her property. And he also resented Kayana cautioning him on how to do his job.

"I'll make certain not to upset her."

Kayana expelled a sigh. "Thank you, Reese."

He waited for her to open the door, and he walked in; Kayana closed and locked it behind them. Reese wanted to get his interview with Cherie over quickly and then go home and sleep. The midnight-to-8:00 shift always screwed up his circadian rhythms, and he much preferred the 8:00 a.m.-to-4:00 p.m. or even the 4:00 p.m.-to-midnight schedules.

Reese came to an abrupt stop, his gaze meeting and fusing with Cherie's. He detected a glimmer of fear in the hazel eyes before she lowered her lids, shuttering her innermost feelings. Within seconds, he realized what Kayana had warned him about. He didn't know what she had exhibited when interacting with her friends, but it was obvious that his appearance was a blatant reminder of what she'd experienced less than twenty-four hours ago. Leah inched closer to Cherie, a motion signaling an intention to protect her.

He nodded to the café's baker. "Good morning."

"Good morning.

Leah had given him what he interpreted as a death stare before she'd acknowledged his greeting. The two women were like lionesses protecting a cub from an approaching predator. However, he hadn't come to harm Cherie. He just needed information from her that he could give to the chief to process the transfer of the prisoner to the county jail.

"Cherie, do you have time to talk to me?"

She smiled, the gesture not reaching her eyes. "Yes."

Kayana gathered the flutes. "Leah and I are going upstairs."

Reese waited for the two women to climb the staircase and motioned for Cherie to sit on the love-seat portion of the sectional; he dropped down next to her. The scent of flowers clinging to her hair wafted to his nostrils.

"Do you mind if I record our interview?"

"No."

Reaching into the front pocket of his jeans, he removed a department-issued, handheld tape recorder. "Before I begin taping, I need to know if you're willing to testify against the man who attacked you." Reese knew interviewing her would be pointless if she didn't want to testify.

"I want to testify and put that piece of shit in jail, where he won't be able hurt anyone else."

That's my girl, Reese thought. She had no intention of letting her attacker go free. He switched on the recorder. "I'm going to ask you a few questions about yourself. Then you can tell me everything you remember about the man who attacked you."

Cherie folded her hands together in her lap. "What do you want to know about me?"

"Where did you live before moving to Coates Island?"

"Cos Cob, Connecticut."

"Where is that in relation to the state capital?"

"It's about thirty-five miles away."

"Is that where you grew up?"

"No. I grew up in New Haven."

Reese smiled. "Is that why you're wearing a Yale sweatshirt?"

There came a lengthy pause. "I graduated from Yale."

He sobered quickly and realized that Cherie Thompson was an enigma. She'd graduated from an elite Ivy League college but worked part-time in a small restaurant. The two facts just didn't add up.

"I suppose you're curious."

Reese shifted to his left and gave her a direct stare. "About what?"

"As to why would someone with a degree from Yale would accept a job as a maintenance worker."

He couldn't believe she'd read his mind. "You're right. I am curious."

Cherie had quickly tired of the ongoing questions. If Reese wanted information on her background, then she would give it to him. "I'm working temporarily at the Seaside Café until I return to college."

"When is that?"

"Next spring. I intend to enroll in online courses for a graduate degree. After twelve years as the parent coordinator for a childcare center, I still want to work with children but as a classroom teacher."

"You couldn't do that in Connecticut?"

"I didn't *want* to do that in Connecticut."

"But why here?"

"I'd vacationed here for the past two summers and loved it. The first summer, I met Leah and Kayana, and when we discovered our love for books, that's when we formed a book club."

Reese ran a hand over his face. "You decided to move here because of a book club?"

Cherie placed a hand over her mouth to stifle giggles when she saw his stunned expression. "Yes. People relocate every day because of something they're passionate about. With me, it's books and loyal friends. Bettina Wilson told me you left the island to enlist in the military. Why did you come back?"

"I came back because Coates Island is my home."

"And now it's mine. Is there anything else you'd like to know about me?"

"That will do for now," he said with an explicit finality. "Is there anything you can recall about the man who assaulted you?"

"What about him?"

"Do you recognize him as someone you may have seen before you began working at the café?"

"No. If I had, I'm certain I would've remembered him."

"It appears that he'd become a regular at the café. Can

you recall how often he came in? And did he ever speak to you?"

Cherie went still as she gave Reese a long, penetrating stare, noticing things about him she'd ignored during their past encounters. They were sitting less than a foot apart, and she saw a feathering of gray in the cropped, straight, black strands of his hair. His features reminded her of a mahogany mask she'd purchased from a street vendor selling artifacts from Africa, India, and Asia. She'd bought several pieces from the man; she planned to exhibit them in her home office.

Reese's eyes—large, dark, and with long lashes women spent money and time in a salon chair to acquire—mesmerized her. It was as if he could see that she wasn't as calm and confident as she appeared. Leah and Kayana's visit had allowed her to temporarily forget that she could've been murdered if Reese Matthews hadn't come along at the exact moment before she lost consciousness. But having to answer questions about the attack brought everything back as she was forced to relive the trauma.

"Cherie? Are you okay?"

She blinked as if coming out of a trance. Cherie wanted to scream at him that she wasn't okay and wouldn't be until the man who attacked her was in prison—and for a long time. "You're firing questions at me as if I were being cross-examined as a hostile witness."

Reese lowered his eyes. "I'm sorry about that. I just want to get this over with so you can try to get on with your life."

"That's not going to happen until that man is in prison."

He nodded. "And that will only happen with our testimony."

"Our?"

"Yes, Cherie. Our. I'll be called as a witness and will testify under oath about what I saw in that parking lot." Reaching over, he covered her hands with one of his. "We're in this together, and because of that, you will get justice."

Reese had said it with so much conviction that she believed him. A hint of a smile parted her lips, and he returned her smile with one she interpreted as wholly erotic. He held her gaze, and Cherie felt as if she'd been caught up in a force field. His warmth and the now-familiar scent of his cologne pulled her in and refused to let her go. He'd created a spell from which she was helpless to escape.

"Reese."

"What is it?"

"I'm ready to finish answering your questions."

It was the only thing she could think of to say when, if circumstances were different, she would've asked him to kiss her to remind her of what she'd been missing for much too long. Five years. That's how long it had been since she'd been in a relationship. She'd been too ashamed to admit to Kayana and Leah that what she'd had wasn't a relationship but an affair.

Weylin married Michelle when Cherie was twenty-two, and that's when she should've stopped sleeping with him. Weylin called her a week following his honeymoon to say that he couldn't stop thinking about her, and like an addict craving her next fix, she'd willingly begun to participate in an adulterous affair.

The instant Reese released her hand, she felt the loss of their connection. Pulling back her shoulders, she stared straight ahead. "No. He never spoke to me. I began working at the Seaside Café a day after they reopened for business earlier this month. My shift didn't start until after they closed, but I always came in early to get a jump on cleaning up. I am familiar with the customers who like to linger until closing time. What I did notice was one man hanging out longer than some of the other folks, and each time, he would have to be told to leave. I caught him staring at me whenever he thought I wasn't looking, but I didn't think much of it. Because I'm new to the island, I thought he was just curious."

"Well, it looks as if his curiosity got him into something

serious; he's going to need a helluva lawyer to keep him from serving more than ninety days."

With wide eyes, Cherie stared at Reese. "What are you talking about?"

He turned off the tape recorder and told her about Clay Lee Adams's extensive rap sheet of petty crimes spanning more than twenty years. Reese said that, despite being arrested, Adams had refused to talk and hadn't requested a lawyer.

"What's going to happen if he doesn't talk?"

"He'll be arraigned and held without bail until it comes time for his trial."

"How long will that take?"

Reese shrugged his broad shoulders under his black, waffle-weave pullover sweater. "It all depends on the court's docket. It may take a few weeks to a couple of months. Meanwhile, you're safe with him locked up."

A shiver of apprehension eddied through her when she thought of the alternative. "What if he does make bail? What would stop him from coming after me again?"

"The sheriff's department. If he is granted bail and he's spotted on Coates Island, you can file for an order of protection that states he can't come within two hundred feet of you, or his bail will be revoked, and he'll be returned to custody."

Cherie sucked in a breath, held it before slowly letting it out. "I suppose I'm going to have to trust you."

Lines fanned out around Reese's eyes when he smiled. "I've taken an oath to protect and serve, and I want you to trust me to protect you."

"I suppose I don't have any other choice," she said flippantly.

"You do have a choice, Cherie. You can stay with your friends until this ordeal is finalized."

"No! There's no way I'm going to let someone, crazy or not, control my very existence. This is my home, and I'm not leaving it."

Cherie experienced a rush of the courage she'd exhibited when negotiating the sale of her baby. She had shocked even herself when facing down the rottweiler attorney representing the Campbells. She'd deflected threats and intimidation to issue her own set of demands, and sensing victory within her grasp, she'd refused to negotiate further. It had become her way or no way.

"That's my girl," Reese said, grinning. He sobered. "You have my number, and I want you to call me whenever you . . . you need someone to talk to. I know you have your book club friends, but sometimes you may need a set of broad shoulders to lean on that your girlfriends can't provide."

"And you believe your shoulders are broad enough for me to lean on?"

Cherie couldn't believe that had come out of her mouth. She was flirting. Yes, flirting with one of Coates Island's most eligible bachelors—and she liked it because it was something she'd never done before. Men had flirted with her, and she'd ignored them because her head and heart belonged to someone unworthy, but she didn't discover that until it was too late.

Reese chuckled. "I have no doubt that they are. Would you like a demonstration?"

"No," she said quickly. Cherie was helpless to stop the wave of embarrassment wash over her as a flush suffused her face. "Perhaps another time." Reese must have sensed her uneasiness when he pushed to his feet.

"I need you to do one more thing for me before I can leave you in peace."

She stood and stared up at him. Standing in sock-covered feet put the top of her head at his shoulders. She stood at five-three and Reese had to be at least a foot taller. "What is it?"

"Walk me to the door, and don't forget to lock it behind me."

"Okay." She walked to the door. "Thank you for everything."

He stared at her under lowered lids. "Just doing my job."

Cherie nodded. Reese was doing his job, yet he'd hinted about going above and beyond those duties when he'd offered friendship. And she wondered if it was something he usually proposed to women he met. She remembered the woman staring adoringly up at him the day she drove to Shelby.

Forget him, Cherie. You're only drawn to him because you're undergoing a sexual drought. She wanted to dismiss the voice in her head, yet knew that wasn't possible. Despite the deputy's overall attractiveness, she knew it would be a mistake to get involved with Reese solely because he'd rescued her from a madman. After all, it was his duty to protect and serve.

Reese opened the door and stepped out onto the porch. "Close and lock it, Cherie."

She did, shutting out his image, and it wasn't until she heard the fading sound of his vehicle's engine that she was able to draw a normal breath and the pent-up tension slowly left her body.

Everything about Reese Matthews was delicious and lethal, like the mimosas she'd drunk earlier that morning. She had to be careful, very careful, because whenever she overindulged, the wall she'd erected to keep everyone at a distance could be easily breached and she might divulge her innermost secrets.

Cherie climbed the staircase to the second story to let Leah and Kayana know that Reese was gone. She found them in the guest bedroom. Leah sat on the cushioned bench seat at the foot of the queen-size bed, and Kayana had selected the armchair in the room's sitting corner. Cherie walked in and sat next to Leah.

"The interview is over."

Kayana stared at her. "Are you certain you're okay?"

Cherie's eyebrows lifted questioningly. "Yes. Why are you asking?"

"I just hope Reese wasn't too hard on you."

A smile parted Cherie's lips. "He wasn't hard at all. In fact, he was quite easy with me."

"That's because he likes you," Leah quipped.

Shifting slightly, she met Leah's eyes. "What are you talking about?"

Leah patted Cherie's back. "Remember when you used to tease me about gawking at Derrick? Well, it's no different with Reese. I'm certain he tried to hide it behind a façade of professionalism, but I'm here to tell you that he failed miserably."

Waving a hand, signaling dismissiveness, Cherie shook her head. "You're mistaken."

"You're in denial," Kayana said, smiling. "You're in as much denial as I was when Derrick mentioned Graeme was interested in me. I'd told him he was crazy, but in the end, I had to admit that my brother was right."

"Well, both of you are wrong about me and the deputy. Besides, I'm not interested in becoming involved with someone." *Even if he's sexy as hell*, she thought.

"That's what I said after I divorced James," Kayana countered. "Sometimes the head refuses to listen to the heart. But there was something about Graeme that was able to shatter the wall I'd put up to keep a man from getting close to me. Everything about him was subtle, unlike some men who'd come onto me like a dog in heat. It even took a while before we slept together."

Cherie smothered a giggle. "A while, Kayana? You married the man six months after your first date."

"That's because we're not kids, Cherie. Both of us are middle-aged, and there are more years behind us than ahead. We don't have children, so there's nothing stopping us from doing whatever we want. And the fact that Graeme is a very wealthy man means he doesn't need my money."

Cherie winced when Kayana mentioned that her husband was very wealthy; it was a reminder of what she'd always wanted: to be married to a wealthy man. However, the route she'd taken to secure one had backfired. "I know you have something to add, Leah."

Leah clasped her hands together. "Now, you know Mama has to dole out advice to our young book club buddy and newest resident of Coates Island. Kayana was lucky to have married two men who didn't have to work a couple of jobs to make ends meet. It was different with me because my family existed at the poverty line, or at times below it. And at no time growing up was I looking for a man to change my lifestyle. That was something I'd planned to do on my own, and that was only possible with a college degree. The degree would give me greater earning power, and in turn, I could help support my parents. And I had no idea who Alan Kent was before I met him."

"You slept with the man who got you pregnant and you didn't know who he was?" Cherie asked, her tone filled with skepticism.

Pinpoints of color dotted Leah's pale complexion. "Let me rephrase that. The first time I met him, and he gave me his business card, with a promise that I would have lunch with him after I graduated from Vanderbilt—it was then that I realized he was a Kent. And even then I had no preconceived notions about hooking up with him because I knew I was out of his league. His intent was to marry someone in his social circle, and I'd become one of his many mistresses. But when I got pregnant and refused to have an abortion, his mother forced him to marry me to protect the precious Kent name."

"You decided to have the baby, even though you weren't in love with him?" Cherie questioned.

Leah made a sucking sound with her tongue and teeth. "I

was never in love with Alan Kent. That's not to say I didn't try to love him, but Alan didn't want to be loved. He wanted to be obeyed, and that was something I refused to do. Alan thought he was using me whenever we appeared at social events as the loving couple, but what the dumb bastard didn't know was that I'd used him whenever he wanted sex. I'd become a prostitute when all that I didn't sell I withheld. That's when he'd buy me expensive jewelry as a peace offering."

With wide eyes, Cherie stared at Leah, recalling the times when she'd asked Weylin for money and jewelry. However, it wasn't because she'd withheld sex from him. Most times, she was too glad to sleep with him, because during that time he was hers and hers alone. She bit her lip to keep from laughing. It was obvious that she and the former headmistress were more alike than Cherie had originally believed.

"What are you going to do with the jewelry now that Alan's dead?" she asked.

"I'm going to give some to my daughters-in-law and save some for when I, hopefully, have granddaughters. Enough about me, Cherie. Now, tell us why you won't give Reese a second look when he has been giving you side-eye glances every time he comes into the café."

"Leah's right," Kayana said, giving Cherie a long, penetrating stare. "We've spilled our guts about the men who done us wrong. Now it's your turn."

She lowered her eyes. "What makes you think someone has done me wrong?"

Kayana frowned. "Stop the bullshit, Cherie! We know the reason you went after Leah every chance you got was that you wanted what she had—a rich husband, the mansion, and all the accoutrements that said you'd made it. But unfortunately, you didn't know what she'd had to go through to maintain that lifestyle. She had a whoring husband who beat the hell out of her when she refused to do what he wanted, while he had the unmitigated gall to bring his young whore to his mother's funeral repast and flaunt her in the presence of his wife and grieving sons."

Cherie put a hand over her mouth. "I had no idea it had gotten that bad," she said through her fingers.

"It was the height of disrespect," Leah spat out. "I didn't care how many women he fucked as long as I didn't see it. But when I had to explain to Caleb that I knew he'd been cheating on me and the look he gave me was not anger but pity, it was enough for me grow a backbone. Disrespecting me behind closed doors was one thing, but disrespecting me in front of my sons took the rag off the bush. That's when I decided not to ask for two million but ten as a divorce settlement. There are some things we let slide and others we say "Oh hell no" to. I knew I could deal with my problems with Alan if they were between us, but once they involved my sons, I knew I had to go for his throat. You don't know how I had to beg them not to lay hands on him once I told them their father had thrown me down the staircase, because right now they would be serving time for murder. Aron and Caleb are six-three, two-thirty, and they were ready to take him apart."

Cherie had no idea what Leah had gone through to live the life she had aspired to. Suddenly, she felt ashamed of how she'd treated the woman who appeared to have had it all. "I'm sorry, Leah."

"For what?" the redhead asked.

"For being a real bitch when I said those nasty things to you."

Leah rested an arm over Cherie's shoulders. "I've forgotten it, and so should you. I'm ready to live my best life, and you should do the same. You have a beautiful house and two friends who will be here whenever you need someone to talk to. And I happen to have one son who's still looking for that special woman."

Cherie laughed. "Thanks, but no thanks."

"Her sons are gorgeous, Cherie," Kayana said, smiling.

"Gorgeous or not, I'd prefer to find my own man."

Kayana nodded. "But are you ready for a relationship?"

A beat passed as Cherie pondered Kayana's question. She'd moved and had established residence in a new state. She was furnishing her home to fit her lifestyle and had planned to embark on a new career as a teacher.

"I think so."

"So, you're no longer carrying baggage from your last relationship?" Leah asked.

"No," she answered truthfully. "I left everything in Connecticut."

"If that's the case, then do you want to tell us about it?" Kayana asked.

Cherie had known it would be only a matter of time before she would have to reveal to her book club friends the events in the past that had made her who she was today. She owed it to them to be truthful with them, as they'd been with her.

"Okay."

Chapter 11

Cherie drew in a breath, held it, and then slowly let it out. It was as if she had to pump herself up to reveal what she'd never told another person. Not even her mother.

"I met this guy when I was fifteen, and the year I turned sixteen, we began sleeping together. We continued to see each other even after he married, and that's something I'm not very proud of."

"Why are you blaming yourself for that?" Leah asked. "After all, he was the married one."

"It still didn't excuse what I did."

"When did you stop seeing him?" Kayana questioned.

Cherie knew she couldn't reveal her lover's name or that she'd had his baby. "It will soon be five years. I'd had enough of being what I considered his side piece. I had wasted so many years wishing, hoping, and praying for something that would never become a reality. The only other thing I'm going to say is that he's very wealthy."

"Wealthy *and* white," Kayana reminded her. "Was it his money or his race that made you stay with him?"

The former psychiatric social worker's question gave Cherie

pause. "His race had nothing to do with our relationship—or I should say our affair. He just happened to be the first and only man I've ever been with. But I can honestly say it was all about money. I grew up in a low-income, crime-infested neighborhood, where many girls were mothers even before they were old enough to vote. That's something I didn't want for myself. I wanted to live in a place where I didn't have to step over drunks and crackheads to get to my apartment or install three locks on my door to feel safe. There was a running joke in my neighborhood about the life expectancy for young boys. By twenty-five, they were either in jail or in the ground. And I knew the only way out of that environment was to get an education and meet someone with enough money to give me the lifestyle I'd always dreamed about."

"Did he?" Leah asked.

A hint of a smile tilted Cherie's mouth. "Yes, he did. It's not that he volunteered to make life easier for me; it was what I demanded. Leah, you said you'd become a prostitute when all that you didn't sell you withheld when it came to having sex with your husband. It was different with me because it wasn't all about sex. For Wills and me," she said, using Weylin's mother's name for him, "it was about a more visceral connection. I understood who he was, and for him, it was the same with me. He knew I didn't want to spend the rest of my life in the neighborhood where several generations of Thompson women had been raised and where they'd chosen to raise their children. So he made it possible for me to rent a studio apartment, and then a one-bedroom so that my twin brothers could spend weekends with me. I gave Daniel and David the bedroom, while I slept on the convertible sofa. It began with weekends, school holidays, and summer recess, which allowed them to see there was another world other than the one my mother had brought them into. I'd lost one brother to the streets, and there was no way in hell I wanted to lose another."

"Where are your brothers now?" Leah asked.

Cherie smiled for the first time since revealing personal things about herself to her book club friends. "They're both graduates of military academies and are now commissioned officers in the army and air force."

Kayana applauded. "That's wonderful! You and your mother must be very proud of them."

"I am, but my mother's doubly proud," Cherie said. "She cried at their graduations, because, I believe, she was grateful they'd made it, unlike my older brother, who had been killed in a drive-by over some bogus BS that he'd been messing around with another dude's girlfriend." She told Kayana and Leah about Jamal borrowing a friend's car to help her move into her dorm room a week before his murder.

Leah draped an arm over Cherie's shoulders and pressed a kiss to her hair. "I'm so sorry, baby."

Fighting back tears, Cherie rested her head on Leah's shoulder; the lingering resentment she'd harbored when first meeting Leah Kent had dissipated like the sun piercing a veil of low-hanging fog. It has taken a while for her to view Leah's life through a different lens. When first meeting the middle-aged redhead, Cherie had wanted what Leah had: children and a wealthy husband, though she was unaware of what Leah had had to go through to maintain a lifestyle that had allowed her to rub shoulders with the social elite of Richmond, Virginia.

Cherie cried without making a sound. Not for herself, but for her older brother, who hadn't been given the opportunity to live out his life. Whenever she was in a funk, it was the loss of her brother and her son that sucked her into a morass of despair that pulled her down like quicksand. It would linger for days, and occasionally weeks, before her inner strength reemerged to remind her that she was a descendant of survivors. That the men and women who came before her had overcome insurmountable obstacles to produce future generations.

Extricating herself from Leah's embrace, she rose and

headed to the en suite bath to compose herself. But instead of stopping, the tears continued to flow, and Cherie buried her face in a towel to muffle her uncontrollable sobbing. After what appeared to be an eternity, she blew her nose, splashed water on her face, and patted it dry with a hand towel. Peering into the mirror over the vanity, Cherie groaned under her breath. Her eyes were red, and there were equally red blotches on her cheeks. She sucked in a breath, holding it for several seconds until she was back in control of her emotions, and then returned to the bedroom. Leah and Kayana were where she'd left them.

"You're still here."

"Where did you think we'd be?" Leah asked.

"I just thought you'd leave," Cherie said.

"Friends don't abandon friends in their time of need," Kayana said, with a slight edge creeping into her voice.

Cherie sat next to Leah on the bench seat. "Sorry about that," she said.

Kayana smiled. "Feeling better?"

Cherie nodded.

"There's nothing like a good cry to get rid of what's bothering you. I've done my share of crying, and I'm here to tell you that I always feel better afterward."

"I can't imagine you crying, Kayana," Cherie remarked.

"Believe me, I have," the co-owner of the Seaside Café admitted. "I thought my crying about failed relationships had ended once I'd divorced James, but little did I know that breaking up with Graeme affected me more than I was willing to admit because he didn't trust me enough to let me know he'd planned to live here permanently. Meanwhile I'd been counting down the days when he was going to return to Massachusetts, and that I would have to wait for the following summer to see him again."

Cherie angled her head. "But now you're married to the man."

Kayana nodded. "Very happily married."

"How does being married to Graeme differ from your first marriage?"

Kayana met Cherie's eyes. "It very different because I trust him. I know I talk a lot about trust, Cherie, but that's the glue that holds a relationship together. You can talk about love all you want, but if you can't trust your partner, it's like having a bell without a clapper. It's useless."

Cherie thought about her relationship with Weylin. She'd fallen in love with him, believing they would spend the rest of their lives together once they graduated college. And now that she looked back, she couldn't believe she'd been that naïve, that gullible when he told her he wanted to keep their relationship secret from everyone until their engagement.

She'd known from the onset that she could never invite him to meet her family until he'd put a ring on her finger, but what Cherie didn't understand was why she hadn't met his. After all, she and their son had attended the same prep school and graduated from the same Ivy League college, even if she had graduated with honors and he hadn't. It had never dawned on her that her race would be a factor if he decided to choose a wife, but apparently it was, along with her social status. When Weylin's parents announced that he was engaged to the daughter of a prominent elected official, Cherie felt as if her whole world had imploded. She'd watched the man to whom she'd given her virginity and her love become the husband of a woman who had been their Yale classmate. That's when she realized Weylin was an expert when it came to keeping secrets. No one had known he was dating Michelle before their engagement, and no knew he was also sleeping with a black woman. He'd carried on two clandestine relationships at the same time, and neither woman knew about the other.

"You're right," she said. "I trusted someone who was so undeserving of it." Cherie sighed softly. "But that's behind me now."

"Good for you," Leah crooned. "Now that you've put

that part of your life in the rearview mirror, it's time for you start over in a new state, a new house, with book club friends who are your older sisters."

Cherie couldn't help but smile. Leah was right. "Do you know what I find ironic?" she said after a comfortable silence.

"What's that?" Kayana questioned.

"We all have something in common. You left Atlanta to come back to Coates Island after your divorce, while Leah left Richmond after burying her husband to move here. And I decided to relocate to Coates Island because it's where I met two women who have helped me discover who I am and what I need to live my best life."

Leah nodded. "How true. But you forgot another thing."

"What's that?" Cherie asked.

"Kayana and I were given a second chance at love. And I know you probably don't want to hear it, but it's time you find that special someone with whom to share your newfound life. You claim it's been almost five years since you've been in a relationship—even if it was an adulterous one—and because you're older and, I hope, a lot wiser, you will know what you're willing to accept or reject when it comes to a man. I told you before that you're beautiful and intelligent, and that translates into men flocking to you like bees to a flower."

"Like that crazy-ass man who tried to strangle me."

Leah rolled her eyes upward. "I'm not talking about crazies, Cherie. And don't forget that I have a son who's a very eligible bachelor."

"I'm here to tell you that Leah's sons are very attractive men," Kayana added.

Cherie laughed. "Thanks, but no thanks. I believe I can find my own man. And besides, Leah's sons live in Richmond, and I have no intention of moving again."

Leah let out an audible sigh. "And I doubt whether Aron is willing to leave Richmond now that he's an associate in the family's law practice."

"He's an associate and not a partner?" Cherie questioned.

"Even though the firm is Kent, Kent, McDougal and Sweeny, Caleb and Aron weren't given preferential treatment. They had to start as associates, and eventually they'll become managing partners."

Cherie suddenly realized, at that moment, that she had no need to second-guess herself about leaving Connecticut to move to North Carolina to reconnect with two women who two summers ago were strangers and whom she now thought of as not only friends but family. Both Kayana and Leah were old enough to be her mother, if they'd had the baby in their early teens, yet she didn't regard them as mother figures, but as older sisters protecting their younger one.

Kayana would occasionally slip back into her psychiatric social worker role when giving her suggestions on how she should look at life, while Leah's maternal instincts translated into wanting to protect and nurture her. And she was certain that, when they'd decided to form their book club, they had no idea how inexorably their lives would become entwined. Leah had come to the island the first time to distance herself from a toxic marriage, and the second time, it was to heal from a domestic violence incident. She'd fallen in love with Kayana's brother, and before the end of the year, she and Kayana would become sisters-in-law.

Cherie really did appreciate Leah attempt's to fix her up with one of her sons, but she didn't want a repeat of what she'd had with Weylin. It would be like making a lateral move because both men were white and wealthy. However, she found it odd that Leah believed race was a priority for her when it came to a relationship when it wasn't. There weren't that many black boys at her prep school, and most of them dated other black, white, and girls of color. For some reason, they hadn't given her a second look, yet she wasn't bothered by that. They knew she was on scholarship and were aware of where she lived, and that meant she wasn't socially and financially their equal.

"I really appreciate the company, the food, and the drink," Cherie said, smiling.

"I know we came over unannounced and uninvited, but Leah insisted we check on you," Kayana stated.

Cherie smiled. "And I'm glad you did."

Kayana pushed off the chair. "I know we said we were going to spend the day with you, but I think you may need some alone time before you come to the café tomorrow."

"Kayana's right," Leah said. "If you need company, just text me, and I'll come and get you so you can stay over with me and Derrick."

"I can assure you two mother hens that I'm going to be okay."

"If you say so," Kayana drawled.

"I'm all right, Kayana. After drinking those mimosas, I'm ready for a nap. And when I get up, I'll probably make some popcorn and watch a couple of movies."

Leah nodded. "Okay."

Cherie closed and locked the door behind her friends, then retreated to the kitchen to wash the flutes. She knew Leah and Kayana were genuinely concerned about her, and she appreciated that, but she didn't want them to view her as a victim; that was a status she refused to accept. Even when she'd made the decision to give up her baby, she'd thought of herself as a surrogate carrying a child for a woman unable to have one, and she had been paid well for it. Now she was not only older but wiser. If or when she found herself in another relationship, it would be vastly different from the one she'd had with Weylin. She'd promised herself she would never sleep with another woman's husband, and if she did become pregnant, she would never again give up her baby.

* * *

Reese returned to the station to transcribe his interview with Cherie, and he printed out a copy for the chief before heading home to get some sleep. He lingered long enough to prepare breakfast for himself, then showered and got into bed.

He was always a light sleeper, and it was the sound of his cell phone vibrating on the bedside table that woke him. Reaching for the phone, he peered at the time. It was minutes after five. He'd been asleep for six hours.

"What's up?" he asked, when he saw his cousin's name on the screen.

"I suspected you were sleeping, but I just wanted to call to tell you to take the night off."

Reese sat up. "Why?"

"I just got a call from the FBI's field office in Tennessee that our resident prisoner's DNA was found on a dead girl in Chattanooga. He'd stalked, raped, then strangled her to death. There were warrants out for his arrest, but he'd managed to evade being apprehended. Federal marshals will be here in the morning to extradite him to Tennessee. So you can tell Miss Thompson that there's no need for her to testify, because he'll be tried there for rape and murder."

"So he goes from petty offenses to rape and murder. How old was the girl?"

"Fourteen."

Slumping back against the pillows cradling his shoulders, Reese blew out his breath. "He's an animal."

"I don't know if he realizes he'll be facing capital punishment, which is a legal sentence under Tennessee law."

"He'll find out soon enough whether he'll spend the rest of his life in prison without the possibility of parole or get a needle in his arm." Reese knew that, if he hadn't come along when he did, Cherie could've become another one of his victims. "Thanks for giving me the night off, and I'll be certain to let Miss Thompson know she will not have to face this monster in court."

"I know you're off for the next two days, so now that you have a head start, try to relax."

Reese smiled, even though Parker couldn't see him. "Thanks."

"No, thank you, little cousin."

"Hang up, Chief, so I can go back to sleep."

He ended the call, his smile still in place. It was a relief not having to work the midnight-to-8:00 shift just before his days off. Reese had told Parker that he was going back to sleep, but he knew that wasn't possible now that he was fully awake. Scrolling through his phone's contacts, he tapped Cherie's number. She answered after the second ring.

"Hello."

"I need to see you." There was a long pause before she spoke again.

"Why?"

"Have some news to tell you, and I'd rather do it in person."

"Okay. You can come on over."

Reese ended the call and headed for the bathroom. He hadn't planned to talk to Cherie again until it was time for her to appear in court, but this was news he knew she would welcome hearing in person.

The doorbell echoed throughout the house, and Cherie took a deep breath, held it, and then let it out slowly as she made her way to the door. She peered through the security eye to see the distorted image of Reese staring at her.

She unlocked the door and smiled. "Hello again." It was the second time that day he'd come to her home. "Please come in." The overhead light in the entryway shimmered off his jet-black hair, and Cherie curbed the urge to moan as his warmth and the sensual scent of his cologne swept over and through her.

"Thank you," Reese said as he wiped his booted feet on the thick mat inside the door. "It's nice and toasty in here."

"That's because I turned up the thermostat. Even though I grew up New England, I don't like cold weather."

"It gets cold here, too, but our winters are nothing like those up North. But if you don't like cold weather, you should've moved to Florida or Southern California."

"I don't think so. I happen to like the change of seasons."

"Well, you will get that in North Carolina."

Cherie clasped her hands together. "I'm forgetting my manners. Would like something to eat or drink?" Reese stared at her under lowered lids. She noticed a hint of a smile tilting the corners of his mouth.

"What's on the menu?"

She didn't know why, but Cherie hadn't expected him to take her up on her offer. "I've been experimenting with cooking, and today I decided to make meat loaf. "I just put it in the oven. Meanwhile, I can give you some loaded-baked-potato soup. I don't know why I bought a five-pound bag of potatoes when I don't eat them every day. They were beginning to sprout eyes, so I made potato soup and salad, and I plan to make mashed potatoes to go along with the meat loaf. You can't have meat loaf without potatoes." She realized she was talking too fast and too much, and hoped Reese didn't think she was one of those women who liked to hear herself talk.

Reese's dark eyes lit up. "You're singing my song. Even though I'm a rice-eating country boy, I do like meat and potatoes."

"What are you doing?" Cherie asked when he bent over to untie the laces on his boots.

"I'm taking off my shoes because I don't want to track dirt over your floors."

She shook her head. "Don't worry about that. I'm seriously thinking about replacing this bleached pine flooring with gray European oak in a herringbone design. I went online and found a store about thirty miles away that stocks what I want."

"That would really complement the blue, green, and pale gray walls. By the way, I really like your house because it's so zen," he said.

"Thank you. You should've seen it before I had it painted. Everything was white and very sterile."

"Do you intend to replace all of the flooring in the house?" Reese asked as he followed her into the kitchen.

"No. Just on this floor."

"Before you buy anything, I'd like to go to the store with you."

Cherie gave him a quick glance over her shoulder as she recalled Kayana mentioning Reese had come from a long line of master carpenters. "Do you want to go with me because you believe that, because I'm a woman, they'll try to cheat me?"

"No," he replied, "it has nothing to do with you being a woman. It's just that I know a lot about wood and will be able to tell if what they're calling European oak is the real deal. I happen to come from a long line of carpenters," he continued when Cherie turned to face him, "and I was able to identify different types of wood before I turned eight. My grandfather was a hard taskmaster, and there were times when he'd give me a pop quiz about the supply of wood he had on hand in the shed."

"I really appreciate the offer, Reese, but I don't want to put you out."

"You won't be putting me out."

She gave him a steady stare. "What about your job?"

Reese's eyes crinkled when he smiled. "I do get days off. I'm off tonight and for the next two days."

Cherie felt a swath of heat in her face. "I didn't mean that you work twenty-four seven, but it's just that I don't want to take up your time when you could be seeing someone else."

Reese crossed his arms over his gray sweatshirt. "Is this your way of asking if I'm involved with someone?"

The heat in her face increased. "Yes and no. Yes, because I don't need some woman in my face because she believes I'm taking time away from her when her boyfriend is out with me. And no, because it doesn't matter whether you are or are not involved with someone."

"Well, I'm not, Cherie Thompson. I'm not involved with anyone on Coates Island, and the last woman with whom I found myself *that* involved I married."

She blinked slowly. She hadn't expected him to be that forthcoming about his relationships with women. "How long ago was that?"

"It was a long time ago. I've been divorced for twelve years."

Cherie nodded. "That is a long time," she said under her breath.

"To be honest, it should have been longer. I kept hoping it would get better, but it didn't. What about you, Cherie?"

"What about me?" she asked.

"Were you ever married?"

Her eyelids fluttered wildly. "No. No ex-husband and no children."

Reese took a step, bringing them less than a foot apart. "It looks as if we have something in common."

Tilting her head, Cherie met his eyes. "What's that?"

"I, too, don't have any children."

Her brow furrowed. "How long were you married?" she asked, believing that Reese and his ex-wife probably didn't stay together long enough to start a family.

"Four years. I wanted children, and she didn't."

Cherie wanted to ask him if they'd discussed having a family before they were married, but decided that was too personal. Just knowing he was single was enough. "You said you had something to tell me," she said quickly before he could ask about her prior relationship.

"You won't have to testify against your attacker."

Her eyes grew wide. "Why?"

"Because United States marshals are coming here tomorrow to extradite him to Tennessee, where he's wanted for raping and murdering a fourteen-year-old girl."

Cherie's legs began shaking, and she would've collapsed if Reese hadn't held her upright. Knowing the man had raped and killed a girl made the reality of his attack even more frightening, and she knew that if Reese hadn't been in the café's parking lot at the time she was being strangled, she could've possibly become another one of his murdered victims.

Reese buried his face in Cherie's hair as he supported her trembling body. He'd debated whether to tell her about the man over the phone or in person, and he was glad he'd decided on the latter. There was no doubt she was experiencing PTSD.

"It's okay, bae. I'm here for you," he said over and over until her trembling eased and then stopped altogether.

"What's going to happen to him?" Cherie asked. Her voice was muffled as she pressed her face against his chest.

"If he doesn't get the death penalty, then he's probably going to spend the rest of his life in prison without the possibility of parole."

She leaned back and stared up at Reese. "So I won't have to see him again?"

"No. When we arrested him, his name and DNA came up in the CODIS database, and that's when the chief got a call from the FBI field office in Chattanooga, Tennessee. We forwarded our report to the prosecutor in Chattanooga, because Tennessee has jurisdiction, and they have an outstanding warrant for his arrest for rape and murder."

Cherie covered her face with her hands. "I'm trying to forget what happened, but whenever I close my eyes, I relive the time when I couldn't breathe."

Reese took her hands, bringing them down. "You're experiencing flashbacks. It's the same with soldiers in combat or someone who has had a traumatic encounter. It's going to take a while for you to get over it."

"What if I never get over it, Reese?"

Cradling the back of her head, he kissed her forehead. "You can, and you will, because I'll be here to help you. That's a promise, and I always keep my promises."

Cherie forced a smile. "That what I used to tell my brothers. Whenever I would promise them something, I'd always come through for them."

Reese kissed her forehead again. "And I've never been one to break a promise. You have my cell phone number, so if or when you need me, I'm only minutes away."

Pulling her lower lip between her teeth, Cherie closed her eyes for several seconds. "If I need counseling, I'll talk to Kayana. There's no need for me to bother you with my problems."

"You're not a bother, Cherie, so I don't want to hear you refer to yourself as one."

"I would've said a pain in the neck if I didn't have one."

He loosened the scarf she'd wound around her neck, sucking in his breath when he saw the darkening red bruises on her throat. "Are you experiencing a lot of pain?"

"Not as much as before. I just can't stand to look at my neck because it's a constant reminder of what could've happened to me if you hadn't come along when you did."

"I told you I was destined to be where I was yesterday afternoon."

A trembling smile parted her lips. "Destiny, fate, and luck."

His smile matched her. "That's definitely a trifecta." Reese adjusted the silky material and covered the bruises.

"Are you ready to sample what I've cooked?"

"Yes. Do you do a lot of cooking?" he asked Cherie.

"I'm cooking more now than I did in the past. Come sit down, and I'll tell you why I've decided to spend a lot of my free time cooking."

"What else do you do besides cooking?"

"Read."

Reese's eyebrows lifted. "You read that much?"

"Yes. I have boxes of books in one of the upstairs bedrooms that I plan to turn into a home office and library. I still haven't decided how I want to decorate it."

"Maybe I can help you out with that. I have some books on different styles. You're more than welcome to come to my place to look at them."

Cherie nodded. "I'll think about it."

Reese wondered if he was moving too quickly by inviting her to his home. It was one thing to interact with Cherie because it concerned police business, but if he were truly honest with himself, he liked her in the way a man likes a woman.

Other than her natural beauty, he wasn't certain what drew her to him, and that was something he intended to find out. He'd dated women since his divorce—some he'd really liked and a few to fill up the empty hours when he was between deployments.

However, there was something different about Cherie Thompson. Although she'd exhibited a modicum of feistiness, he had also detected a vulnerability lurking beneath her bravado. She was an enigma and a challenge, and he'd never been able to resist a challenge. It was why he'd joined the ROTC and spent the next twenty years of his life as an Army Ranger.

"Are you going to have some soup with me?"

Cherie flashed a cheeky grin. "Of course."

Chapter 12

Cherie swallowed a mouthful of baked-potato soup and silently congratulated herself that it'd come out better than she'd expected. The creamy soup—with coarsely chopped potatoes and topped with shredded sharp cheddar cheese, chopped fresh chives, sour cream, and crumbled fried bacon—tantalized her palate with a release of flavor from onions, garlic, and pepper.

"Did you really make this?" Reese asked.

Her spoon was suspended in midair when she met his eyes. "Yes. Why?"

"This is the best baked-potato soup I've ever tasted. And I've ordered enough to say that. Who taught you to cook?"

Cherie set down her spoon and picked up a napkin to touch the corners of her mouth. Sitting across the oaken table in the kitchen's alcove with Reese, there was an atmosphere of intimacy that wouldn't have been possible if she'd had her dining-area table.

"I can't take credit for the recipe," she truthfully. "I found it online."

He angled his head. "Are you saying you don't know how to cook?"

"Oh, I know how to cook, but not like Kayana and her brother."

"Not many folks on the island can compete with the Johnsons. They've had years of experience and use recipes that go back several generations."

"Now that I don't have what I consider a nine-to-five, I've been experimenting with different dishes. Whenever someone hosts a book club meeting, not only do we discuss books, but we always have food and cocktails."

Reese took another spoonful of soup. "How often do you meet?"

"The first summer, it was every Sunday afternoon. Our first meeting was at the café, and Kayana surprised me and Leah when she prepared incredibly delicious hors d'oeuvres and sour-apple martinis. To say we were lit up was an understatement."

"What book did you discuss?"

Cherie swallowed another mouthful of soup. "We didn't discuss books during our first meeting. It was more like a get-together where we familiarized ourselves with one another. However, we did decide what titles we wanted to read for the next few meetings."

"Which ones did you decide to read and discuss?"

"*Kindred* by Octavia Butler, *Pride and Prejudice* by Jane Austen, and *Ethan Frome* by Edith Wharton."

Leaning back in his chair, Reese chuckled. "Did you realize you'd chosen books written by women?"

A slight frown appeared between Cherie's eyes. "Are you intimating that we deliberately selected women authors because we like them better than their male counterparts?"

"No. Not at all. I just thought it odd that you would select those authors. That maybe something in their writing was more appealing than someone like James Baldwin or Tom Clancy."

The fact that they'd selected books written by women during their inaugural book club summer was something she hadn't thought about. "We just happened to recommend some of our favorite books. Last year, it was all men."

"What were they?"

"*The Alienist* by Caleb Carr, *Love in the Time of Cholera* by Gabriel Garcia Márquez, and *Memoirs of a Geisha* by Arthur Golden. *The Alienist* was my choice, and we were only able to discuss that one title because Leah had to go back to Virginia to take care of several personal issues."

"Did they enjoy your choice?"

"Of course they did. We always enjoy each other's choices. Have you read *The Alienist*?"

"No. Should I?" Reese asked.

"I'm only going to say that I highly recommend it."

"If that's the case, I'll order a copy."

"You don't have to do that," Cherie countered. "I have a copy upstairs you can use. I'm willing to lend it to you, but only if you promise not to bend the corner of the pages or read it while eating or drinking coffee. I once lent someone one of my books, and I had to throw it away and buy another copy once they returned it with missing pages, a broken spine, and many pages dotted with coffee stains."

Reese placed a large hand over his heart. "I promise, Miss Cherie Thompson, that I will return your book in the same condition in which it was given to me."

Her smile was dazzling. "As soon as you finish your soup, I'll go upstairs and get it."

"If you don't mind, I'll go with you. There may be other books in your collection that I'd like to read."

"You read?"

"What makes you believe I wouldn't read?"

"I don't know, Reese. I figured that, during your downtime, you'd want to kick back and watch sports."

"That's not all I do," he countered, a slight edge creeping into his voice. "I read, watch television, *and* I build things."

Propping her elbow on the table, Cherie cupped her chin in the palm of her hand. "What things do you build?"

"The last one was a child's wagon. One of the guys at the station had a little boy who was turning three, and he asked me if I would build a personalized little red wagon for his son."

"How long did it take for you to make it?"

"I worked on it whenever I was off, so it was about a week. I had to order the wheels and the handle from a supplier, and I had an artist paint balloons, half-moons, and stars along the sides. Fortunately, it was finished before the child's birthday party."

Cherie closed her eyes and tried to imagine her son sitting in a wagon being pulled by his father. The instant the image popped into her head, she dismissed it. "He must have been overjoyed with the wagon."

"So much so that he wanted to sleep in it."

"That must have been adorable."

"It was," Reese confirmed, "because the little boy is adorable."

She didn't know why the conversation had veered off from books to children. "Whenever you're ready, I'll take you upstairs to look for the book."

Reese followed Cherie up the staircase, and somehow he couldn't stop thinking about the myriad of emotions that had flittered over her features when he'd talked about building the wagon for his coworker's son; he wondered if perhaps she'd wanted or had lost a child, and made a mental note not to broach the subject again.

He'd told Cherie that he had wanted a family when his exwife didn't. However, it hadn't always been that way; otherwise, he wouldn't have married her. But after less than a year of marriage, Monica began complaining that she didn't feel she was ready to become a mother. Reese told her they were young and had time to enjoy each other before starting a family. Then once they'd celebrated their third anniversary, she'd dropped a bombshell when she claimed she didn't want children *and* she didn't want to be a military wife. It had taken time for him to process her complete one-eighty; after all, it was she who had proposed marriage, while claiming she wanted his babies. He'd suggested they see a marriage counselor, but Monica refused. At first, he'd believed she was having an affair, and when he'd confronted her with his suspicions, she said making love made her feel dirty. By that time, Reese knew there was nothing he could do to save his marriage and gave Monica what she wanted—a divorce. After it was finalized, she moved back to Fayetteville to take care of her widowed father.

He walked next to Cherie along the carpeted hallway to the bedroom at the end of the hall. There was a stained-glass casement window that overlooked the side of the house that he hadn't noticed the first time he'd come. "This house is a lot larger inside than it appears from the street," he said.

"It has a lot more room than I need, but I didn't want to wait for a smaller house to come on the market. It's twenty-six hundred square feet, and it has one more bedroom than what I'll need. I wanted a master, a guest room, and a home office, but I suppose having two guest bedrooms will come in handy if my mother and brothers come to visit at the same time."

"Should I assume your brothers are younger than you?"

She nodded. "Yes. I'm twelve years older than they are. They are recent graduates from West Point and the Air Force Academy."

"You're kidding!"

Cherie's eyes sparkled in delight as she flashed what Reese had come to think of as her sensual smile. She'd slightly lower her head and look up at him through her lashes. "No, I'm not. David and Daniel are not only identical twins but are super competitive with each other. They'd graduated valedictorian and salutatorian at their high school, even though they'd earned the same grade point average. And because David is four minutes older than Daniel, he decided to defer to his younger brother and allow him to become the valedictorian."

"They sound incredible."

"They are. I'm so proud of them."

"What about your parents, Cherie? They have to be proud that their children have superior intelligence."

A beat passed. "There's just my mother."

"Well, she's to be commended. It's not every day a single mother can raise three exceptional children."

Cherie opened the door to the bedroom, flipped on an overhead light, and walked in. "What you see will eventually become my office and library." She pointed to boxes labeled BOOKS lining two walls.

"What the . . ." Reese swallowed the curse. "How many books do you have?"

"A couple of hundred—maybe three or four. A lot of them are textbooks, and the others are—"

"I know, Cherie," Reese said, cutting her off. "And the others are romance novels."

Her jaw dropped. "How did you know?"

"Because a lot of women read them. You would really get along with Miss Elizabeth at the station because that's all she reads. She's our clerk."

"Do you think there's something wrong with romance novels?"

He walked into the room and opened the shutter-styled blinds. "No, because my grandmother used to read them. After she passed away, I boxed up the books and stored them in a corner of the garage. But when I discovered our clerk read them, she was gifted with decades of Harlequins going as far back as the sixties."

Cherie came over to stand next to him. "My grandmother was also addicted to Harlequins and daytime soaps. She'd set up the ironing board in the kitchen and iron while watching her favorite soaps on a tiny black-and-white television. If it wasn't ironing, then it was folding laundry. Whether it was cooking, ironing, doing laundry, or reading, her hands were never still."

"Is she still alive?" Reese questioned.

"No," Cherie said after a swollen pause. "I was still in high school when she passed away. I miss her telling me that if I wanted a husband, then I had to learn to cook. She'd get so angry when I told her I didn't need to learn because I could buy frozen foods from the supermarket and heat them up in the oven or microwave or order takeout from a restaurant."

"You're right, and so was your grandmother."

"About me having to cook to land a husband?"

"A husband is optional. No, it's about knowing how to cook for yourself."

"And that is, Reese?"

"It's a feeling of accomplishment that you were able to follow a recipe from the beginning to the end. A prime example is your loaded-baked-potato soup."

"It's not as if I'm completely helpless in the kitchen," Cherie countered.

"Then what is it, Cherie?"

"It's perfecting recipes so that, whenever I have to host a book club meeting, I'll be able to hold my own with Leah and Kayana. The first time I came here, I stayed in the boardinghouse, so I couldn't host a meeting, but I'd assumed the responsibility of making drinks or bringing desserts. Last year, I rented a bungalow, but again I didn't get to host. We had only one meeting, and that was in a converted garden shed at the rear of Derrick's house. We commandeered it as our she-shed while he grilled surf and turf."

"Wow! You guys are really fancy."

Cherie winked at him. "You don't know the half. We go

all out for our meetings. There's nothing better than good friends getting together to eat, drink, and talk about things they really love. And for us, it's books."

"Speaking of books," he said, pointing to the boxes, "do you have to go through all of them to find what you're looking for?"

"Not really. I made notations on the sides of the boxes, so once I get bookshelves, I'll know how to catalog them."

Reese watched as Cherie knelt and shifted several boxes until she found the one she was looking for. She removed the top and held up a thick hardcover book. "Read and enjoy."

He took the book, then extended his free hand to help Cherie stand. "It's a mystery."

She nodded. "It's a combination of mystery, crime, and some horror."

"Are you certain it won't give me nightmares?"

"I don't think so. It's nothing like Stephen King's *It*."

Reese shook his head. "I refused to read that title because I couldn't understand why King made the main antagonist an evil clown. Do you know how that can mess with kids' heads?"

"Don't forget Chucky, Reese. That's enough for little girls to swear off playing with dolls."

"I take it you don't like horror books or movies."

"Not particularly. This year, we've decided to read books with movie tie-ins."

"What have you selected?"

"Our first three will be *Like Water for Chocolate*, *Live by Night*, and *The Jane Austen Book Club*."

Reese leaned closer to Cherie. "What's with you and Jane Austen?" he whispered in her ear.

Cherie rounded on him. "What's wrong with Jane Austen, Reese? Her novels, published two hundred years ago, are still popular today. That should tell you that her work still resonates with today's readers."

He shook his head again. "I still don't understand the obsession with her books after two centuries."

"Would you say the same about Willie Shakespeare?"

Throwing back his head, Reese laughed loudly. "He's Willie and not William?"

Cherie flashed a saucy grin. "Yeah. To me, he's Willie. His plays are two hundred years older than Jane Austen's novels, and they are still performed by famous actors with major theater companies around the world. What's good for the goose should be good for the gander."

"Shakespeare's different because his plays don't focus on desperate women looking to marry wealthy men."

"I'm not denying the man's literary genius, but do I detect a little cynicism when it comes to love? Austen's female characters weren't just looking for wealthy husbands to take care of them because women weren't allowed to inherit property, but also for love. And that's very different from the titled men in Edith Wharton's *Buccaneers* who married American heiresses for their money to save their impoverished estates. Not only did they take their money, but some of the women were treated wretchedly."

"Why did the women marry them?"

"They were daughters of the nouveau riche, and despite their fathers' wealth, they weren't accepted by those with old money. So their fathers negotiated deals with men who had titles and vast estates, along with mounting debts, to marry their daughters. Winston Churchill's mother was one of those women, along with one of Princess Diana's ancestors."

Reese was pleasantly surprised when he heard the passion in Cherie's voice as she discussed books and authors. Aside from his grandmother, he hadn't met or been involved with any woman who had been an avid reader. Some of them were more interested in the lives of movie or reality-television stars.

"Perhaps I need a refresher course in English lit."

"Didn't your high school teach literature?"

He smiled. "Yes, it did, and I did take a literature course in college to fulfill the requirements for English."

Cherie went completely still when Reese mentioned attending college, as she remembered Bettina Wilson saying that Reese had enlisted in the army after graduating high school. "You went to college." The query was a statement.

"Yes. Does that surprise you?"

"Well—I—" she stammered, struggling to get her words out. "I shouldn't be surprised because I really don't know you."

"That's true, but since we both live on Coates Island, I'm certain we'll get to know a lot more about each other."

"I'll suppose we'll have to level the playing field, because, Deputy Matthews, you do know more about me than I know about you."

Reese smiled, and the expression was so sensual that Cherie felt her pulse quicken as she was caught up in a spell of longing that made her weak in the knees. She didn't know what it was about the man that made her whole being fill with a desire for him to make love to her. It had been that way the first time she saw him walk into the Seaside Café to pick up a takeout order. At first, she'd believed he was curious or even suspicious because he'd never seen her before. Yet it had happened again when she'd gone to the mainland to shop for gifts for Kayana and Leah. Just for several seconds, she'd met his eyes before going inside the jewelry store.

Cherie had admitted to Leah and Kayana that she'd only been with one man and, because of that, was wholly unprepared for what to expect if or when a man should express an interest in her. She hadn't dated before leaving home to attend the prep school because she didn't want to get involved with any of the boys in her neighborhood and possibly end up pregnant, which seemed their intent whenever they went out with a girl. It was as if they'd made a pact to see how many children they could father before turning twenty.

And now, in hindsight, Cherie realized she hadn't been prepared to sleep with Weylin, but he'd been so persuasive that she'd found it hard to resist him. After a while, it was obvious she wasn't the first girl he'd slept with, and when she'd told him she couldn't afford to get pregnant, he'd assured her that wouldn't happen because he always used condoms. Even after they'd agreed never to see each other again, she wondered what it would've been like to sleep with another man.

"That's true, Miss Thompson," Reese said, breaking into her thoughts. "But that's only when I'm a deputy asking you pertinent questions about a crime. And that's very different now because I'm currently not in that capacity."

"Which means what, Reese?"

"That I'd like to get to know Cherie."

Their eyes met. It was apparent they wanted the same thing. "I don't think that will be a problem," she said in a quiet voice. An expression of shock froze his features before he nodded. It was obvious he hadn't expected her to agree.

He lowered his head and brushed a light kiss over her parted lips. "Thank you."

Cherie hoped Reese couldn't hear the pounding of her heart through her sweatshirt. "You have your book, and I have to go downstairs and check on my meat loaf before it turns into a brick. You're welcome to stay for dinner."

"I was hoping you'd ask. Thank you."

Turning on her heel, she left the room, leaving Reese to turn off the light. He was hoping she'd ask, and she'd hoped he would accept. Cherie knew she'd turned a corner in purging Weylin completely from her past, now that she looked forward to having an open relationship with a man that wasn't an affair.

Chapter 13

"If I were to grade you on tonight's dinner, I'd definitely give you an A, Cherie," Reese said as he set down his fork.

She'd talked about upping her game to compete with the owners of the Seaside Café, but Cherie didn't realize she had a natural talent for cooking. Not only could she follow a recipe; she also had the wherewithal to modify it to make it her own. She'd used ground beef and veal, and had removed sweet and andouille sausages from their casings to substitute for the pork; the result enhanced the flavor of the moist meat, topped with a savory tomato sauce and Panko bread crumbs. He watched her whip up a bowl of creamy mashed potatoes and sauté freshly washed spinach in garlic and oil.

Cherie lowered her eyes, enchanting Reese with the demure gesture. "If I'd known I was going to have company, I would've made a salad and baked some bread."

"You didn't need the salad or bread, bae. What you made was perfect. If I hadn't eaten with you, I would've heated up some leftovers."

She smiled. "Didn't you say that you cook?"

Reese nodded. "I do."

"Who taught you?"

"My grandmother."

Cherie's eyebrows lifted. "There's nothing like a grand-mama's cooking. Even though we were Connecticut Yankees, I grew up eating southern food."

"What part of the South were your folks from?"

"South Carolina."

"Gullah?" he asked.

"Down to the marrow in my bones. My great-grandmother came north during the Great Migration. She settled in New York City for a couple of years before moving to Connecticut when a municipal hospital advertised for laundry workers. That's where she met my great-grandfather, who worked there as an orderly. They got married and moved into a low-income housing development in New Haven. When they moved there, it was a suitable place for families raising their children. It was where my grandmother was born and where she had my mother, and where Momma had us. Even before my mother was born, the neighborhood had changed, becoming infested with crime and drugs."

"But your family doesn't live there now."

"Not all of us."

Lines of confusion creased Reese's forehead when he frowned. "Are you saying your mother still lives there?"

Cherie emitted an unladylike snort. "My mother wouldn't leave even if she won the Powerball."

"I've known a lot of folks who don't like change, Cherie."

"And my mother is one of those. But she did promise to come down and visit with me whenever she gets some vacation time."

"I'm willing to bet that, once she sees your home and how nice it is to live on Coates Island, she'll change her mind."

"That's what I'm hoping."

"If she's anything like her daughter, she'll go back to Connecticut and begin packing up to relocate. I don't know what it is about this place, but once I left the military I knew I wanted to come back and spend the rest of my life here."

Cherie leaned forward. "It's because you have roots here, Reese. Bettina told me you grew up on the mainland and that you enlisted in the army after graduating high school."

"Bettina got her facts wrong. I enrolled in the ROTC in college, and when I graduated, it was as a second lieutenant. I waited a couple of years before applying to Ranger school. It was the most grueling thing I'd ever encountered, but luckily I made it through and earned my Ranger tab. I served for twenty years, while achieving the rank of captain."

"Why did you leave?"

"There's a lot of truth to the saying that war is hell. I'd lost count of the number of military funerals I attended, and then there were my buddies who had returned home maimed and suffering from PTSD. I felt that if I signed up for one more deployment, my luck would run out. It was like putting one bullet into a revolver and playing Russian roulette. You'd never know when you pulled the trigger whether the live round would come up in the chamber and it was suddenly lights out. I know I shouldn't be telling you this when your brothers are on active duty."

Cherie's eyelids fluttered as she forced a smile. "It's what they signed up for, Reese, although it's not something I wanted for them. Whenever I pray, it's for them to be safe."

Reaching across the table, Reese held her hand, giving it a gentle squeeze. "They'll be all right."

"That's something I've come to believe. That life wouldn't be so cruel that I would lose another brother."

Reese felt as if he'd been punched in the gut. When Cherie talked about her brothers, he'd assumed she was referring only to the twins. Releasing her hand, he rounded the table and eased her up, and then sat on her chair and settled her on his lap. He cradled her head against his shoulder.

"Talk to me, bae."

He listened intently when Cherie revealed the circumstances surrounding her older brother's murder. Her voice was void of emotion as she talked about how his death had changed her and that her sole focus was shielding her younger brothers from the same fate; after she'd moved out of her old neighborhood, she insisted they stay with her whenever they weren't in school.

"I'd made it out, Reese, and at that time, I was willing to do anything to get them out."

"You were successful, Cherie, because they did make it out. Do they realize the sacrifice you made to get them to where they are today?"

Cherie nodded. Unburdening herself to Reese was different from when she'd told Kayana about losing Jamal. Having him hold her, feeling his warmth and strength, was like eating after a self-imposed fast. And he was right when he said she'd made sacrifices to help Daniel and David achieve their goals. She'd made the decision to continue to sleep with Weylin after he'd become a member of Congress because she realized she needed his recommendation to get her brothers into the military academies. She'd also sacrificed having a normal relationship because she'd found herself in too deep when she continued to sleep with a married man.

"I believe they do," she said after a comfortable silence.

"Do you realize how remarkable you are?" Reese asked.

"I'm anything but remarkable. I did what I had to do to shield my brothers from street violence. Where I lived is no different from other neighborhoods, regardless of race or income, when it comes to violence. There seems to be an epidemic of murder and shootings, whether it occurs in classrooms or at shopping malls."

Reese's fingers played in her hair. "Is that why you didn't have any children? That you're afraid of losing them to gun violence?"

She didn't want to tell him she'd lost a child, not to violence but to greed. She traded her baby for a lifestyle that had evaded her, and in the end, she wasn't the winner but a loser.

She'd lost her baby and the man she'd loved unconditionally—for a price.

"No. If I fell in love and married, I'd definitely have a child."

"Would you have to be married?" he asked quietly.

Her head came up, and she gave Reese a direct stare. "Yes."

He nodded and smiled. "Duly noted."

"You need to let me go, so I can clean up the kitchen."

Reese tightened his embrace. "Not yet. It feels good holding you."

Cherie let her head drop back to his shoulder. He had no way of knowing how good it felt for him to hold her, and she couldn't believe how much she'd missed when interacting with a man. Reese was older than Weylin and no doubt had more experience with women; maybe that was why she'd felt an instantaneous comfortableness with him, and it wasn't solely because he'd saved her life.

If she were honest with herself, she knew there had been a vaguely sensuous connection that had passed between them whenever they saw each other, and at the same time, she had been both flattered and frightened by his interest in her. However, his interest in her hadn't escaped the eagle eyes of Kayana and Leah. If Reese liked her, then the feeling was mutual because she also liked him. He made her feel safe—and that was something that had always been missing in her life. She hadn't had a father to protect her, and achieving financial security or living in a gated community wasn't the same as feeling safe.

"When are you going to cook for me?" she asked. Cherie felt Reese go stiff. It was apparent she'd shocked him and herself with the query. *Now where did that come from?* she mused.

"Do you really want me to cook for you?"

"I did ask, didn't I?" she countered.

"I'm off Sunday, so what about Sunday dinner?"

She was also off because Kayana and Derrick didn't open

the café on Sundays during the off-season. "Sunday dinner sounds wonderful. Do you want me to bring anything?"

"Yes."

"What?" she asked.

"Yourself."

"Are you sure, Reese?"

"Very sure."

"My Grammie would haunt me from her grave if I showed up at someone's home empty-handed. Old southern traditions die hard, even for a Connecticut Yankee."

"Okay, Cherie. You can bring dessert."

Smiling, she kissed his jaw. "Thank you. Now please let me go so I can clean up. I have a pet peeve about leaving dishes in the sink."

Reese unwrapped his arms from around her body. "I noticed that you are a neat freak."

She slipped off his lap and stared up at him when he stood. "Does that bother you?"

"No, because I'm also somewhat of a neat freak."

She patted his bicep, encountering rock-hard muscle. "That means we should get along well."

"You can rinse while I stack the dishwasher."

Cherie wasn't going to argue with Reese. The kitchen would be cleaned up faster with two of them working together. "Can you stay long enough to have coffee? I have a coffee machine that makes lattes and cappuccinos." She'd bought the machine to brew cappuccinos, espressos, and lattes to serve with dessert when it came time for her to host her book club meeting.

Reese dropped a kiss on her hair. "Of course."

She wiped her hands on a towel and walked to the pantry to take the machine off a shelf. She hadn't taken more than a few steps when Reese took it from her, carried it back to the kitchen, and set it on the countertop.

"Thanks."

"You should've asked me to get this."

Cherie rolled her eyes. "It's not that heavy."

"Come on, sweetheart. Aren't you used to men spoiling you?"

She went still. Weylin hadn't spoiled her in the traditional sense. He'd given her what she'd demanded if he wanted to continue seeing her. "Not really."

"Well, beautiful lady, be prepared to be spoiled."

"I'm not helpless, Reese," she spat.

He sobered and glared at her. "Did I say anything about you being helpless, Cherie?"

She shook her head. "No."

"Then don't try to put words into my mouth," he said angrily.

Cherie recoiled as if she'd been struck across the face. She'd promised herself to think before she opened her mouth to say something, and she hadn't followed through with that promise. When, she asked herself, was she going to rid herself of the bitterness and resentment that seemed to surface without warning? She had no one to blame for her actions and the choices she'd made in her life. The blame rested solely on her.

"I'm sorry, Reese. I didn't mean it to come out like that."

He extended his arms. "Come here, bae. I know you've been through a lot, and there's nothing to apologize for."

She moved into his embrace and closed her eyes. He was talking about the assault, while she knew differently. It was as if she'd spent a lifetime verbally attacking people when she should've taken stock of her life and corrected it a long time ago. She'd grown up not knowing her father and resented her mother for not telling her who he was. And once the news of Weylin's engagement to one of their classmates was announced, she should've walked away from him and never looked back. But she'd been too weak, too much of a coward to let him go once she realized she'd loved him more than she loved herself.

Cherie curved her arms under Reese's broad shoulders and

held onto him as if he were her lifeline. Why, she asked herself, couldn't she have met someone like him years ago? She knew the answer to that question the instant it formed in her mind. They were different people, living miles apart, and she doubted whether she would have been receptive to a man unable to give her what she'd perceived as a lifestyle for the rich and famous. She knew she'd had to go through what she'd experienced to make her the woman she was now.

Moving to Coates Island had given her second chance to live life by her own rules. Reese Matthews saving her life had made it possible for her become friends with a man for the first time in her adult life. Cherie didn't know where their friendship would lead, and she didn't care because she had options. They could either have a platonic relationship or segue into becoming friends with benefits.

"Can you please do me a favor?"

"What is it?"

Easing back, she smiled up at him. "Will you kiss me?"

She didn't have to wait for his answer when his head came down and he covered her mouth with his, in what was more a caress than a kiss, before he increased the pressure. Her lips parted under his, and she moaned when his tongue found hers as he deepened the kiss until every nerve in her body screamed for release. Cherie moaned again when she felt throbbing between her legs, followed by a gush of moisture, and she knew if she didn't end the kiss, she would beg Reese to take her upstairs and make love to her. She then realized he was as just aroused as she was when she felt his erection pressing against her middle.

Both were breathing heavily when she managed to tear her mouth away from his. "I shouldn't have asked you to do that."

He buried his face in her hair. "I'm glad you did."

"You are?"

"Of course, Cherie. It's no fun when one person does all the liking. And yes, I like you."

"And I like you, too." Cherie couldn't believe how easy it'd been to tell Reese that, while she'd felt comfortable enough with him to ask that he kiss her.

"I'm going to ask for a rain check on the coffee, Cherie. It's time I leave before we do something both of us aren't ready for."

"You're right," she agreed. Although she'd been celibate for years, she wasn't desperate. *Sometimes the head refuses to listen to the heart.* She recalled what Kayana had told her earlier that day. She had allowed her heart to overrule her head with one man, but she had no intention of repeating that with Reese. He was her friend, and he would remain her friend until circumstances dictated otherwise.

Reese kissed her cheek. "I'll be in touch, and you can let me know what you want to eat for Sunday dinner."

"Surprise me, Reese."

"I think we should dispense with surprises until we get to know each other better."

Cherie nodded, smiling. "You're right."

He reached for her hand. "Walk me to the door, and don't forget to lock both of them after me."

She glanced up at him and wanted to ask if that was necessary, now that the man who had assaulted her was behind bars and was scheduled to be extradited to another state. There was an outer storm door and the inner solid oak one, and she tended not to lock the outer door until just before she retired for bed.

"Okay, Reese."

He opened the doors and stood on the porch staring at her through the glass while she secured the lock. She glanced at the black pickup in her driveway before closing the inner door, shutting out the image of the man she looked forward to seeing again.

Reese hadn't realized he'd been clenching his teeth until he opened his mouth and experienced tightness in his jaw. He'd gone to Cherie's home to update her on the details surrounding the man who had assaulted her and wound up spending hours with her. It was as if he couldn't force himself to leave. Why, he'd asked himself, had he allowed himself to be so caught up with a woman that he'd lost all semblance of self-control?

He'd learned to control his emotions as a boy whenever he joined his grandfather in the woodshed. He knew Papa wanted him to sit on a stool and watch him without saying a word while he tutored him in the art of woodworking. His first lesson began the year he'd celebrated his eighth birthday, and it took another two years before Reese was permitted to question his grandfather about why he'd chosen a particular type of wood to make a table or chair. Now that he looked back, he marveled that he'd been able to sit for hours without uttering a single word as he'd watched Raymond Matthews cut, carve, and sand a piece of wood into a piece of furniture for one of his clients.

It wasn't until he was older that he saw Raymond caress a piece of wood, after sanding it, with a motion akin to a man caressing a woman's body. Reese recalled his grandmother complaining that her husband loved wood more than he loved her. Reese had reassured Winifred Matthews that Raymond did love her, but that working with wood was in his DNA, and it was something that gave him pleasure and provided her with a comfortable lifestyle. She didn't have to work outside the house to supplement her husband's income, and she could devote all her free time to raising her orphaned grandson.

Reese never knew his mother or his father. His mother, a college dropout, had been driving from upstate New York to North Carolina to introduce her two-month-old son to his grandparents when a wrong-way driver hit her car head-on. The first responders on the scene found the seriously injured young woman and her infant baby boy crying in his car seat behind the passenger seat. Miraculously he hadn't been injured. Sondra Matthews lingered in a coma for weeks before passing away, and as the next of kin, Raymond and Winifred became the legal guardians of their grandson, listed on his birth certificate as Reese Matthews. Sondra hadn't listed her baby's father's on the document.

Growing up and not knowing his father didn't bother Reese as much as it did not to know the woman who had given birth to him. Grams had told him she was proud of her daughter because she was the first one in her family to go to college. Sondra had earned a partial scholarship to attend Syracuse University in New York. However, her parents were unaware that she'd dropped out at the end of her freshman year to give birth to a baby. She'd finally worked up enough nerve to tell her mother she'd gotten pregnant after sleeping with a boy she'd met at an off-campus party and that she was coming home.

There were times when Reese wondered if the boy who had slept with his mother realized he'd fathered a child, and if he had, did he care, or had he dismissed it as something he'd done before? Then there was his mother, who'd decided to have her baby rather than abort it, and then found the courage to tell her parents that she was sorry she'd disappointed them when they had expected her to earn a college degree.

The only memories Reese would have of his mother were photographs chronicling her life from childhood to when she'd posed proudly in her cap and gown at her high school graduation. There were also photos of her after she'd moved into off-campus housing and her bed covered with some of her favorite childhood stuffed animals. Aside from that last photograph taken of her, it was as if her life had ended the first day she'd left Coates Island, North Carolina, to move to Syracuse, New York.

Reese had had a wonderful upbringing because he knew his grandparents loved him unconditionally. Although his grandfather wasn't overly affectionate, an occasional pat on his head or back was enough for him. It was only in later years, whenever he returned from a military leave, that Raymond would reveal how proud he was of him. It was different with his grandmother, who would hug and kiss him in the presence of his friends, who would tease him, saying he was a mama's boy. He'd accepted their taunting because he knew some of them were jealous because they didn't have the same close relationship with their parents.

Raymond and Winifred Matthews had given him everything he needed to grow up loved and secure, and when he'd lost them, he felt a void that still lingered. He didn't know why, but he always felt their presence when he was in the kitchen or the woodshed. It was as if they were with him in spirit.

Reese drove onto the mainland and turned off onto the road leading to his home. The sun had gone down, and lights were visible in many of the houses. It was the end of January, and the holiday season was over. This is when Coates Island appeared to go to sleep, like a hibernating bear. Except for locals, there was hardly anyone on the streets or browsing in the mom-and-pop shops. This was the time when Reese came to enjoy his hometown best. He was familiar with both old and new residents and had come to regard them as his extended family.

He'd just tapped the remote device attached to the visor of the pickup for his garage when his phone rang, and he saw the number on the dashboard screen. It was Cherie.

"Hey, you," he said, smiling.

Her sultry laugh echoed throughout the truck's interior. "Hey, yourself. I just came up with what I'd like for Sunday dinner."

"I hope you're not thinking about a standing rib roast?"

Cherie laughed again. "No. Nothing that elaborate. Do you know how to make chicken?"

"Does a cat know how to lick its paws?" he teased.

"I suppose I got my answer. I'd like chicken."

"How do you like it? Fried, baked, roasted, poached, braised, fricasseed with dumplings, smothered, grilled—"

"Stop, Reese," she said, cutting him off.

"Oh, I forgot broiled and stir-fried."

"I don't care, as long as it's chicken."

"Okay, sweetheart." There was silence on the end of the connection, and Reese thought Cherie had hung up.

"Do you call all women sweetheart?" she asked.

Reese slumped in his seat. Once again, he felt himself moving much too quickly where it concerned Cherie Thompson; he knew he had to dial it back before whatever he hoped to share with her detonated beyond repair. Yet he wasn't above being anything but truthful with her.

"Only the ones I like. Does that bother you, Cherie?"

"No, Reese, it doesn't bother me. I just wanted to know where you're coming from."

"Do you now?"

"Yes, I do. And thank you for being honest with me."

"Honest is the only way I know how to be."

There came another pause before Cherie said, "I'm going to hang up now. You can text me your address and the time you'd want me to come over."

"Okay."

That was the last word Reese heard before there was a break in the connection. Cherie had hung up. He drove into the garage and tapped the remote to close the door. He reached for the book on the passenger-side seat, got out, and opened the door that led into a mudroom and left his boots on a mat before making his way up four steps and into the kitchen.

Reese glanced at the clock on the microwave. It was a little past six, and because he'd been given the night off, he planned to stay up late to watch the local and national news before channel surfing to see if there was a basketball game. After the game, if he wasn't too tired, he would start reading

The Alienist. Then he recalled his concern about nightmares and decided to forgo the book and watch TV.

Despite having very few nightmares that he could remember, on occasion, when he experienced flashbacks of some of his deployments in Afghanistan, he woke up sweating and shaking uncontrollably until his head cleared.

Reese turned on the bulbs on the table lamps in the parlor and the floor lamp in the dining room to their lowest settings, adjusted the thermostat, then went up the staircase to the second floor. Since his discharge, he had made it a practice not to come home to a darkened house. Most of the lights were set on timers, to come on and go off at different intervals. He lingered in the bathroom to brush his teeth, wash his face, and strip off his clothes, leaving them in a hamper, before walking into his bedroom. It had taken more than six months for him to move out of the bedroom that had been his since childhood and into the one that had been occupied by his grandparents. Not only was it the largest bedroom in the house; it also was the only one with a southern exposure.

He set his cell phone on the bedside table, got into bed, and opened the book to the first page. He read the date and the first sentence. It was apparent the author was going to take him back in time, and this appealed to Reese because he was a history enthusiast. In college, he'd majored in history with a concentration in military history. Within minutes, he was sucked into the underbelly of early-nineteenth-century New York City. It wasn't until he found his eyes burning that he picked up his cell phone to see the time; he'd been reading nonstop for three hours.

He wanted to continue reading, but he had the next two days off and would have time to read and hopefully complete the book so that he could discuss it with Cherie when she came for Sunday dinner.

Leaning over, he opened the drawer in the bedside table,

took out a pad, and tore off a page, using it as a bookmark. Reese remembered Cherie's warning not to eat or drink while reading, and not to bend the corners of the pages when reading her books, and he planned to return this one in the same condition as she'd given it to him.

He turned off the lamp, settled down to a mound of pillows, and pulled the top sheet and several blankets over his body. An unconscious smile parted his lips when he thought about Cherie. There was something about her that was so open and uncomplicated that he wanted to believe she couldn't be real. He'd been temporarily shocked when she'd asked him to kiss her; it was something he'd wanted to do the first time he saw her. Besides her jewellike eyes, it was her full sensual mouth that had captured his rapt attention and had him wondering what it would be like to kiss her.

Well, he'd found out, and he liked it.

He liked kissing Cherie, liked everything about her. Given time, he would show just how much he did and hopefully make her a part of his life and—if he was fortunate enough—his future.

Chapter 14

Cherie sat on a rocker on the porch, bundled up against the cool morning air while sipping a mug of steaming green tea. Derrick had told her to take the rest of the week off, but not doing anything was playing havoc with her nerves. She'd gotten up before sunrise and finished reading *Like Water for Chocolate* and loved it, but she wasn't ready to read another book for at least another week. And she knew Kayana was going to go all out when she prepared some of the recipes listed in the novel.

Unfolding her legs, she walked on sock-covered feet into the house and closed and locked the door. She rinsed the mug and put it in the dishwasher, and then headed for the staircase. She paused halfway up to straighten one of the framed black-and-white pictures on the wall before heading for her bedroom.

Forty minutes later, Cherie pulled into the parking lot behind the Seaside Café. There was only the restaurant's van, Leah's Audi, and Kayana's SUV. It was near closing time, and apparently most or all the diners were gone. On occasion, those living on the beach side of the island opted to walk to the restaurant. She climbed the steps and opened the rear door. A radio blasting Motown tunes meant Derrick was in the kitchen. She walked in, and he suddenly turned and went completely still. Cherie knew he hadn't expected to see her.

"Didn't I tell you not to come in until next week!"

It was the first time she'd witnessed him raising his voice. "I know you did, but I decided to come in anyway."

"Are you working up for me to fire you?"

"Who are you firing?" Kayana asked as she entered the kitchen.

"Your friend!" Derrick spat out. The veins in his neck were visible as he continued to glare at Cherie.

"I had to come in," she said, looking directly at Kayana, "because the longer I stay away, the more difficult it will be for me to come back. I refused to let fear rule my life."

"She's right, Derrick," Kayana said.

Derrick wiped his hands on a towel looped under the ties of his bibbed apron. "I won't feel safe having Cherie here as long as that crazy bastard is still on the island."

"He's leaving today," Cherie stated in a quiet voice.

"Why?"

"Where is he going?"

Derrick and Kayana had spoken at the same time.

"Deputy Matthews told me the man has an outstanding warrant in Tennessee, and federal marshals are coming today to extradite him to Memphis to stand trial."

"What are you guys talking about? Cherie, what are you doing here?" Leah asked.

Cherie noticed Leah was carrying a broom and dustpan. It was obvious she'd assumed the responsibility of cleaning up in her absence. "I came to clean up."

Leah scrunched up her nose. "But weren't you supposed to stay home until next week?"

Derrick threw up both hands. "I'm out! No one listens to me, so you ladies can have this. I'm taking the Audi, so Kay, can you drop Leah off at the house?"

"Of course," Kayana said as she stared at her brother's departing back after he ripped off his apron and threw it on a stool. "He's really in a funk," she whispered.

Cherie grimaced as she shrugged out of her puffy jacket. "And that's because of me."

Leah rested the handle of the broom against a wall. "Don't you dare blame yourself for what that sonofabitch did to you."

Kayana closed her eyes for several seconds. "My brother is blaming himself for allowing the SOB to hang around after he'd finished eating. If it had been the summer, he would've chased him out because we've established a reputation where folks don't have to wait long for a table."

"Well, he's going away where he can't hurt anyone ever again," Cherie said confidently.

"What makes you so certain of that?" Leah asked.

"Cherie said federal marshals are extraditing him to Tennessee," Kayana stated, smiling.

Leah stared at her future sister-in-law, and then Cherie. "How do you know this?"

"Reese came over last night and told me my attacker is wanted for the stalking, raping, and strangulation of a teenage girl."

Kayana sat on the stool where Derrick had discarded his apron and covered her face with her hands. "Oh, sweet heaven," she whispered. "If Reese hadn't come along when he did, he could've killed you, too."

Leah slumped against the wall. "I think I need a stiff drink to steady my nerves."

Kayana lowered her hands. "That makes two of us. Cherie, are you going to join us?"

She shrugged her shoulders. "Why not."

"Y'all go sit in the dining room while I make up a batch of apple sour martinis," Kayana said, reminding Cherie of their first book club meeting, when Kayana had served the potent cocktail along with a variety of delicious appetizers.

Cherie picked up the broom and dustpan. "Are you finished with this?" she asked Leah.

"Yes. We closed early, so I cleaned the restrooms and swept up the dining room. Business was slow today. Derrick said it was probably because news got out about the parking-lot attack and folks were wary about coming here."

Kayana opened the door to the fridge and removed three martini glasses. "Give it a few days, and people will forget about it."

"Did you know your brother was talking about keeping a gun on the premises?" Leah asked Kayana.

"No, and I hope you talked him out of it."

"I did," Leah confirmed, "and then I reminded him if there's trouble here on the island, the only means of escape is the one road to the mainland or the water. And didn't you tell me that with one call to the sheriff's department, they would have deputies set up a roadblock before anyone could cross the bridge?"

"Yes," Kayana replied, "but there's so little crime on the island. Maybe you'll have a woman call the sheriff because her husband or kids are acting a fool, but not much beyond that. No one is allowed on the beach after midnight, and that regulation is strictly enforced by the sheriff's department."

Leah reached for a pitcher from several lining a shelf. "I told Derrick he was being paranoid, but you know your brother, Kayana. There are times when he tends to overreact."

Cherie sat on a stool at the prep table, watching Kayana as she took out the ingredients for the alcoholic cocktail. There were meetings when their drinks were so potent that they'd elected to substitute mocktails. "Y'all know I can't drink without eating something."

"Not to worry," Kayana reassured her. "We have some leftover smoked brisket and mac and cheese."

"I think we also have a few corn muffins left," Leah said.

Cherie didn't know what she liked more: discussing books or eating with her friends. It was like peanut butter and jelly. You couldn't have one without the other. "It's too bad we can't have a book club meeting now. I finished reading *Like Water for Chocolate* this morning."

"I also read it," Leah said, her blue eyes shimmering in excitement. "I loved, loved, loved it."

Kayana smiled. "Well, since it was my book pick, and I've read it, what do you say we host our first Seaside Café Book Club meeting now? I can always make some of the dishes from the recipes in the book once we watch the movie."

"I say yes," Cherie said.

"Count me in," Leah added.

Twenty minutes later, sitting in the enclosed patio, Cherie, Kayana, and Leah sipped icy-cold sour apple martinis in between bites of tender, succulent smoked brisket, with its distinctive reddish smoke ring, and the café's immensely popular macaroni and cheese. Leah had sliced crusty-topped corn muffins baked with corn kernels, topped them with garlic butter, and heated them under a grill until they were crisp and toasty.

Cherie held up her glass. "I'd like to toast this year's first meeting, and may there be many, many more in the years to come."

"Hear, hear!" Leah and Kayana chorused.

Kayana took a sip of her drink, then grimaced. "I think I made them too strong."

Cherie took a sip, holding the cold liquid in her mouth for a few seconds before letting it slide slowly down her throat. "Whoa! It's like nitroglycerin."

Leah pressed her fingertips to her lips after she swallowed a mouthful of the martini. "Damn, Kayana. Are you certain you didn't add napalm? This stuff is truly illegal."

Cherie set down her glass and picked up a fork. "I'm not

going to take another sip until after I've eaten, because there's no way I'll be able to drive home and not run off the road and get arrested for a DWI."

"I don't think you'll have to worry about that," Leah remarked as she touched her napkin to the corners of her mouth. "I'm certain Reese Matthews will squash your citation."

Cherie stared across the table at her redheaded book club member for several seconds and then smiled. In the past, something acerbic would've come out of her mouth, but at the last possible moment, she reminded herself of her promise to think before saying something that would be viewed as a verbal attack.

She knew her friends were curious about her association with Reese, even before the parking lot attack, and she had to admit that she'd been more than curious about him. "I hope it would never come to that, Leah. I've never been stopped for even buzzed driving, and I've made it a practice to limit the number of drinks I have whenever I have to get behind the wheel."

Kayana swallowed a mouthful of brisket. "Why do you sound so defensive whenever we mention Reese?"

Cherie's eyebrows lifted. "Do I?"

"Yes, you do," Leah and Kayana chorused again.

Cherie laughed. "Now I know why you two are about to become related, because you're beginning to think alike."

"Stop trying to evade the question," Leah said, smiling. "What's going on with you and that gorgeous lawman?"

Pinpoints of heat dotted Cherie's face when she recalled how she'd felt when Reese had kissed her. It wasn't as if she'd had several other men to compare him to, and if she were truly honest, she could say that it was the first time a kiss had turned her on so much that it was if her body had taken over control of her mind. That, under another set of circumstances, she would've willingly opened her legs to him. And she knew it would be just a matter of time before everyone on Coates Island knew that their deputy sheriff was spending time at Cherie Thompson's house when it had nothing to do with police business.

"I'm having Sunday dinner with him at his house."

Kayana raised her glass and clinked it with Leah's. "That's what I'm talking about!"

An expression of shock froze Cherie's features. "You approve?"

"It's not whether Lee or I approve," Kayana said, "but that you're finally able to forget about your ex to start over with someone new. And I'm here to tell you that Reese Matthews is quite a catch for any woman who's looking for man who comes from a good family."

Cherie was curious about Reese's family yet had noticed he hadn't mentioned his mother, but his grandmother. She had never been one to pry into someone's life or background because she didn't want them asking about hers.

"I must admit I like him."

"What's not to like?" Leah asked. "Whenever he comes here to pick up food for the station house, he's always friendly and polite."

"If he invited you to his home, then it goes without saying that he likes you, too, Cherie," Kayana said. "When he's not working, he usually keeps to himself."

"How do you know this when he lives on the mainland and you live on the island?" Cherie asked Kayana.

"You come in when we're ready to close, so you get to miss all the gossip. Half the time, I pretend I'm not listening, but folks seem to talk about everybody and everything on Coates Island. I didn't have to wait to read in the *Clarion* that Reese had put in his discharge papers and left the army because someone had overheard his cousin, Chief Parker Shelton, mention it to one of his deputies. Then the news spread like a wildfire that Reese was coming back to live in the house where he'd been raised by his grandparents."

"What happened to his parents?" Cherie asked Kayana.

"I recall my mother saying something about his mother being killed in a car accident when he was just an infant, but no one has ever mentioned his father."

Cherie bit her lip and stared at the contents of her glass, wondering if her life paralleled Reese's, whether both of them were unaware of who had fathered them. However, it may be different for her, because Edwina had known the men she'd slept with to father her children, but had elected to remain mute whenever she or her brothers questioned her about them. And she wondered if the same man had fathered all of Edwina's children, or did each of them have different fathers? The questions had nagged at Cherie for so long that it had become an exercise in futility to continue to ask Edwina about the men she'd slept with. However, her mother had given her an opening when she said, "I'll tell you once you decide to start a family. But not until then." That was going to be a while for Cherie, because she'd planned to earn a graduate degree and become a classroom teacher before she would even consider starting a family.

"Did he marry a girl from Coates Island?"

Kayana gave her a steady stare. "He told you about his ex-wife?"

Cherie lifted her shoulders. "Yes. Why? Was it a secret?"

"I'm just a little surprised that he would've opened up to you like that," Kayana countered. "Like I said, he usually keeps to himself and tends to be very quiet."

"The man saved my life, Kayana, and that created a bond that connects us to each other."

"That connection started even before he saved your life," Leah interjected. "I told you the man couldn't keep his eyes off you whenever he came here. He saw something he liked, and it was just a matter of time before he'd make that known. I don't think he could've anticipated saving your life, but it had to be destiny that he was in the parking lot when you were attacked."

She wanted to tell Leah that Reese believed in destiny,

that he was supposed to be where he was to save her from what could've been certain death. "He's easy to be with and to talk to."

"I know, Kayana, and I don't want to get ahead of ourselves, but we hope you can have a better relationship with Reese than what you had with your ex."

Cherie wanted to tell Leah there was no comparison between the two men. She'd spent nearly half her life wishing, praying, and hoping to become the wife of someone who had been unable to commit and then had deceived her over and over—and still she'd stayed. She'd hoped to marry Weylin, and her hopes were dashed when he'd announced he was going to marry someone with whom she'd shared classes. Then when he'd proposed that they have a child together, her rationale had become that if she couldn't have the man, at least she would have a part of him in their child, and again he'd proven to be duplicitous because he wanted his child for his wife. That's when she turned from sweet, agreeable Cherie Renee Thompson into the greedy ghetto bitch his lawyer had called her and decided that, if she was going to give up her baby, then it had to be financially worthwhile. Any love she'd felt for Weylin died like the extinguished flames of a campfire. There were no smoldering embers, just smoke, until that finally disappeared into nothingness.

"You are getting ahead of yourselves," she said, smiling. "Sharing meals does not necessarily translate into a relationship. Right now, I'm more than happy for us to become friends."

"Have you ever dealt with a man who was your friend?" Leah asked. Cherie shook her head. "Well, neither did I until I met Kayana's brother. I wasn't a virgin when I slept with Alan because I'd had a boyfriend in college. I discovered being friends allowed me to relate to Derrick in a way I'd never been able to do with Alan in nearly three decades of marriage. I was able to gauge his moods, what he liked and didn't like. Then it was discovering what we had in common, and that was a love of cooking. Some of the best memories of my childhood were baking with my mother and grandmother, and when Kayana and Derrick allowed me the opportunity to bake for the café, I knew it was where I wanted to be. As they say, the rest is history," she added as a noticeable flush added color to her pale complexion.

"I think Reese and I have something in common," Cherie stated.

"What's that?" Kayana question.

"He reads. I gave him my copy of *The Alienist*."

Leah and Kayana exchanged high fives. "Maybe we can get him to join our book club, like Jocelyn did with Grigg in *The Jane Austen Book Club*," Leah suggested.

Although Cherie was familiar with the movie, she still had to read the book. "I don't think so, Leah. Reese works different shifts, depending on the week, so there's no guarantee he would be able to attend our meetings."

"I don't think inviting men to attend our meetings would go well when we veer off topic to talk about dildos, droopy balls, and shriveled dicks," Kayana stated, as she struggled not to smirk.

Cherie nodded in agreement. "Once you start talking about a man's junk, he's like a coiled rattler ready to strike. Yet they get together and talk with impunity about the size of a woman's breasts or her behind, and we're supposed to accept that that's okay."

"Preach, my young sister," Kayana intoned. "I've lost track of men commenting on my body when I'm within earshot, but one time I got so sick of it that I shouted out, 'You must really like this ass because you have to take that little blue pill whenever I give you some.' "

Leah covered her mouth at the same time Cherie laughed so hard tears rolled down her face. She picked up her napkin to blot her cheeks. "No, you didn't."

Kayana pushed out her lips. "Yes, I did."

"What did he do?" Leah asked after she'd recovered from laughing.

"He started to come at me, but his boys held him back, saying it wasn't worth it. I used to carry pepper spray in my purse, and he definitely would've gotten a face full of it if he'd attempted to attack me."

"When was this?" Cherie questioned.

"It was when I was in graduate school. I used to stop at this corner store to pick up breakfast before going to class, and a group of men who would just hang there, doing who knows what, would holler at every woman who walked by, and that day I'd had enough."

Cherie nodded. "As they say, that will learn them."

"I don't know if it did," Kayana continued, "but after that time, they never said another mumbling word whenever I walked by."

Leah picked up a forkful of mac and cheese. "I know we're going to discuss *Like Water for Chocolate*, but I really was looking forward to sampling some of the recipes in the book."

"We can still do that," Kayana said. "I was thinking about Super Bowl Sunday."

"Where do you plan to hold the Super Bowl party?" Cherie asked Kayana.

"Graeme and Derrick still haven't decided."

"I wouldn't mind hosting it at my place," Cherie volunteered. "I'm expecting the delivery of my dining room furniture Tuesday morning. Y'all are welcome to come over early next Sunday morning and do what you do best—cook." Kayana and Leah shared a look, and then nodded.

Cherie pressed her palms together. Now she didn't have to wait months to host a book club meeting and entertain guests in her new home. Super Bowl Sunday was a week away, and during that time, she would also plan what she wanted to contribute to the festivities.

"I'm ready to discuss Tita and her tyrannical mother, Mama Elena, before I attempt to drink anymore. Y'all know I'm a lightweight when it comes to alcohol."

"I know you're still being carded when you go out and order a drink," Leah told Cherie.

"Not really. I didn't go out much, and when I did, I rarely drank anything alcoholic."

What she wanted to tell her friends was that she'd never dated. Weylin had never taken her out in public, but had planned for them to meet in out-of-the-way places as far away as midtown Manhattan, Massachusetts, and even Vermont. She would go to a particular hotel, check in under her name a day or two before he'd arrive to meet her. He'd claimed he was considering a career in politics, and he wanted to keep his private life private until he announced his engagement. Like a gullible little fool, she'd believed him. It wasn't until after he'd announced he was marrying Michelle that she began her campaign to get whatever she could from Weylin. Yes, she'd blackmailed him, but he didn't seem to mind because, like Cherie, Weylin wasn't ready to let her go. It had become a win-win for the two of them. She gave Weylin what Michelle hadn't been able or willing to give him, while Weylin gave Cherie the financial stability she'd always wanted.

"Lee and I are big girls, so we like big-girl drinks." Kayana and Leah again exchanged fist bumps.

"Give me time," Cherie teased, "and one of these days I'll be a big girl, too."

Chapter 15

"I know I'm biased when choosing this title," Kayana began, "because of the recipes. And it truly had me thinking about making my own sausage."

"That's a lot," Leah remarked.

"I agree," Cherie said. "Do you think it was right for Mama Elena to stop her youngest daughter from marrying the man she loved because she wanted her to take care of her in her old age?"

"It depends on the culture," Leah said. "It's called ultimogeniture, where the youngest child inherits and is given the responsibility of taking care of the house and their parents, while the older children are free to marry and live their lives by their leave. Look at Jane Bennet in *Pride and Prejudice*. As the eldest, she was expected to marry before her sisters. It was the same with Rosaura in *Like Water for Chocolate*. As the older sister, she was expected to marry before her two younger ones."

"I've read about primogeniture, where the eldest of both parents, especially a son, have the exclusive right to inherit everything. But it's crazy as hell that a girl—even the youngest—shouldn't be allowed to marry or have children until after the mother's death," Cherie spat out angrily. "What if the mother lives beyond the time when her daughter is past her childbearing years?"

"That's more plausible now than years ago," Kayana said, "because people are living longer. Remember, Tita is initially agreeable to her fate until she falls in love with Pedro. That's when everything changes for her because he becomes the love of her life."

"And don't forget that Pedro loves Tita unconditionally," Leah reminded them.

Cherie emitted an unladylike snort. "He loved Tita so much that he agreed to marry Rosaura to be close to her. I think of it as a Mexican Romeo and Juliet where the lovers aren't allowed to be together."

"You're right, Cherie," Kayana said. "Pedro is Romeo, and Tita is Juliet *and* Cinderella. But we have to remember that the book is about how life used to be in Mexico and how tradition imposed rules of marriage during that time."

Leah took a sip of her cocktail. "What I did like was the sexual tension between them. Tita said she would never forget the moment when their hands accidently touched when they both bent down to pick up the same tray; she knew then she was in love with Pedro. There was passion in the way they looked at each other. Whenever they were close enough, they touched each other, and that passion was transferred to Tita's cooking."

"As horrible as her mother was, Tita did have an ally with Nacha, the kindly servant and cook," Kayana reminded them. "I liked that the author turned cooking into a sensual experience. All of Tita's emotions were transferred to her dishes."

Cherie nodded, smiling. "You're right about that. However, I found Rosaura to be as hateful as her mother when she accused Tita of putting something in her wedding cake that made her vomit all over her wedding dress."

"Don't forget, Cherie," Leah said, "Rosaura wasn't the

only one affected when eating the cake. Those who attended the wedding were crying uncontrollably because when Tita made the cake her tears of losing a love went into the ingredients."

Kayana slowly shook her head. "Her mother thought she'd deliberately sabotaged the cake and beat her so severely that Tita had to spend two weeks in bed to recover from her bruises. And when she tried explaining to Mama Elena that she'd only added one extra ingredient to the cake and that was her tears, her mother was having none of it. When she went to find Nacha to back up her claim, she found that the poor woman had died."

"Mama Elena was a real witch," Cherie said. "I believe her husband died two days after Tita was born so he could be rid of her."

"You're probably right," Leah agreed. "There are some people who are never happy no matter what you do for them. Case in point, my former mother-in-law. Adele complained if it was raining or if the sun was shining, and I think it was the same with Mama Elena. There's no doubt Tita was devastated once she discovered Rosaura was pregnant with Pedro's baby, when if she'd been allowed to marry him, she would've had his child."

Cherie thought of herself and Michelle. As Weylin's mistress, Cherie had given him a child when his wife couldn't. "Even if she couldn't have the man, she was there to nurse his baby when Rosaura's milk dried up."

Kayana laughed softly. "My grandmother used to say a half loaf is better than no bread at all. There are times when we must deal with the hand that has been dealt us, then work like hell to change it. What did you like or not like about the book?"

"I like that it was divided into the months of the year," Cherie said, "and, of course, the recipes. The plot was a combination of realism, fantasy, and the paranormal, and I wondered if this was the writer's deliberate attempt to combine all three genres because she couldn't figure out which one she actually wanted."

"Of course, y'all know I loved the book, but what bothered me was why didn't Tita and Pedro run away and elope," Leah stated.

"Sometimes it's not that easy," Cherie said in a quiet voice. She noticed Leah and Kayana staring at her with questioning expressions. "I know this firsthand, and one of these days, I will tell you everything, and I mean everything, about my former lover. That includes his name."

Leah leaned closer. "Are you saying that, when you tell us his name, we'll know who he is?"

Cherie nodded. "I'm almost certain you will."

"Well, damn," Kayana whispered. "You never fail to shock me."

"There are times when I shock myself. But, enough about me," Cherie said, waving a hand. "I'd like to suggest that we reverse the order of reading and then viewing the movie. I ordered the *Like Water for Chocolate* DVD, and while I plan to watch it in a few days, I'd like to watch it without thinking the filmmaker should've put in a particular scene that was so germane to the plotline."

Leah lifted both shoulders. "I don't have a problem with that. What say you, Kayana?"

"I sort of like that idea. But you didn't have to order the movie, Cherie, because I already have it."

"It's too late to send it back, so I'll just add it to my movie collection," Cherie told Kayana. "If I really like it, I'll watch it more than once."

Leah clasped her hands together. "I suppose we've settled where we're going to watch the Super Bowl, and that Kayana is going to prepare some of the food based on the recipes from our first book discussion."

"I'm not so certain of that, Lee," Kayana said. "I've looked over all of the recipes, and there are some I won't be able to duplicate because I can't get the ingredients. What

I've decided is to make Mexican-inspired dishes like chiles rellenos, chicken mole enchiladas, tacos with chicharron and carne asada, and grilled street corn. And of course, I'll make guacamole, and we'll have margaritas."

Smiling, Cherie crossed her arms under her breasts. "Now you're talking."

Leah rolled her eyes. "I love grilled street corn," she crooned before pushing away from the table. "It's time I head home before Derrick wonders what's happened to me."

Kayana stood. "You can't go anywhere because he took your car, so you're going to have to wait for me to put away the food."

Cherie rose to her feet and began picking up dishes and tableware. "I can drive her back. But I'd rather wait so we can all leave at the same time."

They cleared away the remains of their impromptu meal in record time. Kayana armed the security system, and they left the restaurant together. Cherie dropped Leah off at the beach house she shared with Derrick and then drove a short distance to her own home.

It wasn't until she'd parked her vehicle in the garage and climbed the staircase to her bedroom that Cherie realized that the protagonists in *Like Water for Chocolate* reflected her own life with Weylin. She'd promised herself she'd relegate him to the deepest recesses of her mind, yet just discussing the lives of the forbidden lovers had reopened a door to events she emotionally never wanted to think about again.

However, she was realistic enough to know her life wouldn't change until she was able to completely purge her ex-lover from her existence, and that would only become a reality if she found herself involved with another man. She thought about Reese but didn't want to use him as she had Weylin, while she had to remind herself she was no longer the Cherie Renee Thompson who used her wits and body to get what she wanted from a man. Reese didn't deserve that, and she would walk away and never look back before hurting him.

* * *

Cherie peered out the window for the umpteenth time. It had begun raining earlier that morning, and as the temperature continued to drop, it had turned into sleet, coating everything with ice. She'd gotten a weather alert on her phone that driving was hazardous due to icy conditions.

She was looking forward to sharing Sunday dinner with Reese, but it looked as if the weather wasn't going to cooperate. Reaching for her cell phone, she tapped his number. He answered before it rang a third time.

"Hello."

"I don't think I'll be coming for dinner."

"Why?" he asked.

"Because I just got an alert on my phone that only emergency vehicles are allowed on the roadways because of icing."

"Not to worry, Cherie. I'll be there in about twenty minutes to pick you up. And you should pack an overnight bag with enough clothes to last for a couple of days."

"But, Reese—"

"It's okay, bae. Just be ready when I get there."

She heard a tone that indicated he'd hung up on her. Galvanized into action, she opened drawers and took out several sets of underwear, T-shirts, and socks. She opened a closet and took down a quilted weekender from a shelf and filled it with jeans, leggings, and a couple of sweatshirts. Cherie went into the bathroom and gathered grooming, personal, and feminine products, and put them in a large cosmetic bag. She opened and closed drawers in the vanity to make certain she hadn't forgotten anything.

Pulling on a rain poncho over her coat, she slipped her feet into a pair of boots lined with shearling. She was dressed for a New England winter day. Grasping the handles of the weekender in one hand and her ubiquitous tote in the other, she went down the staircase at the same time the doorbell rang.

Cherie opened the door to find Reese wearing a black

slicker and baseball cap. He took the weekender and tote from her, and she picked the cake carrier off the table in the entryway. He waited while she locked the doors and escorted her to his pickup. He hadn't turned off the engine, and the heat and the lingering scent of his cologne wrapped around her like a blanket as she sat on the passenger seat, the cake carrier resting on her lap, and secured her seat belt.

"Should I assume there's something delicious in that container on your lap," he said, as he slipped behind the wheel.

She stared at Reese's distinctive profile. "It's dessert. How are the roads?" she asked when he smiled at her.

"Treacherous. The bridge freezes over before the roadway, so it's really slow going."

"Do you have a lot of ice storms down here?"

Shifting into Reverse, Reese slowly backed out of the driveway. "We get enough. When I was a kid, we had one where the ice was so heavy it brought down power lines. We were in the dark for nearly a week. We had to resort to using candles for light and fireplaces for heat and cooking."

"If there is a power failure, I hope it won't last more than a day." Cherie had experienced power failures after blizzards blanketed the Northeast region, and everyone would huddle in the kitchen, where her mother turned on the oven and cooked everything in the freezer to provide warmth and keep the food from spoiling.

"We don't have to worry about that because I have a generator."

"That's something I'll definitely need to buy," Cherie told him.

"Do you have firewood for your fireplaces?" Reese asked her, as he slowed to under ten miles an hour.

"I found some in the garage."

"Do you know how to light a fire?"

Cherie met his eyes when he gave her a quick glance. "Yes. I went camping overnight with some friends in college, and we stayed at a cabin that was unheated. Some of the guys who had been Boy Scouts made quick work of lighting fires in the fireplaces."

"You went camping in the winter?"

"No," she said, laughing. "It was late spring, and sometimes nighttime temperatures dip below forty."

Reese turned the wipers to the fastest speed. "I would never take you for someone who would rough it in the woods."

A slight frown appeared between her eyes. "Why would you say that?"

"Everything about you screams big-city sophisticate. Your tote and shoes are a definite giveaway."

She glanced down at her Kate Spade Jemma booties. "I happen to like shoes and bags."

While Tory Burch and Kate Spade were her favored designers, Cherie didn't tell Reese that she'd made it a practice never to shop retail. If she saw a pair of shoes she liked, she'd wait for them to go on sale at the company's outlet store, where they would be discounted as much as forty percent. It was the same with handbags, and she prided herself in not paying full price for whatever she wore.

"Do you have a problem with a woman spending a lot of money for her clothes?"

"No. If it's her money, she can spend it any way she chooses."

"What if it was your money, Reese? Would that pose a problem for you?"

"I don't know," he said after a long pause. "If the shoes made her happy, then I wouldn't care how much they cost."

Cherie was slightly taken aback with his explanation. "Are you saying it's all about her happiness?"

"It's always about her happiness, Cherie. I'm certain you've heard the expression happy girlfriend, happy life."

Shifting on her seat, she gave him a long, penetrating stare. "I thought it was happy wife, happy life."

"Same difference, Cherie. Why should a man treat his girlfriend any differently than he would his wife?"

Reese's question gave her pause. "He shouldn't." He smiled, and it wasn't the first time that Cherie noticed the length of his silky eyelashes.

"I'm glad you agree." He sobered. "I remember my grandmother telling me that whenever you date a woman, you should always think of her as a potential wife. If she doesn't fit that criteria, then don't take up her time."

"That's good advice."

"What about you, Cherie?"

"What about me, Reese?"

"Did you consider the men you dated potential husbands?"

Cherie looked out the side window that was fogging up from her warm breath. "There was only one man," she admitted truthfully.

"What happened?"

She exhaled a soft sigh. "He married someone else."

Reese chuckled. "Good for him."

Cherie gasped, unable to believe Reese would say something so insensitive. "What a horrible thing to say."

"No, it's not, Cherie. Think about it, bae. If you'd married him, you wouldn't have met Kayana and Leah. And you wouldn't have come to vacation on Coates Island not once, but twice, and loved it so much that you decided to move here. And if you'd married your ex-boyfriend, I wouldn't have been able to invite you to my home for Sunday dinner."

She did not want to believe a man as attractive as Reese lacked for female company. "How many women have you invited to your home since your return?"

Reese's hands tightened on the steering wheel, and he decelerated as he drove onto the bridge. "Only one."

"I'm the second?"

"No, Cherie. You're the first."

She slumped back against the leather seat. "Oh, I see."

"Do you?" he asked.

Cherie's eyelids fluttered. "Yes. Should I assume you want us to continue to see each other?"

"It's called dating. And yes, I'd like to date you."

She knew Reese was offering her something she'd never gotten from Weylin in all the years she'd known him. Even when they'd hung out together in high school and college, it was always in a group. They were actors, with roles in which they were able to give award-winning performances. No one, not even any of their classmates, had suspected they were sleeping together.

Cherie did not want to believe she'd had to wait until she was almost thirty-five to experience a normal relationship with a man where she didn't have to meet him in secret. There were times when, after spending the night with Weylin, she'd felt dirty and ashamed, but not so much that she'd refused to see him whenever he contacted her. His cryptic emails were always followed up with a telephone call from a phone booth with instructions as to where they should meet.

"And I'd like to date you, too," Cherie said after a comfortable silence.

"I'm glad we're able to settle that."

In that instant, Cherie felt as if she'd been reborn, that Reese was allowing her the opportunity for her to become whole again. It wasn't until after she'd sold her son that she'd had an epiphany and knew she had to change her life. She had resisted the advances of men who expressed an interest in her, stopped joining her coworkers for Friday night happy hour, and stopped speaking to her neighbors. She had become not only withdrawn, but also angry and bitter. It had taken her driving from Connecticut to North Carolina to check into a boardinghouse on an idyllic island for the summer for her to realize she had to get away to begin the process of healing and repenting. Kayana and Leah were the integral pieces she'd been looking for to add to the puzzle of her transformation. She didn't know how Reese would fit in her life, but she was open to finding out.

She smiled. "Me, too."

Chapter 16

Reese felt the tension in his body ease as he tapped the remote device on the pickup's visor to raise the garage door. The drive from Cherie's house to his, which should've taken about ten minutes, because of weather conditions had taken twice that long. He hadn't encountered a vehicle leading onto or off the bridge, and driving on the bridge was akin to attempting to walk on an ice-skating rink without skates. Once he entered the downtown business district, he noticed all the shops were closed and the only vehicles patrolling the streets were from the sheriff's department. He was glad his next shift didn't start until late Monday night, and he hoped weather conditions would improve by that time.

He maneuvered into the garage, parking next to a Lincoln Navigator. His grandfather had purchased the SUV when it debuted in 1998, and had kept the vehicle as pristine as when it'd rolled off the factory's assembly line. Reese took it out several times a month and had it serviced regularly by a trusted mechanic.

Reese tapped the remote, lowering the door, then rested a hand on Cherie's shoulder. "Don't move. I'll help you out."

He got out and came around to assist her down, smiling when he noticed she clutched the cake carrier close to her chest. He was curious to see what was in the container. Reaching behind the seats, he grasped the handles to her overnight bag and tote.

Cherie pointed to the motorcycle in a corner of the garage. "Do you ride?"

"Yes." He'd bought the Yamaha as a gift for himself for his forty-second birthday. "But only in the warmer weather. Have you ever been on a bike?"

"No-o-o."

Reese laughed when registering Cherie's trepidation. "Don't worry, Cherie. I'll get you a helmet and promise not to go too fast." She gave him a you've-got-to-be-kidding-me look. "I always keep my promises."

"Let debate this when the weather gets warmer."

Reese winked at her, thinking at least she hadn't said no. "Let's go inside, where it's warm," he said, leading the way up the stairs and into the mudroom, where he left his cap and poncho on a wall hook and his boots on a mat. Then he held the cake container while Cherie took off her outer garments. He didn't know what to expect she would be wearing under her slicker and coat, but it wasn't the black ribbed turtleneck sweater and black stretchy pants that hugged every curve of her petite body. The sweater outlined the roundness of her breasts, which were fuller than he'd expected, but then he had to remind himself that the other times he'd seen or been with her she'd worn baggy sweaters or sweatshirts.

Reese knew he had to be very careful now that he'd invited Cherie to sleep under his roof. What he did not want to do was take advantage of her. On the other hand, he didn't want their relationship to become so one-sided that he was the only one doing the pursuing. If possible, he wanted Cherie to want him as much as he wanted her.

From the moment he'd walked into the Seaside Café to pick up a takeout order for his colleagues and seen Cherie,

Reese had asked himself what there was about her that had him so enthralled with her mere presence. And he knew it couldn't just have been her face. Yes, she was beautiful, but he'd lost count of the number of beautiful women he'd seen during his lifetime. While he didn't like a particular type when it came to a woman, there was something about the way Cherie looked at him and then demurely lowered her eyes that he'd found so seductive that he'd been unable to draw a normal breath.

Seductress. She'd managed to seduce him without uttering a word, and he wondered if she'd practiced the mannerism or did it unconsciously. It no longer mattered to Reese if the gesture was feigned or deliberate because he'd found himself captivated by a woman who appeared to be as carefree as she was confident. However, there was something about her that made him believe that she was an old soul, that she'd experienced a lot more than some women her age.

Leaning against the wall, Cherie bent slightly to unlace her boots, leaving them on the mat next to his. Reese stared at her small, bare feet with bright red polish on the toes. "You can't walk around barefoot."

She pointed to the bag he'd slung over his shoulder. "I have a couple of pairs of shoes and socks in my overnight bag."

Reese set down the cake carrier and slipped the bag's straps off his shoulder. "Why don't you look in there and get some shoes before we go inside. The mudroom is called that for a reason."

No matter how often he swept the area, there was always a light layer of dust on the cement floor. There had been a time when his grandmother had the washer and dryer installed in the space, but Reese decided, once he'd become a civilian, to purchase more updated, energy-saving models and had them installed in a space off the kitchen. He pushed his sock-covered feet into a pair of worn moccasins, and after

Cherie had slipped her feet into a pair of ballet-type flats, Reese led her into the kitchen.

Cherie closed her eyes as she drew in a deep breath. "Something smells delicious."

"That's the rosemary and garlic chicken you smell."

Her smile was dazzling. "Ohmygod. I can't believe I've hooked up with a gourmet cook." She noticed Reese frowning. "What's the matter?"

He set her bag and tote on stools at the cooking island. "I really don't like the implication that we're hooking up."

Her eyebrows lifted slightly. "Would you prefer if I'd said courting?"

A hint of a smile played at the corners of his mouth. "That sounds a little old-fashioned, but it's better than hooking up."

Suddenly, Cherie recalled Kayana mentioning that Reese had been raised by his grandparents after the death of his mother, so she assumed he'd adopted some of the behaviors and values that were standard in his grandparents' generation. And spending twenty years in the military had prepared him well for a second career in law enforcement. His entire adult life had been shaped by discipline and regimentation, and Cherie wondered if he would get along with Derrick Johnson and Graeme Ogden if she invited him to join the others for Super Bowl Sunday.

"Maybe I should've said I'm going to enjoy my boyfriend cooking for me."

He winked at her. "That sounds a lot better. Come with me, and I'll show you where you can put your things."

Cherie picked up her tote, while Reese took the quilted bag. "Do you have time to give me a tour of your beautiful home before we eat?"

When Reese had turned into the driveway of the large two-story, farm-style house with a wide front porch, she was surprised to find it was only one of two structures standing on an open expanse of land.

Reese glanced over his shoulder at her as he led the way up the carpeted mahogany staircase with carved spindles. "There will be plenty of time for that after we eat. It's not as if we're going anywhere tonight."

Cherie knew he was right. She was stuck at his home until the ice storm was over, and there was no guarantee that, once it was, she would be able to return home. Reese electing to come and get her solved the dilemma of not freezing if or when the power went out because she didn't have a generator. She shivered when recalling the times when the boiler in the building where she'd grown up would need to be repaired and they would have to heat water on the stove to fill up the bathtub to take a bath. When many of the tenants had had enough of not getting the services outlined in their leases, they'd formed a tenants association and conducted a series of rent strikes.

Once the building's owner realized he was losing money and that the tenants had hired a lawyer to represent them in court, he instituted major capital improvements that included installing a new heating and cooling system. Although the services in the buildings had improved their quality of life, her old neighborhood hadn't kept step with the upgrades; crime had continued to escalate unabated. Cherie knew most of the residents were aware of who was dealing drugs, but were reluctant to talk to law enforcement because they feared reprisals from various street gangs.

"This will be your bedroom."

Reese stepped aside, and she entered a room with a large antique spindle bed covered with handmade quilts and mounds of pillows. A chaise lounge covered in white Haitian cotton was positioned in a corner near a trio of floor-to-ceiling shuttered windows. She touched a wall and discovered it wasn't covered with wallpaper but a sunny-yellow print fabric, before she glanced up at the blades of the mahogany ceiling fan, which were reminiscent of large leaves. A small desk doubled as a bedside table with a pale jade-green ginger-jar table lamp. The space was more than a bedroom. It was a retreat.

"It's perfect."

Reese set her bag on the bench seat at the foot of the bed. "I'm glad you like it. You can put your things in the dresser drawers and hang up what you want in the armoire." He pointed to a door. "That was a closet, but now it's a bathroom with a commode, vanity, and shower stall."

Having access to a bath in the bedroom indicated she didn't have to share one with Reese. "When you take me on the tour, I'd like for you to give me the history on everything in this house."

He smiled. "There's a lot of history attached to every piece in this house."

"I'll put my things away later. Right now, I'm willing to help you in the kitchen anyway I can."

Reese caught her hand, gently squeezing her fingers. "There's not much to do. I turned the temperature down on the chicken, and it should be done by now. The sweet potato casserole and the collard greens are in the warming drawer. I wanted to wait until you got here to ask if you want cornbread or biscuits."

"You are really full of surprises. I know you said that your grandmother taught you to cook . . ." Her words trailed off when she realized the man with whom she found herself involved was truly an enigma. Kayana said he came from a long line of master carpenters, and no doubt he was one, but he also cooked.

"Gram was an exceptional cook," Reese said as they left the bedroom and headed for the staircase. "Some said she was almost as good as the Johnsons."

"Derrick and Kayana are phenomenal cooks," Cherie stated matter-of-factly.

"That's because they come from generations of phenomenal cooks. Their recipes for mac and cheese, Creole chicken and buttermilk waffles, potato salad, and lasagna are family secrets that they've pledged never to divulge on pain of death."

Cherie laughed. "I know exactly what you're talking about. The first time I ate their mac and cheese and lasagna, I truly had an out-of-body moment. I was moaning like Meg Ryan in the restaurant scene in the movie *When Harry Met Sally*."

Reese chuckled. "Were you alone when you had your moment?"

"No. Kayana and Leah looked at me as if I'd lost my mind until I had to explain to them that it was the food."

"Some dishes can trigger sensual overload."

"You're right," Cherie agreed. "Whenever I watch period dramas, there's always an abundance of food. It could be hunks of beef, different birds, fruit, wines, and desserts."

"What else did the nobles have to do but put on elaborate dinners for their families and guests? It was all about who could outdo the others."

"You're right about that, Reese. I've seen the same at weddings. After the cocktail hour, there's a four- or five-course dinner, followed by a Viennese table with an assortment of desserts that's almost sinful when there are millions of starving people, not only in this country but all over the world."

"Have you gone to many weddings?"

"Enough," she said. "Some of my classmates in high school also attended Yale, and we managed to keep in touch with one another. There was a time when I attended two to three weddings every year until it trickled down to one, and then they stopped altogether by the time we turned thirty."

Cherie couldn't tell Reese that she'd been invited to Weylin and Michelle's wedding and, like a lovesick fool, had attended because she didn't want to raise a red flag with her former classmates, who had known she and Weylin were close friends. She'd become the consummate actress when she laughed and danced with many of the men in attendance. Several had asked for her number so they could get together at another time. She'd given it to them, yet when they'd called she'd made the excuse that she was now dating someone and thanked them for their interest. Unbeknownst to them, she'd continued to sleep with the groom only days after he'd returned from his honeymoon.

"Have you attended any of your class reunions?" Reese asked.

"I missed my tenth-year reunion, but hopefully I'll make it to the twentieth." She couldn't tell Reese that she missed the reunion because she was in the early stages of her pregnancy; because she was spotting, her doctor recommended she limit her activities.

"I missed both my tenth and twentieth because of deployments."

"Where were you deployed?"

"Afghanistan."

"How many deployments, Reese?"

A beat passed. "Four."

"That's a lot," Cherie whispered.

He nodded. "After the last one, I swore not to sign up again, and now that we're out, I hope we'll never have to go back."

Cherie knew he was talking about the complete withdrawal of all American military personnel from the Middle East country. "Do you think we'll get into another war like we did in Afghanistan and Vietnam."

"Who knows, Cherie. There have always been wars and rumors of wars since the beginning of mankind, so no one knows until shit happens and we're drawn back in."

"I don't know why, but I keep thinking about my brothers."

Reese rested a hand at the small of her back. "Your brothers will be all right. One of these days, they'll meet the loves of their lives and make you an auntie."

She smiled up at him. "An auntie who will spoil the hell out of my nieces or nephews."

"A niece who will be wearing designer shoes and carrying a designer bag before she's two."

"That's not nice, Reese."

"Okay. Maybe I should've said when she's twenty-two, so she can strut and profile with her gorgeous auntie."

"By that time, I'll probably be close to or over sixty, and I doubt I'll be wearing four-inch stilettos."

"You wear heels that high?"

Cherie walked into the kitchen with Reese and sat on a stool at the island. "Yes."

"How tall are you?"

"Five-three. If I were wearing heels you wouldn't appear that much taller than me."

"I'm six-four, so I'll always appear a lot taller than you."

She rested her elbows on the island's quartz countertop. Reese was tall and all muscle without appearing bulky, and she wondered if he worked out to stay in peak condition. He'd also worn all-black, and the black mock-V-neck sweater and slacks made him look more imposing.

"Are you certain I can't help?" she asked again.

"I've set the table in the dining room, so there isn't much else for you to do."

Cherie wanted to tell Reese that she wasn't used to sitting and doing absolutely nothing. Whenever she sat down, it was either to eat, read, or watch television. "What are you doing Super Bowl Sunday?" she asked when television popped into her head.

Reese turned to look at her. "I'm scheduled to work the eight-to-four shift."

"Eight at night to four in the morning?"

"No. Eight in the morning to four in the afternoon. Why?"

"I'm hosting a Super Bowl party at my house, and I'd like you to come. Kayana and her husband and Leah and Derrick will so be there. We've decided on a Mexican-inspired menu because we just finished discussing *Like Water for Chocolate*."

"Are you certain you want me to come?"

Cherie rested a hand at her hip. "If I didn't want you to come, I never would've said a mumbling word to you, Reese."

"Okay. Count me in. Is there anything you want me to bring?"

"Yes. Yourself," she repeated what he'd told her when inviting her to his house.

He wagged a finger at her. "Remember, we southerners don't come to one another's homes empty-handed."

Cherie knew she, Leah, and Kayana would have everything under control when it came to the menu. "I don't want to argue with you, Reese. Bring whatever you want," she said in a harsh, clipped tone.

He turned and glared at her. "I don't argue, Cherie, so please don't confuse me with some of the other men in your past."

Cherie recoiled as if she'd been slapped across the face. She didn't know why Reese had brought other men into the conversation when it wasn't about them. "You had no right to say that to me."

He took a step and leaned over the island. "Yes, I do. If we're going to have any semblance of a normal relationship, then we did need to get something out in the open."

"And what's that?" she spat out angrily, praying she could hold her temper in check before she said something that would shatter the fragile bond holding them together.

"Every once in a while, you verbally attack me without provocation. And if you want an argument, then I'm not the one. I went through hell and back, and I've done things in war that I'll spend the rest of my repenting for, so right now, I need peace in my life, and that includes not sniping and arguing with a woman I just happen to like more than I should. You're not someone I need to pass the time with when I'm not working, Cherie. The first time I laid eyes on you, something told me to ignore you and walk away, because if I got involved with you, I'd be in a world of hurt. But instead of listening to the instincts that allowed me to sign up for multiple deployments, I found myself so inexorably entwined in your life that when I walked into that parking lot and found that crazy pervert attacking you, I knew then it was beyond what I could control. So, right now, I'm offering you an out. If you don't want to continue to see me, then say it now, and I'll stop pursuing you."

Cherie felt as if Reese had suddenly ripped out her heart, leaving her to bleed unchecked. He was everything she could want in a man, yet a lingering bitterness wouldn't permit her to let go of her past to accept all of him.

Tears welled up in her eyes as she struggled not to cry. "Are you giving me an ultimatum?"

"No, sweetheart. I'm giving you a choice."

"The choice is I want you. You can't imagine how much I want you."

"How much?"

She sniffled and knew it was truth-telling time. She was rapidly approaching her thirty-fifth birthday, and that made her a grown-ass woman. And as a woman, she had to tell the man staring at her what she wanted.

"I want you in and out of bed."

Reese rounded the island and gently eased her off the stool. "How long has it been?" he asked.

Cherie knew he was asking how long it had been since she'd slept with a man. "It's been almost five years."

His arms tightened around her body. "Did he hurt you that much?"

She nodded, rather than tell him she also had been responsible for her own pain and disappointment. Weylin couldn't have used her if she hadn't allowed it. After all, she did have free will to stop seeing him if she'd wanted. But she hadn't because she believed he'd cast some spell over her, making her helpless to refuse his demands.

"Will you please kiss me?" she whispered.

Cradling the back of her head, Reese buried his face in her hair. "You know what's going to happen if I kiss you, bae. It's not going to end there."

"It doesn't have to end there. Please don't make me beg you to make love to me."

His fingers curved under her chin until she met his eyes. "I don't ever want you to beg me for anything. All you have do is ask."

A sense of strength filled her as she smiled through unshed tears. She didn't want to use Reese to erase what she'd had with Weylin, but making love with him signaled not only a new beginning, but a chance for her to heal. "I want you to make love to me."

Reese dropped his arms and walked to the oven and turned it off, then returned to sweep her up in his arms and take the stairs two at a time.

Chapter 17

Cherie felt as if she'd entered an alternate universe when she met Reese's steady gaze as he knelt over her on the bed to remove her clothes. The events that had brought her to this intimate moment flashed through her mind like frames of film. It had only been two years ago when she'd found herself in a funk with the approach of her son's birthday, and she knew she had to get away from Connecticut or have a complete emotional meltdown and possibly be hospitalized.

Weeks later, she'd flipped through a food magazine to read the classified section advertising vacation properties. She'd read the blurb on Coates Island and decided to contact the rental agent. After the childcare center's director approved her leave of absence, she got into her car and headed south.

It had to be providence that brought her to sit at a table with Leah Kent the first time she'd entered the Seaside Café, and after apologizing for sniping at the redhead, she and Leah discovered their love of books. It was Leah who had introduced her to Kayana Johnson, and after the three had formed the Seaside Café Book Club, the rest was history. She'd returned to Coates Island the following year and realized it was where she wanted to live and start over with a new career. What she hadn't planned on was meeting a man who would make her question what she wanted in her life, including her future.

It'd only been weeks since she'd first glimpsed Reese Matthews, unaware that their lives would be so inescapably linked that she wanted him to be the last man in her life. She wasn't certain whether she was falling in love with him because what she was beginning to feel for Reese was so different than what she'd experienced with Weylin.

Cherie closed her eyes when she heard his intake of breath once he'd removed her sweater and pants. He hadn't turned off the bedside lamps, and the illumination allowed him to see what her clothes had concealed.

She felt his warm breath on her throat as he pressed light kisses on the fading bruises. Her arms went up and encircled his neck, bringing him closer as she kissed his ear, breathing in the lingering fragrance of his masculine cologne, which blended sensuously with his body's natural scent. Cherie knew she would never tire of smelling him. Her hands were busy pulling the hem of his sweater up and over his shoulders as his mouth covered hers in a possessive kiss that stole the breath from her lungs.

What had begun as a slow exploration changed to a frantic need to feel skin against skin. Within seconds, her bra and panties lay on the floor beside the bed, and Cherie discovered she couldn't pull her gaze away from Reese as he undid the waistband on his slacks and pushed them and his briefs off his hips at the same time. She bit her lip when seeing him fully aroused. Everything about this man was so different from her former lover, and raising her arms, she silently welcomed him to claim what she was willing to give him.

Supporting his greater weight on his forearms, Reese

forced himself to go slow when he lowered his head to taste every inch of Cherie's body. He couldn't believe her clothes had concealed a lushness that sent his libido into overdrive. He kissed her mouth, then moved lower to her full breasts, and then even lower to her belly before burying his face between her thighs. She moaned as if she were in pain, the sound making the hair stand up on the back of his neck. Her moans escalated to whimpers when his tongue tasted her essence.

"Please, Reese."

"Please what, baby?" he mumbled as his tongue continued to feast on her labia.

"I need to feel you inside me," Cherie gasped.

He reversed his position, moving up her trembling body, and he kissed her again. Reese reached over and opened the drawer in the bedside table to remove a condom. If Cherie hadn't slept with a man in five years, he doubted whether she was on birth control. He slipped on the condom, and when he attempted to penetrate her, he was met with some resistance. She was tight, and he took his time pushing into her celibate body, inch by inch, until he was fully sheathed inside her.

Raising his head, he saw her smile. "I'll try not to hurt you."

"I'm not worried," she whispered.

Those were the last words spoken as they began the dance of desire reserved for lovers.

Cherie felt as if she were swept up by the powerful force of a twister spinning her around and around until she feared passing out from an onslaught of multiple orgasms holding her captive. She'd heard people talk about *la petite mort*, but this was her first time since becoming sexually active that she'd experienced it.

She'd barely returned from her free-fall flight when she heard Reese's groaning and felt his quickened motions as he thrust inside her, he ejaculated, and breathed the last of his passion into her mouth. They lay together, limbs entwined, waiting until their breathing slowed to a normal rhythm.

Cherie wound her arms around his moist back. "Thank you," she whispered, unable to conceal her grin.

Raising his head, Reese kissed the end of her nose. "I should be one doing the thanking. You were more than worth the wait."

Her eyebrows lifted questioningly. "Has it been as long for you as it's been for me?"

"No, but it has been a while."

"I think I can get used to sharing a bed with you," she whispered.

It was Reese's turn to lift his eyebrows. "You think or you know?"

"I stand corrected," she said. "I know."

"That's more like it. I'd love for us to stay like this, but I'm going to have to pull out and throw away the condom."

Cherie wanted to tell him not to move because having him inside her made their physical connection even stronger. And when he did pull out, she felt the loss immediately. She turned and stared at Reese as he slipped out of bed and headed for the en suite bathroom. His body was magnificent, clothed or nude. He would've been the perfect model for Michelangelo to sculpt his David in onyx rather than marble.

She grimaced as she attempted to flex her leg, and the slight tightness in her groin was a blatant reminder of how long it'd been since she'd used those muscles. Reese was heavier and anatomically much larger than her ex-lover. Now that she'd slept with Reese, it felt good for Cherie to think of Weylin as her ex. After making love with Reese, she was finally able to mentally exorcise, eradicate, eliminate, and exterminate everything she'd had with the man, and that included giving up her son.

Cherie saw movement out the corner of her eye and watched Reese approach the bed in all his naked splendor.

Extending her arms, she welcomed him into her embrace when he got into the bed with her. He shifted her body until they lay facing each other.

"How are you feeling?" he asked,

She looped one leg over his. "Wonderful."

"I didn't hurt you?"

Cherie vowed to be truthful with Reese as she recalled Kayana's lecture about trust. That it was more important in a relationship. "I have a little discomfort in my groin area."

Reese gave her a direct stare. "Are you sore down there?"

She smiled, knowing he was referring to her vagina. "No. Down there feels just fine."

He also smiled. "It's going to take a while for you to stretch out those muscles."

"Maybe I should do some squats."

"One of these days, after you have a long soak in the tub, I'll give you a massage that is certain to make your body as loose as al dente pasta."

"How much are you going to charge me for the massage?" she teased.

"Massages are always free," Reese countered. "By the way, are you hungry?"

Cherie had forgotten about food. "No. I can wait a little longer before my belly starts making noises."

Reaching down, Reese pulled the sheet and blankets up to their shoulders. It was apparent he wanted to stay in bed a little longer, and so did she; she snuggled closer to his body, gasping softly when her thigh grazed his semi-erect penis. Cherie closed her eyes and forced herself to think of anything but the need for Reese to make love to her again. It had been years since she'd shared her body with a man, and she was realistic enough to know she wouldn't be able to make up those lost years. She'd always known of the strong passions within her, yet had denied her own needs because she preferred to live in the past.

"Reese?"

"What is it, bae?"

"Do you think I was shameless when I asked you to make love to me?" Laughter floated up from his throat, and Cherie couldn't stop the wave of heat beginning at her hairline and moving lower to her breasts. "Why are you laughing?"

"Because your question borders on ridiculousness, Cherie. If the roles were reversed and I'd asked you to sleep with me, would you have thought me overstepping what we have because we haven't known each other that long."

"No, because it's what I wanted."

"You asking me to make love to you is also what I wanted," Reese retorted. "We're both adults, and we should feel comfortable enough with each other to say whatever is on our minds. I told you before that I value truth in a relationship over all else. And if you can't be truthful with me, then that's a deal breaker."

"What if you're not truthful with me, Reese?"

"If you ask me something, I'll always tell you the truth. The only time that won't happen is when I don't have the answer."

Cherie's mind was in tumult. She so wanted to tell Reese about her prior relationship with Weylin, then thought better of it. What if what they had was too new? More importantly, she didn't want him to judge her.

It was different with Kayana and Leah because, as women, they were cognizant of the sacrifices they'd made to save their marriages, even if what they'd had to give up was for naught. Leah had married a man who sought to control every aspect of her life, while Kayana had put up with her first husband turning their home into a club where she was expected to play the role of hostess, while unaware that he'd been having an ongoing affair with one of their invited guests. Even when Cherie admitted to them that she'd slept with a married man, they hadn't judged her.

Cherie knew her grandmother would've said she'd taken the rag off the bush and was Boo Boo the fool once she'd made the decision to continue to sleep with a married man *and* become a surrogate for his wife.

She closed her eyes and sighed softly, knowing that not only had she turned a corner in her emotional growth, but she was grateful that she'd waited for someone like Reese to come into her life. Her breathing slowed until she fell asleep in the embrace of the man who had unknowingly given her a second chance at love.

Reese reclined on a cushioned chaise in the enclosed sunroom at the rear of the house, drinking beer and watching the rerun of a basketball game from the night before; despite knowing the final score, he pretended interest in it, because it kept his mind off the woman sleeping upstairs in his bed. When Cherie asked him about inviting women to his home since he'd returned to Coates Island as a civilian, he'd been forthcoming and admitted she was the first one. What he hadn't admitted to her was why it was her. Why her and not some other woman?

He knew the answer as surely as he did his own name. She wasn't like any of the women with whom he'd had a platonic relationship or those he'd slept with, or even the woman he'd married. And he had loved Monica enough to want to spend the rest of his life with her even when he'd become aware of the cracks in their marriage. It wasn't until after their divorce that he realized he'd been in denial; his wife had been dropping hints about being unhappy, while he'd attributed it to their moving from one base to another when she'd just formed friendships with the wives of other officers. She'd also resented that she had to put her goal to become a lawyer on hold and her growing concern with her father's failing health.

It had been twelve years since his divorce, and since that time, he'd been able to control his emotions when it came to women. There were some he liked more than others, and whenever they mentioned they wanted a commitment, Reese was truthful when he told them that wasn't possible because, as an active-duty soldier, his commitment was to serve his country.

His marriage to Monica had taught him that he wasn't emotionally equipped to deal with oppositional issues affecting his personal life at the same time that he was responsible for the lives and safety of the men and women under his command whenever they embarked on a mission.

Then there was Cherie Thompson. The first time he saw her in the Seaside Café, he realized she was the same woman he'd seen talking to Bettina Wilson during his patrol of the island. He'd tried, although unsuccessfully, not to think about her while attempting to rationalize that she was just another woman. But the truth was she wasn't just another woman. However, he didn't want to make the same mistake with Cherie that he'd made with Monica and let his heart overrule his head, thinking that he was the answer to all her problems.

When he first met Monica, they were both students at Duke University, and he'd sensed a vulnerability under her sometimes overly animated demeanor. A part-time student, she worked as a legal secretary during the day, while attending evening classes. He'd gone to the college library to study for finals, found an empty chair at a table where Monica sat with two other students, and opened his textbook on European military history. He'd been so engrossed in reading that he hadn't realized the other students had left and only he and Monica had remained.

She introduced herself, and then revealed she was a freshman and pre-law. Her eyes appeared to light up when he told her he was a junior in the ROTC. They'd spent the two hours talking rather than studying; when Monica revealed it was getting late and she had to leave—she didn't want to miss her bus and have to wait more than an hour for the next one—that's when Reese offered to drive her home to a rented room in a house with other students.

They'd begun dating during his senior year, and he was instantly drawn to her upbeat, carefree personality, unaware it was a foil for deep, unresolved childhood issues. Her mother had walked out on her father, leaving him to raise their four children. Her father hired a woman to look after his three sons and daughter whenever he went out on the road as a long-haul trucker.

Monica told him the woman favored her brothers and treated them as if they were royalty, while she was considered an outsider. And whenever she complained to her father about the mistreatment, he claimed she resented the live-in housekeeper because she wasn't her mother. It wasn't until years later that Monica learned that her father had been cheating on her mother with the woman he'd invited into his home to care for his children, flaunting his affair until her mother had had enough and left.

When her father was diagnosed with Parkinson's, Monica forgave him and moved back to Fayetteville to take care of him after the woman with whom he'd cheated deserted him because she hadn't signed up to take care of an invalid.

Reese put the bottle of beer up to his mouth and took another swallow. It had been years since he'd thought about Monica, and despite what she'd put him through, he still wished her well. She'd been the one to propose marriage while declaring she wanted to become the mother of his children. At twenty-two and as a newly commissioned officer, he knew he wasn't ready for marriage. He told Monica he wanted to wait for her to finish college, and two years later and a week following her graduation, they were married on base by a military chaplain.

And when he called and told his grandparents that he was married, their first question was were they about to become great-grandparents. Reese had laughed and said that wasn't going to happen for a while, unaware that it would never come to fruition.

He was now forty-two, single, and with no children. His mother was gone. His grandfather and grandmother were also gone, leaving him with a house filled with warm and wonderful childhood memories he would take to his grave. It was those memories that had sustained him whenever he'd faced imminent death from enemy fire, and that's when he'd imagined hearing his grandmother's voice praying for his safe return.

When he was granted family leave to return to Coates Island to bury his grandfather, his Gram had pleaded with him to leave the army because she couldn't bear it if she had to bury him beside his mother. He reassured her he would submit his discharge papers once he completed his last deployment. Seven months later, she was gone, and Reese blamed himself for not being there for her as she grieved the loss of her only child and the husband with whom she'd shared sixty-one years of marriage.

Reese detected movement behind him and stood up. Cherie hadn't made a sound when she entered the sunroom. His instincts were still on full alert, and it was obvious he hadn't lost his edge. He could smell what he'd come to recognize as her bodywash as she approached him.

"How was your nap?"

She smiled. "It was longer than what I intended. I had no idea I'd slept more than three hours."

Reaching for her hand, Reese pulled her close to his body. She looked different with her hair off her face and styled in a ponytail. And with her bare face and wearing a sweatshirt, pants, and thick socks, she appeared no older than a college student. "Maybe it was because you needed the sleep. By the way, what time do you go to bed at night?"

"It varies. Sometimes I'm in bed before ten, and then it could be as late as two or three. But I have an internal clock that wakes me when the sun comes up."

"Which means you never have to set an alarm?"

"Very rarely. I only set it when I'm expecting an early delivery. And that reminds me. I'm expecting a delivery of my dining-area furniture before ten Tuesday morning."

When she'd ordered the table and chairs, the salesman told her he had a set with seating for eight but not the six she'd wanted. Like the house, the beautiful table was larger than she needed, but she decided to purchase it and the comfortable chairs it came with because she didn't want to wait another four months for the one with seating for six to become available.

"Speaking of furniture," Reese said, "have you given any thought about what style you want in your office?"

A slight smile touched her lips. "Are you asking so I could commission you to make the furniture?"

His smile matched hers. "That is a distinct possibility. It's been months since I've made anything, so I am offering my humble services."

"Don't play yourself, Reese Matthews. You're anything but humble."

He sobered. "What do you think I am?"

Cherie bit on her lower lip as she appeared deep in thought. "You're brave, chivalrous, generous, well-mannered, and generally good-natured. I like that you're honest, and you're someone I'd trust with my life."

Reese laughed. "That's a lot."

"You don't think you're deserving of the accolades?"

"I'll accept some but definitely not all of them." He paused. "Now, do you want to hear how I think of you?"

Cherie took a deep breath and nodded. "Yes, let me have it."

Reese felt as if he was drowning in pools of gold and green as the overhead light slanted over Cherie's face when she looked up at him. "You're beautiful, crazy smart, loyal to your family and friends, and you're sexy as hell in and out of bed. And I'm glad your ex was so undeserving of you that he couldn't appreciate what he had, or you wouldn't be here with me."

Cherie buried her face against Reese's sweatshirt. She wanted to tell him Weylin knew what he had, but his future had been mapped out for him from birth. He was heir to a real estate empire, and he was expected to take over once his father retired or go into politics like his maternal uncles. He'd chosen the latter and, as such, needed a wife with a similar background to help launch his political career.

Cherie knew she had the intelligence to hold her own as the wife of a politician, but not the pedigree. It hadn't mattered that she'd graduated magna cum laude from one of the most prestigious colleges in the country, because there was the stigma to being raised by a single mother who had children from several different men. And if she had married Weylin and he'd entered politics, there was no doubt his opponent would've vilified her family, similar to what the British press did to Meghan Markle before she married Prince Harry. Reese was right. Weylin did her a favor by marrying Michelle, because it spared her the humiliation of having her life played out in the tabloids.

"And you don't know how happy I am to be here with you," she admitted.

Lowering his head, Reese pressed a kiss to her forehead. "Thank you, sweetheart. I don't know about you, but I'm ready to eat. What say you?"

"I say yes."

Chapter 18

It had taken less than a week for Cherie to realize she could have an open relationship with a man without experiencing guilt or fear that someone would uncover their clandestine liaisons. She'd spent Sunday night and Monday afternoon with Reese before returning home. He'd taken her on a tour of his home and pointed out the tables, chairs, and head- and footboards that were crafted by several generations of Matthews carpenters.

His grandfather had bought the land behind the house with the intent of putting up a bungalow and selling it, but that plan died with Raymond Matthews when he'd passed away in his sleep. Reese said he'd planned to begin to fulfill his grandfather's dream of building the two-bedroom house and renting it to vacationers when he went on vacation later in the year. He also showed her the woodshed where his grandfather had taught him all he knew about carpentry. Although small, it was well-ventilated when all the windows were opened. Reese said it was where the magic of turning a piece of wood into a functional item began.

He was currently scheduled to work the midnight-to-eight

shift until Wednesday, then to take the eight-to-four afternoon shift on Thursday for the following two weeks. She knew her neighbors were aware that his pickup was parked in her driveway at odd hours, and when she'd mentioned this to him, he claimed he had no intention of sneaking around to see her, and if anyone had a problem with it, then it was theirs and not his.

He'd come over to measure the room for her would-be office. They'd discussed whether she wanted bookcases built into the wall or ones that could be moved, and when she couldn't make up her mind, he suggested built-in ones because of the number of books, CDs, and DVDs she'd collected. She'd watched as he drew different configurations on a pad for the shelves, and now she knew what Kayana had talked about when she said Reese came from a long line of master carpenters. He planned to use one entire wall for floor-to-ceiling bookcases and suggested installing a railing and a ladder for easy access to the upper shelves.

When she'd asked him how much he was going to charge her, he gave her a death stare that had momentarily rendered her mute. Then, when she offered to pay for the materials, he put his tools away and walked out.

Cherie knew she had insulted Reese because he had volunteered to put up the bookcases and making them would give him something to do during his days off. She didn't see him for two days, then without warning, he showed up with a bouquet of flowers and several bottles of wine as a peace offering. He claimed he'd walked away before saying something he would later regret and hoped she would forgive him for being rude.

She did forgive him in the most intimate way possible. The downside was they'd made love without using protection, and Reese reassured her if she did become pregnant they would have to discuss whether they wanted to marry right away or wait until they were certain if it was what they wanted, and not because of the baby.

Cherie had been expecting to see her period within days and breathed a sigh of relief when it came on schedule. They'd dodged a bullet, and because she didn't want any more slipups, she'd driven into town to buy a supply of condoms to have on hand.

It was Super Bowl Sunday, and Leah and Kayana had come over early in the afternoon to begin preparing the menu for later that night. Cherie could not believe the amount of food Kayana had planned to serve. "Who's going to eat all this stuff?" she asked.

Kayana smiled. "My man, Lee's man, and your man, Cherie."

"Why are you blushing when Kayana mentions your man, Cherie?" Leah asked.

"You know about that?" Cherie questioned.

Kayana continued to take items out of several large canvas bags. "Chile, please. Everyone on the island and half the folks on the mainland know about you and Reese. It was the same with me when I used to park my car at Graeme's house. Nothing escapes these wannabe secret agents."

Cherie sat on a stool and drew imaginary circles on the breakfast bar's marble countertop. "When I mentioned it to him, he said it wasn't a problem what folks say about him."

Kayana met her eyes. "You have to remember that Reese is a grown-ass man who doesn't have to answer to anyone about where he goes and what he does, and I feel sorry for anyone who broaches the subject with him, because I'm certain they'll get an earful of something they don't want to hear."

"Do you like him?" Leah questioned.

"Stop it, Lee," Kayana chastised her future sister-in-law. "If she didn't like him, do you think he'd be spending nights at her house."

"Days, nights, and afternoons," Cherie quipped smiling, "and between his shifts."

Kayana narrowed her eyes. "So, that's why we rarely see him come into the café."

"We've begun sharing meals together," Cherie said.

"That's not all they're sharing," Leah said under her breath.

"I heard that, Leah Kent soon-to-be Johnson."

The redhead scrunched up her nose. "And I wanted you to hear it. I'm glad that you finally got over that loser you were mooning over for so many years and found someone that you don't have to share with another woman. Maybe now you can think about what you want for your future."

"And that is?" she asked Leah.

"A husband and children."

"Have you two talked about marriage and or children?" Kayana questioned.

"Not directly."

Kayana turned and stared at her. "What do you mean not directly?"

Cherie knew it was time to level with her friends, because she could always count on them to offer advice that forced her to consider another viewpoint. "The last time, we made love without using protection, and when I told him it was the wrong time of the month, he said we'd talk about it if I were to become pregnant; we could marry right away or wait until we decide if it is what we really want."

Leah and Kayana stared at her. "What did you say?" Kayana asked.

"I told him I needed to think about it. He told me he wanted children when he was married, but his ex-wife didn't. So I'm under the impression that he still wants them."

"Do you think you are pregnant?" Leah asked in a quiet voice.

"No. I got my period yesterday."

Leah came over and sat on the stool next to hers. "Did he tell you why his wife didn't want children?"

Cherie shook her head. "No. He's never opened up about his marriage, and not wanting to pry, I've never asked."

"Is that because you don't want him to pry into your past?" Leah questioned.

Cherie nodded. "Yes. My past is my past, and I'd like it to remain there."

Kayana came over and propped her elbows on the countertop. "I'm going to give you some advice just this once, then the topic is moot. If you're sleeping with the man and you're having unprotected sex, I suggest you tell Reese about your past and insist he tell you about his, because if something comes up that you're hiding, then whatever you'd share with the man will be shot to hell. And it's the same with him. Graeme and I were very open with each other when we talked about our first marriages; we were given the option to continue to see each other or walk away. This is not to say that Graeme placed all the blame on his wife for their failing marriage, but he did accept some of the responsibility for not understanding what she'd been going through.

"It was the same with me and James. I married him knowing his family believed I wasn't good enough for their son, but I was so madly in love with him that I didn't care what they thought of me. It was the reason I allowed James to turn our home into a place where his friends could hang out as if it were a social club; he knew his parents didn't approve of me and were reluctant for me to mingle with their fake-ass friends."

Cherie's jaw dropped. "You mean they never invited you to their home?"

"I could count on one hand the number of times I crossed over their threshold during the nineteen years of my marriage. But, to be honest, I didn't give a shit about them because I felt they were morally beneath me. James's father also cheated on his bougie wife, and what makes it so sad is that she knew it. I was nothing like my mother-in-law because I'd told James even before we were married that if I found out he was cheating, it was over. Apparently, he'd forgotten who his wife was; when I discovered he'd gotten another woman pregnant, I was out."

Cherie thought about her affair with Weylin. There was no doubt his parents would not have approved of or accepted her, and that was evident when the Campbell family lawyer called her every low-down epithet he could think of.

She closed her eyes and said a silent prayer for strength, because what she was about to tell her book club friends was something she'd never revealed to another living soul. "I'm going to tell you everything about the man with whom I had an affair for years, but I'm still not ready to divulge his name."

Kayana held her hands. "We don't have to know his name, Cherie." Her voice was low, soothing.

Cherie nodded, smiling. In that instant, Kayana became her therapist, and she trusted her enough to bare her soul. "I . . . I was fifteen when I was awarded an academic scholarship to a prestigious prep school." She took a deep breath, held it, then slowly exhaled. She told Kayana and Leah everything from giving a fellow student her virginity to continuing to sleep with him throughout college and then beginning a week following his honeymoon. The more she talked, the easier it was for her to reveal the incidents that had turned her into a jealous, manipulative woman who used her wiles and her body to get what she wanted from her adulterous lover. There were gasps from Leah and Kayana when she told them she'd sold her baby to his father because his wife was unable to give him a child.

Leah's eyelids fluttered wildly as she struggled to blink back tears. "I can't believe he tricked you into having his baby when it was his original intent for you to become a surrogate."

"I know it sounds crazy, but when he told me, I went ballistic and threatened to go to the press about our affair. Then, once I cooled off, I realized women agreed to become surrogates for different reasons. Wills comes from a very wealthy family, as does his wife, so I quoted an outrageous figure I was certain he wouldn't accept. I was shocked when he did, but when I met with his lawyer to draw up the contract, the supercilious little man called me names I won't repeat, so I doubled, then tripled the original amount. Wills wanted his child, so he was forced to give me whatever I wanted. I got a two-bedroom condo in an exclusive gated community and stock in his family's company. I held onto the shares before selling them back to Wills for more than they were listed for on the stock market. When I sold the condo, I was able to pay cash for this house and invest what was left over in a retirement account."

Kayana was grinning like a Cheshire cat. "Girl, I really like your style."

Cherie inclined her head in acknowledgment. She was not only book smart but also street smart. As a young girl, she'd overheard women talk about how they were able to get over on the men with whom they were involved, never thinking that one day she would use their tactics to get what she wanted from a man. Weylin may have thought he was manipulating her when it'd been the reverse. She had become the winner when he gave her money, precious jewelry, the condo, and stock in his family's real estate conglomerate. She may have given him a son, but every time he looked at that child, he would be reminded of how he'd gotten him, and it wasn't out of love. Fast-forward five years, and now she had a second chance to right the wrongs. A chance to fall in love with someone worthy of her love. Someone she could trust completely.

"Do you ever hear from him?" Leah asked.

Cherie flashed a wry smile. "We had an agreement never to see or talk to each other again once I delivered the baby. He'd conveniently forgotten about that when he called me a day before I closed on this house to complain that I didn't tell him I was selling the condo."

"The SOB had a lot of nerve to complain about something that belonged to you," Kayana stated angrily.

"Exactly," Cherie drawled. "I told him to fuck off and hung up. He called back and left a voice mail, but I deleted it without listening to it. He wanted a son, and I gave him one. Case closed."

Leah rubbed Cherie's back. "I'm so sorry you had to give up your baby."

Cherie lowered her eyes. "Either I was stupid or under some crazy spell when Wills said he wanted me to have his love child. And looking back, I know that now I never would trade my son for all the money in the world."

"Did you get to see the baby?"

Cherie shook her head. "No, Leah. I was given a sedative before giving birth that made me loopy, so I never got to see or hold the baby. But I do remember hearing him cry."

Kayana squeezed her fingers. "You say this man is very wealthy. Are there photos of him and his wife and *your* son?"

Cherie had divulged a lot of her past, but knew she had to choose her words carefully because she wasn't ready to name William Weylin Campbell III as her former lover. "Not really. They tend to keep their personal life very private." Weylin had released one photo of his wife holding their adopted infant son wrapped in a blanket. Michelle had held the baby at an angle to conceal his face.

Kayana let go of her hands. "You said he called you. How long had it been since y'all had decided to sever all communication?"

"It will be five years in May."

"And you didn't change your number?" Kayana questioned.

"Maybe she was hoping he would call her," Leah interjected. "And he did."

"That's where you're wrong, Leah," Cherie countered. "I allowed Wills to control half my life, and not changing my number allowed me to take back some of the power I surrendered to him. I could make the decision to talk or not talk to him. Even after he called, I decided I wasn't going to block his number. He can call and leave as many messages as he wants, but I'm not going to talk to him or listen to any of his voice mails."

"Cherie's right, Lee. Her ex was like a puppet master, pulling the strings to make her do whatever he wanted. He probably expected her to change her number or block his calls, and I'm certain he was shocked when she didn't."

Leah rubbed Cherie's back again. "I'm glad you got out of it when you did, or the selfish bastard could've come back and demanded you become a brood mare for him and his wife."

"That definitely wasn't going to happen," she stated firmly, "even if we hadn't agreed to sever all contact with each other, because I no longer trusted him. I know sleeping with a married man was wrong, and I paid for it when I sold my son."

"You have to stop saying you sold your baby," Kayana snapped angrily. "You'd become a surrogate, and you were paid to carry a baby to term and then give it to his parents." She held up a hand when Cherie opened her mouth. "Please let me finish. It would have been the same if you'd donated an egg and Wills his sperm that, when fertilized, was implanted in your body. And you had a right to ask to be paid because you were deceived into becoming pregnant, and the duplicitous snake was made to pay for his deception."

Cherie chewed her lip. "I know where you're coming from, Kayana, but I can't shake off the guilt that easily."

"It's a process," Kayana said in a quiet voice. "If you've carried this guilt for five years, then you can't expect to wake up one day and discover it's no longer there."

"I do know one thing. If I become pregnant again, I'm going to keep my baby, like Leah did with her sons."

"I wish I'd had your strength, Cherie," Leah said. "If I'd known what I was going to go through with Alan, I never would've married him. And he was as manipulative as your Wills. The first time I had a date with him, he promised to use his influence to get a teaching position for me at the school where, years later, I'd become the headmistress. He'd set up an interview for me, despite my being not much older than the students I would teach. When I got the notification that I'd been hired and I called to tell him, he suggested we go back to the inn where we'd had our first date and celebrate. The first time, he'd been the perfect gentleman, but that was to gain my confidence and before he'd morphed into predator mode. He ordered champagne, knowing I was too young to drink, and after several glasses, I was in no condition to tell him I didn't want to have sex with him.

"So there's no need for you to feel guilty about pimping his ass for money, jewelry, stocks, and your condo. You more than earned it for putting your life on hold to be at his beck and call. I was only nineteen when I married Alan, but it didn't take long for me to discover his weaknesses. He wanted to be obeyed, and he also wanted his ego stroked, and I did that when I told him he had the best cock in the world. That really made him feel good because he knew I wasn't a virgin when we first slept together."

Cherie laughed hysterically. "Was he good?"

Leah sucked her teeth. "He was okay. Most times, I'd fantasize about making love with my old boyfriend, who looked like a nerd, but he was the complete opposite when it came to making love. He told me that his parents had had a maid who not only took his virginity, but taught him how to please a woman."

"Good for you," Cherie said, smiling. "It was different for me, because I had no one to compare Wills to."

"What about Reese?" Kayana questioned.

Cherie waved her hand in the air as if she were in church testifying. "No comment."

Kayana applauded. "You don't have to give us any deets,

but judging from this new and improved Cherie Thompson, I know Daddy must know what to do for you to blush whenever we mention his name."

Leah slipped off her stool. "I forgot to bring your housewarming gifts in from the car."

Cherie also stood up, thankful she didn't have to go into detail about her and Reese. It was enough that she'd admitted they'd had unprotected sex. "Y'all know I don't need anything."

"We know, Miss Martha Stewart," Leah quipped as she walked out of the kitchen.

Cherie shared a smile with Kayana. "I don't know where I'd be without you and Leah." There was a thread of sadness in her voice.

Kayana slipped on an apron over her blouse and jeans. "You'd be just where you are today, Cherie. There are times when we question why things happen to us, but I'm of the belief that they happen because they are supposed to, so we can move from one place or situation to another. You met and fell in love with a man who not only used you but had a hidden agenda. When I miscarried early in my pregnancy, I was truly devastated after the doctor told me I would never have children. He had to perform an emergency hysterectomy because they weren't able to stop the bleeding. It left me depressed for a long time, until I realized I wasn't less of a woman because I couldn't bear children. There are women who opt never to become mothers, and they are quite content with their lives. James sleeping with another woman and getting her pregnant was the wake-up call for me to realize my marriage was on shaky ground and had been for a while. And it was the impetus I needed to take control of my life and return to my roots. If I hadn't come back to Coates Island, I never would've met Graeme, and I know for certain that I never would've married again."

Cherie nodded. "You're right about my coming to Coates Island. I feel as if I've been reborn. Yesterday I got up early and walked along the shore to think about where I'd been and where I am now. I know in my gut I'm not ready for motherhood, but I did feel a little disappointed when I saw my period."

"Don't worry, Cherie. It's all about timing. When the time is right, you'll have your baby, and this time your baby's father will be there for you."

She sighed. "You really believe Reese and I are going to be together for the long run."

Kayana angled her head. "I believe it even if you don't want to. You deserve a lot of happiness after what you've had to go through. My grandmother used to say opportunity is like a bald-headed man. You must grab it as it's coming toward you, or your hand will slip off and it's gone forever. Reese Matthews is your opportunity for happiness, Cherie. Please don't blow it by hiding things from him."

Cherie wondered if Kayana was able to discern things about Reese that weren't apparent to her. Kayana had grown up on Coates Island, and so had he, which meant she was more than familiar with him and his family. Then it was Leah's reference to his interest in her even before they'd introduced themselves to each other. Was it because her friends were older, more worldly, and had had more experience with men than she had that made them more aware of the interactions between a man and a woman.

She'd noticed Reese looking at her whenever he entered the café, but so had the man that had attacked her. Cherie wasn't vain when it came to what people claimed were her so-called exotic looks, but she knew men were drawn to her because on occasion they would ask if she was a Latina or mixed race, and her comeback would be that she was a black woman. Their curiosity as to her racial makeup stirred up her frustration with her mother because she'd refused to tell her about the man who had fathered her.

Leah returned, cradling a large, gift-wrapped box against her chest. "There's one more in the car that I have to get."

"I'll come with you," Cherie volunteered. She followed Leah out of the house to her car. She waved to Bettina, who was sitting on her porch knitting. Bettina returned the wave and went back to knitting. "I'm wondering whether I should invite her and her husband to join us," she whispered to Leah.

Leah lifted another shopping bag from the trunk. "Are you friendly with her?"

"Not really. But I suspect she's lonely. When I first moved in, she told me she was an empty nester, and now that her husband's retired, he expects her to wait on him hand and foot."

"If I were you, I would invite her, Cherie. Maybe being around other folks will make her feel better."

"What about hubby?"

Leah rolled her eyes. "What the hell. Invite him too. I know firsthand what it means to be an empty nester. Once Caleb and Aron became teenagers and were old enough to drive, they were in and out of the house like folks going through a revolving door. That didn't bother me because I knew they were always coming home. It wasn't until they left to attend college that it really hit me that I was truly alone. I dreaded them coming home during semester breaks because I knew I would only have them for a little while. That's when I'd go up to New York to visit whenever I could. It has taken me a long time, Cherie, to emotionally let my sons go so they can live their own lives. Now that Caleb is engaged, I'm ready to become a grandmother."

"You have changed, Leah."

"Why would you say that?" she asked Cherie.

"Because when we first met, you used to refer to your sons

as 'my boys,' and I wanted to tell you that they weren't boys but grown men."

"You're right. But then, I could've said my babies. Do you know how many women refer to their adult children as their babies?"

"Too many. That's probably because they didn't give them what they needed to grow into mature, independent adults."

She didn't want to tell Leah that many of the young men in her old neighborhood who had fathered children still lived with their mothers, grandmothers, or aunties. However, she had to give Edwina credit for threatening her sons about getting a girl pregnant when they were unable to take care of themselves.

Cherie closed the Audi's trunk for Leah. "I'm going across the street to invite Bettina and Andrew Wilson to join us later."

Leah smiled. "The more the merrier."

Although she knew Bettina was a gossiper, Cherie felt sorry for the woman. It took less than three minutes for her and her husband to agree to come over later that afternoon for a Super Bowl party. She'd just returned to the house when her cell phone rang.

"Hey, you," she whispered into the mouthpiece as a smile spread over her features.

"Hey, yourself," Reese said in greeting. "I'm having a dilemma because my cousin was under the impression that he was coming to my place to watch the Super Bowl, and right now he's cussin' up a blue streak because—"

"Bring him with you," Cherie said, cutting him off. "There's plenty of food, so one more will just add to the merriment."

"Are you sure he won't be imposing?"

"Stop it, Reese. He's your family, and that means my door is always open to him."

"I'll be certain to tell him that. We'll see you later."

She set the phone on a shelf under the breakfast bar and then met Kayana's eyes. "I hope you don't mind that I invited my neighbors from across the street and Reese's cousin."

Kayana rested a hand at her hip. "Do you really hear yourself, Cherie? You're asking me if you can invite people into what is your home. You suggested hosting the Super Bowl party, and I volunteered to cook, so there should be no debate as to who you can or cannot invite."

Cherie felt properly chastised. Kayana was right. It was her home, and who she would permit to enter was at her discretion. "I'm going to put out the plates and serving pieces, and then when you're finished prepping, I'm going make some spinach-bacon, blue devils, and pimento-cheese deviled eggs. And I know you southerners love your pimento cheese." She'd made three dozen hard-cooked eggs earlier that morning, and made up the fillings and stored them in different containers in the fridge before piping them into the egg halves.

"Well, aren't we fancy?" Kayana crooned, smiling. "Lee and I aren't the only southern girls. You show your country when you say *y'all* instead of *you all*."

"I won't deny that I have southern roots, but when I open my mouth, folks know right away that I'm not from down here."

"Well, you're here now. And to stay."

"You've got that right," she said confidently.

There had been a time when she'd felt like a nomad moving from place to place. First, it was to move into a dorm room at the prep school, followed by another dorm room at Yale. After graduating, it was to a small studio apartment, then a one-bedroom apartment, and then into the condo unit with two bedrooms. Now it was into a house along the shore on Coates Island, North Carolina. A house where she planned to spend the rest of her life.

It was as if she had to keep moving to find herself and her rightful place in the universe. And Kayana and Leah were right; she'd had to go through what she had with Weylin to appreciate the woman she'd become. Kayana had called her new and improved, and she was going to embrace that assessment of herself. She knew instinctually that, if she hadn't improved, she could not have imagined having a positive relationship with Reese or any man.

Chapter 19

Reese parked his pickup on the street in front of Cherie's house rather than in the driveway behind an Audi or Range Rover. He shut off the engine and got out at the same time Parker opened the passenger-side door.

"Nice place," Parker drawled.

"That it is," Reese confirmed, reaching into the back of the pickup to remove two crates, handing one to his cousin. "You need to get out of the station house more often."

"You're right about that."

Hoisting the crate onto a shoulder, Reese walked up the path leading to Cherie's house and climbed the porch steps. He was looking forward to the get-together because it would keep him from thinking about the possibility he could've gotten Cherie pregnant. He didn't know what had possessed him to make love to her without using a condom; he knew that, if it had been at his house, it wouldn't have happened. Now, even days later, he could hear her whisper in his ear once he'd recovered from the most unbridled lovemaking he'd ever experienced: "You picked the wrong time of the month to make love to me without a condom."

It was the first time he'd slept with a woman without using protection. The exception had been with Monica when they were married because she'd used a contraceptive. Even when some women claimed they were on the pill, Reese still didn't want to take the risk they weren't being truthful. However, Cherie wasn't some woman or any woman. She was special, and special enough for him to want to spend all his spare time with her.

She was intelligent, sexy, uncomplicated, and unpredictable. He liked that she didn't take herself too seriously; for him, that was a breath of fresh air. He'd finished reading *The Alienist*, and they spent hours discussing the novel—something he enjoyed and looked forward to with other books.

He peered through the glass on the storm door and then rang the bell. Derrick came to the door and opened it. "Please come in, Reese. What's up, Chief?" he said to Parker.

"There's no chief business today, Derrick. It's just Parker."

"Who's minding the station house?"

"Assistant deputy chief Ian Burrows," Parker replied. "I doubt whether there's going to be any arrests or citations tonight because everyone will probably be watching the game."

Derrick flashed a dimpled smile and opened the door wider. "You guys are just in time to get your eat on."

Reese gave the owner of the Seaside Café his crate. "We bought some libations just in case you run short."

Derrick stared at the bottles in the crate, then rolled his eyes upward. "There's enough booze in this house right now to open *and* stock a bar."

Reese took his cousin's crate. "What's good is it won't spoil."

"You've got that right," Derrick drawled. "The ladies went upstairs to change, and as soon as they come down, we'll eat. Meanwhile, Graeme is in the kitchen tending bar. I have to warn you that he has a heavy pour, and if you have a problem navigating it back to the mainland, Parker, you're more than welcome to crash at my place." He shot a glance at Reese. "I don't have to tell you where you'll be sleeping."

Reese slowly shook his head. "Damn! News appears to travel around Coates Island at warp speed."

Parker rested an arm on his cousin's shoulder. "Don't act so shocked, Reese. Everyone and his mama knows you're keeping company with Cherie Thompson."

Derrick's eyebrows lifted. "It's been a while since I've heard the term *keeping company*."

Reese wanted to tell Derrick it was because his cousin was a throwback to his grandmother's generation. Parker's father had been a fire-and-brimstone preacher who raised all his children in the church; less than a week following his high school graduation, Parker walked into a Marine Corps recruiting station and enlisted. The military was a good fit for him, and he'd served for thirty years, rising to the rank of master sergeant. He'd been a hard-nosed, no-nonsense drill sergeant with an impeccable reputation for turning young boys into men in the tradition the Corps was known for. Once a marine, always a marine.

He followed Derrick through the entryway, past the living and family rooms, and into the kitchen, where Kayana's husband was busy measuring ingredients into a shaker. The large flat-screen mounted over the fireplace in the family room was muted and tuned to ESPN, and he barely caught a glimpse of two banquet tables with cold and warming trays that were emitting mouthwatering aromas. The table in the dining area was set for nine. Cherie had added a leaf, expanding the table, and had set out another chair. It was obvious she was expecting more people.

He set the crate on the floor next to the breakfast bar. "Here's some more to add to your stash," he said to Kayana's husband. Reese had had very little interaction with the former high school teacher who had vacationed on the island

and liked it enough to purchase property and retire here. Graeme was tall and slender, with large gray eyes, and Reese noticed that his cropped, sandy-brown hair had acquired more silver since their last encounter.

Graeme set down the shaker, wiped his hands on a towel, and extended the right one to Reese. "Thanks. It's nice seeing you again. And especially out of uniform."

Reese took the proffered hand. "Same here. Right now, work is the farthest thing from my mind."

Graeme pointed to three mason jars of margaritas lining the countertop. "Take one and let me know what you think."

"I'll also have one of those," Parker said, as he set down his crate.

Graeme handed Parker a jar. "Drink up, Chief."

Reese noticed his cousin's frown when Graeme had addressed him by his official title. Most folks called Parker "Chief," while he was Deputy Matthews. He touched his glass to Parker's and then took a sip. He swallowed the ice-cold liquid, and then, without warning, it detonated in his chest. Derrick had warned him that his brother-in-law had a heavy pour.

He blew out a breath. "How much tequila did you put in here?"

Graeme wiggled his eyebrows. "Nice, isn't it?"

"No, you didn't!"

Reese turned to see Cherie standing only a few feet away. It was obvious the alcohol had temporarily dulled his senses because he hadn't detected her approach. She wore a white man-tailored blouse with a pair of fitted jeans and ballet flats. She'd styled her hair in a ponytail and applied a light cover of makeup. It was the first time he'd seen her without a bare face. The smoky shadow on her lids made her eyes appear even lighter than they were, while he couldn't pull his gaze away from the raspberry color on her lush mouth.

He moved closer and kissed her cheek. "Hey, bae."

Cherie rested a hand on Reese's chest before she walked over to Graeme. "I thought Derrick was going to tend bar."

"He decided he'd rather take care of the food."

"For a math teacher, you definitely have a problem measuring liquids." Kayana had revealed that Graeme had earned a reputation for concocting very strong drinks.

Lines fanned out around Graeme's eyes when he smiled. "Former math teacher."

"Graeme, you have to lighten up on the alcohol, or everyone will be drunk even before the game begins."

"Graeme Norris Ogden, step away from those bottles!" Kayana ordered as she entered the kitchen.

He held up both hands and struggled not to laugh. "I was just trying out some samples."

Kayana glared at her husband before she forcibly took the jars from Reese and Parker. "Just because my beloved husband has learned to cook, he now believes he can become a mixologist."

"They are rather strong," Reese confirmed.

"And I know that from past experience," Cherie admitted. "The one time I had one of his cocktails, I felt as if I was drowning in the Bermuda Triangle." The doorbell rang, and she smiled at Reese. "Can you please walk me to the door?"

He nodded. "Of course."

Cherie took his hand, and when they were out of earshot of everyone, she leaned in closer to him. "We dodged a bullet," she whispered. She'd wanted to get him alone to give him the good news.

"No baby?" he said sotto voce.

"No." Cherie saw a myriad of expressions flitter over Reese's features and wondered if he was as relieved as she'd been when seeing her menses. It's not that she didn't want to become a mother, but only when the timing was right. She and Reese had known each other a little more than a month, and she still wasn't ready to tell him about her past. Once that was behind her, she knew she'd be ready to talk about or consider a future with him.

Bettina and husband stood on the porch; she held a foil-covered pan. Cherie opened the door. "Welcome, Bettina."

The redhead blushed. "Thank you for inviting us. This is my husband, Andrew Wilson."

Cherie stared at the man with a receding hairline and what she thought of as nondescript features. It was her first time meeting him face-to-face. "It's nice meeting you, Andrew."

His lips parted in what could pass for a smile. "It's nice to finally see you up close." He extended his hand to Reese. "Deputy Matthews."

Reese took his hand. "Mr. Wilson."

"Please call me Andy. Whenever someone calls me Mr. Wilson, I think they're talking about my father."

Bettina handed Cherie the pan. "I know it was short notice, so I decided to make what I had on hand. It's my grandmother's recipe for sausage and peppers. Not too many people know it, but Nona came here from Italy as a young woman and brought her cooking skills with her."

Cherie smiled. "Thank you so much, but you didn't have to bring anything. We've prepared enough food to feed a football team."

"I'm sure you did, but I didn't want to come empty-handed."

"Please come in, and I'll introduce you to everyone before we have cocktails and appetizers. After that, we'll sit down to eat before the game begins. Everything will be served buffet style."

Cherie handed the pan of sausage and peppers to Derrick, and then made the introductions, although everyone was familiar with the Wilsons, especially Bettina. "The beverages include various margaritas, beer, wine, pop, and water."

Bettina clasped her hands together. "What kind of margaritas can you make?" she asked Kayana.

"You can have the classic margarita, or a strawberry spritzer, sweet tea lime, mojitarita, cranberry, or apple cider."

Bettina's brow furrowed. "What is a mojitarita?"

"It's a combination of a mojito and a margarita. You have the tequila from the margarita and the mint from a mojito."

"I think I'd like the strawberry."

Kayana was busy mixing cocktails, while Graeme became her assistant and handed her the ingredients for the drinks. Cherie shared a smile with Parker when he came over to stand next to her.

"I see why my cousin is so taken with you," he said in her ear.

Cherie smiled up at the solidly built man, looking for some resemblance between him and Reese, and could not find any, despite their sharing DNA. His khaki-brown complexion was dotted with a light sprinkling of freckles, and his light-brown eyes were friendly. There was something about his round face that made her think of him as a teddy bear. However, she knew her assessment of him was quite the opposite of reality, because Reese had mentioned he ran the sheriff's department as if he still were a Marine Corps drill sergeant.

"I happen to like him a lot, too," she whispered.

Parker put a can of beer to his mouth and took a deep swallow as he stared at Cherie over the rim. "My cousin has survived a lot of losses in his life, so please don't hurt him, Cherie."

She went still and met the eyes, which were now anything but friendly. "What makes you think I'll hurt him?"

Cupping her cupped her elbow, Parker led her out of the kitchen and into the dining area. "Reese is not one to open up about his feelings, but when I asked him about you, he didn't hold back."

Cherie's respiration quickened as she felt her heart rate tick up. "What did he say? Are you or aren't you going to tell me?" she asked when he hesitated.

Parker stared at something over her head. "He's falling in love with you. And it's only when you're in love that you become vulnerable."

Her gaze narrowed as her hands fisted. "What makes you think I'm going to hurt him?"

"I don't know," Parker admitted.

"Then why mention it?" Cherie struggled not to lose her temper. She resented Parker's interference, wondering if he'd said what he did to sabotage his younger cousin's relationship. And if that was his intent, she wanted and needed to know why.

"I'm just trying to look out for my cousin."

"Really? In case you haven't noticed, Reese happens to be an adult capable of looking out for himself. And I resent your interference."

Parker's broad shoulders slumped. "I'm trying not to interfere, Cherie."

She bit her lip and counted slowly to five. "Pray tell, exactly what *are* you attempting to do, because right now you're giving me double messages. Are you saying that you don't want me involved with your cousin?"

"No, I'm not saying that."

"Then what is it?" she spat out. Cherie's frustration with the chief of the sheriff's department escalated when he didn't answer her question. "I'm going to say this once, and then I never want you to approach me again with this nonsense. Reese isn't the first man in my life, and right now, I can honestly say I would like him to be the last one." She wanted to say *bullshit* rather than *nonsense*, yet knew that would make a bad situation worse.

Parker crossed his massive arms over his chest. "You really don't bite your tongue, do you?"

"You just don't know the half," she retorted. The man didn't know she'd tried to keep her resolution to pause and think before allowing something nasty to come out of her mouth. Bitter, cutting words, once spoken, could not be retracted. She forced a saccharine smile when Reese joined her and Parker.

"It's nice to see you two getting acquainted," Reese said as he looped an arm around her waist.

Cherie's smile didn't slip when she said, "Your cousin and I were just discussing a few things."

Parker took another swallow of his beer. "I must say our conversation has been very interesting."

"Yes, it has," she confirmed. "Reese, can you please get me something to drink?"

He dropped a kiss on her hair. "What do you want?"

A beat passed. "That's okay. I'll get it myself."

"No, bae. You can stay and continue your conversation with Parker."

Cherie wanted to tell Reese there was nothing more she wanted to discuss with his cousin. "That's okay. I think we've said enough."

Reese stared at Cherie's back as she walked in the direction of the kitchen. He'd felt the tension in her body when he'd put his arm around her waist. "What did you say to her, Parker?"

"I just told her not to hurt you."

"Why in hell would you tell her that?"

"Because I can recall how devastated you were when you broke up with Monica. Do you remember when you told me you wanted to leave the army? And I had to talk you out of it because you'd gone through hell to make it through the training to become an Army Ranger."

"For your information, I didn't break up with Monica. She broke up with me when she admitted she wasn't cut out to be a military wife."

"Why didn't you give her the option of not living on the base?"

"It was more than that."

"How much more?" Parker questioned

"She didn't want to be married, and she didn't want children."

Reese told his cousin the details behind his failed marriage, seeing an expression of shock freeze Parker's features. When he'd returned home on leave without Monica, he'd told everyone a half truth, that he and Monica had grown apart and that he had filed for divorce. He hadn't wanted his grandmother's prediction to manifest itself. When he'd initially refused to agree to a divorce, Monica had gone to his superior officer to accuse him of rape after she'd refused to have sex with him. He'd been summoned to a meeting with the top brass, and he was forced to reveal everything going on in his marriage. He'd managed to convince them he wasn't on the base during the date and time of the alleged rape, and was ordered to put in for a leave and get his personal life in order before returning for duty.

"Why didn't you say that before?"

"Because it was none of your business," Reese countered. "What goes on between a man and his woman in their relationship is none of anyone's business."

"You're right, Reese. I'm sorry."

"It's a little late for an apology. But make this your first and last time you get into my personal business."

"Okay." Parker drained the can. "I think I'm going to need something a little stronger than a beer."

Reese watched Parker walk away. He could not understand what had made him warn Cherie about something that had nothing to do with him. And what upset Reese was that Parker was a guest in Cherie's home. He wanted to remind his cousin that this wasn't the station house, where he gave orders and could expect them to be followed without question. He loved Parker like a brother, had always looked up to him, and knew he was trying to protect him, but what his cousin didn't understand was that he didn't need protecting.

Now Reese regretted telling him that he was falling in love with Cherie.

He loved everything about her and knew that, if she'd told him she suspected she was pregnant, he would've proposed on the spot. What he didn't want was a repeat of what his mother had gone through when she discovered she was pregnant. Not only hadn't she known the father of her baby, but she'd been too ashamed to tell her mother that she was going to be a grandmother until after she'd given birth to a son. And Sondra knew that, even if she disappointed her mother, because she was expected to graduate college, her mother would never reject her grandchild.

Reese realized Parker wasn't the only one who needed a drink. He returned to the kitchen to find Cherie laughing at something his cousin had said to her. Going on tiptoe, she kissed Parker's cheek. Reese also smiled. It was apparent they'd worked out their differences.

Cherie lay in bed with Reese, smiling. She knew she couldn't accept all the accolades for the success of the first social gathering in her home, because it never would've happened if she hadn't had her book club buddies to help her. Yes, she'd contributed a few appetizers, but it was Kayana's Mexican-inspired dishes and Derrick bringing over a tray of Creole chicken wings that made it a true, quintessential Super Bowl party with wings, beer, and guacamole. Reese and Parker had contributed two dozen bottles of assorted spirits, including several bottles of champagne that she'd stored in the pantry.

Her initial misunderstanding with Reese's cousin was defused when he apologized to her for overstepping. She'd accepted his apology because if she was going to continue to date Parker's cousin, she wanted to do so without any hint of acrimony between them. After all, blood was thicker than water, and she didn't want to become a source of contention between the two men.

Even Andy Wilson morphed into party mode after a few drinks and had shocked Bettina when he urged her to sit while offering to bring her a plate. Cherie realized he'd been shamed into waiting on his wife when Graeme told him that if the women cooked, it was incumbent for their men to serve them. And she had to admit that Bettina's contribution of sausage and peppers was phenomenal; she had gone back for a second helping before all of them were gone.

"What are you thinking about, bae?"

Cherie shifted on her side and rested her arm over his flat belly. After he'd dropped Parker home, he'd returned to her house to help with the cleanup. He'd admitted to her that his cousin wasn't much of a drinker; after downing a couple of margaritas, he was two sheets to the wind.

"The Super Bowl party was a rousing success. Thank you for helping out."

Reese wound his fingers in her unbound hair. "The kudos go to you and your book club sisters. And I can't believe there weren't any leftovers."

"Because of you, Parker, Derrick, Graeme, and Andy eating like piranhas, I had to change my mind that Kayana had made too much food."

Reese chuckled. "That's because everything was beyond delicious. And I must give it to Bettina. Her Nona's sausage and peppers were incredible."

"Tell me about it. When I went back for seconds, there was hardly any left."

"I think Andy really enjoyed himself."

"That's because after he'd had a couple of drinks, he was able to shed some of his inhibitions and get down with the get down. Did you see him dancing in his seat during the halftime entertainment?"

Reese laughed again. "I did. I think the man needs a hobby or a part-time gig because I don't believe he's adjusting well to retirement."

"Wasn't he a teacher?"

"Yes. He was the technology teacher at the high and middle schools. If there was a problem with a computer, you just had to call Mr. Wilson, and he'd solve it in a matter of minutes."

"Maybe he should advertise in the *Clarion* that, as an IT specialist, he's available to troubleshoot and fix computers."

"That's a wonderful idea," Reese said. "Why don't you approach him about it?"

"No, Reese. The man's a chauvinist, and it would sound better coming from you now that you're besties."

"We're not besties, Cherie."

"Well, you two seemed to have a lot to talk about whenever there was a commercial."

"That's because he was my teacher in high school. We were reminiscing about some of his colleagues who were teaching during his tenure."

"And because of that connection, it would sound better if you talked to him."

"I'll think about it. Wait a minute. Are you suggesting this for Andy or for Bettina?"

Cherie kissed Reese's bare shoulder. "Both." She told him about Bettina complaining that she'd become her husband's personal maid since his retirement.

"That's a lot to ask of anyone, especially your wife, if you're not an invalid."

"That's a lot to ask of any woman, even if she's not your wife." Cherie countered.

"I'd never do that to you, Cherie."

"I know you wouldn't, because I'm not the one to wait on a man hand and foot."

"Is that why you broke up with your ex?"

Cherie closed her eyes and exhaled a soft sigh. She still wasn't ready to reveal the circumstances behind the breakup with Weylin. "No. I told you he'd decided to marry someone else."

Reese shifted positions until he was facing her. "What was there about her that made him choose her over you?"

The glow from the table lamp wouldn't allow Cherie to make out Reese's features because his back was to the light. "Money. She had the right pedigree, and I didn't."

"That's crazy!"

"No, it's not, Reese. People from different social classes rarely marry one another. First, they don't circulate in the same social circles, and if a man or woman wants to marry up, they continually must prove their worth. It hadn't mattered that I'd been granted a full academic scholarship to a prestigious prep school and then Yale, because I still was Cherie Renee Thompson from the ghetto, although I could walk their walk and talk their talk."

Reese dipped his head and brushed his mouth over hers. "Their loss and my gain."

She smiled. "Before you turn off the lamp, I want you to open the drawer in the bedside table."

"What's in there?"

"Open it, and you'll see."

Reese untangled their limbs and turned and opened the drawer. "Damn woman! How many condoms did you buy?"

"As many different kinds as I could find. I didn't know which brand you used, so you can have your pick."

Throwing back his head, Reese laughed uncontrollably, and Cherie found it so infectious that she also laughed. That was something she'd rarely done with Weylin once they'd enrolled in college; she had been unaware he'd been conflicted because he was sleeping with one woman while knowing he was expected to marry another.

Reese was right. Losing Weylin was the best thing that had ever happened to her, because the man in her bed had given her a chance to live and love openly, without a hidden agenda.

"I know you have to go to work at eight, so if you get up early enough, I'll make breakfast for you," she said, after recovering from her laughing fit.

Reese turned off the lamp and gathered her close. "Thank you, love."

Chapter 20

February 15

Yesterday was Valentine's Day, and it was the first time I was able to celebrate it in public with a man. Reese had made reservations at an upscale Italian restaurant in Shelby, and after we shared a romantic candlelight dinner, we went back to his house, where he gifted me a gold bracelet with a diamond heart charm. He'd had the charm engraved with our names and the date. My gift to him was a silk tie in a platinum shade that he could wear for a special occasion. I refused to tell him what that special occasion could be, saying he would have to use his imagination. And I know if he'd asked me to marry him, I would've accepted because I love him just that much.

Cherie reread what she'd written. It had been months since she'd written down her thoughts because she was no longer plagued with the angst that had held her captive for so long that she didn't believe she would ever rid herself of it.

She'd fallen in love with Reese Matthews and could imagine herself married to him sometime in the future. Kayana was happily married to Graeme, and Leah and Derrick were talking about getting married sooner rather than later. Leah had finally given up the notion that she wanted to wait a year after becoming a widow to marry again.

Cherie had just capped her pen when her cell phone rang. She glanced at the screen and smiled. It was her mother.

"Hello, Mama."

Edwina's laugh came through the earpiece. "I don't know why I love it when you call me Mama rather than Mom."

"Now you sound like Biggie Smalls when he said he liked it when he was called Big Papa."

"I don't know about Biggie, but I'm willing to admit that I prefer you call me Mama."

"Okay, Mama. How are you?"

"I'm ready to take some time off and head down your way. This cold weather is getting to me. It seems as if we get snow every few days. It's not enough to close schools, but it's what I call nuisance snowfall."

"When are you coming?"

"When do you want me?"

"How much vacation time do you have coming to you?"

"A week, but I'm going to take two. My tips have been good, so I can afford to take the extra days."

Cherie didn't know why, but she felt like crying. She couldn't believe she was going to see her mother again, and this time it would be different from their last encounters. She wanted Edwina to know she could exist in a world that was different from the one she feared leaving.

"I'm going to go online and buy your ticket. You should let me know the date you plan to leave, and I'll also arrange for a car service to pick you up and take you to the airport. You'll fly into Wilmington International, and I'll be there to pick you up."

"Tomorrow. I'm going to pack tonight, and I'd prefer an early-morning flight. Oh, I forgot. Should I pack winter clothes?"

"It's a little cool down here, so bring something warm. And whatever you don't have you can borrow from me. There's an advantage to having a daughter who wears the same size as her mother."

"That's true," Edwina said, laughing. "Text me after you make the reservations."

"Will do."

"Love you, baby."

It was several seconds before Cherie said, "I love you, too."

She ended the call and powered up her laptop to search for flights from New Haven, Connecticut, to Wilmington, North Carolina. Cherie grimaced when seeing the inflated ticket prices, but she would willingly to spend twice that much, because spending the next two weeks with her mother was priceless. It took forty minutes for her book the tickets and reserve a car service to take Edwina to the airport. After she received the confirmations, she sent her mother a text with the information.

Her next text was to Reese.

Cherie: My mother is coming down tomorrow for a couple of weeks. I can't wait for you to meet her.

Reese: That's wonderful. And I can't wait to meet her and let her know she has an incredible daughter and that I love her very much. I'll see you later tonight, and I'll bring dinner.

Cherie: Later.

She had signed off because she didn't know how to respond to Reese's declaration of love. It was the first time he'd admitted he loved her. Then she recalled Parker telling her Reese had confessed to him that he was falling in love with her. It was one thing to tell his cousin and another to admit it to her. But why in a text message?

Perhaps she was overthinking, and whenever she did that, it usually foretold a problem for Cherie. Why couldn't she just accept that the man loved her and leave it at that? Maybe she hadn't turned the corner in her life and completely exorcised the years she'd spent with Weylin, because in her mind she'd continued to make comparisons between the two men. However, she had to admit it wasn't easy to wipe away fifteen years of her life like erasing what had been written on chalkboard. And what had been written was a chronological timeline of her life that had begun at fifteen and ended abruptly at twenty-nine.

Cherie knew she would never escape her past until she told Reese everything. But she would wait until after her mother returned to Connecticut to tell him everything.

Cherie sat between Reese's outstretched legs on the chaise in the family room, watching a cable news channel. He'd stopped by the café earlier that afternoon to pick up dinner. "Have you planned what you want to do with your mother while she's here?"

"Not yet. We have a book club meeting in a couple of weeks, and hopefully she'll still be here for that."

"Why do you say hopefully?" Reese asked.

"I'm praying my mother will like Coates Island enough for her to decide to stay."

Reese rested both hands on her belly. "Well, if she does decide to stay, you have more than enough room in this house for her to live with you."

Cherie glanced over her shoulder at him. "That's not going to happen."

He frowned. "Why not?"

"Because my mother likes being independent. I told her that, if she did move, I would subsidize a rental or even buy her a condo." She felt the tension in Reese's body with her pronouncement.

"You have it like that?"

"If you're talking about money, then yes. I didn't earn a lot of money when I worked for the childcare center, but I have a sixth sense when it comes to investing." Cherie didn't want to tell Reese she hadn't invested nearly fifteen years of her life in a man without earning some dividends. "I'm not saying I'm wealthy, but I can admit that I am quite comfortable."

He smiled. "You never cease to amaze me."

"Would I continue to amaze you if I were predictable?"

"Nah! Being predictable translates into boring."

It was Cherie's turn to freeze when she heard the news correspondent mention Weylin's name. Her eyes were glued to the screen as the candidate who had been chosen by his party to challenge the incumbent president announced that the woman he'd selected as his running mate had dropped out and was being replaced by William Weylin Campbell, the immensely popular and charismatic representative from Connecticut. Cherie prayed that Reese couldn't detect the rapid pumping of her heart against his arm.

"Do you know him?"

"Yes." The single word came out breathless, and she knew she had to pull it together and quickly. "We were at Yale together and shared some of the same classes. When he first ran for elected office, I and some of our other classmates worked as volunteers for his campaign, working the phones and mailing out campaign literature."

"There's no doubt he'll get the female vote, because he looks a lot like Brad Pitt."

Cherie wanted tell Reese that girls fawned over him because of his marked resemblance to the man twice voted Sexiest Man Alive. Weylin was the trifecta: looks, brains, and money. "He's done a lot for his constituents."

"Do you think he has a chance of becoming vice president?"

"I don't know, Reese. That all depends on if his running mate can win the presidency."

"Do you plan to vote for them?"

"Of course."

"Talk about loyalty."

Cherie detected some cynicism in the three words and wondered if he suspected she would vote for Weylin because they had history. Weylin running for national office didn't bother her; she doubted that his opponent would be able to uncover anything about his son because it had been a closed adoption, and Michelle had been successful in shielding her son from public scrutiny.

"He was a friend and classmate, Reese, so why shouldn't I be loyal?"

"You're right, bae. I suppose there will be no sleepovers while your mother's here," he said, changing the topic of conversation.

"Just because she'll be here doesn't mean we can't see each other."

"Cherie, sweetheart. I didn't say we wouldn't see each other. It's just that I wouldn't feel comfortable sleeping with you with your mother down the hall listening to her daughter moaning and groaning when we make love."

Shifting on the chaise, she turned to glare at him. "I don't moan and groan."

"You don't realize that you do. But I have to admit it turns me on."

"Keep it up, Reese, and I'll turn you off."

He lifted her effortlessly and slipped off the chaise. "If this is going to be the last time I make love to you in a while, I intend to make the best of it."

Cherie wrapped her arms around his neck. "It better be good."

"When is it not good, baby?" Reese bent slightly, picked up the remote, and turned off the television.

She kissed his ear. "Let me think about it."

Their coming together was rushed and frantic, as if they had to get it over with before they were discovered. Cherie pushed Reese's hands away when he'd attempted to undress her; she was able to accomplish it in under a minute. She couldn't pull her eyes away from him when he stepped out of his boxer briefs fully erect. There was no need for foreplay, as she felt a rush of moisture bathe the folds of her labia. Never had she been so aroused, so ready to feel Reese inside her.

She didn't have to wait. Reese slipped on a condom and then entered her with a powerful thrust that sucked the breath from her lungs. He had aroused passions she didn't know existed, while shamelessly moaning aloud with the erotic pleasure that took her beyond herself.

Reese was stunned by the pleasure Cherie offered so selflessly, and he never tired of making love with her. Even after ejaculating, he still wanted more. Her warmth, the feel of her silken skin, was a reminder that he wasn't truly alive until he was inside her. Cradling her face, he kissed her mouth until her lips parted and his tongue plunged in and out of her mouth at the same time his hips kept pace. Skin to skin, they'd again become one with each other, and when he felt the walls of her vagina contract around his penis, Reese knew he couldn't hold back any longer. Releasing her face, he buried his against the side of her neck and groaned out his passion as they climaxed together. He collapsed on her body, unable to move, even if his life depended upon it.

"Reese."

"What is it?"

"You're crushing me."

He loathed moving because he didn't want to sever their connection. "Okay. I'll be back as soon as I get rid of the condom."

"I'm going to miss making love with you," Cherie whispered when he returned from the bathroom and got into bed next to her.

"It's only going to be for a few weeks. Once your mother returns to Connecticut, we can always pick up where we left off."

"Now that sounds like a plan."

Reese reached for her hand, threading their fingers together. "Don't you think it's time we begin making plans."

"About what, Reese?"

"About us, Cherie. I'm not a kid, and I know what I want."

"And that is?" she asked.

"You." He heard her intake of breath.

"Are you talking about marriage?"

"Yes. Not now, but sometime soon."

Cherie had waited for years to hear those words from Weylin. They'd spent enough time together, and she wanted him to commit. But the man in her bed wasn't Weylin. He was everything Weylin wasn't and couldn't be. "Can we talk about this after my mother leaves? And I promise to give you an answer at that time."

"Of course. And I don't want to put any pressure on you."

"Then please don't, Reese," she countered. "I'm not going anywhere, and neither are you. I don't want to rush into anything I might come to later regret. You have to know I love you, even if I don't say it."

"You've never said it."

Cherie extracted her hand and straddled his body. Resting her chin on his breastbone, she smiled down at him. "I love you, Reese Matthews, and I'm almost certain that one of these days, I'll become Mrs. Matthews and the mother of your baby."

"Baby? What about babies? I grew up an only child, and I always wanted a brother or sister."

Reese had just given her the opening she needed to ask him about his mother. "You always talk about your grandmother, but never your mother."

"That's because I know so little about my mother. She died a few months after she had me."

Cherie listened intently, struggling not to cry when Reese revealed what his mother had told his grandmother after she delivered a baby boy. "So she never told anyone who fathered her baby?"

Reese closed his eyes. "No. If she'd just met the guy at the party, then I doubt if they were familiar with each other. Off-campus and frat parties are breeding grounds for male students trolling for women to have sex with. I have photographs of my mother, and I look nothing like her, so I assume I resemble my father."

"Did you ever take one of those DNA ancestry tests to see if you're connected to someone you don't know or never met?"

"No. And I don't want to know. Gram and Papa were the best parents a kid could ask for. My grandfather wasn't overly affectionate, but I knew he loved me and would say on occasion that he would walk through hellfire to protect me. I know he was disappointed that his daughter had dropped out of college, but at least he lived long enough to witness my college graduation. I've heard folks say he was never the same after losing his daughter. He stopped attending church services and spent all his free time in the woodshed."

"What about your grandmother?" Cherie asked.

"My Gram was an angel. She was kind, gentle, and sometimes overly affectionate. She was known as a hugger and always had a kind word for everyone except Monica."

"Who's Monica?"

"She was my ex. I'd brought her home on leave to meet my family, and she openly insulted my grandparents when she complained about spending her vacation on Coates Island when we should've gone to the Caribbean."

"She actually said that in their presence?"

"Yup. We were sitting at the dinner table, and when Papa asked her how she liked Coates Island, she didn't even bother to hide her disdain; she said she'd prefer spending the holiday in the Caribbean rather than in a dead-ass town with a bunch of boring-ass folks. Papa got up from the table and walked out, and once I was alone with Gram, she warned me to divorce Monica because she was going to try to ruin my life."

"Did she?" Cherie asked yet another question at the same time she rolled off Reese to lie beside him. Once again, she was shocked by Reese's ex-wife's out-of-control behavior. "If my older brother had brought a girl home and if she'd opened her mouth to say what your ex said, my Grammie would've reached across the table and slapped the taste out of her mouth. My grandmother spoiled the hell out of her grandchildren, but she was old-school and didn't believe in sparing the rod. It was different with my mother; she didn't believe in spanking her children, and that became a source of contention between the two of them."

"Your grandmother spanked you?"

"What she called spanking was one slap on the behind. It never hurt, but we pretended to cry because we knew she would feel bad about punishing her grandbabies."

Reese chuckled. "Did it work?"

"Every time."

"So you guys didn't mind making Grandmama feel guilty about punishing you?"

"Not at the time. It was only after she passed away that I realized how we'd manipulated her. I can honestly say we were good kids who didn't get into trouble like some of the other kids in the neighborhood. We were in the house just before the streetlights came on, and there was a rule that we all had to share meals together. There was also a hard-and-fast rule that we weren't allowed to have kids in the house when no adults were present, and if someone came over to study, we had to stay in the kitchen. The one time my mother discovered that Jamal had invited a girl over to study for an exam and they wound up in his bedroom, all hell broke loose. Mom told the girl to leave and never darken her door again, and then she read Jamal the riot act. Jamal was trying to plead his case that the girl insisted they go his bedroom even though he'd told her they had to stay in the kitchen, but my mother was past listening to reasoning. Her greatest fear was that her sons would get caught up in the cycle of fathering children out of wedlock, like so many other young men in the neighborhood. This girl must have had some fixation with Jamal, because a year later her name was mentioned after he was murdered."

"You think she had him killed because if she couldn't have him, then no one would?"

Cherie took a deep breath, held it, and then let it out slowly. "I don't know. What I do know is that Jamal had begun dating another girl at the high school, and they had enlisted together after they graduated."

"Did this girl's name ever come up in the police investigation?"

"I don't know, Reese. The police came around asking questions, but after a couple of weeks, it was listed as a cold case. It was know nothing, see nothing, hear nothing, and say nothing, and after a while, Jamal Thompson's name was added to the growing list of young men who have lost their lives due to street violence."

"Now I truly understand what you had to do to save your younger brothers."

"Jamal's death hit my grandmother hard, and most folks said she died from grief. Starting a week after Jamal's funeral, Grammie never left her apartment again and barely touched the food my mother left for her. Three months later, she was gone. The death certificate listed her death as natural causes, but I believed she willed herself to die because Grammie literally and figuratively worshipped her first grandchild."

"Life is fickle, Cherie, that's why we have to let the ones we love know they are loved. And I'm glad your mother is coming for a visit, because it must be lonely for her with her children living in different states."

Cherie recalled her mother's complaints, when she told her

she was moving to North Carolina, that her children were deserting her. "I know," she said in a hushed tone. "That's why I'm going to try to convince her to move closer to me."

Reese shifted and rested his head on his forearm. "Do you want to make a bet?"

"What on earth are you talking about?"

"Do you want to bet that, when your mother comes down here, she'll think about relocating."

Cherie turned to face him. "Are you really that sure?"

His smile was dazzling. "So sure that I'm willing to put some money on it."

Cherie ran her finger down the length of his nose, the brilliance of the diamonds on the charm dangling from the bracelet on her wrist catching the light from the table lamp. "Put up or shut up."

"Can you spare a Benjamin?"

She wanted to tell Reese that she'd amassed thousands of hundred-dollar bills. However, that would remain her secret. "I think so. But on one condition."

"What's that, Miss Money Bags?"

"That if you win, you'll donate the money to a worthy cause."

Reese smiled. "I was hoping you would say that, because I happen to be a monthly donor to the Wounded Warrior Project."

"Ego aside, then I wouldn't mind losing." Cherie touched her mouth to his. "I think it's time you try to get some sleep before you go to work." Whenever Reese had to work the late shift, he usually brought over his uniform and gear so he could shave, shower, and get dressed at her house.

"Are you going to sleep with me?"

Cherie sat and pulled the sheet over her breasts. "No. If I go to sleep now, I'll be up all night prowling around the house like a vampire. Besides, I have to leave early to drive to Wilmington to meet my mother's flight."

"What time is she coming in?"

"A little after nine. If her flight is on time, then I'll be able to get back here before I have to go to work." Cherie was glad her mother was coming in on Saturday because that would give them all day Sunday to hang out together.

Reaching over, Reese ran his hand down her back. "Once your mom gets settled, let me know when I can meet her."

"Okay. Now I'm going to go shower in the other bathroom, so I won't disturb you."

"Kiss me before you leave."

Leaning down, Cherie brushed her mouth over his, holding back because she knew their kisses usually ended with them making love.

She slipped off the bed and gathered a change of clothes before walking out of the bedroom, feeling the heat of Reese's gaze on her nude body. Although it'd been weeks since they'd first shared a bed, Cherie still didn't feel completely comfortable walking around without her clothes in front of him.

Reese wanted to meet Edwina Thompson, and there was no doubt her mother would be shocked, because it would be the first time she would get to meet a man with whom her daughter was involved. Whenever Edwina had asked her about boyfriends, Cherie told her she didn't have time for a man, when the truth was that the man she wanted belonged to another woman.

She'd moved to North Carolina to forget one man and start over with another, but now that Weylin was slated to become the running mate for the popular candidate seeking the highest office in the country and would soon begin campaigning, Weylin's name and face were certain to dominate the political news. He'd become a stalker in her mind, showing up when she didn't want or least expected him. And she didn't want to think of him winning the election; then she would have to hear his voice and see his image often over the next four years.

Hopefully, before that time, she would be married and have her own family on which to focus all her attention. Reese wanted to talk about their having a future together, and she'd promised to give him her answer once her mother returned to Connecticut. Barring any unforeseen events, she knew she was more than ready to accept his marriage proposal.

Chapter 21

Cherie spotted her mother as soon as she entered the baggage claim area. She had a wheeled carry-on and a large leather tote, which meant she'd packed light. She waved to Edwina to get her attention.

She hugged her mother. "How was your flight?"

Tiny lines fanned out around Edwina's hazel eyes, and it was the first time Cherie had noticed them. "It was nice. Thankfully, it took off as scheduled. You know I don't like waiting, especially in an airport terminal."

Cherie knew what her mother was talking about. Their flight to Colorado had been delayed twice before takeoff. Edwina had prowled the terminal like a caged big cat, complaining she didn't want to miss her son's graduation.

"Well, you're here," Cherie said, taking the handle of the carry-on. "I'm parked across the street in the lot."

Edwina untied the scarf around her neck. "It's a lot warmer down here than back home."

"It's expected to hit the mid-fifties today."

Edwina unzipped her coat. "I sweated all the way down. It's probably hot flashes."

Cherie glanced at her mother as they walked out of the terminal. "You're menopausal?"

"I have been for a couple of years. The last time I had a flow was a month after I turned fifty."

"Have you seen a gynecologist?"

"Yes."

Cherie wanted to ask her mother if she went for her annual checkups, but then decided to wait until Edwina was open to discuss things and events they would've been talking about all along if they'd kept in touch with each other.

"I see that you changed your plates," Edwina said after she was seated in the SUV.

Fastening her seat belt, Cherie tapped the START button. "I'm now a legal resident of North Carolina."

"Do you like living here?"

"I love it, Mama. No rush, no stress."

Edwina settled back on the leather seat. "My grandmother left the South to escape Jim Crow and for better employment opportunities. Fast-forward ninety years, and her great-granddaughter makes the reverse migration."

Cherie heard an emotion in her mother's voice that sounded like regret. "It's a different time, Mama. It's by choice that I decided to move here, not because I was forced to."

"I know that. I'm not begrudging you for wanting to make changes in your life. In fact, I'm a little jealous of you because I should've done the same after David and Daniel left home."

Cherie pressed her lips together to keep from grinning like a Cheshire cat. Hearing Edwina talk about changing her life meant there was the possibility she would consider moving. "You're still a young woman, Mama, and weren't you talking about going to college?"

"Yes."

"I intend to start grad school next spring, so what if we do it together? You can study for the SAT and then apply to different colleges for an online degree."

Edwina nodded. “That’s something for me to think about.”

“Don’t think too long, Mama. What you have to do is set a goal.”

“Yeah. That I’d like to graduate college before I turn sixty, then become a nurse.”

Cherie accelerated into the flow of traffic and followed the signs that would take her to Wrightsville Beach and then south to Coates Island. “I never heard you talk about nursing.”

Edwina took off her knitted hat. “I’ve always wanted to be a nurse.”

She gave her mother a quick glance before returning her attention to the road. “You cut your hair.” The salt and pepper pixie cut hugged her head.

“Do you like it?”

“I love it, Mama. It makes you look like a young girl.”

“Not quite. I thought about dying my hair, then changed my mind, because I tell everyone that I’ve earned these grays.”

“The gray looks like highlights, and it goes well with your complexion.”

“Your hair is longer than it has been in years, Cherie.”

She fluffed up the loose curls on her nape. Edwina hadn’t known she’d let her hair grow to her shoulders during her pregnancy; after she had the baby, she instructed her stylist to cut off the curls that once were her signature look.

“I’ll probably cut it before the weather gets too hot.”

“You hair looks very shiny. Are you using product on it?”

“No. But I did change my shampoo and conditioner. What did your boss say when you told him you were taking an extra week off?”

“He didn’t like it, but I knew he wasn’t going to fire me because he’s already short-staffed for the late shift. If he wasn’t so damn cheap and paid his workers a little more, he would be able to keep his staff. When he starting complaining about me taking off, I reminded him he was going to save a week's pay, and that the diner wasn't going out of business because I wasn't there."

"It sounds as if you're sick of it," Cherie said.

Edwina sucked her teeth. "I'm more than sick of it."

"I didn't tell you that I'm working part-time in a café so that I can keep busy before I go back to school. I work a couple of hours a day six days a week. And that means you'll be home alone during that time. I'm going to give you a set of keys to the house and my car. Once you're familiar with driving around the island, you can drop me off at work."

"How will you get back?"

"My friends can drop me off."

The sunlight coming through the window and glinting off the bracelet on Cherie's left wrist caught Edwina's attention. "That's pretty."

"What are you talking about?"

"The bracelet on your arm. I've never seen you wear any jewelry except your earrings."

Cherie touched the small diamond stud in her lobe. Her grandmother had given her the earrings as a congratulatory gift when she'd been awarded the scholarship to the prep school. "It was a gift."

"From a man?"

"Yes, Mom. From a man."

"Do you want to talk about him, or he is a secret?"

Cherie's fingers tightened on the steering wheel. Had her mother known she'd had a secret liaison with a man, or was she just probing for information? "He's not a secret. He knows you're coming down and says he wants to meet you."

"How serious are you and this man?"

"Quite serious. We're in love with each other." It felt good for Cherie to admit that to someone—and, even more importantly, her mother.

Edwina clasped her hands in a prayerful gesture. "You

don't know how long I've prayed for you to meet someone who will make you happy. Whether you realize it or not, whenever we used to get together, you'd look so sad, and I wanted to ask you what was going in your life that had made you so unhappy."

"I saw someone for a long time, and I kept hoping it would get better, but it never did, so we decided to break up."

"How long, Cherie?"

"I said a long time, and please just leave it at that," she said defensively. "It's my past, and I'd like it to remain there."

Edwina stared out the side window. "I hope you told your boyfriend about him, because you don't want to start over with someone new while you're still carrying baggage from a prior relationship."

"I told him the truth. That he decided to marry someone else because I didn't have the right pedigree."

Edwina's head swung around. "That's crazy, Cherie. What does family background have to do with anything when you love someone?"

"Apparently everything to some people, Mama! Why do you think I never invited him to come and meet my family? I'm certain if he'd parked his luxury car on the street and come upstairs to the apartment, it would've been stripped and sitting on crates in under fifteen minutes."

"Are you saying you were ashamed of where you grew up?"

"Yes. I was ashamed *and* scared that you were going to bury another son or sons. Why do you think I had Daniel and David stay with me whenever they were out of school? I'm not saying there aren't good and honest people in the neighborhood, but it was the ones who feel they have nothing to lose that have made it a cesspool for crime and drugs. That's why I sent you the money for Christmas because I want you to move to a safer neighborhood."

"I haven't touched a penny of it. I'm going to look for a place as soon as my lease expires."

"When's that?" Cherie asked.

"September, but I plan to stay on until October to live out my security."

"Mama, stop! September is more than six months away, and a lot can happen before that time. Look at Jamal. He was killed days before he was to be sworn into the army. I told you before that if you find a suitable apartment, I'll help you, and I'm willing to cover the remaining months on your lease."

"I didn't have my children so they could take care of me."

"There you go again, Mama, with your false pride. I won't take care of you. I just want to help you out."

"You bought me the car."

"I gave you the car as a birthday gift. And if I offer to pay the remaining months on your lease, I want you to think of it as an early Christmas present."

"I still remember the times when I asked you for money and you gave it to me. But I also can't forget the one time you told me that, if I need money, I should look for one of my baby daddies and hit them up for some cash."

Cherie recalled the incident as if it had occurred the day before, and that had been the last time her mother had called to ask her for anything. "I'm sorry about that. It was rude and uncalled for."

Only hours before her mother called, Weylin had told her he wanted her to become a surrogate for his wife. She'd just completed her first trimester when he dropped the bomb that the baby she was carrying wasn't going to be their love child, but a son or daughter for him and his wife. She hadn't been just angry when Edwina called, but enraged to the point where she'd been totally unreasonable about everything.

"I'm glad you said what you did. It was a wakeup call for me to stop playing cards every weekend where I'd lose more than I'd win."

"Do you still play cards?" Cherie asked.

"No, because I work weekends. I've learned to put myself

on a budget. After I pay rent and utilities and put gas in the car, I add what's left over from my paycheck to my tips and put it in the bank."

Cherie signaled and left the parkway when she saw the traffic sign for Shelby. "What about food?"

"I eat at the diner. I have a dinner break, and one of the cooks will occasionally surprise me with a takeout container."

"How occasionally, Mama?" she teased. "Everyday?"

"There's nothing happening. The man's just trying to be nice."

Perhaps because she'd never seen her mother with a man, Cherie couldn't conjure up that image. However, Edwina was only fifty-two and very pretty, and she could see why men would be attracted to her.

She entered the city limits for Shelby and slowed to allow Edwina to sightsee. "Shelby is our county seat and where we come to shop if we need something sold only in big-box and chain stores."

"You don't have stores on Coates Island?"

"The mainland has stores, and there's only one business establishment on the island side, and that's the Seaside Café."

"What do you do there?"

"I clean up after it closes. They're open from ten to two during the off-season."

"You went to Yale to do maintenance work?"

"Now you sound like an elitist. I'm helping my friends out until I begin classes." Cherie told Edwina how she'd met Kayana and Leah and, through their love of reading, had formed a book club. "They're one of the reasons I decided to move here."

"What's the other reason?"

"You'll see," she drawled mysteriously.

Cherie stood on the porch with Edwina. "Mama, you need to come inside and relax."

"I just want to hang out here just a little longer, then I'll unpack."

She knew her mother was overwhelmed with the beauty and serenity of the view of the beach and the ocean off in the distance. The porch had also become her favorite spot to begin and end the day. The smell of saltwater, the screeching of gulls fighting one another for scraps of food, and the hypnotic sound of the incoming surf had become an aphrodisiac she never tired of.

Edwina pushed away from the railing. "Now I know why you said you feel alive here. It's peaceful and beautiful. You did good, baby."

"Thank you, Mama. Are you ready to eat something?"

"Sure."

"I'm going to show you to your room. If you want to shower or change before eating, just let me know."

"I want to get out of these heavy clothes and change into something lighter. But I do want to shower first."

"Come. The bedrooms are upstairs." Cherie picked up Edwina's carry-on and tote.

Edwina stared at the open floor plan. "How many rooms are in this house?"

"It has four bedrooms and three and a half baths."

"Did you really want a house this big?"

"No. But it was the only one on the market at the time, and I didn't want to wait for one with two or three bedrooms to come up for sale."

Edwina followed her up the staircase. "You've really decorated it beautifully. I had no idea you were this talented because you never invited me to your condo."

Cherie glanced at Edwina over her shoulder. "That's because I was still pissed at you. Whenever we argued, it was about my wanting you to move, and your excuses for why you wanted to stay. After a while, I gave up because I knew I was just wasting my breath."

"You know I didn't want to leave my friends."

"You know those heifers weren't friends, Mama. They saw you as a mark. They were known to cheat at cards, but you didn't believe it because y'all had grown up together and you believed that friends don't cheat friends. And the few times you did win, it was because they let you win. Grammie used to tell you to stay away from them, but for you, it went in one ear and out the other."

"That's over, because I'm working too hard to save money and not turn around and give it away."

"Good for you." Cherie walked into the bedroom where she'd slept before the delivery of the furniture for the master suite. She set the bags near a walk-in closet. "You're in here."

Edwina slowly entered the room. "Did you hire someone to decorate your home?"

Cherie laughed. "No. However, I admit that when I lived in the condo, I did have a decorator give me tips on colors and feng shui."

"Well, it's really working here."

She curtsied. "Thank you, ma'am. Your bathroom is through that door, and the remote for the TV is in the drawer of one of the bedside tables. There are fresh facecloths and towels in the bathroom, along with grooming supplies. Room service is always available, so if there's anything you're missing, just text the front desk, and we'll provide it for you."

Edwina burst into laughter. "You are so silly."

"I'm glad you're here," Cherie said in a quiet tone.

Edwina sobered, her eyes filling with tears. "So am I."

Cherie turned on her heel and walked out of the bedroom, closing the door behind her. She hadn't lied to her mother. She was glad Edwina had come to stay with her—if only for a couple of weeks. They wouldn't be able to make up for the years they'd been estranged, but she hoped and prayed it would signal a new beginning, a time to start over when they could have a positive and rewarding relationship as mother and daughter.

* * *

"Something smells delicious."

Cherie glanced over her shoulder as Edwina walked into the kitchen. "I'm broiling bacon."

Edwina came over to stand next to Cherie. "Can I help with anything?"

"No, Mama. You just sit and let me wait on you." Her mother had taken her advice and had changed into a pair of blue cotton cropped pants and a loose-fitting, blue-and-white-striped blouse.

"Are you sure you don't need my help?" she asked again before covering her mouth to stifle a yawn.

"No. After you eat, you should go to bed and try to get some sleep. I know you had to get up early to catch your flight. I'm going to leave here around one, and I should be back no later than three. The fridge is stocked, and so is the pantry. I'm not expecting any visitors or deliveries, so if the doorbell rings, you don't have to answer the door."

Edwina's eyes grew wide. "Are there break-ins around here?"

"No, Mama. The island is quite safe. Many of the folks who live here are retired and vigilant; they monitor who's coming and going."

"Something like a neighborhood watch."

Cherie laughed. "Yeah. It's something like that. I know you like omelets, so what kind do you want?"

"A Western is okay." Edwina pointed to a device on the countertop. "Are you growing herbs?"

"Yes. That's an AeroGarden. One of my friends gave it to me as a housewarming gift. I just set it up last week, and already I see some of them sprouting. I can't wait for the basil to come up so I can make pesto. My other gift is that crystal fruit bowl on the dining-area table."

"You had a housewarming party?"

"No. They brought over the gifts when I hosted a Super Bowl party. Reese and his cousin brought enough bottles of liquor to last years. I'd rather have mocktails than cocktails."

"I stopped drinking a couple of years ago because I'd wake up depressed and headachy. I can't remember the last time I had an alcoholic drink. But getting back to your herb garden. You've really turned into a domestic goddess. I remember my mother telling you that if you wanted to get a husband, you had to learn to cook."

"Grammie was old-school. Men nowadays cook as well as or some even better than women, and even if they're not chefs, they don't mind being seen in the kitchen."

"Does your boyfriend cook, Cherie?"

"Yes, he does. And quite well." She knew she had to give her mother a little background on Reese before she introduced him. "He was raised by his grandparents after his mother passed away."

Edwina rested a hand on her throat. "Oh, how awful."

"Reese doesn't remember his mother because he was an infant when she was killed in a car crash."

"What about his father?"

Cherie knew her mother had opened a Pandora's box with the topic of fathers. She didn't know hers, and Reese didn't know his. "He doesn't know his father."

Edwina's expression had become a mask of stone. "And you don't know yours."

"And I don't want to know until you're ready to tell me. And if you decide to keep it a secret, that's okay with me. When I moved here, I decided to leave my past behind, and the nagging question about the man that was my father is no longer relevant. Unlike Reese, I do know my mother. I know our relationship hasn't always been warm and fuzzy, but at least we both have been given a chance to try and get it right."

"I told you before, and I'll tell you again that I am so proud of you. You are everything I'd wanted to be but . . ."

"Enough, Mama. We're not going down memory lane and end up crying and souping snot. You know that I cry ugly, and I don't want my friends to think something's wrong when I walk into work." Whenever she cried, her eyes puffed up, and her cheeks were dotted with red blotches.

"Your friends sound like incredible women."

"They are, and so are you. You raised four children who were never arrested or had to go to rehab because of an addiction."

Edwina's expression brightened. "I never thought about that."

"Well, you should, because I don't believe I would've been strong enough to go through what you have. And you're still standing."

"We're still standing, Cherie, because we are descendants of survivors, and I don't ever want you to forget that. My mother preached that to me because her mother had said the same thing to her, and it probably goes back generations."

"I'd better get back to cooking so you can eat."

Cherie sat in the alcove with Edwina, eating a fluffy omelet, crispy Applewood bacon, and buttered wheat toast, and laughing about some of the quirkier characters in their apartment building. She noticed her mother's attempts to suppress her yawns, and after a cup of coffee, Edwina excused herself and went upstairs to rest. After cleaning the kitchen, Cherie exchanged her jeans for a pair of leggings and left a set of house keys on the kitchen countertop for Edwina.

She decided to get to the café more than hour before closing because warmer temperatures always brought out more diners. She entered the restaurant through the rear door and walked into the kitchen to see Kayana slicing brisket.

"You're here early."

Cherie hung her jacket on a hook and slipped a bibbed apron over her clothes. "My mother came down this morning, and I wanted to get a jump on cleaning—"

"What are you doing here?" Kayana said, interrupting her. "Go home and spend time with your mother."

"Who's a mother?" Derrick asked when he entered the kitchen from the storeroom at the back of the restaurant.

"Cherie's mother is in town, and she should be spending time with her instead of hanging out here. By the way, how long will she be here?"

"Two weeks."

Derrick pushed his cap off his forehead. "Now it's time for you to take a two-week vacation."

Cherie's jaw dropped. "When you hired me, there was no mention of a vacation."

"As the co-owner of this venerable establishment, I can make and break the rules. Now, if you don't take off and spend time with your mother, I'll fire you."

"You like saying that, don't you?" she asked Derrick. "I can recall you threatening to fire me after that incident in the parking lot."

"This time I'm going to agree with my brother," Kayana said. "I know you and your mother haven't always agreed on a number of things, so if you're given the opportunity to bond with her, then please do it."

"Now it's two against one," Cherie spat out.

Kayana winked at her. "I've got to have my brother's back or he'll be quick to call me a traitor. If the warmer weather holds, we plan to cook out at his place tomorrow. Why don't you come and bring your mother, and we can have an impromptu book club meeting in the she-shed, which is now equipped with a heating and cooling system."

"Does it have a television and a Bluetooth player?"

Derrick nodded. "Leah was relentless when she said it had to have all the accoutrements of a man cave. But I had to put my foot down when she said she needed a fully stocked bar."

"It's apparent you didn't put it down hard enough," Kayana said under her breath.

Derrick gave her an incredulous look. "What did you say?"

"Nothing. So, Cherie, what do you say we watch your movie selection tomorrow?"

"Yes. What time should we come over?" she asked Kayana.

"Any time after noon. We can watch the movie before we eat, because if we eat and drink before, you know the movie will be watching us rather than vice versa."

Cherie took off the apron and put on her jacket. She was grateful that Derrick and Kayana had given her time off to be with her mother. "I'll see you guys tomorrow."

Cherie crawled into bed with Edwina, and the two laughed uncontrollably as they watched *Tower Heist*. There had been a time when they had shared a bed and bedroom; with five people living in a two-bedroom apartment, space was at a premium. They applauded as if in a theater when the credits rolled up the screen.

"I'm going to bed now. Remember, you're going to meet my friends tomorrow." She kissed Edwina's soft cheek. "Good night."

Edwina smiled. "It's after midnight, so it's good morning."

Chapter 22

The weather cooperated with brilliant sunshine, and the early-afternoon temperatures were predicted to reach sixty. Cherie introduced her mother to Derrick, Leah, Kayana, and Graeme, and she was warmly greeted by the quartet, which she knew surprised Edwina.

Kayana took her arm, steering her away from those who had crowded around Edwina. "Your mother is stunning. I see where you get your beauty."

Cherie blushed. "My mother has always been a head turner when it comes to men."

"There's no doubt about that. My brother and husband are cheesing at her like teenage boys meeting Jennifer Lopez for the first time. It has to be her eyes, and I hope when you Reese have babies, they'll inherit their grandmama's eyes."

"Whoa, Kayana. You're getting ahead of yourself. Reese and I aren't even engaged, and you have us married with children."

"You don't have to be married to have kids, Cherie."

"Well, I'd like to be married," she said firmly.

"Have you talked about marriage?" Kayana questioned.

"Not yet. But I told him we will talk about our future once my mother leaves."

"Are you really thinking about marrying him?"

"Why the twenty questions, Kayana?"

"I'm just asking what everyone has been talking about," she said, lowering her voice to just above a whisper. "The looks you gave each other at the Super Bowl party said y'all wanted us gone so you could be alone together."

Cherie blushed. "Were we that obvious?"

"Yeah! His eyes were eating you up."

"That's because we don't get to see that much of each other because of his crazy work schedule. It changes every two weeks."

"You can solve that problem if you live together."

Cherie shook her head. "I don't think that will solve our problem. I have my house, and he has his."

"You'll have to decide where you want to live. It's going to come down to that once you're married."

"I'll cross that bridge when we come to it. Meanwhile, he's been spending more time at my place than I am at his. Besides, I'd rather live on the island than the mainland."

"Me, too," Kayana agreed. "I grew up here. Fortunately, Graeme had bought property here, so it was a win-win for us."

Cherie knew she would have to bring up the issue of their living arrangements before agreeing to an engagement and or marriage. Having to give up her home was certain to be a deal breaker for her. Living on the island was the reason she'd moved to Coates Island.

"Derrick turned on the heat in the she-shed and set up the TV so we can watch *Live by Night* anytime you want."

"I'm ready." Cherie didn't know why she liked the movie so much when it had been panned by most critics. She motioned for her mother to come with her as they followed

Kayana and Leah out to the rear of the house and a converted garden shed.

Kayana tapped a keypad on the shingled garden shed and opened French doors to the structure, which had been converted into a bedroom, with painted cornflower-blue shutters matching the door frame. The tiny cottage was filled with homey touches and garden accents, plus a hutch displaying items usually found at flea markets or lawn sales. Two Depression-glass vases were filled with green-and-white dried hydrangeas. Wrought-iron chairs, an antique desk, a twin bed with a pale-green wicker headboard, and framed prints of Audubon birds and flowers made it the perfect space to nap and while away the hours doing absolutely nothing.

Derrick had explained that he set up the space as a go-to guest bedroom whenever his teenage daughter, Deandra, had friends and family over. He also had a plumber install a commode, vanity, and shower stall behind the door in the corner next to the wardrobe. But that was before his teenage daughter moved to Gainesville, Florida, to live with his mother and sister. Deandra was now in her first year at the University of Florida.

"It took a while," Leah said as she flopped down on a cushioned chair, "but I was finally able to convince Derrick to buy a club chair that seats two, because we needed more seating."

Kayana shook her head. "It appears as if you do a lot of negotiating with my brother when you want something, Leah."

Leah blushed. "When negotiating doesn't do it, I have to resort to my feminine wiles."

"Yeah, right," Cherie drawled. "I'm willing to bet it was Eve's feminine wiles that got Adam to eat the forbidden fruit, and look where it got him and the entire human race."

Leah scrunched up her nose. "Adam had free will, and if he didn't want to eat the fruit, he should've rejected it. It's the same with me and Derrick. There are times when he does say no, and that's when I don't push the issue."

"Like when you wanted him to install a bar in here," Kayana reminded her.

"I didn't want anything monstrous, just an itty bitty thing with enough room for a few bottles and a shelf for bar accessories."

Cherie noticed a smile tilting the corners of the redhead's mouth. "You went and did it, anyway, didn't you?"

Leah pressed her palms together. "I asked Reese to make one, and he's bringing it over later this afternoon. I'm certain Derrick will read me the riot after everyone leaves, but it will be worth it, because he's not going to tell Reese to take it back."

Cherie felt her stomach muscles tighten when Leah mentioned Reese's name. This was the first time she was hearing that he'd been invited to come to Derrick's house. But she shouldn't be surprised, she realized, because, after all, they'd known him a lot longer than she had. Well, it looked as if her mother would meet Reese sooner than she'd planned.

The movie ended two hours later, and Cherie watched the reactions of her book club friends and was shocked to see that both were moved by the death of the Zoe Saldana character.

"Why did Graciela have to die?" Leah asked, sniffling as she pressed a tissue to her nose.

"I asked myself the same question," Cherie said, "but I think it was because Joe Coughlin had to pay for his many sins."

"Have you read the book?" Kayana questioned.

Cherie nodded. "Yes. And it reads like the movie."

"What I don't understand, Cherie," Edwina said, "is why did Joe Coughlin call himself an outlaw rather than a gangster, because his behavior demonstrated he was indeed a gangster."

"I think he believes he's someone who lives outside the law or legal system, while a gangster is more a mobster and will commit a crime because he's been ordered to do so. Jesse James, John Dillinger, and Bonnie and Clyde were outlaws, while Al Capone and John Gotti were gangsters."

"I think it accurately portrayed race relations in the South during Prohibition, with the KKK's resentment of Joe Coughlin living with a black woman," Edwina remarked.

Leah nodded. "You're right about that, Edwina. But what the writer did was portray all races equally as villains in the film. You had the Irish and Italian mobs, and the KKK. The police chief with the drug-addicted daughter turned evangelist was crooked, and the Cubans in Ybor were running speakeasies and selling illegal booze. Even the Boston police were on the take. And don't forget Emma Gould, who was supposed to be Albert White's girl while she was sleeping with Joe and then betrayed him."

"She only betrayed him once Albert White discovered she was two-timing him," Cherie explained.

Edwina shook her head. "I have to disagree with you, Cherie. Albert White knew Emma was sleeping with Joe all along. He was just waiting for a time to exact revenge. He planned to take Joe somewhere and kill him when Joe's father and the police showed up. Of course, his father had to step aside and allow the police to beat him because he'd been involved in a bank robbery where they'd lost one of their own. And then later in the movie, when Joe discovers Emma isn't dead, she tells him that Albert had put out a hit on her, but she managed to escape and flee to Florida. And although he was married to Graciela, I think he was really crushed when Emma told him that she'd never loved him, that he was just someone with whom to pass the time."

"The male ego can be very fragile," Leah drawled. "And I'm speaking from experience. Joe was so caught up with her so-called passion that he let the other, wrong head think for him. Sneaking around and making love in out-of-the-way places was heady for Joe when he knew he was sleeping with a gangster's woman."

"You're right, Leah," Cherie said. "He got what was coming to him when the cops cracked his head open to the white meat and then was sentenced to serve time in prison."

Kayana laughed along with everyone at Cherie's reference to white meat. "What's the expression? A hard head makes for a soft behind. It was obvious Joe didn't learn his lesson after he was paroled because he went from being an outlaw to a gangster. If I'd taught a course on deviant behavior, I would consider using this film."

"Have you thought about teaching online courses?" Cherie asked Kayana.

"No. Number one, I don't have the time, and secondly, I'm enjoying my life because it comes with so few responsibilities. I know what I have to do at the café, and when I come home, I get to enjoy my downtime with my husband."

"It sounds as if you're living the dream," Cherie said.

"Right now, it feels as if I am. I don't know why the critics panned the movie because it's beautifully shot and in all probability is historically accurate."

Cherie shared a smile with Kayana. "You're right. Following the Great War, there were Irish, Italian, and Jewish gangs all vying for power and money. Which of the characters did you like best and least?"

"I liked Dion Bartolo," Edwina stated, "because he had an infectious swagger that made you want to like him even though he was a cold-blooded killer."

"I have to agree with your mother," Kayana said. "It was hard to take your eyes off Dion because you never knew how he was going to react. I thought the character of Digger Pescatore was the opposite of his mobbed-up father, Maso Pescatore. He was silly, tried too hard to come across as tough, and failed miserably. Maso knew his boy was a joke, and that's why they called him Digger; the only thing he was good for was digging graves to bury their enemies."

Leah pushed her wavy hair behind one ear. "I liked Graciela. She was the only one in the film who came close to possessing a redeeming quality. She knew her brother and Joe had amassed their wealth illegally, yet she wanted to use the money to set up homes for abandoned women and children."

"But isn't it ironic that she was the only one doing good deeds, and she had to die?" Cherie asked. "Meanwhile, the man she'd married was an outright killer and the one responsible for turning the chief's daughter on to heroin when she went to Hollywood for her screen test, in order to blackmail her father into lending his support for him to put up a casino. He lives to raise their son, while his wife is shot to death by the very man he'd blackmailed."

"That's called karma, Cherie," Leah said with a wide grin. "What goes around comes around. I'm glad you recommended this film because I can't wait to read the book. I know we could go on for hours critiquing it, but I think I smell grilling meat, so I suggest we close this meeting and eat."

Cherie returned to the house to find Graeme, Derrick, and Reese in the family room watching a basketball game. Reese stood, along with the other two men. She saw him staring at her mother.

Reaching for Edwina's hand, she waited for Reese's approach. "Mom, this the man I've been telling you about. Reese, my mother, Edwina Thompson."

Edwina extended her free hand, but Reese ignored it and instead dipped his head and kissed her cheek. "I'm Reese Matthews, and I'm honored to meet you."

Edwina lowered her eyes, the demure gesture mimicking Cherie's. "I'm the one who's honored to meet you. And I want to thank you for making my daughter so very happy."

Cherie knew her mother had embarrassed Reese when he averted his gaze. "I didn't expect to see you here until Leah mentioned that you were bringing over a bar table."

"It's a bar cart, and it's in the pickup. I'm waiting for Parker to bring over a drill bit so I can attach one of the wheels. It fell off when I picked it up, and then I discovered I'd misplaced the bit."

"Is Derrick aware that you have it in the truck?"

"He cussed for a while when I called to tell him I was bringing it over, then he calmed down and asked if I wanted to watch the game with him and Graeme."

"And, of course, you said yes," she teased.

"Football is over, so now we're into college and professional basketball."

"And don't forget hockey and baseball."

He smiled. "We still have several weeks before spring training begins for baseball."

"Yo, Reese. When's your cousin going to get here because everyone's ready to eat," Derrick called from the kitchen.

"Don't wait for Parker."

"If that's the case, then everyone grab a plate and dig in."

Reese extended his arm to Edwina. "Mrs. Thompson."

Edwina rested her hand on his forearm over a long-sleeved sweater. "None of that Mrs. Thompson business. Either it's Edwina or Mom."

Cherie shrugged her shoulders when Reese stared at her. What did he expect her to say? If he'd hoped to have any kind of a relationship with her mother, it was up to him establish the ground rules.

"Mom it is," he said after a noticeable pause.

Edwina gave him a warm smile. "I was hoping you would say that."

Cherie followed them into the kitchen, not wanting to believe that her mother was flirting with her boyfriend. She'd admitted to Kayana that men were drawn to her mother not only because of her looks and petite body, but also because of the intelligence she refused to downplay for anyone; there were times when Cherie wondered how far Edwina could've gone if she hadn't dropped out of high school at fifteen to become a mother. The year she'd celebrated her eighteenth birthday, she'd earned a GED several weeks before delivering her second child. Edwina had placed her goal to become a nurse on hold for thirty years, but now that all her children were living their own lives, she could look forward to fulfilling her dream.

Cherie smiled when she saw Reese dip his head to listen to what Edwina was saying. He picked up a plate and filled it with whatever she pointed to. There was no doubt her mother had assumed the role as the fragile, vulnerable, virginal heroine Cherie had read about in her grandmother's romance novels, and it was obvious Reese had been taken in by Edwina's flawless performance.

Dial it back a little, Mama, Cherie thought as she approached the table to pick up a plate.

Leah sidled close to her. "I wonder if Reese is asking your mother's permission to marry you," she whispered in Cherie's ear.

"Why are y'all rushing me to the altar," she whispered back, "when Reese and I haven't talked about marriage?"

"Once you do, I hope you won't have a long, drawn-out engagement."

Cherie rolled her eyes at Leah. She knew her book club friends wanted to see her married, although she didn't feel the need to rush into it. "All I have is time."

"You claim you're over this Wills dude, Cherie, but that's a bald-faced lie. You won't be completely rid of that duplicitous bastard, who still has a home in your head, until you carry another's man name and his baby."

An icy shiver eddied down Cherie's back as she replayed Leah's impassioned statement. She knew she was right. There were times when she did think about Weylin, and now that he'd announced his candidacy for the office of vice president of the United States, he would no longer be a distant memory. But what she feared most was seeing footage of her son and not being able to keep her composure.

"What were you and Leah whispering about?"

Her head popped up when she saw Reese looming above her. Dressed entirely in black, he appeared slimmer, yet more imposing. "We were talking about you and my mother," she said as she moved along the table to fill her plate with grilled chicken, vegetable and shrimp kabobs, and peaches.

Reese reached for a plate and selected two skewers of vegetables and grilled salmon. "What about me and your mother, bae?"

"Y'all seemed rather tight."

"Jealous, sweetheart?"

"No."

"That's good, because you're the only woman who has a lock on my heart."

Cherie knew without a doubt that Reese loved her as much as she loved him. She'd just claimed a seat at the dining room table next to Graeme when Parker walked in. Derrick slapped his back and invited him to sit and eat.

Parker executed a snappy salute. "Good afternoon, good folks. It look as if every time I get together with y'all, there's always food."

"If you're not hungry, you can just leave the drill bit and leave," Reese called out.

"Did I say I wasn't hungry, little cousin?" Parker retorted. He picked up a plate, filled it, and then sat down next to Edwina. Smiling, he extended his hand and introduced himself.

Parker's grin was so wide when he stared at Edwina that Cherie believed she could see his wisdom teeth. Maybe if she'd seen her mother interact with men in the past, she wouldn't have been so taken aback witnessing their reaction to her. As a young girl, she'd noticed men staring and whispering under their breath whenever she and Edwina walked down the street, but her mother always looked straight ahead and pretended they weren't there. She stared at the contents on her plate and smiled. At fifty-two and the mother of three adult children, Edwina still had the ability to turn men's heads.

Graeme asked Cherie about the book club meeting, and she told him they'd watched a movie with a book tie-in, and when she mentioned the title, he admitted he'd read all of Dennis Lehane's books. Cherie was riveted by Graeme's interpretation of the characters, allowing her to see them from a male's point of view. Kayana had revealed that Graeme was an aspiring writer and spent hours a day at the computer, working on several manuscripts that he had yet to complete. She was so engrossed in her conversation with Graeme that she hadn't noticed the interaction between Edwina and Parker until they stood.

"Cherie, I'm going to take your mother on a tour around the island. I promise not to keep her out too late."

She stared at the chief of the island's sheriff department and realized he was serious. He'd just met Edwina and had already appointed himself her tour guide. "Okay." She registered a series of collective soft murmurs when Parker escorted Edwina out of the dining room.

"Well, it didn't take him long to let everyone know he liked what he saw," Kayana drawled.

"Do you think your mother should have a chaperone?" Derrick teased.

Cherie couldn't stop a wave of heat sweeping over her face. "If we can't trust the police, then we really have a problem. Right, Reese?" she asked, giving him a direct stare.

Reese exhaled an audible sigh. "I'm certain Parker will be the perfect gentleman."

He'd been as shocked as the others sitting around the table when Parker offered to take Cherie's mother on a drive, because his cousin was usually indifferent when it came to women. He was aware that Parker had had several long-term relationships, but none of them were serious enough for him to consider marriage. The one time he'd asked Parker about marriage, his cousin admitted he was married to the Corps, and it was a jealous mistress.

A mysterious smile parted Reese's lips. Maybe there was something about the Thompson women that he and Parker were helpless to resist. And he couldn't blame his cousin if he found himself enthralled with Edwina, because it was the same with him and Cherie.

He sat across the table watching her with Graeme Ogden, and Kayana's husband appeared totally engaged with her and their conversation. Reese had asked her if she was jealous of the attention he'd paid to her mother, and if she were to ask him if he was jealous seeing her in deep conversation with another man, his answer would've been a resounding yes.

His gaze lingered on the bracelet on her wrist. It had taken him more than a week to think about what to give her for Valentine's Day. He wanted to give her a ring, but dismissed that notion because he hadn't wanted to send the wrong message. And the other problem was he didn't know her ring size. When he asked the local jeweler for ideas, the man had suggested the bracelet and charm.

Picking up a glass of sweet tea at his place setting, he emptied it and then pushed back his chair. "Leah, I'm going to get the bar cart and put it in the shed for you."

"You're the best," Leah crooned.

Derrick grunted. "There's nothing else you can put in that shed because it's beginning to look like a hoarder hut."

"Not if I contract with Reese to expand it," Leah countered.

Reese threw up both hands. "I'm sorry, Leah. I'm booked up with other projects that will take months to complete."

Leah blew Derrick a kiss. "I think I'm good now."

"You should be," her fiancé mumbled.

The last thing Reese wanted was to become embroiled with the couple's disagreement. He needed his focus to be on his own relationship with a woman who occupied his thoughts day and night.

Chapter 23

"Why the long face, bae?"

Cherie and Reese sat on the porch, watching the sun sink lower and lower toward the horizon before it disappeared altogether, leaving streaks of orange and purple hues across the darkening sky. "I can't believe I took two weeks off from my job and I haven't been able to spend one full day with my mother."

"Does it bother you that she has been spending so much time with Parker?"

"Yes and no," she replied. "My mother and I haven't been particularly close for a while, and I thought having her visit with me would improve that. But I had no idea your cousin would take off from his job to occupy all her time."

Reese stretched out his legs, crossing his feet at the ankles. "When I asked Parker about him and Edwina, he said he found her fascinating, and that she was the first woman whom he thought of as a friend."

"A friend or girlfriend?" Cherie questioned.

"He said friend, Cherie. And I left it at that."

Parker had usually come to the house early in the morning to pick up Edwina and drove her back later that night, most times after Cherie had gone to bed. She knew she had no right to question her mother about her comings and goings, because Edwina was an adult capable of making her own decisions, and it had been apparent she enjoyed Parker's company enough to see him every day. The chief had even volunteered to drive Edwina to the Wilmington airport for her return flight.

Cherie closed her eyes and rocked back and forth, and hoped she hadn't overreacted when it came to her mother. If she'd changed since moving to Coates Island, so had Edwina during her brief stay. Edwina had hinted that there was a possibility she was considering leaving Connecticut. Cherie didn't want to read more into Edwina's statement, and then realized it wasn't her daughter, but a man that was influencing the older woman's decision.

She didn't know Parker, and her initial interaction with him hadn't been positive when he'd attempted to insinuate himself into her relationship with Reese. However, he did apologize, which she'd accepted. Now he was at it again, this time with her relationship with her mother.

"You promised we would talk about our future after your mother left."

Cherie opened her eyes and smiled. "Yes, we did. What do you want to know?"

"I love you, Cherie, and I want to marry you, so I need to know if this is what you also want."

"I want the same thing you want, but I need time to take in everything."

Reese leaned forward. "Time for what?"

"I'd like for us to continue to see each other before announcing an engagement."

"When do you want that to happen?"

Cherie bit her lip, counting back to when she first saw Reese. "June."

Reese flashed a white-tooth smile. "That sounds reasonable. What about marriage?"

A beat passed. "Next year on Valentine's Day."

He nodded. "That's also doable."

She exhaled an audible breath. "There's something else we need to discuss."

"What's that?"

"Where we're going to live after we're married. I just bought this house, and I don't want to sell it."

Reese reached out and covered her hand resting on the arm of the rocker next to his. "You don't have to sell your house. I can move in here with you."

"What are you going to do with your home?"

He smiled. "I'll ask Parker if he's willing to move in. Right now, he's renting a small house on the mainland."

"Do you think he wouldn't mind moving?"

"Are you kidding? Parker and his family used to come to our house every week for Sunday dinner and family reunions. I was still a young kid, but I remember that, whenever Parker came home on leave, we would have a fish fry in his honor, because there was a time when Parker would only eat fish. Gram said she wanted to call him Shrimp, but he was too large for that moniker, so he became Crab."

Cherie sighed in relief. She and Reese had solved the dilemma of where they would live as a married couple. She still was in awe of how smoothly her relationship with Reese was going. This is not to say they agreed on everything, but when they didn't, they were able to discuss it rationally. They'd settled when they would announce their engagement and had confirmed a wedding date and where they would cohabitate. The only issue left was children—if or when they would start a family.

Cherie knew she also had to select a college from a list she'd researched and forward the necessary transcripts for acceptance. She had a lot on her plate for the coming year: engagement, marriage, and college.

Cherie sat on the chaise in the family room watching the national news when a BREAKING NEWS alert flashed across the screen. She sat riveted, unable to move or breathe when the anchor announced that the wife and son of vice-presidential candidate William Campbell were killed when a private jet crashed during a flight from Connecticut to the Caribbean; the two were en route to vacation with the candidate and other family members.

Cherie heard a scream and realized it had come from her because there was no one else in the house with her. Tears streamed down her face as she cried without making a sound. Her son was gone. The woman who had claimed him as her own was also gone.

She didn't know how long she'd sat, staring with unseeing eyes at the television screen. Minutes became more than an hour when Cherie finally got up and turned off the TV. It wasn't until later the following morning that text messages on her cell phone chimed in rapid succession. They were from her former Yale classmates, sending condolences for Weylin. There were questions about funeral services, and their class president wrote that he would contact Weylin and let everyone know if there would be a funeral or a memorial service.

A week later, on a cold rainy day in late March, Cherie found herself back in Connecticut to attend a memorial service for William Weylin Campbell III's wife and young son. The Campbells had decided on a private funeral and had opted to hold a memorial service for family and close friends.

It was the first time Cherie had been inside the Campbell family mansion, and she knew it would be the last. Her legs nearly buckled when she saw the blown-up images of Michelle and her son resting on easels. The boy Weylin and Michelle had named Elijah, after his mother's grandfather, had been an incredibly beautiful child. He'd inherited Cherie's dark hair, and his large round eyes were a shimmering blue-gold that complemented his tawny-brown complexion.

She couldn't believe how cruel life had been to her. She hadn't seen or held her baby when he drew his first breath, yet she was given the opportunity to see him in death. Reaching for a tissue, she dabbed the corners of her eyes. *Rest in peace, baby boy.*

When she'd gotten the information for the memorial service, her first impulse had been not to attend, but Reese had encouraged her to go. He told her it was the least she could do for her friend, who needed the support of his former classmates. She'd made a reservation to fly into New Haven and stay overnight at a hotel before flying out the following afternoon.

"You came."

Cherie went completely still when she recognized the voice of the man who had been so inexorably a part of her life that he'd shaped her into someone she hadn't wanted to become. Turning around, she stared up at Weylin, seeing grief in his eyes and etched around his nose and mouth. It was obvious he was taking the loss of his wife and son hard.

"Yes, Weylin, I came because it was the proper thing to do. That's what friends do. Support one another in their grief."

He leaned closer. "What do you think of *our* son?"

"He's not my son," she whispered. "He stopped being that when I signed that contract giving him to you and Michelle. And I'm sorry for your loss."

Those were the last words she said to the man she'd once loved unconditionally, and she walked out of the house. She tapped her phone to hire a car service to take her back to her hotel.

Reese had noticed the difference in Cherie when she returned to Coates Island. The smiling, light-hearted woman he'd fallen in love with was now replaced with one who rarely smiled, and when she did, it resembled a grimace. He knew she was grieving because she'd also shared several classes with the politician's wife.

He knew what she was going through because he'd attended his share of military funerals, and they were something he knew he would never forget. It had taken him weeks, if not months, to stop dreaming about them. The one time he woke up screaming at the top of his lungs, Reese knew it was time to leave the military.

Reese noticed the most profound change in Cherie on Mother's Day. She refused to see him, saying she needed some alone time. He nearly lost his temper because he felt she was spending too much time alone, but he honored her wish and stayed away for the next week.

Cherie woke one morning and scrambled out of bed and raced to the bathroom to purge her stomach. Once she began vomiting, she couldn't stop until she collapsed on the floor. She couldn't remember what she'd eaten to make her so sick and wondered if she'd picked up a stomach virus. She brushed her teeth and rinsed her mouth with a minty mouthwash and went back to bed. When she woke hours later, she sent Reese a text that she wasn't feeling well, and that he should stay away because she suspected she had picked up a stomach bug.

* * *

Reese parked his cruiser in the driveway and rang the bell to Cherie's house. He'd been troubled by her text. Yes, she'd been acting strangely, and he thought it was the result of losing her college friend, yet he didn't want to believe there was something physically wrong that she didn't want to tell him about.

He noticeably recoiled when she opened the inner door and he saw her face. There were dark circles under her eyes, which appeared haunted. "Open the door, Cherie."

She shook her head, the profusion of black curls moving with the motion. "No. I don't want to get you sick."

"Open the damn door, Cherie, or I'll kick it down!" He must have gotten through to her, since she complied. "How are you feeling?"

"How the hell do you think I'm feeling? I told you I have a stomach virus."

"Did you go to the doctor?"

"Not yet."

"When, Cherie?"

"When I'm feeling better." All the brown hues in her eyes were replaced by streaks of gold and green, indicating she was angry. "Now will you please leave?"

Reese shouldered his way into the house. "No. I'm going to fix something for you to eat, and then I'm going to call a doctor to make an appointment for you to see him."

"I told you before I'll see one when I'm feeling better."

"You won't need a doctor when you're feeling better. You need one now."

Cherie felt too exhausted from barfing a second time that morning to get into a debate with Reese. He was in full uniform, and that meant he was on duty. "Okay. You can make some soft scrambled eggs, and hopefully I'll be able to keep that down."

Reese followed her into the kitchen. "When did you start throwing up?"

"This morning."

"Maybe you're pregnant."

"Very funny. You know I get my period every month. And after that first time, we've always used protection."

"I was just thinking it may be a possibility."

"Keep thinking."

Reese intimating that she might be pregnant made her recall the time when she was pregnant. Since she'd first begun getting her period at twelve, it came on time like clockwork, and the first time she'd missed it, she'd known for certain she was pregnant without taking a home pregnancy test or having it confirmed by a doctor. She experienced morning sickness for the first three months, and then it went away completely.

Reese removed his gun belt, leaving it on a chair in the alcove, and washed his hands before taking out several eggs and bread. He quickly scrambled the eggs and made dry wheat toast and set the plate before her at the breakfast bar.

"I'm going to make you some tea; maybe that will help settle your stomach."

She smiled. "Thank you." Cherie ate everything on her plate and drank a cup of tea, which did make her feel better.

Reese kissed her forehead. "Go back to bed. I'll clean up here."

Cherie didn't know why, but she felt like crying, something she'd rarely done in the past. Maybe falling in love had made her vulnerable, and she remembered what Parker had told her the day of the Super Bowl. *And it's only when you're in love that you become vulnerable*. Not only had she fallen in love with Reese, but she loved him unconditionally. He was everything she wanted and needed in a partner for the rest of her life.

"I love you," she whispered.

"And I love your life," Reese said, before kissing her forehead again. "I'll text you later to see how you're feeling. And if you need something, I want you to call me. Promise?"

She nodded. "Yes, I promise."

The next day, Cherie did feel better when she saw her menses, but still decided to make an appointment with a gynecologist for a checkup. The receptionist gave her an appointment for the following week, two days before the start of the Memorial Day weekend and the beginning of the Seaside Café's summer hours. Now, with the café opening seven days a week, she would no longer have a job because of the return of the restaurant's summer help.

She filled out the necessary paperwork and gave a urine sample before a nurse took her vitals and then drew blood. Then she was led into a dressing room, where she exchanged her street clothes for a gown that revealed more than it concealed.

Cherie was sitting on an examining table when the doctor walked in with a nurse. "I'm Dr. Phillips, and I've scheduled a sonogram to determine how far along you are."

"Far along? What are you talking about?"

"You're pregnant, Ms. Thompson. I know you indicated you haven't missed your period, but there are some women who have their menses throughout their pregnancy, and in your case, I need to know when you may have become pregnant."

Cherie closed her eyes. "We had unprotected sex one time in January, but not since that time." It was now the end of May, which meant she had to have completed her first trimester.

He flipped through pages in her file. "You indicated this is not your first pregnancy. Did you experience similar symptoms then?"

She shook her head. "No, the first time I missed my period, I knew I was pregnant."

"Not all pregnancies are the same, so I want you to lie back on the table, and a technician will conduct the sonogram."

Cherie drove back to Coates Island, attempting to process what she'd gone through in the doctor's office. The sonogram indicated she was pregnant, and her estimated due date was mid-October. The doctor faxed a prescription to the pharmacy on Coates Island for a three-month supply of prenatal vitamins and gave her an appointment to return the following month.

She picked up the prescription from the pharmacy and went home. It took more than two hours for her to work up enough nerve to tell Reese she had to see him. He sent a reply that he didn't get off until midnight and would come by then.

Cherie opened the door when she heard his pickup pull into the driveway. The familiar scent of bodywash wafted to her nostrils when he walked into the entryway. "Hey, you," he crooned before he lowered his head to kiss her.

"Hey, yourself," she whispered against his mouth. "Come with me into the family room because I have something to tell you."

Reese held her hand. "Why do you sound so mysterious?"

"Because what I have to tell came as a shock to me." Cherie sat on the love seat, and Reese's body's followed hers down. She took a deep breath. "I went to the doctor today, and he ran some tests."

Reese's hand tightened on hers. "What is it?"

She heard a tremor in his query. "I'm pregnant." Cherie felt her heart stop and then start up again when he closed his eyes and slumped against the back of the leather sectional.

"Are you certain?"

"Very certain. I had a sonogram and saw the baby. I'm at least four months along."

Reese released her hand and put his over his mouth. "So I wasn't that far off the day you were hurling your guts out when I joked about you being pregnant."

"No. I still don't believe it because I never missed my period."

"You know what this means, Cherie? We'll have to skip the engagement and get married as soon as possible."

"Hold up, sport. I thought we decided we would talk about this."

"We are talking."

"No, we aren't, Reese. You're telling we must marry next month. Don't I have any say in this?"

"Weren't you the one who said you had to be married before you had a baby. Now is your chance."

"Why do you make it sound as if you're doing me a favor?"

"Am I?"

"Yes, Reese, you are. Let's wait until next week before we discuss this again. I haven't even told my mother that she's about to become a grandmother."

Reese nodded. "Okay, bae. Whatever you say. Meanwhile, I want you to take it easy." He rested a hand over her flat belly. "Remember, you're carrying around precious cargo."

"Okay." She wanted to remind him that, despite her condition, she hadn't had to modify her daily activities. "It looks as if I bought all those condoms for nothing," she teased.

Dropping an arm over her shoulders, Reese pulled her into an embrace. "You can't imagine how much I love you."

"I think I can."

He pushed to his feet and swept her up in his arms. "It's time for Momma to go to bed and get her rest."

As Reese undressed Cherie, he looked for the obvious signs that she was pregnant, but didn't find any. Her breasts weren't fuller, and her stomach was still flat. He'd heard stories about women carrying to term without realizing they were pregnant. Perhaps Cherie was one of those women. Sitting on the side of the bed, he bent over and kissed her belly. The shock that he was going to be a father still hadn't sunk in, and he didn't care whether he had a son or daughter. He just wanted it to be healthy.

It was only after Cherie told him she'd informed Edwina that she was going to become a grandmother that Reese felt it was the appropriate time to tell Parker that he and Cherie were expecting a baby. He'd begun sleeping at her house every day and spent time at his home on his days off to work on the bookshelves for her office. His next project included designing baby furniture. He had to talk to Cherie about turning one of the guest bedrooms in her house into a nursery and storing the queen or twin beds in the attic at his house for future use.

He was relieved that she'd stopped working at the café and was now devoting her free time to planting flower, herb, and vegetable gardens in the backyard. They still hadn't decided on a date for their wedding, and Reese had to constantly remind himself that Cherie wasn't going anywhere, and neither was he.

When he'd gone into the café to pick up lunch for Miss Elizabeth and himself, Kayana had pulled him aside to congratulate him on his impending fatherhood. It stood to reason that Cherie would tell her book club friends about her condition.

He'd utilized the backyard kitchen for the first time, and it felt good not to heat up the house now that the average daily temperatures peaked around eighty-five degrees. After dinner, he and Cherie walked along the shore, then returned to the house to use the outdoor shower to wash off the sand.

It was mid-afternoon, and Reese had just started up the staircase to get dressed for his four-to-midnight shift when the doorbell rang. He reversed his steps and walked to the door, hoping it wasn't Bettina Wilson. The woman had had the audacity to ask if he and Cherie were living together, and he knew he'd shocked her when he told her they were experimenting to see if they could get it right.

He opened the door and froze as if he'd been impaled by a sharp object. The man standing on Cherie's porch was William Campbell, and behind him two men who were obviously Secret Service.

"Is this Cherie Thompson's residence?"

You know it is, otherwise you wouldn't be here, Reese thought. "Yes, it is. May I ask who's calling?" he asked, even though he knew exactly who he was.

"Tell her it's Weylin. She'll recognize the name."

"Who do you think you are coming to my home? And how did you find me?"

Reese turned to find Cherie standing only a few away. He knew she was upset because her hands were shaking. "Should I leave?"

"No," she spat out. "But I want him to leave," she said, pointing at the man in the doorway.

"I'll leave, but there's something I'd like to say to you. Please, hear me out." He turned to say something to the two agents, and they stepped back. Weylin removed his sunglasses, and he gave Cherie a long, penetrating stare. "May I come inside?"

"You have five minutes," Cherie said.

Reese opened the door, and the smartly dressed man with perfectly cut blond hair stepped into the entryway. He glanced at the watch on his wrist. "Your five minutes starts now."

Cherie didn't want to believe Weylin had shown up at her home without warning her he was coming. And she didn't want to listen to anything he had to say, because they'd agreed what now seemed eons ago that whatever they'd had had ended when she handed over her baby.

He flashed the smile that at one time she hadn't been able to resist. "I work for the government, so it was easy enough for me to find your address." His smile faded. "I want to thank you for coming to the memorial service, but you left before I could tell you that."

"You've just told me. Now please leave."

Weylin pointed to Reese. "Are you involved with this man?"

"That's none of your business."

"Does he know we have history?" Weylin continued. "Does he know that you had my baby, and that if circumstances had been different, I would've married you instead of Michelle. That every time I made love to my wife, in my mind it was you that I was making love to." He paused. "Now that my wife and your son are gone, I'm proposing we start over. I'll wait a year, and then announce that I'm marrying a friend from our college days, and together we can become a new power couple. We'll have more children—"

"Get the fuck out my house!" Cherie screamed. "And if you attempt to contact me again, I'll go to the press and tell them everything, Mr. Wannabe Vice President." She walked over to the door and opened it. "Get out!"

"Your five minutes are up," Reese warned in a low tone that indicated he was quickly losing patience.

Weylin turned and walked out, and Cherie slammed the door and locked it. She looked at Reese, and he stared at her as if she were a stranger. "I'm sorry, Reese."

"So am I, Cherie. I told you that lying to me was a deal breaker."

"I didn't lie to you."

"Why couldn't you tell me that you'd been involved with that piece of shit? He's lucky I didn't kick his ass, because he felt his privilege gave him the right to show up unannounced and attempt to pick up where he left off with you."

"There's no picking up, Reese. I walked away from him more than five years ago, and I never looked back."

"Well, it looks like you left quite an impression on him because he wants to marry you and have more children."

"Where are you going?" Cherie asked, when he turned on his heel.

"Upstairs to get dressed so I can go to work. I think we both need some alone time to figure out how we're going clean up this shit show.

Chapter 24

Cherie sat on the porch, watching rain come down in torrents. A weather depression had stalled out in the Atlantic Ocean, bringing wind and rain that had been falling steadily for three days.

Reese was right about a shit show. And Leah and Kayana were also right when they suggested she tell Reese about her affair with Weylin. Well, now it was out in the open, and it had become a waiting game of who would blink first.

She knew she would've eventually opened up about her past, but it never seemed to be the right time. And now, in hindsight, she was glad they hadn't married because it would have been more emotionally devastating to have her husband leave her before she delivered their baby. Now, she'd resigned herself to be a single mother, like millions of other women all over the world. She had the resources to take care of herself and her child without child-support payments.

It had been three weeks since Reese had walked out of her house, and she had grown used to not seeing him or hearing his voice. He did send her a text or direct message every day, asking if she needed something, and she had yet to reply because there wasn't anything she needed from him that she couldn't get from her friends. She told Leah and Kayana that Weylin had come to Coates Island and that Reese had witnessed the exchange between her and the politician and about his reaction to her former lover.

As Leah had predicted, Edwina lost her shit when Cherie told her about her affair with Weylin, and she had to make her mother promise never to breathe a word to anyone because she had been a willing participant in everything that had happened between them. The exception was his ruse as to why he wanted to get her pregnant.

The sound of a car's approaching engine brought her to her feet. It was a taxi from Shelby, and Cherie was overwhelmed with emotion when she saw her mother emerge from the car. Her tears mingled with the falling rain as she walked off the porch to meet her. She hadn't known how much she needed her mother until that moment.

"Thank you, Mama. Why didn't you let me know you were coming?"

Edwina smiled. "I wanted to surprise you. And, this time, I'm staying long enough to hold my grandbaby boy or girl."

"You quit your job?"

"Hell, yeah. That cheap bastard tried to short me a day's pay, and I told him I was out."

"Good for you. What about your apartment?"

"I put everything in storage, withdrew some of the money you sent me for Christmas, and paid the rent up to the end of the lease. I know you probably need your space, but I've made arrangements to live close by."

"What are you talking about?"

"Parker asked me to move in with him."

Cherie didn't know what was more shocking—seeing her mother show up unexpectedly or the news that she was moving in with Parker Shelton. The driver removed three bags from the trunk of the cab and set them on the porch.

Edwina gave the man a seductive smile. "Can you please be a dear and set the bags inside the house?"

"Of course." He winked at Edwina when she handed him several bills. Cherie shook her head. There was no doubt her mother had charmed yet another unsuspecting man.

Wiping her feet on the mat, Edwina left her rain boots on a mat inside the door. "As soon as I shower and change, we'll sit down and put our heads together to figure out how we're going make things right between you and Reese."

"Let it go, Mama. If it's meant to be, then it will work itself out."

Edwina stared at her with her catlike eyes. "Is that what you want?"

"Yes, it's what I want."

Parker walked out of his office and motioned to Reese as he entered the station house. "My office. Now, Deputy!"

Reese met Elizabeth's eyes, hoping for a hint about why the chief wanted to see him, but she shrugged her shoulders. He headed for the office and closed the door. "Yes, Chief."

Parker sat on the corner of his desk with his massive arms folded across his chest. "When was the last time you saw Cherie?"

Reese felt as if he'd been blindsided. He'd thought the chief wanted to talk to him about something that was work-related. "That's none of your business."

A rush of color suffused Parker's complexion, turning it a ruddy shade. "What?"

"You heard me," Reese shot back. "I said if it's not police business, you have no authority to question me about my personal life. Not here! And not now!"

Parker dropped his arms. "Then let's go someplace where we can discuss it. We'll take my car."

They walked out of the office, and Parker instructed Elizabeth to contact the deputy asking for overtime to come in and work Reese's shift, because there was something important they had to take care of.

Reese sat in Parker's tiny kitchen, staring at his cousin, as he poured a jigger of bourbon into each of two glasses and handed him one. He touched his glass to Reese's, then downed the amber liquid in one swallow. "Drink up."

Putting the glass to his mouth, he tossed back the smooth liquor. "That's nice."

The lines around Parker's light-brown eyes crinkled when he smiled. "It is nice. Now that I have your attention, we need to talk about a few things."

"What about?"

"Your baby's mother. How long has it been since you've seen her?"

"How do you know about this?" Reese had answered his question with a question.

"Her mother told me."

"So now we're involved with mothers."

"Edwina told me everything, Reese. She told when and how Cherie met this Campbell dude and what he did to her. The man was nothing but a predator-in-the-making when he set his sights on a fifteen-year-old girl, seduced her and took her virginity, and then set out to make her his mistress. A week after he returned from his honeymoon, he came sniffing around her like a dog. He'd convinced her to have their love child, then turned the tables on her to give up the baby because his wife couldn't have kids. Do you realize how devastating it must have been for her when he strong-armed her to give up her baby? Even though he couldn't have Cherie, he still was connected to her because of their son. The man's obsessed with her, and that's why he came here to see if he could get her back, unaware that she'd moved on and was now carrying another man's child."

Reese ran a hand over his face. "Why didn't she tell me this?"

"Maybe she was afraid that you would reject her, or she was waiting for the right time to tell you. Edwina told me that Cherie had told Kayana and Leah about everything. She trusted them, but felt she couldn't trust you, Reese. And she was right because you walked out on her, like the man who fathered you walked out on your mother. Even if their encounter had been a one-night stand, he could've contacted her to find out if he'd gotten her pregnant. Don't let history repeat itself, Reese. I know you love the girl, and she loves you, so let go some of that stiff-necked pride, and stop that flipping texting and talk to her."

"What's up with you and Edwina?"

"I asked her to move in with me.

"No shit!"

"Yes," Parker confirmed smiling.

"What did she say?"

"She said yes, but only if I marry her."

"Will you?"

"Of course, fool. I've waited fifty-five years for a woman that makes me laugh and not take life too seriously, and you think I'm going give that up? Yes, I'm going to marry her and use my GI benefit for the first time to buy a house because this place is too small for two people."

"You don't have to do that, Parker. I told Cherie that, when we marry, I'm going to move in with her and that you can have my house."

"Stop messing with me, Reese. You know I love your house."

Reese smiled. "I know. That's why I'm giving it to you. Why not keep it in the family?" He pushed back his chair. "Now drive me back to the station house so I can pick up my truck and drive over to the island. Wish me luck."

"You don't need it, little cousin. Let's go."

Reese cursed under his breath when he pulled up in front of Cherie's house to find Graeme's Range Rover parked in the driveway. He'd hoped to find Cherie alone, but it was too late to turn around. Getting out of the pickup, he walked up to the porch and rang the doorbell. The inner door opened, and Kayana glared at him through the glass.

"What do you want?"

"Open the door, Kayana." She must have heard the threatening tone in his voice because she unlocked it.

He brushed past her and stalked into the family room to find Edwina and Leah sitting next to Cherie, sipping from cups of hot liquid. The scene reminded him of another time when he'd come to her home to interview her about her attacker, and the two women had flanked her like lionesses protecting a cub. But they'd added another lioness to their pride, and it was Edwina's narrowed gaze that nearly unnerved him.

"I'd like to talk to Cherie. Alone, please."

Cherie stood up. "It's all right."

"Are you sure?" Edwina asked her daughter.

"Do you actually believe I would harm the mother of my child?"

Edwina straightened her shoulders. "I don't know."

"Mama, please. Reese and I need to talk."

"All right," she said, walking out of the family room and following Kayana and Leah up the staircase.

Reese waited for Cherie to sit, then sat opposite her. Never had he seen her look so alluring. A few stray curls had escaped her topknot and floated around her neck. "How are you feeling?"

"I'm good. My period stopped, so I'll probably begin to put on weight."

"You should let me know when you have your doctor's appointments, because I'd like to go with you."

Cherie nodded. "That can be arranged."

He stared up at the ceiling. "I know everything, Cherie, about you and Campbell, beginning with you attending the same prep school and how he tricked you into becoming a surrogate for his wife."

"Who told you?"

"That doesn't matter. What matters is I love you, and I shouldn't have been so quick to judge you. And I knew eventually you would've told me everything, but only when you felt comfortable."

"You're right. There were so many times I'd thought about it, and after I found out that I was carrying your baby, I planned to tell you just before we went out to shop for an engagement ring. That would've given you the option of going ahead with the engagement or backing out."

"Do you actually believe I would've backed out, Cherie? I would've married you even if you had a dozen kids. I love you just that much."

She smiled for the first time. "That's a lot of babies."

"Yes, it is. And there would be enough love from both of us to go around for every one of them."

Cherie pressed her palms together. "I'm not proud that I slept with a married man, and I paid for it by having to give up my baby."

"That's your past, Cherie, like Campbell is your past. When he lost his wife and son, he also lost the last thing that connected him to you. He knows it's over, and that's why he came here to see if you were the same vulnerable young woman he could manipulate all over again."

"He wasn't the only manipulator, Reese." She told him about the money and jewelry he'd given her. "Close your mouth," she said when his jaw dropped. "I just want you to know what kind of woman you want to marry."

"Baby, I like your style."

"You like that I hustled him?

"You didn't hustle him, bae. He wanted a child, and surrogates are usually paid for carrying a couple's baby. And it's same with becoming a wealthy man's mistress. Gifts are the norm."

"So you believe I did nothing wrong?"

"Cherie, it's not about right or wrong. However, Campbell was wrong for continuing to sleep with you after he married his wife. And when he asked you to have his love child, he knew he had an ulterior motive to take it from you."

Cherie realized Reese was attempting to absolve her of her past indiscretions, similar to Edwina telling her she'd slept with men for money. Jamal's father had been Edwina's first boyfriend, while Cherie's father had been a middle-aged white widower who had hired her to babysit his children. When she told him she was pregnant and refused to have an abortion, he gave her eight thousand dollars and then moved his family across the country to Oregon. The man who had fathered her twin sons was a college professor she met online. He was into BDSM and paid her to restrain him before having sex. She told her mother she did what she had to do to support her children, and none of the men with whom she'd had relationships were married. Edwina had also been given a chance to find happiness with Parker Shelton. She'd admitted that she and Parker spoke to each other every day, even if it was for only a few minutes.

"Let's begin again," Reese said, breaking into her musings. "What do you want to ask me?"

Going to one knee, he held her hand over his heart. She felt the material of his bulletproof vest under his shirt. "Miss Cherie Renee Thompson, will you do me the honor of becoming my wife?"

Cherie slipped off the sofa and knelt in front of him. "Yes, Reese Matthews. I will marry you."

"I'm not going to ask you when. Just knowing you will is all I need to know."

Leaning closer, Cherie kissed him with all the passion and love she felt for the man who'd saved her life and created the new life growing inside her.

Epilogue

Reese hadn't thought his life could get any better. He and Cherie were married on the beach on July Fourth, with their family and friends witnessing the event, before they returned to the house for a reception that didn't end until after midnight.

Parker had the honor of being his best man, and Edwina was Cherie's attendant. Edwina and Parker had moved into the house where Reese's grandparents had raised him and had made plans to marry later in the year. Leah and Derrick had decided to wait until Christmas to exchange vows in Florida and then honeymoon on an island in the Caribbean.

The Seaside Café book club was on hiatus until the following spring and had welcomed Edwina as their newest member. She offered to babysit her granddaughter once Cherie began her online courses to earn her degree in early childhood education.

Reese couldn't wait for his daughter to begin walking so he could take her with him whenever he strolled along the shore of the island that generations of his family had called home for centuries. He lifted strands of hair off Cherie's moist forehead. She'd closed her eyes, and the gentle rise and fall of her breasts indicated she'd fallen asleep. He knew she was exhausted, and he was elated. Reese had taken a leave from the sheriff's department, and he was looking forward to spending the next six weeks with his new family.

Samara Lian Matthews made her entrance known late one October night, weighing five pounds, four ounces, and crying at the top of her tiny lungs. Her mother had been in labor for more than sixteen hours, while her father had alternated holding Cherie's hand and massaging her lower back.

"Who does she look like?" Cherie asked Reese.

"She's beautiful, just like her mother."

Cherie smiled when she saw the tiny, red-faced baby, who suddenly stopped crying and opened her eyes. They were an odd shade of green, a color that would probably change, but it was the tufts of straight black hair, which reminded of bristles on a brush, that made her laugh. Her daughter had ten fingers and toes and a pair of strong lungs.

"She's perfect, Reese."

He leaned over and brushed a light kiss over her parched lips. "So are you."

Don't miss Kayana and Leah's stories in
The Seaside Café
and
The Beach House
Available now from
Dafina Books
Wherever books are sold